READY THE EIGHT

READY THE EIGHT

Jae Gordon

To Colby
Enjoy!
With much love
Jae
S

iUniverse, Inc.

New York Lincoln Shanghai

Ready the Eight

iUniverse, Inc.

For information address:
iUniverse, Inc.
2021 Pine Lake Road, Suite 100
Lincoln, NE 68512
www.iuniverse.com

ISBN: 0-595-28808-1

Printed in the United States of America

For Mihal & Jess
My life's inspiration

PROLOGUE

▼

Jordan, September 1998

Six comrades boarded half a dozen flights to the same number of cities.

They set out from Ramallah, Jenin, Nablus, Akbat Jabbar, Jericho and Abu Jibril, crossed the Jordan River and headed for Amman. From there, the six devotees, unknown to one another, set off on a common mission guided by a master plan, fueled by an unshakable faith in Allah and unswerving loyalty to his messenger, a man they called Al Rasuul, the Deliverer.

The voice over the loudspeaker announced the flights.

"Final call for TWA flight 842 now boarding for Rome at gate 41."

"American Airlines flight 33 now boarding at gate 35 for New York."

"Swissair flight 003 now boarding for Paris," British Airways to London, TWA to Los Angeles and Tokyo.

As the six comrades boarded their flights, a customer seated at a rickety table in an East Jerusalem café crushed out his cigarette in an iridescent tin ashtray and a young man stood at the edge of an old quay in Jaffa, meditatively inhaling the night salt air of the Mediterranean Sea just below him.

Eight comrades. Eight cities. Eight martyrs. One cause.

Stage IV had begun.

Pentagon, 2:00 AM

The handler's head jerked up as his computer beeped, rousing him from a heavy slumber. Glancing at the clock, he sighed with relief. He'd slept only ten minutes. He took a swig of cold coffee from the mug set on the desktop beside the computer, rubbed his eyes and peered into the monitor.

The gentle beep, alerting him that a message had been retrieved and decoded, was unexpected. It had been months since anything had been picked up.

"Good morning, Darlin'," he said softly, almost coaxing, as he scanned the screen. "What'cha got for me here, hon?" In the darkened room, unfurnished but for the oversized gray metal desk and swivel chair, the letters on the computer monitor glowed bright.

He read the message, hit the Print button, then read it again. Now fully awake, chills crept down his spine like swarms of advancing insects.

"Oh, shit," he swore to himself.

In one swift move, he grabbed the printout, stuffed it into a manila folder marked "Top Secret" and shot out the door.

CHAPTER 1

▼

Jerusalem, May 1998

As she ran, she felt a tug at the muscle of her inner thigh.

"Not yet," she whispered to herself, only three miles into her evening run. The air was hot and her limbs felt heavy. The *hamsin* had arrived early this year and its pervasive dry heat threatened to cut her workout short. She raised her eyes from the track in front of her and focused instead on the treetops above. Immediately, her lethargy lifted off and she propelled herself into a steady, comfortable stride.

Half an hour later, evening gave over to the cool mountain night, infusing the air with a sudden chill. Soaked with sweat, the crisp breeze made Nadine shiver. She sprinted past the eight-mile mark, then slowed into a lope, inhaling deeply and slowly, acutely aware of her racing pulse. She walked briskly around the track until the blood pounding through her veins quieted, then dropped to the ground. Body taut, hands firmly planted on the grass directly beneath her shoulders, she quickly counted out twenty-five push-ups.

Back on her feet again, she raised her arms high over her head, took a long, slow breath and pulled on a sweatshirt discarded earlier in her run. Satisfied, she headed up the hill towards Fouad's kiosk for a cool drink before he closed up for the evening. Their rendezvous had become a nightly ritual and the old Arab was waiting as she approached.

She raised her hand in greeting and slid onto a stool next to a counter overstocked with candies, nuts and chocolates.

"*Ahalan*, Fouad," she said, smiling as he handed her a Gatorade.

"*Salaam aleichem*, Nadine," Fouad responded in greeting.

Nadine was always amused by the incongruity of seeing him whisk the all-American sport drink from the small cooler tucked between Middle Eastern pastries and a rack filled with periodicals printed in Hebrew, Arabic, French and English.

"*Shukran*," she added, offering Fouad her thanks.

Nadine raised the can in salute, then drained it of its contents and lightly tossed into a plastic bin behind the counter.

"What's the trouble, Fouad? You don't look so good."

"I made the mistake of reading the newspaper," he complained, handing it to her. The lead editorial decried the round of terror and retaliation that had rocked the tiny country the week before.

He studied her for a moment before responding to her questioning gaze. "I am an Arab, Nadine. My family has lived on this land for five generations. It is my home. I am also an Israeli, a citizen of this country. I vote for my representatives to the Knesset and I carry an Israeli passport. So who am I? I am angered by the slaughter of innocent Israelis by Arab fanatics. Then I am anguished, and despair with my people, when Palestinian homes are leveled in retribution for the sins of their sons."

She finished her drink in silence, stilled as much by her friend's personal dilemma as by the realization that there was no simple solution to this conflict.

Fouad turned off the lights and together they stepped outside. With a wave, Nadine trotted off in the direction of home while Fouad turned to secure the metal shudder that rolled across the front of his kiosk.

Each night, as she climbed the hill, she marveled at the beauty of the city around her. Sculpted from Jerusalem stone, it rested like a giant bas relief mounted on the crests and slopes of seven emerald hills. Awash in warm rays dancing and leaping off the stone's notched surface, the city glowed pink in daybreak's rising sun and turned to a burnished gold in the evening sunset.

She spied the flat that she shared with her two boys in a new neighborhood just southeast of Jerusalem's Old City. Perched on the summit, it overlooked the Judean Hills and on a clear day, she could see the Dead Sea glittering in the distance from her terrace.

Nadine took the stairs two at a time up to their apartment. She couldn't wait to get into a hot shower. She pushed open the door only to hear the phone start ringing at that same moment.

"Anybody home?" she called. Almost in unison, two voices responded from different ends of the flat.

"Hi, mom."

"Yeh, here."

The shrill ringing of the hallway phone insisted that she answer it. Whoever it was had better be brief, she mumbled to herself as she picked up the handset. She had started to shiver despite the heavy sweatshirt she wore, as her body temperature readjusted after her run.

"Did I call at a bad time?" the caller inquired in response to her abrupt greeting.

A wide smile creased her unlined face. "It's never a bad time for you, Brad," Nadine responded, happy to hear the familiar voice. Since Jeremy's death, his mentor, General Bradford McKenzie, called often.

"Couldn't help thinking of our friend today. This morning, for the first time in close to a year, I scheduled a day off. I packed my gear and headed out for the Dolomite Mountains to revisit some of the trails we used to climb. I was barely off the base when I was nearly clipped by a chopper carrying a load of Washington VIPs. My immediate thought was that this has got to be another one of Jeremy's practical jokes." Brad paused. "He was probably looking down at me with an ear-splitting grin on his face, watching me squirm."

Nadine could only laugh. It beat crying. It seemed Brad missed him almost as much as she did.

A short silence filled the space between them before Brad ventured further. "You know, Nadine, we still need you here. There aren't too many with your expertise."

Unconsciously, Nadine bit at her lower lip. She knew the ropes. She couldn't do that. Not yet.

Her voice dropped. "I'm sorry, Brad."

They spoke for a few more minutes then Nadine gently placed the phone on its cradle. The United States Department of Defense had done quite well before Dr. Nadine Kanner came along, she rationalized, and would continue to do so from now on. With that, she headed for the shower, determined not to give the conversation another thought.

Brad replaced the handset. He felt as he often did after speaking with Nadine; suspended, as though part of him was missing.

He squeezed his eyes shut. What was it about her that wouldn't allow him to let go? Everything, he answered himself, exhaling as he did.

The void left in her wake was infinite. Brad shook his head vigorously, as if to shake off his unpleasant brooding to reveal the truth. What would he do to bring her back into his life? Would he leave the Air Force for her?

He sank into the leather armchair facing the fireplace. The dying fire cast dancing shadows across his rugged skin, illuminating tiny rivulets around steel gray eyes, testimony to years outdoors often squinting into the sun. His chin rested on the tips of his long fingers and he thought back to their first meeting.

"*Meet Major Jeremy Kanner. Major Kanner, this is our base commander here at Aviano AFB, General Bradford McKenzie.*"

As Brad stepped out from behind his desk, Jeremy extended his right hand. Brad's met his in an equally firm grip. The bond was immediate.

"*And this is his wife, Dr. Nadine Kanner.*" *Brad turned to greet her. At that moment, he knew his life had changed forever.*

Brad could still feel the grip of fate as he walked hand in hand with his father through the cavernous hallways of the Pentagon. Even as a six-year-old, he knew that the Air Force was his future and it had remained all he had ever wanted. Apparently, his ex-wife knew that too. She had left him years ago, for reasons he no longer cared to remember.

A seared log toppled in the fireplace, crackling loudly. Brad started at the sound. Freed of his melancholic reverie, he stared into the blaze. Jeremy was the best friend he'd ever had, and now Nadine, the woman he yearned for, was a thousand miles away.

The fire's yellow flames licked blindly in a frenetic search for prey to fuel their insatiable appetite, as they had consumed Jeremy almost one year ago.

Dr. Sami Nasser unlocked the door to his apartment on Central Park West and headed straight for the study. The light tapping sound of his shoes on the polished wood floor ricocheted off high ceilings as he strode down the long hallway towards the back of the flat. Without pausing, he passed through the study door, dropped his jacket and briefcase on the soft leather couch to his right and sat down at the desk opposite. Despite its expanse, the antique desk topped with leather inlay was adorned with only one item—a computer. Behind him, floor to ceiling leaded glass windows displayed the grayish brown city beyond. He did not bother to turn on the lights and the room was illuminated only by the murky evening dusk.

Dr. Nasser flipped on his computer and waited impatiently as it whirred and beeped into readiness. A few moments and several keystrokes later, he'd retrieved the document he needed. With his right hand ever so gently yet skillfully caressing the trackball, Nasser clicked on a series of icons, abandoning the orb only momentarily to type in the secret password that gained him immediate access to the Internet. He knew exactly where he wanted to go in that virtual universe of information and web sites. Another series of clicks and he was there. Hooked up to a site in the Middle East, he attached the document retrieved only minutes earlier and hit the SEND button. Before he could blink, confirmation flashed on the screen.

Nasser exhaled as he leaned into the high back of his leather swivel chair and rotated to gaze out at the New York City skyline, now ablaze with a myriad of tiny lights.

CHAPTER 2

▼

There was a light knock on her open office door at the Israel Strategy Institute. Nadine turned from her computer to see Shlomo Cohen, president of the prestigious Jerusalem think tank, step in with a stack of documents.

"Good morning, Nadine," he said, as he set the stack down on her desk.

"Good morning, Shlomo. What's that?"

Shlomo smiled. "It's the reason I hired you. This is a collection of recent publications and papers presented on regional security regimes. We just pulled them off the Internet. Pretty dry stuff really, but with your background, you should be able to get through it relatively quickly and judge whether there is anything of significance."

With a wave, he was gone as quickly as he had come. Nadine leaned back into her chair. Her work at ISI was fairly mundane, but that suited her just fine these days. The last thing she had wanted after Jeremy died was a demanding job. Shlomo seemed to sense that and was letting her break into the work at her own pace.

Even now, it was hard to believe that five years had passed since the Casablanca Economic Summit where they'd first met.

The resounding applause from the audience of government leaders and top ranking business people representing the United States, Russia, Israel and most of the Arab world, followed Nadine as she stepped away from the podium. The enthusiastic response to her presentation on political shifts in the Middle East based on changing economic trends, far exceeded her expectations. She forced herself to contain her excitement as she walked across the stage, down the five steps to the auditorium floor and headed towards the double-door exit. Hands reached out to shake hers. Thrilled by the energy around her, she forcibly suppressed a childish urge to skip.

Once in the large lobby just outside the auditorium of the Casablanca Sheraton Hotel, she paused to take two long deep breaths, then headed for the bank of telephones set back in one of its many carpeted arteries. She walked briskly, checking her watch as she did. There was still time to catch Jeremy. Halfway there, she was intercepted by a slightly winded, somewhat rumpled looking man with light blue eyes, sandy hair and a warm smile.

"Dr. Kanner, I'm Shlomo Cohen," he said handing her his card. She looked at it briefly, then extended her hand.

"Dr. Cohen, your reputation, and that of your Institute, precedes you. It's a pleasure to meet you."

"The pleasure is all mine. Your paper was brilliant. I won't keep you. I just want you to know that I would be honored to have you visit our Institute in Jerusalem, anytime. You will always be welcome." A mischievous glint lit his blue eyes. "I don't suppose I could hope to steal you away from the Department of Defense, but if you ever need a change of climate…"

"Nadine," a voice called out from behind her. The heavy scent of musk assaulted her nostrils. She turned to see Dr. Sami Nasser approaching and an imperceptible shudder ran through her.

The fact that he was a highly regarded economist in the academic and business world, a tenured Columbia University professor and a member of the American delegation to the conference as well, did nothing to ease the sense of discomfort Nadine felt in his presence.

Stop it, she chided herself. He was always polite and charming, and his close contacts at every level of business and government in the Middle East made him an exceptional asset to the American team. Admittedly, he had a compelling presence and she could not help but notice that he was often in the company of several beautiful women. But his intense dark eyes, hooded by a set of thick eyebrows, always seemed to bore right through her.

"Your paper was excellent," he said shaking her hand. "You had some very practical ideas that I think we can really put into motion. I'd like to talk to you about them before the end of the conference. We need to look at the subject of cultural and economic trends creating predictable political shifts more closely. Certainly, some of the Israeli and Palestinian delegation members will want to take this further."

Nadine smiled appreciatively and introduced him to Shlomo Cohen. "We have a member of the Israeli delegation right here."

"I am quite familiar with your Institute," Dr. Nasser said as he shook Shlomo's hand. "I've relied on your research on many occasions."

After a quick pose for a passing photographer, the three parted ways. Nadine crinkled her nose, slightly annoyed by the lingering scent of Nasser's cologne. She steered towards the telephones and as she neared them, thought again about Shlomo Cohen.

Cohen was a consultant in great demand by Israeli businessmen, investors and government officials, well known and widely admired for his quick mind and understanding of the Arab psyche. He had been one of the first to develop contacts with the Arab world when the peace talks began. His open manner had made him a trusted ally by both sides.

Quiet inquiries and unofficial prospects were often confidentially broached through him, and his negotiating savvy had made him a favored link between Arab and Israeli governments and businessman. As she reached the phone bank, she thought that she just might take him up on his invitation.

As he headed down the hallway back towards his office at the Institute, Shlomo's mind was on the Summit, too. Nadine had impressed him immediately. A Ph.D. in Middle East Affairs and fluency in both Hebrew and Arabic, were enough for him to try to entice her to the Institute. But her status as a senior intelligence analyst with top security clearance at the United States Department of Defense Intelligence Agency, privy to classified and often sensitive material, made her irresistible. Many of the Institute's research projects were funded by the Israeli government and carried a high security classification. He quickly recognized the potential that she could bring to his Institute and he had made it clear to her that if she ever wanted to work at ISI, all she had to do was call.

He surmised that her departure must have been a blow to the Pentagon. Nadine's theories on the spread of global Islam were taken seriously and the Department of Defense used her analyses in its dealings in the region. He could not help but think that they had lost a very valuable asset—and he had gained one. He'd be surprised if Israel's own intelligence agency, the Mossad, didn't have its eye on her. He more than expected 'Y,' the Mossad chief, to say something about her at their last meeting, but he was conspicuous in his silence.

Shlomo shook his head slightly as he reached his own office. Tragedy had brought her to his doorstep. She was biding her time on the academic stuff, Shlomo knew, but he was also convinced that with her sharp mind and keen analytical skills, it would not be long before she was itching for a role in one of their more challenging assignments, and for his part, he was anxious to get her there.

The young engineering student with the wire-rimmed glasses entered his cubicle at Beir Zeit University on the West Bank. He closed the door to the tiny room gently and flipped on the power switch to his computer. While it slowly booted, he opened his backpack, extracted a stenographer's notebook and a sharpened pencil. The room was sparse, devoid of decoration except for a small shelf on one wall stacked with a few engineering books and a Qu'ran. The walls were painted institutional beige, long in need of a touch-up. The table and chair, where he now sat, were the cubicle's only furniture.

The computer was ready for his command. Accessing the Internet, he typed in the web site address for the International Association of Economists and Scientists for World Peace, downloaded a recently posted paper, transferred it to his word processor and began to read.

For the next several hours, Sabri patiently decoded instructions for the next phase of the holy crusade that would ignite the spread of global Islam, free the Palestinian people from Israeli occupation and restore to them their rightful homeland, free of Jews, Zionists and Western abominations.

Ready the eight. Materials and supplies set for assembly at all destinations. Final targets: New York, Los Angeles, Washington, D.C., Paris, Rome, Tokyo, Jerusalem, Tel-Aviv. Simultaneous detonation. Exact time for each zone to follow. Maps and sites attached. Maintain anonymity at all levels.

He followed some additional instructions for pinpointing hidden photos, maps and information pertaining to the specific site locations, downloaded and printed them out. Then he leaned against the back of his wooden chair and smiled. Even now, he could see the eight human bombs bursting into flame without warning, showering grief upon their victims around the world. Eight martyrs across the globe invoking the name of Allah as they ascended to heaven. Their hallowed voices rang in his ears as if he could hear them at that very moment.

With a few deft movements, he packed up, left his cubicle and locked the door behind him. There was much work to be done.

CHAPTER 3

▼

Nadine surveyed the runners at the track as she went through her warm-up routine. There were only three others this evening beside herself and she recognized each of them. Though they rarely spoke, they shared a camaraderie by virtue of their love of the sport. One runner, at six foot five, towered over the others. He was well built with long muscular legs and blond hair, cut so short that it resembled peach fuzz. Nadine admired his speed and grace. He flew effortlessly around the track as if fired by some internal engine, and never broke a sweat.

As she trotted onto the track, she was passed by a compact Ethiopian woman of indeterminate age, whose form and speed had her convinced that the woman was a professional runner. Her running had spirit and she filled Nadine with motivation on days that her energy flagged.

Finally, there was 'Red,' so nicknamed for the red tank top and pinstriped running shorts he wore. His runs were sporadic, leaving Nadine to surmise that he traveled on business a great deal. Still, she mused, he manages to stay in shape and red does suit him.

Nadine ran her first mile, always her hardest, more slowly, picking up speed as she started into mile two. She focused on the surroundings to keep her mind free. East of the track was a stretch of the Jerusalem Forest criss-crossed by well-packed trails. Some of them, she knew, led to a neighboring Arab village, Abu Jibril, where Fouad lived. To the south was the recreation center that housed a gym, a pool, classrooms and a movie theater. Just beyond the recreation center was a playground and the field where Daniel, Zak and their friends met to play soccer. It wasn't unusual for Nadine to catch up with them there at the end of her runs.

One-half kilometer northwest of the track, the hills were dotted with flats that included Nadine's.

Red moved up alongside Nadine and signaled to her to join him. She gave him a puzzled look, then shrugged and fell in alongside him. The forest was pine and a welcome reprieve from the open track. They ran in silence. Swept away by the beauty and calm of the surroundings, Nadine's soul soared. Her legs propelled her forward but she did not feel them. She was exhilarated by the green scent and seemingly endless trail.

She positioned herself so that Red was slightly ahead of her and she could see him without turning her head. He was a vision of *the* Mediterranean male featured in the glossy tourist brochures that papered the walls of every travel agency in town—tall, handsome and inviting. Perfect white teeth shone brightly against mocha skin. His brown eyes were flecked with green and his dark hair, trimmed back over his ears, fell in small waves to the nape of his neck. Individual locks freed themselves and mingled with beads of sweat that dotted his brow. He carried himself with confidence and exuded a sense of purpose that she guessed carried over into everything he did. Still, he seemed devoid of arrogance.

Forty minutes later, Nadine spied the clearing and broke into a sprint. Red followed suit and they raced triumphantly to the far end of the track.

"Thank you," Nadine said as they walked back towards the recreation center. "I enjoyed that."

"I thought that you might. I don't recommend you go it alone though," he cautioned.

She bristled at the warning. She did not like being patronized and had already decided that she would venture there again. Red caught her look and said, "Listen, whenever I can get down here, we'll run it again."

She was about to protest but privately admitted that it was better to get to know the trails from a veteran than risk getting lost. Once she felt comfortable with a few of the routes, she could run there as often as she liked.

"All right," she agreed. "By the way, do you have a name?"

He nodded. "Barak."

Lightning. His name meant lightning.

A warm wind caressed the young man's unshaven face as he exited the international terminal at LAX. The balmy breeze and scent of eucalyptus so resembled that of his homeland he could hardly fathom that he had traveled halfway around the world. His eyes lighted on the taxi line. Hoisting his duffel bag, he approached the purser and gave him an address in Hollywood.

The purser signaled the next cab. He slid into the back seat and joined the stream of cars, buses, shuttles, limousines and vans that clogged the airport ramps. Minutes later they were heading north on the 405 Freeway, traveling at a nice clip. Century City office buildings gleamed brightly in the California sun against the green backdrop of the Hollywood Hills. No sign of the smog ring he had seen from the plane on descent was visible here. An omen. The young man nodded to himself with satisfaction. He was a man on a mission. Soon, it would be complete. His family would receive much honor and lifetime support for his contribution to the cause.

Three quarters of an hour later, the young man stepped out of the cab and paid its driver. He scanned the area. No need for concern. He would not be noticed in the city of glitz and glitter where all but the current studio celebrities remained anonymous. And if he was, well, by then, the world would be turned on its head.

Kabir picked up the key to his room at the Hollywood YMCA. First, a phone call, then some rest. He stepped into the hallway, dropped two coins into the slot, dialed a number and waited. It rang for a long time but the young man had patience. When the call was finally answered, the young man said, "I have arrived," and hung up.

CHAPTER 4

▼

Nadine felt heavy as her legs slogged through the first mile around the track. She had been exhilarated for a week after the foray into the woods but as the days went by, her exhilaration turned from spirited anticipation to irksome disappointment. Ten days had passed since her run with Barak. Irritated with herself for assuming that their detour had held as much delight for him as it had for her, she pushed her humiliation aside and picked up her pace. She had considered returning to the forest on her own when his warning, like a conscience, urged her to wait another day.

Intent on getting the most out of her run, she focused on her form, pace and breathing. Her feet pounded the gravel track, heel-toe, heel-toe. She made sure her stomach muscles were slightly contracted and her rear tucked in. She brought her back into alignment with her neck and head, dropping her shoulders and tucking her chin just slightly. Elbows bent, hands loosely clenched, her arms swung in controlled movements, back and forth, timed to each breath. Within minutes, her momentum took over and she felt both relaxed and energized as her body propelled itself forward into the warm evening wind.

Thus engrossed, she was unprepared to see Barak's tall form approaching as she rounded the north end of the track. He waved to her as he warmed up alongside, then beckoned to her to join him as he headed for the forest. Her heart leapt involuntarily, rendering any efforts to maintain indifference, useless.

On muscular legs, she veered towards the trail leading into the woods. They ran in silence but their bodies spoke myriads, each attuned to the other's rhythm. Their feet touched down and left the ground in a perfectly timed allegro dance.

Glimpses of bright sunlight trickled through the pine canopy washing a gentle warmth over their glistening bodies, soaked with the dew of their efforts.

As they ran, Barak occasionally pointed out landmarks and changes in foliage. He identified a variety of birds too, mostly from their calls, as they were hard to spot in the thick trees.

"Can you sense our direction?" he asked after a while.

Nadine was thoughtful. They had entered the woods east of the track. There had been some slight curves in the trail but it seemed to her that they were still running east.

She said so.

Barak pulled a small compass from his pocket, glanced at it, then handed it to her. It's needle vibrated rapidly as she held it and ran, but the reading was clear. "South-west," she said aloud, surprised. "When did that happen?"

"Actually, about fifteen minutes ago." Barak slowed to a stop. Nadine trotted up alongside him and stopped too. They stood on the crest of a low hill. "The trail veered right as we were running downhill," Barak explained, pointing behind them. "It's tricky because of the trees. Trails branch off in so many directions, you have to be careful about which one you're on."

"The residents of Abu Jibril and the other villages cut through these woods all the time to get to Jerusalem. The buses take a more circuitous route. Often, it's easier, maybe even faster, to cut straight through the forest and catch a bus on the Jerusalem side."

He stood close to her, his shoulder almost touching hers. Suddenly she was aware of nothing but his overwhelming presence. His warm breath tickled her neck and her entire body responded. Every nerve ending came alive and she knew that if she turned to him, his mouth would be on hers. She didn't.

His gently touched her arm and directed her gaze to the area below them. Terraced olive trees spread out before them. Their shade looked inviting. He was saying something but she no longer heard him. She was aware only of her intensified breathing and the pounding of her heart. He'd stopped speaking. She turned to him and smiled. His arm encircled her waist and his other hand lifted her face towards his.

Eager, his eyes asked her permission and she moved in closer to grant it. His body was rock solid and familiar. She closed her eyes. *Jeremy.* Without warning, she broke free and began to run.

When they exited the woods an hour later both felt a mixture of exhaustion and energy. They cooled down silently then stopped at the water fountain near the recreation building.

"That was beautiful," Nadine said appreciatively.

Barak soaked a small towel under a nearby tap and drew it across his face, then took a long drink from the fountain.

"You're a strong runner," he said with open admiration. His eyes squinted in thought. "I can be here again on Thursday. How about you?"

Returning his gaze, Nadine said, "Sure. See you then."

Before she could refuse, he placed a gentle kiss on her forehead. Rooted to her spot, she watched him walk away. Halfway up the hill to the road he turned around and called out to her. "Wait for me. You don't know the trails well enough yet."

He was gone with a wave.

Outside the Bronx tenement, the air was so hot and heavy with humidity, it was visible, rising from the grimy pavement in undulating, serpentine waves. Somewhere in the not too far distance, the El whizzed by on rickety tracks. The windows of her room shook slightly, but the young woman was not aware of either the stifling heat or the roar of the elevator train. Rigorous training in military camps under blistering Syrian sun and through frigid desert nights in Iran had long since erased her awareness of hardship. Impervious to her surroundings, her concentration focused entirely on the task before her. She gave no thought to the past or the future. Only to her mission.

One by one, she took stock of the items laid out on the wobbly bridge table set before her, then she knelt down and inspected its underpinnings. Slipping a packet out of her left pocket, she gently pinched off small amounts of an off-white gummy material that she pressed into each of its four joints. She ran her eyes down the length of each leg. Earlier, she had wedged the table into a corner of the room as best she could and now she slid a thick magazine under the table leg diagonally opposite the corner. Better.

She stood and caught sight of her reflection in a small mirror hanging carelessly on the wall. Her face was pale and a bluish tinge outlined her full lips. She turned away quickly and returned her attention to her work. She tried to shake the table lightly. It didn't move. Satisfied, she returned to the task at hand. The checklist was in her head, the items neatly stacked and arranged before her. Metal piping. A carton of matchbooks. Several boxes of one-inch screws and tiny nails. Razor blades. Electrical wire. One D battery. A dozen night-light bulbs.

She picked up a tube and sat down on an old sofa shoved up against a wall marred by cracked and peeling paint. Using a small, sharp utility knife, she began cutting vertical lines into the pipe. With deft movements, she expertly carved the metal cylinder, and as she did, she saw her mother in her mind's eye. Tears had streamed down her mother's face as she sewed twelve pockets inside her eldest daughter's flak jacket and thanked Allah for giving her only daughter this gift of redemption. One for each tube. A dozen in all. She would rise to heaven a martyr.

Meticulously etching even lines into the tube, first horizontally then vertically, a waffle pattern began to appear. The young woman nodded to herself in satisfaction. The creases would intensify the explosion, hurling the force of its contents in every direction. Maximum thrust. Maximum devastation.

Indifferently, she wiped the sweat from her brow, only to be immediately replaced by scores more of the tiny droplets. Among the items she had purchased was a small fan, but the humidity kept her brow moist. To keep the salty water from gliding down into her eyes, she tore a long strip of cotton from a pile of clean rags, wrapped it around her forehead and tied it behind the mane of rippling, mahogany-colored hair that cascaded past her shoulders, halfway down her back.

Making the devices was slow and laborious, but they were safe until detonated—and extremely effective. As she labored she remembered their many successes. Her own cousin had martyred himself on a Jerusalem bus. To maximize the number of victims, he'd waited until another bus, similarly packed to standing room only in the early morning rush hour traffic, pulled up alongside the one he rode before detonating himself. The few who weren't pulverized were left maimed or paralyzed. But the commuters were not the human bomb's only victims. The entire country was traumatized. Peace negotiations froze. Another drop of water fell against the stone.

She smiled. Her bomb too, would take many lives. Twelve interconnected mini-bombs joined by a single fuse would light the night sky like Fourth of July fireworks. But more than that, it would take democracy with it. Zeal lit her black doe eyes and she worked with renewed ambition.

The oppressive heat of the late Indian summer did not discourage her. The heat would not last. And it did tend to get windy on the little islands just off Manhattan's south end, where the East River meets the Hudson.

CHAPTER 5

▼

Fingers intertwined, Barak guided Nadine through the narrow alleys of Jerusalem's Arab quarter. Beyond its thick, stone perimeter, the morning was bright and clear, but within the walled Old City, the *shouk* was dim, as if cast in the shadows of late afternoon.

They navigated their way through the sea of shoppers. Tourists, modestly robed women, playful children and holy men of the many faiths that called Jerusalem their home, mingled in the crowded marketplace. The bitter aroma of Turkish coffee laced with sweet smelling tobacco, eased the assault on their nostrils from the more powerful scents of the *shouk*—aromatic spices, pungent sheepskin and slabs of meat. The gentle songs of the wind chimes dangling in the breeze competed with blaring transistor radios from neighboring shops. The mix gave rise to a symphony of discordant yet exotic sounding music. As they made their way down the sloping alleyway toward the central square, hawkers called out, promising them the best prices in the Middle East.

"Look here," one shopkeeper offered. "Feel this olive wood. It's smooth as silk. Come. Buy the lady a gift."

Nadine stopped to admire a satchel hanging from an overhead rack, above a narrow stall. Immediately, the shop owner appeared at her side. In one quick movement, he released the satchel from the hook and handed it to her. Nadine turned it over in her hands then slung it across her shoulders. She shot a questioning glance in the direction of the shop owner.

"Fifty," he said in English. She shook her head.

"Twenty five," Nadine responded in Arabic. As he recovered from his initial surprise, a wide grin creased the shop owner's face, then he let out a hearty laugh.

"An American who speaks Arabic. For you, a special price. Forty."

Nadine shook her head and held the bag out to shop owner. "No more than twenty eight." A small group of merchants from neighboring stalls gathered to listen to the friendly haggling between the American woman and the shop owner.

"Thirty five."

"Hey, I have a brother in New Jersey," one called out. "Maybe you know him."

"Thirty."

"It's yours," the shop owner responded. "Only because you are so beautiful." He slipped the satchel into a bag, handed it to her and said, "Use it in good health."

They exchanged farewells with the onlookers and exited the narrow alleyway into a large open square awash in sunlight. As she stepped into the daylight, a small figure gently nudged Nadine's shoulder, mumbling something as he breezed by. His words seemed to float alongside her, hanging suspended just long enough for her to hear them before fading away into the recesses of the *shouk*. She turned to see the rotund figure of an elderly man quickly retreating into the shadows of the narrow lanes from which they had just emerged. He was dressed in the traditional black suit and hat of an Orthodox Jew. Curling sidelocks and the loose edges of a long, full, gray beard flew back over his shoulders. She watched him for a moment until he disappeared. Then she shrugged and turned to follow Barak across the square to an outdoor café.

They sat on white plastic folding chairs beside a small table covered with a vinyl red and white checkered tablecloth. On it, lay an almost flat, iridescent, tin ashtray. They ordered Turkish coffee and a honey-dipped pastry to share.

"I'm leaving for Paris tomorrow," Barak said when the waiter departed.

"Shopping spree?" she teased.

He winked at her. "If things go as well as planned, it very well may be. But I wanted you to know that I won't be around the track for a while."

She nodded. "Do you enjoy traveling so much?"

"Goes with the territory, I guess. The satellite technology my company develops is unsurpassed. We're setting industry standards. But Israel is too small to support an entire industry so most of our technology is sold abroad. Our biggest clients are in the U.S. and Europe, but we're expanding into China and the Persian Gulf. That will probably turn out to be one of our more lucrative sources." He flashed her a smile. "But no worries, I make sure to travel in style."

Their steaming black coffee arrived in short glasses set in silver holders. Then, the waiter set a delicate pastry of filo dough, honey and chopped nuts, on the table between them.

"So, tell me about the theory that made you so famous amongst our Middle East scholars," Barak said as he heaped teaspoon after teaspoon of sugar into the bitter coffee. Nadine watched him, wide-eyed.

"Having coffee with your sugar?" she ventured.

"My only vice."

Nadine shook her head. "What theory?"

"It's common knowledge that Shlomo Cohen doesn't just invite anybody to think at his think tank. So you must have come up with something that peaked his interest."

"Economic trends and predictable cultural shifts?"

"No, that doesn't sound like the one. Something more global, like the New World Order and terrorism."

"Have you been checking up on me?" Nadine asked lightly, but an imperceptible wariness crept into her deep green eyes.

Barak chuckled. "I was at the Casablanca conference with about a thousand other businessmen. The Gulf States are very anxious to purchase our technology. There was something familiar about you, so I pulled out my file. The program listed your name."

"I gave a talk on economics at that conference."

"Which, by the way, I did not hear," he said through a mouthful of the gooey dessert. "But I hear you contributed significantly to the study of a growing anti-Western ideology."

Nadine chewed her pastry thoughtfully. Much of the information for public consumption on post-Cold War ideologies and terrorism was issued by her own Department, but her work on that subject had never been published. Its sensitive nature and the potential for misinterpretation kept her research and analyses on that subject tagged for internal use only. Still, plenty of people had access to it. The Defense Intelligence Agency and other members of the established Intelligence Community who dealt with anti-terrorism were privy to it. Even Shlomo, with his IC contacts, had read much of her work. She was not naïve enough to believe that her economic theories were the goods that had enticed him.

She brought her thoughts back to Barak. She wanted to trust him. She enjoyed his company, his boyish charm and especially their runs together that were somehow intimate. He surprised her constantly with the breadth of his knowledge and he seemed to care—about people and about her. She liked the way she felt in his presence, the way he made her feel; something she hadn't felt since she first met Jeremy. Her mind was racing. She looked towards a citadel off to her left and tried to quell the alarm bells. She wasn't ready to let go just yet. He was worth a measured risk. She always saw things more clearly after she'd had a chance to mull them over.

"There is an anti-Western ideology developing that I see as something of a backlash. The abrupt end of the Cold War coupled with the spread of the global village phenomenon through technology has changed fundamental concepts and allegiances all over the world. Because of the Internet in large part, places like Syria, Iran and the former Soviet Union are suddenly awash in a free flow of information, exposed to Western ideas and values. To some extent, the exchange was inevitable and welcome. But, to many, especially on the heels of Bush's New World Order, the influx was abhorrent. There are those, and they are not few in number, to whom this flood of Western thought and culture is perceived as an attempt to destroy other peoples, cultures or even governments. This is the prevailing view now, in the Balkans for example, and elsewhere across the globe."

"So the West is the evil empire."

"Quite frankly, yes, that is the belief in many parts of the world. The United States in particular doesn't recognize its forays into other countries as the bad boy exploits the local residents view them to be. But Western good intentions are not the right solution worldwide. Somalia is the perfect example. We went in to save the Somalis and restore peace to the people. Instead of gratitude, we were greeted with hostility. We were clueless about their internal feelings toward the West."

"I would think that considering the state they were in before the fall of the Soviet Union, they would be grateful for a little Western ingenuity."

"So Western of you to say so, but yes, the expectation was that the end of the Cold War would usher in an era of global peace and prosperity in the information age. That hasn't quite succeeded as planned. The road to capitalism has been full of potholes. The people are hungry."

"But hasn't it always been that way? There are the 'haves' and the 'have-nots.'"

Nadine shrugged in acquiescence. "Perhaps. But right now there is a competing cause. Since the success of the Islamic Revolution in Iran in 1979, Islam has taken a very solid hold well beyond Middle East, all across Asia, North Africa, Pakistan, Bangladesh, Malaysia, Indonesia and much of the former Soviet Union. The removal of Soviet controls long in place, left a gap. The Islamic Movement quickly filled that gap. Charity is a strong tenet of Islam. The movement not only provides an ideology, but also puts food on people's plates, provides for basic needs. Many of the once-Soviet satellite countries now have entrenched Islamic governments."

Having polished off the baklava, Barak ordered another, then said, "But they're hardly a threat to the Western world."

"No, *they're* not. However, some extremist militant sects have interpreted jihad as armed uprising against Western dominance. With that, we've entered a new age of terrorism, quite unlike terrorism of the past."

"New age?"

Nadine sipped her Turkish coffee and nodded. "In the '60s and '70s, terrorists were members of organized groups with specific goals, coherent causes, generally secular and nationalistic like Germany's Bader Meinhoff Gang or Italy's Red Brigade. After a particular terrorist act, the group would claim responsibility, issue demands.

"Today's terrorists are strikingly different. They are sophisticated, privately financed networks whose goal is to attack Americans, Israelis and other targets sympathetic to the West. The perpetrators issue no claims of responsibility, no demands, no manifestos. As true believers, they act simply to harm a perceived enemy, in this case, the West."

"Meaning, what? Does that make it more dangerous?"

"Vastly. The constrained terrorist of the past carried out an act of violence to draw attention to a particular grievance or to make a demand, seizing a 'bully pulpit' so to speak. Today's terrorists, by their silence, send a message of overwhelming fear and vulnerability. It is that very vulnerability, whether perceived or real, that weakens the West. Easy access to advanced technology, anonymity and the wide reach of the media makes the impact of the attack much greater."

"And who are these terrorists that are so hell bent on destroying the West?"

Ignoring his attempt at levity, she leaned in towards him and replied, "They are simply everyday people, like you and me, highly skilled killers, many of them freelancers, who travel the globe, establishing links with loosely organized terrorist cells to carry out plots against the U.S. by targeting Americans around the world. They are extremely dangerous. They form diffuse autonomous cells for the purpose of carrying out a specific act of terror. After the deed is done, the cell dissolves. New groups re-form with different members to carry out new acts of terror."

"That would make it very difficult to counter."

"Yes, but there is one thing working in our favor. In the past, governments turned a blind eye to terrorist acts when the cause was thought to be sympathetic.

Today's terrorism is almost universally recognized as a pure crime so there is greater international cooperation in pursuing and prosecuting them. And the United States has become more aggressive, arresting suspects even on foreign soil."

"Where do these nouveau terrorists get their training?"

This time Nadine allowed herself a smile. "Ah, now you've asked the $64,000 question. Syria, Iran. The CIA trained many in Afghanistan during the insurrection against the Soviet Union. One evil empire fell and now they've trained their sites on the other, the United States. Others are trained by terrorist organizations and governments that officially support terror."

"Are you saying that the CIA trained the rebels in Afghanistan and now they are planning a campaign of terror against the United States?" Barak's tone was incredulous.

"Yep," she replied matter-of-factly.

"Who's paying for all this?"

Nadine shrugged, as if the answer was obvious. "There are any number of sources. Wealthy Middle Eastern businessmen sympathetic to anti-Western sentiment. Often, contributors to Islamic religious organizations are an unwitting source. *Zakah*, giving to Islamic causes, is a religious duty. The charitable contributions of many Muslims to legitimate causes are diverted to terrorist groups.

"Then there is state-sponsored terrorism from Iran, Libya, Syria, the Sudan, in the hundreds of millions of dollars. The U.S. is the primary focus. Big Satan as it's called. But as you know, Israel, also known as Little Satan, and the PA are similarly at risk."

Barak practically smirked. "Israel has been the focus of terrorism for fifty years. But the Palestinian Authority? How is the PA threatened?"

"Fundamentalists within the Islamic Movement are not happy with the way the Palestinian Authority has been governing. The Iranian Supreme Leader openly called Arafat a traitor. They haven't taken overt action against the Palestinian Authority, but it may just be a matter of time."

"How so?"

"There are many reasons. But most relevant to us is that they believe that Arafat and his ministers are puppets of the United States and Israel. Arafat established a secular government, also considered an enemy of Islam. They believe that Palestine must be liberated by true believers and founded upon Islamic fundamentalist ideology. *Jihad* is the duty of the true Muslim. Terror is a means to confront God's enemies."

Nadine thought she saw Barak's jaw stiffen just slightly. "Israel can defend itself against terror."

"Perhaps so. But if terror takes on any measure of success against the United States, Western ideology and democratic principles will lose credibility creating an atmosphere ripe for the introduction of a new doctrine. If we are complacent, it could happen, and sooner than you think. History has seen it happen before."

"The Crusades all over again?"

"Some of the imams would like to see it that way. Calls for the destruction of America and Israel emanate loud and clear from Iran's highest clerics. Still, there is room for a scenario that is the result of more purposeful manipulation."

Barak straightened and locked her gaze.

"I see I've finally gotten your attention," she joked, but she was intrigued by his body language. He didn't underestimate its relevance. She made a mental note.

He relaxed slightly. "What kind of manipulation?"

"The fundamentalists have declared war against Western dominance and that war is in full force in a number of countries. The most obvious are Algeria and Egypt who have elected secular governments. Turkey, also a Western-oriented Muslim country has avoided the conflict by reaching a political solution with its Islamic parties. There is a keen sense of community, *umma*, within Islam, that supercedes political disparity. Terrorism against the United States for its support of Israel or a perceived opposition to Islamic governments is an easy sell. A savvy rogue government, in a strategic alliance with a well-organized terrorist organization, could create the catalyst that would see the demise of the dominance of Western culture."

Barak looked skeptical. "Why hasn't it happened until now? I mean, could a handful of loose cannons really pose a threat to the Western world?"

Nadine felt an intensity that she tried to subdue as she responded to Barak. "Westerners have a glaring weakness for ignoring realities that do not mesh with their thinking. They have yet to accept that there is a different logic at work here. They will not acknowledge events that don't make sense to them, so they dismiss them, and their predictable fallout, as unlikely, or as having very low probability."

She leaned towards him. "But they are starting at the wrong starting point. There is another mindset at work here, one that reasons along very different lines. This is not about money, political gain or even justice. This is about anger, frustration, most of all, humiliation. And they want to visit it upon the rest of us." Her shoulders dropped as she leaned back and sighed. "The world has become a very small place. We are setting ourselves up for a surprise. A very big surprise."

Barak stretched his long body and smiled at her. "Israel has all the purveyor's of doom it needs. What do you say we continue on our naïve way, shall we? And enjoy the rest of this lovely morning ignoring world events and taking in the sunshine."

Nadine relaxed a bit. "Yes, let's do that," she said, relieved for the moment, not to pursue the subject further.

"*Ain haor nicar ela mitoch hachoshech.*"

"Light cannot be perceived except out of darkness." That was what the old man had said as he brushed by her earlier that day in the shouk.

Now what did he mean by that? Nadine wondered aloud standing under the hot, steady stream of the shower.

She loved long, hot showers. Her mind opened and her thoughts roamed freely in the billowing mist of the steamy cubicle. Must've been talking to himself, she concluded and promptly forgot his existence.

CHAPTER 6

▼

Nadine eyed the wood with growing excitement. She circled the track two or three times to warm up and then took off for the forest. She had her route down pat and the afternoon heat encouraged her to seek refuge in the shade of the pines. As she entered the cool canopy, she momentarily recalled newspaper spots she had read about trail runners attacked by mountain lions in California, or bears in Alaska.

"Well, none of that to be worried about in the Jerusalem Forest," she reassured herself.

Nadine was a little tense as she got her bearings, but as she ran, the tension dissolved and flowed from her like rippling liquids. Once released, the powerful muscles of her legs moved her ahead of their own accord. Shoulders relaxed and breathing even, her body and soul were in complete harmony with the surroundings. Inhaling the pungent aroma of the evergreens, she had no thoughts as she ran. Her steps were light and touched the ground almost noiselessly as they carried her further and further through the wood.

All of her senses were in a state of heightened awareness, fine-tuned to their utmost. She was utterly in the present, completely a part of the scene, moving through it and breathing with the trees.

The glint of sun on steel blinded her momentarily. She stumbled as her toe snagged the edge of a rut, but caught herself and managed to react before the knife completely cleared her right shoulder. Regaining her balance, her right wrist blocked as her left hand swept the striking forearm and locked it between her own. With one swift cross motion, she heard her attacker's elbow crack. As he howled, she turned one hundred eighty degrees to her right. Half-crouched on her left leg for support, she let her right heel fly straight out and explode against his spleen in a powerful side kick. As he doubled over, she place her right hand on his shoulder, swept her leg behind his lower shin and dropped him to the ground with a thud. Almost before he landed, her foot was in his groin.

She was struck for a moment by a shock of red hair that peeked out from under the black and white checkered *kafiyah* that framed his young face. Then she ran without looking back, finally exiting the woods at the far side of the track.

Think! she commanded herself as she ran towards the recreation center. Where were the phones? By now, the office would be locked. Her mind was racing and she was gasping for air.

"Damn!" she thought as she reached the public phone near the entrance of the center. She had no idea whether she could dial an emergency number without a token or a phone card. They didn't take coins and anyway, she didn't have one.

Her sudden stop sent her into a fit of wheezing, nearly choking her as she tried to slow her pulse. It was still way too high and the blood rushed to her head as she doubled over at the waist, hands heavy on her thighs. About to faint, she raised her chin and inhaled noisily. Finally, she straightened up.

Nadine grabbed the receiver, but her sweaty fingers slipped off the keypad as she tried to press '1-0-0,' the police emergency number. Three tries later, she forced herself to take a deep breath and press each key long and hard. It was ringing! About to hyperventilate, she cupped her hands over her nose and mouth and drew another deep breath. Finally, a voice came on the line and asked her to describe her emergency. Moments later, she could hear sirens wailing in the distance.

Nadine ran over to the squad car as it pulled up to the recreation center. Quickly, she described her route and her attacker to the two officers. She'd only gotten a momentary look at his face, and he at hers.

One headed for the grove while the other took her report.

"We'll go to the station when my partner gets back," he said. "Maybe you'll be able to identify him from the photos."

Nadine nodded numbly and wondered how she was going to keep this from Daniel and Zak. In Jerusalem, this was news. Tensions were riding high. An assault by a young Arab, most likely Palestinian, was not going to be ignored or quietly forgotten.

They waited only a short time before the officer returned from the forest.

"No sign of him. I'll radio for one the guys from the lab to come back and we'll inspect the area more carefully. You go back to the station."

He hesitated a moment, then said, "Have them send a dog, too. We may find something that it can get a scent on that'll help us out later. Tell them to make it quick. We've got a couple of hours before nightfall but it's already pretty dark in those woods."

"Right," said the officer who had taken Nadine's report.

She began to shiver. A chill replaced the heat she had generated while running and her muscles began to ache. Reluctantly, he agreed to let her go home first but warned, "I want to see you at the station in one hour, got it? Or it's my ass, O.K.?

Quietly, Nadine slipped into the apartment. She was streaked with dirt and sweat, and hoped to get into the shower before calling anyone's attention to her. She was so wound up that she nearly fainted when she saw the note on the table.

The original 'Die Hard' was playing at the old Edison Theater, it said. Her neighbor, Mrs. Wolf, sixty-three years old and a die-hard Bruce Willis fan, had taken Daniel and Zak to see the movie with her. They would not be home until well after ten.

"Bless you, Mrs. Wolf," she whispered aloud, momentarily relieved.

Standing under the streaming hot water for what seemed an eternity, the rushing torrent mingled with the flow of her tears that she couldn't seem to stop. When the water finally began to turn cold, she forced herself to step out of the shower, dress and head for the station.

Detective Shimoni led her into a small room and seated her at a table piled high with loose-leaf binders jammed with mug shots. Shimoni, tall, slender and forty-ish spoke to her reassuringly.

"Take your time," he said quietly. "Go through them carefully. We will find him." He paused, then added, "And he'll pay."

Shimoni's last remark jolted her into a flash of understanding. This was not about her. This was about survival. She was not the victim. The entire Jewish nation was the victim. This was Arab against Israeli. Israeli against Arab. When he attacked her in the forest, she thought, that young man was attacking every Israeli, venting his hate for every Jew. When she was attacked in the forest, the Israeli people experienced collective trauma, as they did after every individual assault. And once again, they were united in their determination to repel the aggressor.

The realization unnerved her. She had been drawn into a war being waged at ground zero; a war that was slowly chipping away at the armor of the Israeli people like drops of water, persistent and determined, falling one by one against a mighty rock, until the armor is finally pierced and its heart exposed.

Perhaps, she thought, that was why so many young Palestinians were willing to martyr themselves. Each one was a drop of water, but together, they made a waterfall. And the wear was beginning to show in the frayed nerves of the Israeli people. With each terror victim, came more fear and renewed distrust. They were clearly torn. Even when the peace negotiations were at their height and it appeared that the Palestinians were well on their way to independence, bombs were exploding on buses and in malls. Now, with a right wing government in place and the negotiations between the Palestinians and the Israelis at their most strained level since the talks began, everyone was on edge.

She turned the pages slowly finding herself unwillingly drawn to each photo, probing, wondering what each had done, what horrendous crimes had been committed, to be included between the covers of these heavy blue binders. None resembled the childlike, almost angelic face of the youth who had attacked her.

An hour and a half later, Nadine stepped out of the room and walked down the hallway in search of Detective Shimoni. She stopped in front of the information desk and waited for the officer to finish an obviously personal call. He saw her waiting, but made no effort to assist her.

Annoyed but knowing better than to show it, she turned and headed towards a set of double doors marked "Authorized Personnel Only."

"Hey, where are you going?" the officer called after her.

"To find someone who will help me."

"You can't go in there."

"I know," she said as she kept walking. Abruptly, she halted and turned. "Never mind. I'm going home."

She had already exited the glass doors at the front of the building and was stepping quickly down the concrete stairs to the street when she heard a voice call her name.

"Mrs. Kanner, please. Just a moment." It was Detective Shimoni.

"I'm sorry. He's not there. I need to go home."

"Are you all right? Can you drive? I can have one of my men give you a lift."

"No thanks."

"Listen, we have a lot of paperwork and more photos…" His voice trailed off. "OK. Tomorrow's another day. But first thing in the morning."

Nadine nodded her thanks and stepped into the quiet night. It was only eight o'clock when she unlocked the door to her apartment but the incident had already been reported on the evening news.

At least Daniel and Zak weren't home to hear it, she thought. And maybe by tomorrow it would be forgotten.

That was wishful thinking, Nadine knew. In Jerusalem, the City of Peace, solitary souls could walk her cobbled streets and narrow alleyways without thought of harm. But a recent spate of terrorist attacks in the holy city had the public seething. Tonight's attack on her only added fuel to the fire. No, this was not going to fade quietly. Drained, she curled up on the sofa and watched muted figures and faces parade across her television screen.

She jolted at the shrill peal of the doorbell. Heart pounding, she peeked through the peephole in the door. Immediately, she swung it open and Barak wrapped his arms around her. He held her until he felt her heartbeat slow down and her breathing become more regular.

"Let's go get a drink," he said. It was more an order than an invitation.

Neither spoke. Barak opened the passenger door of his car for her, walked around it and slid into the driver's seat. It was only then that she noticed his khaki uniform and officer's insignia.

"You're a career officer?" she blurted out.

"I was," he answered. "I 'retired' last year. I'm on reserve duty this month."

The legacy of a country always at war, she thought. Three years in the army, some went on to become officers, but they all stayed in for life. And tonight she thought she almost understood why.

They drove in silence past the Haas Promenade toward downtown Jerusalem. Nadine could see the ancient walls and parapets of the Old City awash in a soft white light on the opposite hill. What would David, King of the Hebrews, who inaugurated the city as his capital 3000 years earlier, think of it now?

When they reached the city's center, Barak parked the car, took Nadine's hand and led her halfway down a cobblestone street of artisan's shops and cafes. They turned left into an alleyway and ducked as they stepped down four stone stairs into Shaul's Pub. The room was dim and the mellow tones of a jazz trio permeated the warm air, sweetly scented by night blooming jasmine that clung to the outer walls of the pub. A cushioned bench traversed the wall of the club and they settled into a quiet corner.

Barak watched her in the mellow light. He was astonished that she had escaped the deadly assault unharmed when most victims did not survive at all. He had had his own experience with terrorists. Brutal and driven, they were possessed of unstoppable determination to carry out their carnage at all costs. Yet, here she was, a hair's breadth away from him, close enough for him to be aware of the scent of her skin.

He went over her every feature. Her dark hair was short and seemed to glisten. Her eyes were green and set widely apart above a nondescript nose. Her lower lip was fuller than the upper and Barak resisted the urge to lean over and kiss her. Her tan complexion was smooth and clear, and she had broad cheeks that tapered gently to a delicate chin. Her athletic physique gave her the bearing of a person of strength and confidence, yet her movements were feminine and graceful.

Power and grace, he thought to himself. She's like a tiger.

Barak flashed back to his former wife, Zoe. When they married, he was already a decorated officer in the Israel Defense Forces. Zoe was twenty and launching a successful modeling career. They had been married for several years and he thought that they were happy until he discovered that she'd been routinely unfaithful. But what hurt him most was her indifference to his discovery. A week later she was gone. A flicker of pain crossed his face. He returned his gaze to Nadine. Zoe was beautiful, but Nadine had obvious intelligence and sensitivity, matched by a deep, authentic laugh that came easily and often.

"Are you all right?" she asked quietly.

Nadine's look brought Barak back to the present.

"Sure," he said and smiled. "Just thinking."

He ordered a bottle of wine. They listened to the trio until the wine arrived and Nadine laughed as they went through the 'taste and approval' ritual.

"The subtle distinctions between wines of fine vintage are not my forté," Nadine confessed.

"Ahh, then a trip through the vineyards of Israel is in order." A hint of a smile crossed his mouth.

"Never mind. I'd be so drunk after the first two glasses, it would all be lost on me."

"You don't drink the wine, Nadine, you spit." They both laughed then, but sobered quickly.

Softly, Barak asked, "What happened?"

Nadine took a quick, sharp breath, exhaled slowly and began. "I had been running for close to an hour. We were all one, the road, the trees and I, and I felt like I was flying."

She closed her eyes for a moment and a look of calm crossed her face as her mind's eye returned her to the verdant wood.

"I felt utter serenity," she continued, opening her eyes. "The instant that changed, I reacted. Something foreign and threatening shattered the tranquillity of the moment and I was aware of it immediately. I could feel, hear, even smell the attack coming. I just protected myself. Tyler was right. Timing is everything. I just never really believed I would ever find that out."

"Who's Tyler?" Barak asked.

"Sergeant Tyler Moore, U.S. Air Force, one of my trainers and instructor par-excellence in martial arts and hand-to-hand combat. Tyler would say, 'In a real attack you don't have time to think. You have to feel the attack before it happens. Your reaction must be instinctual, from the gut, and your timing, perfect. If you have to stop and think, you're dead.' Nadine paused and shrugged. "Well, I'm not dead."

They were quiet for a moment. Then she said, "I worked for the Department of Defense and was married to an Air Force officer, so you see, the military is not at all unfamiliar to me."

"So that explains the jeep parked outside your house," Barak commented.

Nadine nodded. Jeremy's jeep had been presented to her as a farewell gift just a few days before her departure and was shipped to the port of Haifa via one of the U.S. Navy ships that docked there regularly. She and the boys had picked the jeep up at the dock and miraculously cleared Israeli customs without a hitch. They drove south down the coastal highway back towards Jerusalem. When they reached the ancient city of Caesaria they stopped for a swim in the inviting Mediterranean.

"This city was built 2000 years ago in honor of the Roman Emperor Augustus," Nadine began lecturing, but before she could go on about its aqueduct and amphitheater, the boys ran whooping and hollering into the blue-green waves.

Starving after the exertion, they ate *shwarma* and *humus* at one of the country's famous gas station-restaurants while filling the jeep's tank, then continued on their way. They reached the foothills as dusk began to settle. Handling the steep curvaceous climb with ease, they rounded the last curve twenty minutes later to a spectacular view of the glittering metropolis appearing like a cache of jewels carelessly flung across the mountaintops on which the city was built. Nadine knew she had come home.

"What made you decide to become an officer?" Nadine asked Barak.

"I'm a patriot," Barak stated simply.

Nadine gave him a questioning look, prompting him to go on.

"I rose through the ranks pretty quickly. And there I was, in my mid-thirties with a great pension plan and my whole life ahead of me. I decided that it was time to start living." He paused as if debating about whether to continue. "In the army, I became an expert in satellite technology and mapping. Now, I'm an executive in my own hi-tech firm developing satellite technology."

The jazz trio took a break. They sat silently for a while, as if the music had acted as a shield, which, now lifted, prevented them from speaking.

"Nadine," Barak said finally, "that attack was not an accident. This was no madman or rapist you happened to come across in the woods. It was planned."

He picked up his napkin, leaned towards her and began to draw with a pen he lifted from a passing waiter. "That part of the Jerusalem Forest is bordered on the east by the village of Abu Jibril, an Arab village that became part of Israel after the 1967 Six Day War. For the most part, they are good citizens, but many of these villages have terrorist cells. Our runs, no doubt, did not go unnoticed."

Nadine saw the muscles of Barak's jaw, tense. He continued, "Taking out an Israeli proves loyalty and sincerity. It's often used as indoctrination into one of those cells. Palestinians fingered as collaborators also hunt Israelis to prove their loyalty. To be a Palestinian accused of collaboration with the Israelis is a death sentence. Whoever they were, they were waiting for an opportunity and you gave them one."

"Them? There was only one," Nadine protested.

Barak shrugged. "Your attacker probably wasn't alone. Having witnesses to such 'bravado' is an important element. Besides, from the sound of it, this guy needed help getting home and he was gone fairly quickly."

Something he said unnerved her. Sensing her alarm he said, "Listen, Nadine, these things don't strike in the same spot twice. You're safe. The danger is to his next victim." He did not mention that the first victim usually did not survive.

"What now?" Nadine asked.

"Try to identify him. Though chances are good that he will be found soon. He needed medical care and the police will know where to look. Would you recognize him if you saw him again?"

"Barak, my only prayer is that I will forget that I ever saw him."

CHAPTER 7

▼

Fouad felt troubled as he made his way home that evening. Nadine had waved to him on her way to the track, but an hour later, he'd heard sirens and seen a patrol car, followed by another a little later with dogs and she did not return as usual. No, he did not feel good about this at all. He was unsure about leaving at all without seeing her, but by the time he closed up, the park was quiet.

He had first spotted Nadine more than half a year earlier, shortly after she'd moved into the neighborhood. The melancholy in her eyes and the desperation in every muscle of her body struck him as she passed his kiosk each evening on her way downhill to the track. There she ran, pounding out the miles, at first, to find deliverance from her despair, and later, as the months passed by, for the sheer joy of it. He loved her spirit and her untarnished acceptance of this old man. He also knew that she found a special solace in his presence each evening. A bond had been forged.

He rode the Jerusalem city bus to the interchange where he caught the Arab line into his village. He still thought of Abu Jibril as a village despite the fact that the village had become a small city in the thirty years since Israel gained sovereignty over it. The two were now socially and economically intertwined. Like him, many residents of Abu Jibril worked and shopped in Jerusalem. And each weekend, many of Jerusalem's residents descended upon Abu Jibril's restaurants and shops. Local merchants bought and sold Israeli goods. Most of Abu Jibril's residents spoke Hebrew and a number of its young men studied at the university in Jerusalem. Yet one of those men turned himself into a human bomb in an attack against the Jews only a few weeks earlier.

Fouad heaved a sigh. As he rode the bus, an expression of disapproval mixed with sorrow shadowed his naturally good-humored face. Try as he might, he could not ignore the tensions that swirled about him, setting off explosive bursts of pent-up anger and misdirected violence. As he saw it, the confrontations would only weaken chances for a Palestinian state. Not that he was unhappy under Israeli sovereignty. In the scheme of things, Israeli rule had worked out quite well for him. Indeed, he might have preferred to leave things the way they were. But all around him there was too much resentment. Too much unrest. The Palestinians needed recognition. A state would bring respect, prosperity and order. Had they been wiser in 1948, the Palestinians would have a state now, too.

Another deep sigh filled him. So much death. He too had lost family members, but who hadn't? Yes, they would have their state, but fifty, maybe sixty years and a lot of hate later. This war for peace, and it was a war, would be no less painful than its predecessors.

He alighted the bus and walked slowly toward his home. Normally, he savored this time of the day to clear his thoughts and enjoy the sweet scents of the many night blooming plants along the way, but tonight a heavy foreboding invaded his usual evening calm. A few minutes later, the stone house that he'd built with Amir, his eldest, came into view. They added two more rooms to the house when Amir married and his wife joined them. Amir now had a young son of his own who was the joy of Fouad's life. Fouad's spirits lifted just thinking of the chubby three-year-old climbing onto his lap and pinching his generous chin. Amir was followed by three daughters and finally, another son, Naji, Fouad's youngest, now seventeen. Yes, he thought as he walked the path to his home, something had to change so that his grandchildren could live in peace.

Fouad was greeted at the doorstep by his wife, who seated him in his favorite chair, exchanged his dusty shoes with a comfortable pair of slippers, then presented him with a feenjon of steaming tea and a plate of dried fruit to relax with before the evening meal.

As he sipped his tea, Fouad heard a chorus of agitated voices coming from the garden. Distracted from his repast, he stepped outside. Naji and several of his friends were in the throes of a heated discussion. They quieted almost immediately as he approached.

"*Salaam aleichem,*" the young men greeted Fouad.

"*Aleichem salaam,*" Fouad responded. "What's going on here?"

A teen by the name of Youssef spoke up. "Muhammad Ibn Assad was crossing through the forest late this afternoon when he was attacked by murderous Israelis. They broke his elbow and beat him. Now, he is bleeding to death. His family is enraged. They have sworn vengeance against the attackers and their families."

"Why does his family not take him to the hospital?"

"He refuses. His life is in Allah's hands. He is a martyr and will ascend directly to heaven," another teen offered.

Fouad felt his throat constrict and a pit form in his stomach. As he tried to make sense of it, their conversation became increasingly militant.

"The Zionists will yet be shoved into the sea. Our *jihad* will not be victorious until we have returned all of the land to *Allah* and his holy servants," seethed a dark-haired man with flashing eyes under thick eyebrows. The man was unfamiliar to Fouad but something about him sent a chill down Fouad's old spine.

"Individual glory is meaningless," the stranger continued. "Through sacrifice, we shall destroy the Jews and restore Islam as the law of the land."

Fouad could see that the man's tempered passion was having an effect on the small group. The stranger kept his voice low when he spoke but its tone was filled with determination. He had the group's rapt attention.

"*Shwaya, shwaya*, slowly, slowly, we are regaining our towns and our cities. Allah smiles upon us and turns history in our favor. We have many battles to wage and the greatest still lies before us. The streets of Jerusalem will yet flow with the blood of the infidel Jews." The speaker's upper lip curled back baring gleaming white teeth. His bushy eyebrows lowered over black eyes narrowed into slits, as if in readiness to devour some unsuspecting prey. The stranger's ominous glower repulsed Fouad.

In many of the local mosques the *imams* were preaching violent action against Israel and even calling for another *intifada*. They organized and harbored small terrorist cells that were responsible for many of the suicide attacks inside Israel.

He was careful to steer Naji clear of those mosques, but he had no control over Naji's friends. The fever of nationalism that fired these young men of no experience and no memory, made them hot headed and unreasonable. He had heard enough. Fed up, Fouad stepped in.

"You spew rhetoric without understanding," he said. "We live in a prosperous town where you young men have been educated and trained. You come from fine Palestinian families. Killing yourselves and others along with you will not change anything. Your thirst for revenge is a mockery. Violence will not help our brothers who live in the squalor of refugee camps in Gaza. Use your voices, not your tempers, to make your point. They need work, not martyrs, to better their lives. The real hope of the Palestinian people lies with jobs and money that buy better education and bring security. Where is your national pride? With the fools who have joined Allah?" He lowered his voice just above a whisper, locking each boy's eyes in his own. "Show me where it is written in the Qu'ran that blowing yourself to bits and taking the lives of innocent people with you, is a holy act? We are an intelligent people. Let us behave intelligently and build a nation whose mothers can be proud of their sons, not grieve for them."

The light in the stranger's eyes dimmed and his eyebrows lowered further. The change in his expression was imperceptible to those around him, but would have been telling had they noticed.

Al Rasuul walked the deserted streets of the sleeping village flanked by three of his senior advisors, his thoughts on the afternoon's events. Despite intensive mental and physical training, the indoctrination of the new recruit had gone awry.

'Dirballak!' he swore to himself.

His thick brows knit together furrowing his high forehead. His visit to Abu Jibril was meant to maintain high morale among his loyalists here. Now, a young man lay bleeding to death. Hospitalizing him was out of the question. The authorities were on the alert and would swarm into the village like ants at a picnic. He would have to let the recruit die and hold a martyr's funeral, generating more hatred for the Israelis and spawning a dozen new recruits in their fight for Palestinian nationalism.

There remained the issue of the woman. Barretta raised, he had been mesmerized, almost aroused, by the power and grace of her movements as she repelled her attacker. She had hesitated for a split second after dropping the recruit to the ground. At that moment, he could easily have put a bullet through her. Indeed, he now regretted not doing so, but he had been momentarily stunned when he caught a glimpse of her face.

His eyebrows lowered slightly as they did whenever he was deep in thought. He had already turned the disastrous day's end to his advantage. Guided by the premise that one must be prepared to make the most out of the unexpected, he used it to fuel smoldering anti-Israeli sentiment and to add several new young men to the local cell. Though he believed in no higher calling than himself, Al Rasuul used the unifying voice of Islam to gather his forces. Now he headed an organization more widespread, militarily adept and politically powerful than any outsider dared to imagine.

Still, there remained one wrinkle that he had not yet fully resolved. He had spent the last two years planning every detail of the next, and final, operation; the act that would give him complete and irrevocable control over the Palestinian people and the new State of Greater Palestine that he would declare in place of the State of Israel. While this was not the time to introduce unnecessary variables, the dying recruit's family and his own freedom fighters were calling for revenge. It was critical not to disappoint them at this delicate stage. He had to be very careful not to shake their faith. His people were fickle, changing direction like leaves in the wind.

"*Shwaya, shwaya.*" "Slowly, slowly," he said to himself. "Soon I will be *al rais.*"

CHAPTER 8

─────────── ▼ ───────────

Nadine was calm by the time Daniel and Zak got home. Zak gave her a blow-by-blow account of the movie as he got ready for bed.

When he finally quieted down, Nadine said, "Listen, guys. A friend of mine said he'd like to take us on a hike to a hidden oasis. What do you say we go this Friday to avoid the weekend hikers?"

"Who's your friend, Mom?" asked Zak.

"Barak," she said in a tone as nonchalant as she could muster.

"You mean that guy from the track? The one you call Red?" Zak asked. "Sure, yeah, great mom, let's do it."

Nadine looked at Daniel. He returned her gaze, nodded and turned to go to his room.

Later, when they were asleep, she stepped out onto the balcony. Here she could forget the distractions of the real world and for a little while, literally leave them behind her. An outline of the mountains was just visible under the moon lit sky. Suddenly, she felt tired. She slid down to the stone floor of the terrace, leaned back against the balustrade and closed her eyes. The night breeze felt soft against her skin. She took a deep breath and let it out slowly. A tear slid down her cheek. Was it self-pity or resentment? It didn't matter.

She saw his face and smiled. "Jeremy," she said aloud. She liked to hear the sound of his name. It soothed her and made her feel less alone. She reached out to caress his cheek. At her touch, he disappeared, leaving her alone with the wind in the trees.

Nadine did not let go of her reserve when Jeremy died. She buried her grief somewhere in the caverns of her heart where her pain remained invisible. Now, alone under the shield of darkness, she shed her carefully crafted reserve and let the sorrow rush through her.

She hugged herself tighter as the blades from the chopper whipped the cold air around her into motion. Jeremy waved to her and smiled as the chopper took off. He would be back from the routine reconnaissance mission in a day. The chopper lifted and hovered above her, suspended momentarily as it readied to speed south and east.

But instead of soaring toward the waiting hills, the chopper heaved and rocked, shuddering violently before bursting into angry plumes of calid flame. The inferno surged upward and outward, raging against the Italian night sky. Scorching heat whipped across her flesh as shock waves from the blast lifted her body and hurled it from the tarmac onto a grassy patch fifty feet from where she just stood. Sirens screamed and lights flashed. Unable to move, her eyes desperately sought out the bent metal skeleton of what had once been a helicopter. They bored through its blackened shell where the charred remains of the only man she had ever loved shriveled into smoldering ashes. The stench of burnt skin and scorched rubber filled the air. Helpless to bring back the life that disintegrated in a fiery instant, Nadine welcomed the black.

That was one year and a lifetime ago. She sucked in a deep breath of air and resolutely shook off the melancholy. She was tired of feeling resentful.

Her shield lifted itself back into place. "Nothing good lasts forever," she told herself and went to bed.

Nadine awoke early the next morning and was dressed by the time the boys got up. They staggered in for breakfast and she sat down with them as they buttered fresh rolls delivered to their doorstep at dawn. Not knowing exactly where to begin, she launched right into it.

"I didn't want you to hear about this on the news first so listen up for a minute. Yesterday, I went for a run in the forest. Someone tried to jump me but as you can see, I'm OK. Tyler did a good job training me and I hope that you guys are still practicing."

Daniel glared at her. On his face she saw the angry look she had come to know so well since Jeremy's death. Zak was clearly frightened. Nadine felt a momentary twinge of regret but she'd had no choice. It was the morning's top news story.

He hugged her, as if to make sure she was still there. "Did they catch him?" asked Zak, his face buried in her chest.

Stroking his head, she felt his vulnerability and the weight of motherhood. "Not yet. But they will." She released him gently. "I have to go to the police station and look at photos. They think they know where he's from and he's going to need some medical attention so they're pretty sure that they're going to find him."

"You hurt him?" Zak was incredulous.

The ringing of the telephone interrupted them.

"Nadine, it's Shlomo Cohen. I tried reaching you last night but you weren't home. Are you all right?"

"I'm fine Shlomo," Nadine responded, "but I'll be a little late this morning. I have to stop at the police station on my way in."

"Don't worry about it," Shlomo said. "Take as much time as you need. Just keep me posted."

"I'll be in later, Shlomo. We'll talk then," she said and hung up.

She had tried to keep her name out of news reports of the incident but the media had its sources and she resigned herself to the fact that there would be at least a few days of publicity.

She drove Daniel and Zak to school on her way to the police station. Zak let her give him a bear hug before running in to join his classmates, but Daniel leaped out of the jeep without saying good-bye. She could only hope that her face did not reflect the pain that shot through her as she watched his retreating back.

She fiddled with the jeep's radio on her way to the station trying to find one that wasn't debating the effectiveness of Israeli security in the wake of the previous day's attack on the runner in the Jerusalem forest. Nadine searched futilely for another topic of discussion to accompany her on her drive downtown. She finally turned the radio off in frustration and resolved to install one with an FM band as soon as possible.

Nadine spotted Detective Shimoni and the Chief of Police answering reporters' questions on the steps leading up to the police station as she pulled into a parking space opposite the municipal complex. Almost immediately, one of the officers she'd met the night before appeared at her side.

"Detective Shimoni asked me to bring you in through the side entrance to avoid the reporters," he said, moving between her and the steps to block their line of vision. "Try not to draw their attention."

Nadine accompanied him silently, but glanced sidelong at the small crowd of newspaper and television journalists gathered there. Reminding herself to thank him, she wondered how he knew that she did not want to face them. Perhaps word had gotten back to him that she had refused to take their calls or agree to interviews. Or maybe he was just a sensitive guy she mused as she caught a glimpse of his face. The black of his hair and eyebrows, his sharp nose and jaw, and rough, dark complexion augmented his serious deportment. He caught her look, but did not acknowledge her. Turning away, she was surprised by the softness of his glance.

She could hear some of the sharp and angry questions directed at the Chief of Police.

"What are you going to do about ensuring personal security?"

"Why haven't you established checkpoints at Abu Jibril?"

"How are you going to stop terrorists from operating within our borders?"

Raising his hands in a gesture requesting silence, the Chief responded, "We have launched a full scale investigation. We hope to complete it swiftly. We are committed to routing out terrorism from within our borders so that every man, woman and child can walk freely without fear for personal safety. However, only when the investigation is complete will we know whether instituting new security policies are in order. Thank you."

The morning passed no differently than the night before and she left the station as ignorant about her attacker's identity as when she had arrived. At the Institute, concentration eluded her. Her phone rang incessantly, alternating between calls of concern and inquiries from the press, while a steady stream of colleagues crossed her threshold. She finally gave up all hope of a routine day at the office and headed for home.

At the entrance to her apartment building, she turned and looked down the hill to Fouad's kiosk and the track beyond before climbing the stairs to her apartment.

The next two days were no better than the first as she endured hours of questioning by police, photographs and a physical examination that some bureaucrat suddenly remembered was necessary to document her condition. By the third day, Nadine had had enough. Her running shoes came out of the closet and as she slipped into her sweats she thought longingly of the release the miles would bring.

She waved to Fouad on her way down to the track. Planting her feet in its pebbly surface, she thought of nothing but the wind in her face and the tension in her legs as she stretched her still cold muscles. Trotting in place, she counted to sixty, then launched into a run, using her breath to pace herself. Her stride was long, slow and rhythmic. Her spirits rose as her momentum grew and before long she felt freed of the burdens that had plagued her for the past three days. At the five-mile mark, she burst into a sprint that took her halfway around the track then she loped to the spot where her sweatshirt and towel, carelessly tossed aside half an hour earlier, still lay.

She trudged up the hill to Fouad's kiosk, grateful for the return to routine. Fouad, however, did not return her smile as she dropped onto the stool and looked forward to a cool drink.

"I am relieved to see that you are well, Nadine," Fouad said. "But there are some in the village who are angry and will not let this die so quickly." He did not mention the meeting at his house several evenings previous but discreetly slipped her a piece of paper with a name scrawled in Arabic as he handed her a soda.

The note brushed her palm and her fingers grasped its crumpled edge. At that very moment Fouad had sealed his own death sentence, and guaranteed punishment for all those dear to him. Stunned, she did not know what to do except to stare at him in disbelief. He returned her gaze with a steadiness and conviction that she had not yet encountered in the old man of whom she had grown so fond.

"Fouad," Nadine breathed. "You could be killed for this."

"I have no choice," Fouad said heavily. "They have chosen the wrong path. They will destroy themselves and our people in the process. This is not just for your safety. Some people want to stop the hate. I am one of those people. My failure to act will allow another act of violence and for this I could not live with myself."

"Thank you, Fouad. May God be with us all."

"*Allahu Akbar*," Fouad responded. "God is great."

Once at home, she closed her bedroom door, sat down on the edge of her bed and stared at the name. A chill ran down her back as the stranger with the bright red hair took on an identity. He was so young! Surely not even twenty, yet he was filled with hate and had wanted to kill her. Instead of feeling frightened, she was overwhelmed with pity.

She began tossing the options around in her mind. Fouad could hardly have gone to the police himself. As it was, just passing the name on to her was enough to have him killed for collaboration by Palestinian extremists. His family would be marked, too. But she couldn't go waltzing into the police station with the name, either. They would want to know who gave her the information. Could she do it anonymously? She wasn't sure. She had the feeling that anonymous tips just didn't stay anonymous for long. Once an investigation began, she was sure that the trail would easily lead back to Fouad and his family. The risk was too great.

No, she resolved, for her, this is over. It wasn't worth his life. With that, she stood up, walked over to her dresser, opened the top drawer and shoved the tiny scrap underneath some clothing.

He saw the Eiffel Tower pointing skyward through the early morning haze. He peered through the dirty panes, then back at the belt carefully placed on a small bare table in the corner of the rundown room. He had just finished the painstaking process of packing it with explosives and it was now ready for wear. Soon he would be riding the jammed elevator to the top, but a little more than halfway there, the ride would end, democracy with it.

He thought better of smoking a cigarette. He would fly to heaven as a martyr, not the remains of a foolish accident. Others had died that way twice before. An apartment in the Philippines burnt to the ground in the flames of an explosion meant to bring down an American airliner and a hotel room in East Jerusalem was blown to smithereens by the explosives meant for a bus packed full of Israelis in the morning rush hour.

His head moved slowly from side to side. No, not him. He caught his reflection in the window. His large dark eyes were calm beneath long thick lashes and his full mouth was relaxed. Once, he had considered a career as a model. Heads turned, even here in Paris. But then he met Al Rasuul and understood his destiny. He was a *shaheed*; one of more than two hundred trained to become living bombs, martyrs who would rise directly to the heavens. Ready to deploy when called upon. Could there be a higher calling?

He was a natural choice for Paris since he spoke French as well as Arabic but also because beautiful people were above suspicion. He smiled. Even white teeth lit his dark handsome face. How foolish were the children of democracy to whom physical beauty was an icon and personal wealth a measure of holiness. He, and seven others, would prove that democracy was but a weak shell filled with degenerate, superficial values. Their overzealous dedication to protecting individual rights and personal freedom left them thoroughly exposed, completely vulnerable. Didn't that prove that the West had chosen the wrong path? Now he had been sent by Allah to wipe all traces of evil and immodesty away, to be destroyed like Sodom and Gomorra.

He, and seven others, were setting the stage for *umma*.

CHAPTER 9

▼

Friday morning finally arrived. None too soon as far as Nadine was concerned. The phone had not stopped ringing all week. She was still a high priority on the media list and her refusal to give interviews did nothing to deter them. Even her colleagues seemed unable to abandon the subject. They dropped into her office more often than necessary, always finding new ways to extract more details of the incident.

She stuffed her backpack with sandwiches and fruit, and filled the water canteens. Today, at least, she'd be out of telephone range, and was grateful for the temporary reprieve. Only the warning she had received from Fouad disquieted her.

Barak arrived at seven. They piled into the jeep and drove out of Jerusalem, down through the Judean Hills toward the Negev Desert and the Dead Sea. Though the road was paved it was never straight for long. It rose and fell with the hills, winding its way among them, as if the engineers who designed it were loathe to change any part of the existing landscape. Looking at it now, Nadine could understand why. The rolling alabaster hills dotted with nettle and ancient sandstone always made her feel that she was in another place in time. It seemed a magical place and she could not resist the impulse to share her fascination with Daniel and Zak.

"This entire region," she told them as they sped south, "from these mountains down into the desert, belonged to the tribe of Judah, reputed to be the strongest of the twelve tribes of Israel. The oasis we're heading for is mentioned all through the Bible, in Genesis, Chronicles, the Book of Samuel and the Song of Songs, just to name a few. David stayed there when he fled from King Saul. Soldiers hid in caves in the rocky slopes above it during the Bar Kochva revolt in 135 CE. The oasis remained populated until the Byzantine period, then was left wild, inhabited only by a few Bedouin families of the Rashida tribe. In 1949, the Israelis established a kibbutz nearby and made it a nature reserve. And today," she concluded with an air of triumph, "it's a hiker's paradise of endless trails, hidden streams and *wadis*."

She knew that it sometimes annoyed them, but she still shared her encyclopedic knowledge with them whenever possible. Zak rolled his eyeballs and gave her a half smile. He really didn't mind when she went off on stuff like that. He actually thought it was kind of cool, he just wasn't ready to let her know that. Daniel stared stone-faced at the passing vista.

Nadine had inherited her father's awe for the rich, if often tumultuous, history of the region. He was a professor of ancient history and she had spent much of her teenage years with him in the Middle East. Both had left an indelible impression. Almost everywhere she turned she could visualize events that took place centuries, even thousands of years earlier, unfolding before her eyes. It was, in fact, her uncanny ability to see beyond the obvious that had made her analyses so valuable to the Department of Defense. That fact was never lost on her.

"These hills look pretty barren from the road," she continued, "but because of the springs, thousands of species of plants and animals live here. Tropical plants grow alongside desert and Mediterranean ones. You'll be amazed at the variety of birds there are and we may see some hyrax or ibex. Luckily, the leopards are nocturnal."

Her last comment got Zak's attention and she went on to describe the other inhabitants of the reserve. He was relieved to hear that it's only snake, the whip snake, was nonvenomous. As she spoke, she thought she saw Barak trying to suppress a smile.

"What?" she asked, feigning insult.

Barak broke into a grin and said, "I'm impressed. You sound like the pioneers who settled here half a century ago. They could tell you something about every kilometer of this desert."

An hour later, they reached the Ein Gedi Reserve on the Dead Sea's western shore. An abundance of sweet water running through the arid Judean desert created an oasis of phenomenal beauty and diversity, and the largest oasis in the region. They planned to hike along Nahal Arugot, one of the rivers fed by the reserve's four springs to a hidden pool and waterfall.

They left the paved two-lane highway and drove down an unpaved desert road that led to the trailhead. They parked at the mouth of the stream where it emptied into the Dead Sea, 350 meters below sea level, the lowest point on earth. The sea's extremely high salt content made it impossible for any living thing to survive in it, but it was immensely popular with bathers who came for the salt's therapeutic treatments and sulfur baths.

They started down the path in single file, walking at a good clip so they could reach the pool before the day became scorching hot. Zak took the lead, leaping ahead like a mountain goat. The cloudless sky was bright blue. Rocky cliffs, the color of sand streaked with gold and orange, rose straight up on either side of them. The stream below ran through a gully thick with plants and trees. The differing vistas created a stark contrast. Nadine hiked briskly along the trail behind Zak. Daniel followed with Barak in the rear.

Shortly into their trek, Barak let out a whistle. They turned to see him picking fresh figs from a small, gnarly tree. They stopped for a short break to enjoy the oozing, sweet fruit and a few swigs of cool water. Then Zak was up and gone and the others quickly followed.

Nadine focused her thoughts on Daniel. Physically, he resembled her more than Jeremy. He had her deep green eyes and dark hair. He was tall for his age and the Israeli sun had deepened the tone of his skin to a soft mocha. Bright, introspective and wise beyond his years, he had Nadine's analytical sense and her easy laughter. But he was devastated by Jeremy's death. The laughter stopped and a veil of anger descended upon him with no sign of lifting. Nadine had been unable to penetrate it so far and after trying all she knew, she decided to just give him time and space, and her unconditional love. She hurt for him. Her own pain was deep, but the pain of seeing her child suffer was sometimes more than she could bear. Zak was the resilient one. Outgoing, energetic and funny, he rolled with every punch.

Nadine threw a glance back over her shoulder. Barak and Daniel were hiking together. Barak gestured at something and she saw Daniel nod.

A moment later, she heard a whoop from ahead followed by a loud splash. Zak was the first to reach the pool and was in the water before she rounded the bend. A few yards later, she stopped in her tracks and admired the waterfall cascading into the pond below. Then she dropped her backpack, quickly stripped down to her bathing suit, kicked off her hiking boots and followed Zak into the pool.

Relief from the hot, dry desert sun came instantly as the cool water hit her face and flowed through her hair. She shimmied through the refreshing pool, resurfacing at the base of the fall. They were joined minutes later by Daniel and

Barak who were mercilessly showered by Nadine and Zak as they struggled out of their clothes and sought refuge from the deluge under the blue waves.

"This is heaven on earth," Nadine murmured as she floated on her back, gazing at the desert rocks looming overhead and the azure sky above. The cliffs hid the cove and she relaxed knowing that nothing could touch her or her family in this idyllic isolation.

CHAPTER 10

▼

Nadine dove into her research at the Institute with a vitality that she hadn't felt for months. The trek into the desert took her away from the chaos of the preceding week and shifted her into high gear. She had forgotten how a day's hike could rejuvenate her.

Later in the day, she took a coffee break with two of her colleagues, Rona and Ehud. They sat in the courtyard adjoining the Institute's cafeteria, surrounded by a stone wall covered with blooming red bougainvillea. Nadine wanted to know how it was that Israelis seemed to have time to do it all. They worked hard, socialized several nights a week and still spent 'quality' time with their families.

"It's an attitude," Ehud responded. "We're a very nosy people, you know, and we all have to know each other's business so how better to do that, than to get together and talk about everyone else?"

Nadine knew he was teasing her and laughed. Ehud had been with ISI since its inception and was the most senior researcher at the Institute other than Shlomo Cohen. But there was no doubt where the authority lay.

Rona was young, intelligent and fresh out of graduate school. Nadine liked her high spiritedness but mostly she liked Rona's live-and-let-live-attitude. No pretenses. She was a straight shooter. Nadine sensed she was someone who could be relied upon.

"We sleep less," Rona said. "We go home in the evening for a while and head out the door again around midnight to visit with our friends. Maybe it's the army. We get used to functioning on very little sleep."

"We compartmentalize a bit more too," Ehud added more seriously now. "We assign time for work and time for play and that's that. No questions asked. And time with family is sacred.

"I must admit, I can't complain about the lifestyle," Nadine seconded.

They sat quietly for a few minutes enjoying the last drops of coffee before getting back to work. Life was indeed close to idyllic and Nadine wondered at the irony that she was back here without Jeremy, *because* she was without Jeremy. She wished he could have been a part of this but that wouldn't have happened. Their career paths weren't heading this way. She sighed involuntarily.

"Are you O.K.?" Rona asked.

"Fine, fine," Nadine answered quickly. "I just had a thought." Her voice trailed off. Rona didn't push it and they parted a few moments later.

The sun began to dip below the horizon casting a shadow that slowly crossed her desk, shading the page before her. Nadine was ready to call it a day. She started to pack up her things when the ringing phone stopped her. She hesitated before answering, then lifted the receiver.

The sound of Barak's voice raised a flush in her face and her heart beat a little faster. Pretending that he didn't mean anything to her wasn't working any more. She knew his kiss the night of the attack was more than a friend's concern. Until then, they'd maintained a comfortable distance. Their runs together were random and pure fun. But Barak's arrival at that very moment when someone to lean on was welcome, created another sort of bond between them. She'd been trying not to think of how close she'd come to death, of her two sons alone, and his strength greatly added to hers. She tried not to let him under her skin, but there he was. That evening's rendezvous had taken their relationship beyond the limited realm of easy camaraderie and replaced it by something else; she wasn't yet sure with what.

He was saying something about a dance festival in the North, near Haifa. "There's nothing quite like it. I was hoping we could drive up for a couple of days."

Nadine's mouth opened. She heard herself say, "I can't. I'm married," but no sound came out.

Jeremy's death had not changed her feelings. She thought they would keep her safe. She wanted to focus completely on Daniel and Zak. Sole parenting left little room for self-indulgence. Still, she felt her reserve bending in the face of her undeniably physical response to his voice.

"Nadine?"

She had to refuse. It would be easy enough to make up an excuse. But as if some other part of her was speaking for her, she found herself agreeing.

"Great," he said, not leaving her a moment for second thoughts. "I haven't had a break in a long time. I'm looking forward to this *and* spending a little time with you off the track. I know an inn on the shores of the Kinneret where we can stay."

His voice was deep and warm. She felt a flush rise in her face and fluttering in her low stomach. They said goodbye and Nadine gazed at the photo of Jeremy and the boys on her desk. He was gone, but his look seemed to say, "Go for it, Nadine." He was like that.

"Well," she said aloud, "that was then and this is now."

She decided not to hang around and ponder her schoolgirl reaction to Barak's call.

"It's nothing that a five mile run won't cure," she told herself reassuringly. She grabbed her bag and headed for the door.

The atmosphere was upbeat and exhilarating as she and Barak sat in the amphitheater waiting for the afternoon performance to begin. Karmiel, nestled in rolling green hills that overlooked the northern Mediterranean port of Haifa, was brimming with dancers and spectators from around the world. Nadine felt buoyed by the festive atmosphere and was glad she agreed to come. What good fortune, too, to have a neighbor like Mrs. Wolf. She was like a grandmother-on-call.

Barak hovered closely, lightly touching her arm, shoulder or the base of her back. When he took her hand to lead her through the crowd to their seats, his touch sent light waves of pleasure coursing through her.

They had been in their seats for fifteen minutes now and there was still no sign that the performance was to begin. Barak entertained Nadine with his latest repertoire of jokes from his business trip to Europe. Then he switched gears and asked her why she'd come back.

She wished that she had a light quip that could sum it all up quickly, but it just wasn't so. At the time, it seemed that there was nowhere else to go.

"When I was thirteen, my father and I came here, to Israel, for a sabbatical, an extended one as it turned out. He's a history professor and he loved it here and so did I. Those were the happiest years of my life. I didn't want to go home; I *was* home. But of course, the time came and that's what we did. When Jeremy died, being in the States was unbearable. There was too much of him everywhere I went. He was very well liked and everyone felt sorry for me. I could see the looks on their faces, friends, family, even at the Pentagon. Some didn't even know how to talk to me anymore. And at Aviano, it was the same. So when I started thinking about our future, mine, Daniel's and Zak's, I thought why not take them to the place I loved most, where I had been happiest as a child. Shlomo Cohen had already called to express his condolences and offer me a job. It seemed like the right thing to do, at the time."

"And does it still?"

Nadine grinned. "Hmm, no regrets so far."

She turned away from him and looked out towards the hills and the blue Mediterranean in the distance. Her thoughts were with her father. She missed him even more in this place where they had shared his passion for history and his dreams for the peoples that lived here. He had understood the enormous complexities of their lives that were, unwillingly or otherwise, so entwined in the conflicts of its past, present and future. He was warm-hearted and wise, comforting and familiar, like the old blue sweater he had worn for as long as she could remember. It gave her solace to know that he approved of her journey, of the time she was taking for herself and her sons to heal, and of the place she had chosen to replenish their family unit.

Yep, she admitted to herself as the afternoon's performance finally began, so far, so good.

A couple of hours later, they were heading east towards the Kinneret, the ancient Sea of Galilee. Once again, she felt the awe of history well up inside her. She resisted sharing her thoughts with Barak. Instead, she gazed at the tiny sea's glassy surface where the Christian faithful gathered to see the waters on which it was recounted that Jesus had walked. Looking up, she could see the Church of the Beatitudes atop the hill where he gave his famed Sermon-on-the-Mount and she imagined its grassy slopes dotted with followers.

Twenty minutes later, they stopped at a museum on the water's edge. During a severe drought a few years earlier, local fisherman had discovered a fishing boat that dated back to that very time. Gazing at the nearly perfect canoe, Nadine was humbled by thought that two millennia had changed little in this place of remarkable beauty where people like herself had lived and worked.

Night had fallen by the time they reached the inn on the lake where Barak arranged for them to stay. Nadine walked down to the rocky beach and listened to the waves gently lap over the small, smooth stones while Barak went into the main building to pick up the key. Black hills rose above the lake and the sky was thick with stars. Looking around her, she spied several neatly spaced cabins, separated by carob trees. Her heart quickened a beat and she felt a flush rise in her face. When she was with him, a sense of pleasant tension enveloped her. Every touch of his long fingers made her feel light. Her gaze was met by his own tender look from eyes, large and brown, fringed with thick dark lashes. They held a warm softness but she had also seen them blaze with an intensity that could penetrate the thickest armor. She inhaled deeply as if the night air were filled with his scent and reluctantly let it go. Tenderly, she tucked Jeremy away into a hidden corner of her mind, and thought she saw him wink at her even as she did.

A few minutes later, Barak was walking towards her with their bags slung over his shoulder. Hearing the sound of the stones crunching underfoot as he approached, she turned to meet him. He guided her to a cabin set apart from the others at the north end of property.

They stepped inside to a room awash in the silvery glow of the full moon. Gently, almost silently, Barak closed the door behind them. Neither of them wished to disturb the subtle aura that filled the room. He set their bags down noiselessly, took Nadine's hand and pulled her towards him. His warm breath gently caressed her ear as he whispered tender reassurances. Though she barely heard them, she could feel his words spill softly, rhythmically, from his lips, dancing like poetry upon her willing torso.

His fingers traced the lines of her shoulders and back. Her breathing slowed and harmonized with his murmuring. She succumbed to his warmth and the cocoon of tender devotion that he spun around her. The rise and fall of his breath became hers.

They undressed one another slowly, deliberately. With each layer of clothing, Nadine shed a ghost of the past, and once naked, allowed herself to be drawn into a new dimension of time and space where their souls mingled in passion and pleasure.

She had almost forgotten the luxuriant feel of skin against skin. She let her fingers roam down Barak's strong back, hips and muscular thighs. His chest pressed lightly against her breasts as he eased her down onto the waiting bed. She accepted the gentle kisses he bestowed on her face and lips, awakening long dormant senses that washed over her like the softly lapping waves of the sea outside their window. Their persistent rhythm seemed to urge her onward. Wrapping her arms around Barak's strong neck, she heeded the now incessant demands of her own strong body and gave herself fully to the moment.

Had it been minutes or hours? He was smiling at her. He closed his eyes and kissed her forehead, then rested his head against the white down pillow. She watched the muscles of his face relax as he slid into sleep. Only when the mourning dove began to sing and the sun reddened the hills of Jordan, did Nadine, too, drift into sleep.

He punched in the untraceable telephone number and waited. The number would be changed the next day, as it would be every day thereafter.

"Voice I.D.," came the indifferent demand.

He stated his identification and asked for "Y," the Mossad chief, known only by the first initial of his first name, his identity a secret to all but a few.

"Yes," the chief said.

"She's hooked," he reported.

A click. A dial tone.

Barak replaced the receiver and retreated into the night.

CHAPTER 11

▼

After the morning staff meeting, Shlomo pulled Nadine aside.

"I'm promoting you, Nadine," he said. His tone was serious but his eyes were smiling.

Nadine liked Shlomo from the moment she met him at the Casablanca Economic Summit four years earlier. Outgoing and witty, he was a tough-as-nails negotiator with unshakable loyalty for his friends. She had benefited greatly from his support and patience and was anxious to hear what he had in mind.

"I'd like you to work with Ehud on a project for the Government. It's classified but with your U.S. security clearance, I don't anticipate a real problem getting clearance for you here. They may balk at first, but this is a private institution. I should be able to push it through."

"Can you give me a hint?" asked Nadine, her curiosity piqued. She hadn't thought so until now, but she suddenly realized that she missed the excitement of working on top-secret assignments.

"I'll do better than that." Shlomo said. "I'll have Ehud scan unclassified parts of the project into your computer. Start with that material and let me know what you think. We'll meet again at the end of the day. In the meantime, I'll get to work on your status."

An hour later, Nadine was engrossed in the material before her. A summit was scheduled to begin in one month, this time right here in Jerusalem. Setbacks in the peace talks with the Palestinians had negatively affected some of the progress made at the Casablanca Summit. The Jerusalem Summit, the fourth Arab-Israeli economic meeting of its kind, it was hoped, would re-infuse some of the other Arab nations with their previous enthusiasm.

Nadine frowned. Odd. There was no mention of this in the media at all. Security, perhaps. Yet, other summits had been widely publicized. Still, Jerusalem was a controversial site. Despite normalization of their relations with Israel, many Arab leaders refused to recognize Jerusalem as its capital. Puzzled, she decided to plow ahead and ask questions later.

Ehud had been working on strategy with the government for several months now. Fending off nagging feelings of having been left out, Nadine's mouth formed a little pout. She had only herself to blame. Since coming to the Institute shortly after Jeremy's death, her message to Shlomo had been clear: keep it academic. She was glad now that he had changed her course and she felt her adrenaline kick in at the anticipation of attending another summit.

She turned her attention back to the monitor and continued reading. The material outlined project developments since the Casablanca summit, especially in Gaza, and their anticipated effects on the economies involved. Something was bothering her but she could not put her finger on what it was. Was she forgetting something? No, it was something else. She couldn't shake the feeling that she had seen this before. She continued reading.

A few paragraphs further, she felt her throat constrict and her pulse quicken as the pencil in her hand began to jot down the letters, first the third, then the fourth of the next word, then the last of the next. It was slow, painstaking work. Beads of sweat broke out on her forehead and dripped slowly down her brow. She pushed her bangs off her face as she deciphered. Words began forming on the pad before her.

Ready the eight.

Snap! The tip of her pencil broke under the pressure of her hand and went flying across the room. Startled, she jumped, then exhaled audibly and sat back. This was not going to work. She needed the computer program they had used at the Department of Defense, and fast.

In her state of alarm, her mind went immediately on alert. Years of training in covert conduct, most of which she had pretended to tolerate with amused suffering but which the Department took very seriously, kicked in automatically. Without trying to appear openly suspicious, Nadine's eyes roamed around the room, searching every crevice of her small office. Was she being watched? She didn't see any signs of a hidden camera. Nonchalantly, she ran her hand under the desktop.

"You're being paranoid, Nadine," she chided herself. "The Israelis are more sophisticated than that anyway."

She returned her focus to the document still staring at her from her computer monitor. Were the Israelis aware of this? Could it be that they weren't? Had Shlomo purposely given her this document to test her? Or was it a coincidence?

Think! she commanded herself. No, she decided. There's no reason for me to believe that they know. Israeli intelligence was good, the best. They had access to the same materials and were analyzing them for content, she reasoned. What was the likelihood that they had picked up the messages?

Nadine's head was pounding. What was the connection? Think, think, think!

"Come in." It was a command.

Knocking gently, Nadine cautiously opened the door to General Bradford McKenzie's office at Aviano AFB and stepped into what felt more like a library than the office of a general. She noted the bookcases lining the entire west wall of his office. Shakespeare's Othello, several titles by Kurt Vonnegut, Jr., and treatises on military strategy and history all showed signs of repeated reading.

Though she had been in the office only once before, she was impressed by the room's warmth. If she felt any trepidation when she entered the room, his demeanor put her at ease.

"I'm sorry to bother you. I meant to set something up with Anne, but she's not at her desk. Do you mind…?"

"Let's have it." His voice was assertive yet had a velvet quality to it.

"For a while now, I've been tracking studies on economic trends in the Middle East. I've read a lot of papers, and there aren't that many experts in the field. A researcher's writing style is often as distinctive as his signature. Reading a paper, I can almost tell who wrote it." Nadine paused to take a breath and regroup.

"I recently noticed that one particular researcher seemed to be publishing quite a bit. When I checked to see who it was, I was surprised to find that the author named on each paper was different." Nadine pressed her lips together and shook her head.

"I was positive that the same person was involved so I checked to see whether they were coming from the same academic institution. They weren't, at least, they're not named as such." Nadine stopped, then said, "I was at a loss."

She looked directly at General McKenzie. "When I was a kid, my sister and I communicated secretly, through codes. It was a great game and we were so good at it, that we could leave notes with hidden messages to each other right out in the open."

He shifted in his seat. Nadine hurried to continue.

"What I am saying, sir, is that someone is sending messages through these papers by using a very simple code, a concealment code."

He straightened in surprise. "How do you know that?"

"I've deciphered a few myself," Nadine responded, stepping forward to show him some cryptic penciled phrases scribbled on a legal pad.

He appraised Nadine as he accepted the notepad from her hand. Her reputation had preceded her, as did her classified file. She was a 'favorite-child' at the Pentagon, a Middle East expert with an incisive, analytical mind. Her husband, Captain Jeremy Kanner, was one of the Air Force's finest pilots. The Department had agreed to her request to accompany him, with their two boys, on his present stint in Northern Italy. She was still working with the Department from the base by computer, but strictly on unclassified projects. Meeting her eyes, she did not strike him as someone given to fantasy.

"Do you know who the real author is?" he asked as he handed the notepad back to her.

"Unfortunately, I can't tell."

"Have Anne set up a meeting for 08:00 in my office with Lt. Col. Harper and yourself. Be prepared to discuss the content."

"The code system being used is extremely simplistic," Nadine reported at the following morning's meeting. "It's a concealment code, a system for hiding words within words. The hidden message is revealed by stringing together letters in a previously designated position of each word," she continued as she extracted some typewritten sheets from her briefcase.

"The code used here is simple and repetitive, clearly being employed by someone intelligent yet amateur, at least in this area. However, that is purposeful, I believe, since it appears that this type of code is being used far more for its facility than for its real ability to conceal. The sender is almost certainly operating under the assumption that there is virtually no likelihood of discovery. Here, I'll give you an example."

Nadine handed out copies of a sheet of paper with three sentences printed on it.

"Begin Phase II. Shipments en route. Ready positions."

"It's not much, but its very existence implies more. Why is it there? Who is it intended for? How are they going to be used? And where? Are there consequences that concern us?" Nadine looked from Lt. Col. Harper to General McKenzie and sat back, indicating that she had concluded.

"What is your assessment, Jim?" Brad asked, addressing Harper.

"I'd like to get Jordan from the computer lab in on this and have him design a program that can decode much more rapidly, to see what we have here."

"Alright," Brad agreed.

He was about to signal the conclusion of the meeting when Nadine said, "There is one more thing."

All eyes were on her. "The possibility of plants. We are working on the assumption that whoever is sending these messages is an amateur but it would be foolish and possibly dangerous to presume that he is stupid, too."

"What kind of plants?" Col. Harper asked.

"To avoid detection, whoever this is might send messages that are false, say only every third message would be genuine. Or, the genuine messages might be tagged with a key word."

Brad nodded. "Make sure to go over all of that with Jordan," he ordered and the meeting concluded.

Nadine reached into the top drawer of her desk and pulled out a blank sheet of paper. Meticulously, but succinctly, she summarized the results of their five-month surveillance as she best recalled them before referring the entire project back to the Pentagon. She wrote, *What do we know?* at the top of the page followed by a list:

The messages dealt with 1. money transfers of moderate sums, mostly in the hundreds of thousands of dollars; 2. orders for weapons purchases; 3. operational instructions (sketchy) for training missions; considering all factors, most likely terrorist. Destination: West Bank, under split control: Israeli and Palestinian Authority. One shipment intercepted before docking in Amsterdam. Contents: Arms including missiles. All recipients used code names. No identifications made. Messages halted. Matter referred back to Pentagon.

What she recalled most clearly was that the messages were simple and sinister. Nadine glanced at her watch. It was one o'clock. She decided not to do anything out of the ordinary. She would work until the end of the day, go for a run and call Brad after dinner. It was paramount that she not break routine or do anything to call attention to herself. Even phoning Brad would have to wait until an hour at which they normally spoke.

She finished reviewing the basic plan for the Summit and attended an afternoon brainstorming session with Shlomo and Ehud, suggesting strategies and pointing out where the Israelis might best focus their attention first.

At four o'clock sharp, she left the Institute for the track. Luckily, Barak was in Northern California attending a satellite technology conference. Nadine was well trained and had a strong survival instinct, but she did not enjoy being deceptive. Barak had keen eyes. Today, she was glad that she would not have to put her skills to the test.

At the end of her run, she joined Fouad for a refreshment and was truly grateful for the reprieve. Quietly sipping her drink at the counter, her back against the wall, Nadine relaxed for the first time that entire day. As she watched Fouad take care of his last few customers she recalled the afternoon that he had handed her the slip of paper with her attacker's name scrawled on it.

They never spoke of the attack upon her again. Nor did she mention that she had never passed the young man's name on to the police. Nadine pulled herself out of her reverie and off the stool, thanked Fouad and jogged home.

CHAPTER 12

▼

"Let's get started," Barak heard Y say. He had been staring into his coffee turned cold. Lately, he'd been distracted.

By any standards, he had an enviable life. A terrific apartment, a few very close friends, interesting, and most would agree, important work. And he was busy, always busy, too busy to feel. He made sure it was that way ever since Zoe left. But something had thrown off the pace. This assignment perhaps, meant to be a break from the undercover work he had been doing for so long. He still supervised the team but was staying out of the territories himself for a while.

"Barak, begin."

Barak straightened and looked at Y. His bald pate shone under the florescent light and his bright blue eyes focused entirely on Barak. Even when still, Y appeared to be in motion. An aura of energy flowed from his very being, injecting those around him with the same vitality he was known for himself.

"Two of my men have infiltrated the Liberation Brotherhood Army on the West Bank. Their intelligence has already proven invaluable. We've intercepted three LBA members crossing into Israel from the West Bank to execute terror missions." Barak's voice took on an edge. "Two were on their way to carry out a kidnap-murder. The third was on a suicide mission."

The Palestinian Authority's creeping control over Gaza and parts of the West Bank had virtually wiped out Israel's intelligence gathering network in the region. Formerly the eyes and ears of the Israeli security apparatus in the terrorist world, West Bank Arabs suspected of informing Israel of potential terrorist activities or attacks were imprisoned and tortured. Vigilante groups and terrorist organizations like the LBA and Hamas made sure that Palestinians sympathetic to Israel did not see the light of day.

Left with no choice but to infiltrate the enemy themselves, two of his team members were now in dangerous territory, risking their lives every moment for the security of their tiny country.

Barak tried to keep his frustration in check knowing that all the while, these punks thumbed their noses at them. They were determined to succeed. And they often did. For every dozen terrorist attempts stopped, one got through. And each one was deadly. It was a vicious cycle fueling his conviction that the most effective weapon against terrorism was to penetrate their organizations and gather intelligence from within. Only that conviction was accompanied by a price that was becoming increasingly difficult to pay. Barak winced mentally. It was a war neither side was going to win. They could only hope to stem the tide.

"Did you learn anything of substance from them?"

"Zip. Its members really know nothing about the hierarchy of the organization. Its scope is as elusive as its leader, Al Rasuul. It has been so carefully designed that we actually know more about it from the little intelligence that we do have, than its own recruits will ever know. They think that their entire organization is made up of patriotic young Palestinians ready to fight to the death for a Palestinian state. The rank and file are hardly aware of the existence of the upper echelons."

"Very wise," Y nodded. "He's compartmentalized the organization. A breakdown in one area will not affect the rest. His organization remains intact."

Barak agreed. "The fact that we do not know his real identity is obviously hindering our ability to predict his movements and counter his actions. But I have received some valuable information from our insiders. They report that Al Rasuul himself makes periodic visits to each of the cells. He's a virtual legend. They worship him. He makes them feel that he is one of them, a freedom fighter, not some far-removed leader with his own agenda. Though not one of them could identify him. He wears a kafiyah and dark glasses at all times, and has a beard, completely masking his facial features. He's manipulated them beautifully. They'll do anything for him."

"What's their setup?"

"Each cell has an *imam*, a spiritual leader, and an operational cell leader. The cell leader reports to the next level of operations and so on, but each level only knows its contacts in the level immediately above its own. The cell members don't even know of the existence of the more sophisticated military and intelligence units. Those members are quietly hand-picked after close and careful scrutiny at the training base camps."

"What's the focus of your current mission?"

"We're hoping to get some information that will bring us closer to positively identifying who Al Rasuul really is. Once we know who he is, we'll be able to track his whereabouts, learn more about his contacts and be positioned to get advance intelligence on their worldwide operations."

"Do you know anything about his agenda?"

"We think that last month's suicide attacks were meant as a morale booster, but possibly also to distract us from something much bigger."

Barak saw Y stiffen. He did not like bad news.

"Give me your indications."

"Stepped up recruitment efforts, increased meetings and activity, a tidal wave of propaganda, more intense training. They're sending a whole slew of their new recruits to training camps in the Beka'a Valley and Iran."

Y nodded knowingly. The Iranian backed Hizbollah, the Party of God, was making mincemeat of the Israel Defense Forces on its northern border. Even the notion that an Iranian-backed group might be operating from the West Bank called for immediate and compelling preventative measures.

Barak continued. "The 'talk' has gotten more militant. There is renewed interest in jihad and Islamic governance. Al Rasuul is exploiting the general population's disillusionment with Palestinian Authority. The PA is cracking down on the Liberation Brotherhood Army's activities but the Brotherhood's popularity is immense. The movement is on."

"Where are your men? Which cell have they infiltrated?"

"Abu Jibril. I'm suspending any expansion of their mission until we've had a face to face. We have a rendezvous set for a debrief."

Y nodded. Barak could see that he was satisfied, but personally, he would not be at ease until both of his men were back in one piece.

"*Hal'a.*" Next.

"Kanner, Nadine. Ph.D., expert in Middle East Affairs. Defense Intelligence Agency, top security clearance…"

Y waved a hand. "I remember her profile. Just update me."

"I've gained her trust but she's a quick one. She doesn't miss a thing. She's on guard even when she doesn't know it. The Americans did a good job. Her training has become second nature. It accompanies her everywhere."

"Does she suspect?"

Barak hesitated. Yes, he thought to himself, she does, but she's not afraid. She knows how to take care of herself. Aloud, he said, "She doesn't want to suspect."

"What do you think?"

"Too soon to tell."

Y nodded. Again, Barak noted his satisfaction. Maybe she *was* just a smart lady who needed some time away from old wounds, he thought to himself. Who knew better than he did what it was like to face daily reminders of pain you were trying to forget, to put behind you?

Barak shifted in his chair and asked, "What about Shlomo Cohen?"

Y responded with a dismissive shrug. "He continues to insist that she's here solely at his invitation to participate in academic research at his think tank, but I still say she's too close to the top of the U.S. intelligence ladder for us to ignore."

Barak said nothing.

Preoccupied by the events of the day, Nadine left her plate untouched. She drank a cup of coffee and watched the boys eat.

"Any e-mail from Brad lately, Daniel?"

Daniel shrugged. Without lifting his eyes from his plate, he said, "He invited me to spend the winter break with him in Italy."

Nadine eyed him thoughtfully. She would let him decide. That was still several months away. Daniel got up from the table, put his plate in the sink and started to head for his room.

"What's the rush?" she asked. She resisted chiding him for leaving the table unexcused. Too often, she found herself walking on eggshells. The shock waves of anger that Jeremy's violent death had sent ricocheting through him still gave no sign of letting up. She would have to do something. She wasn't going to lose him.

"Brad said he was going to upload some software that he wanted me to check out," Daniel replied without looking back.

Nadine perked up. Could she risk downloading the decoding program? She certainly couldn't have it sent to the Institute. Their computers were networked. The entire Institute would have access to it. But she could have it sent to Daniel.

At a quarter past eight, Nadine dialed Brad's telephone number and listened as the phone rang. The fourth ring was cut off by a voice politely requesting that she leave a message.

"Damn," she thought, but began speaking. "Brad, it's Nadine, just called to say…"

Brad picked up. "Nadine! I just walked in. Hold on a minute while I turn this contraption off."

She moved the phone away from her ear momentarily as the machine at the other end beeped and clicked.

"Hey, Nadine, just got in from a late staff meeting. What's going on?"

"Oh, I'm fine. I just called to ask *how's Julie?* she said, slipping into code meaning *I need help.* It was an old one and she hoped he still remembered the sequence. Brad hesitated for the briefest moment.

"She's well now," came his response. *Are you in immediate danger?*

"That's good. I was just checking." *No, but I need a secure line.*

"I'll be having breakfast with her tomorrow morning at 8:00." *I'll call you at eight.*

Nadine thought for a moment. 7:00 AM in Israel. Good.

"Give her my regards." *I'll be here.*

"I will." *Confirmed.*

They moved out of code and after some small talk, Nadine said, "I'll put the boys on now. I'm sure that Daniel wants to talk to you about that new software he downloaded and Zak's team just won its latest soccer meet."

She turned the phone over to them and stepped out onto the balcony with a cup of steaming black coffee in hand. Resting her elbows on the railing, she looked out over the valley below. The twinkling lights of Abu Jibril glittered like a tiny trove of diamonds spilled haphazardly onto the valley floor. There, she thought, lived her dear friend Fouad and the young man who had tried to kill her.

She welcomed the cool mountain breezes, inhaling the sweet night scents like an addict. Pungent and stimulating, the combination of pine and jasmine sent her senses reeling, rushing in through her nostrils and coursing through her every cell until her body was saturated with the exotic fragrance. Despite the hot coffee warming her, an involuntarily shiver scurried down her spine. Uncertainty was an unfamiliar guest. She couldn't be sure whether the chill invading her now was the cold night air seeping into her limbs or grim foreboding evoked by the morning's discovery.

She leaned back against the balustrade and scanned the night sky. Above her, celestial lights blazed indifferent to her confusion. She couldn't help feeling that it was going to be a long night.

When the phone rang the next morning, Nadine got right to the point.

"Brad, is the line secure?" Nadine's voice took on a slight quiver whenever she was tense and Brad picked up on it right away.

"We're all alone, baby," Brad said lightly. "Tell me about it."

Nadine quickly recapped the previous day's discovery.

"I need the decoding software, Brad. Confidentially."

Brad let out a low whistle. Removing the decoding program was clearly a security breach but that was not what worried him.

"Do the Israelis know?"

"I have no idea. It's hard for me to believe that this was just another coincidence, but maybe nobody else is looking. As far as I can tell, I'm not under surveillance."

"Listen, Nadine. It's Wednesday. I haven't seen you and the boys for a while and it's only a three-hour flight to Tel-Aviv. Any objection to my coming in for the weekend?"

"Just let me know when you're landing."

"See you Friday."

CHAPTER 13

▼

He watched Nadine leave the Israel Strategy Institute, then let another five minutes go by before he rose from the bench on which he had been waiting, and walked towards it. He had just one more thing to do before catching his flight back to New York. He straightened as he strode confidently through the entrance to the Institute and approached the horseshoe shaped information desk in the center of the lobby.

Addressing the security guard in flawless Hebrew he said, "Dr. Nadine Kanner, please."

At the mention of her name, Haim Mizrahi lit up. Such a lovely young woman. And her two boys, fine young men, too. Gingerly, he checked his pocket for the sweets that he always kept handy just in case they happened to drop by at the Institute when he was on duty.

"I'm afraid you've missed her. She left early today."

Displaying serious disappointment, the stranger said, "Listen, I'm leaving for New York late tonight and it's imperative that I see her before I go. Can you tell me how to reach her?"

The old watchman appraised the gentlemen. He looked like an intelligent man, though the eyebrows were a bit imposing. A bouquet of flowers wrapped in colored cellophane hung nonchalantly at his side. Perhaps he was a suitor. Heaven knows, a beautiful girl like Dr. Kanner should be married. He himself had married at a young age and had many children and grandchildren. A lovely lady like Dr. Kanner shouldn't be alone.

It was a serious breach of ISI rules to release the address or phone number of any ISI employee. In his twenty-five years with the Institute, Mizrahi had never violated them.

"I'll see if I can reach her for you," he offered instead.

The gentleman smiled his thanks and laid the bouquet on the marble top of the information desk. As he did so, his elbow knocked over a black lacquer vase perched there, spilling its contents onto the desk below. Apologizing profusely, the gentleman rushed around to the opposite side of the desk.

"Never mind, never mind," Mizrahi insisted, placing his rotund body squarely in front of the stranger's. "Please sir, move back around to the other side of the information booth."

A janitor appeared as if out of nowhere and began to clean up the mess. The stranger quietly complied, but not before memorizing Nadine's personal information in view on the computer monitor directly over Mizrahi's shoulder. He waited patiently as Mizrahi called Nadine's home and the phone rang in her apartment. When the call was picked up by an answering machine, the guard offered him the handset.

"Perhaps the gentleman would like to leave a message?"

With a disappointed smile, he politely declined and left. Odd, thought the guard. He was anxious enough to see her, but did not leave a name or a message. Well, he would describe the unexpected visitor to Dr. Kanner on Monday morning. No one could forget those eyebrows.

Nadine, Daniel and Zak waited for Brad at Ben-Gurion International Airport. The atmosphere was charged with expectation as friends and relatives craned their necks to catch a glimpse of the arriving passengers streaming through the double doors from customs to the outdoor waiting area.

Brad's height and Anglo features made him easy to spot. Zak jumped up and down, waving his hands from their position at the periphery of the crowd. Daniel whistled through his teeth and Brad turned. Spotting them, he smiled, waved back and headed towards them. When he reached them, Brad hugged the boys, slapped them on the shoulders, then leaned over and kissed Nadine on the cheek.

"Nadine, you are positively glowing. I see the Mediterranean air suits you!"

Pleased, Nadine blushed and offered, "I've been running. It does wonders for the soul."

And legs, Brad couldn't help thinking, noticing that Nadine was dressed in a short skirt and sandals. They took a moment to survey one other, but their silent reverie was quickly broken by loud taxi drivers demanding to know if they needed a lift, and the shifting of the crowd as more passengers joined the melee and headed off with their escorts in all directions.

"C'mon, let's get going. The jeep isn't far and I want to get back to Jerusalem before sunset."

Brad threw his grip into the jeep and climbed into the passenger seat next to Nadine. The boys clambered into the back and they pulled out of the busy airport. The highway to Jerusalem was practically deserted this late Friday afternoon.

"This is great," Brad commented. "Everywhere else in the world, Friday afternoon is a traffic nightmare."

"The holiest city in the world is preparing to greet the Sabbath," Nadine said. "By the time we get there, the streets of Jerusalem will be completely empty, except for a lone car or taxi. Actually, I like it. Jerusalem is insane all week long. Then Friday afternoon arrives and a hush descends over the entire city that's almost otherworldly. It's very calming. You'll see."

The jeep cruised up the into the foothills, effortlessly passing smaller cars and heavy trucks shifting into low gear to haul themselves up the incline.

"What's that?" Brad inquired, pointing at the remains of a burnt out vehicle on the roadside among some trees.

"A memorial, of sorts. In 1948, Jerusalem was under siege. This was the only road leading up to the city. The vehicles that you see along the way were used in attempts to get supplies to the trapped Jews. They've been left here as a monument to the men and women who died trying to get through."

The four sat in silence as they rounded the last curve bringing the first homes of Jerusalem, scattered across the hilltops, into view.

"I'll never get tired of this view. Every time I see it, it's like I'm seeing it for the first time," Nadine said, almost reverently. Casting a sidelong glance in Brad's direction, she was pleased to see his obvious awe of the panorama spread out before them.

They reached the city limits and sped down Shazar Blvd., whose eight lanes, normally jam-packed with buses and cars, were empty. They passed Binyanei Ha-uma, the Jerusalem concert hall and convention center, and site of the upcoming summit. They continued past Sacher Park, up Rambam Blvd. through Rehavia, then right to Yemin Moshe, an exclusive artist's colony built into the mountainside directly opposite the plateau on which the ancient City of David was perched. A windmill marked the entrance to the terraced community, beyond which was a neatly manicured park, crisscrossed by winding paths, fountains and flower beds. Nadine pulled up in front of a quaint inn at the top of the hill covered in bougainvillea and surrounded by wild flowers.

"I thought you would like it here. Why don't you check in? The boys and I will wait, then we'll head over to our place for dinner."

"You don't have to bother, Nadine. We can go out to dinner. I'd love to treat you," Brad responded.

Nadine laughed out loud. "Forget it, Brad. This is Friday evening in the Holy City. There's barely a restaurant open. I'll explain later. Hurry up. I want you to catch the sunset over the Judean Hills from our terrace."

Brad checked in and was guided to a small, but immaculately clean room. It had a single bed, an antique dresser and matching night stand with a curved brass reading lamp as its only decor. At the far wall, narrow French doors led to a tiny balcony with barely enough room to stand on. Brad stepped outside and caught his breath. Right below him was a small deep valley just beyond which, perched on the opposite hill in all of its majesty, was the ancient walled city of Jerusalem.

"So that's what all the fuss is about," he murmured to himself. He stood for a moment recalling the battles that had been won and lost fighting for the three thousand-year-old city and began to understand Nadine's enchantment with the place.

Brad pocketed his room key and headed back outside to the waiting jeep. The sudden drop in temperature as the sun began to set left a chill in the air.

This is indeed a place of extremes, he thought.

He dropped into the passenger seat and Nadine pulled out of the gravely circular drive then sped up the empty boulevard, bearing left at the old train station and up another steep hill into the winding streets of their neighborhood.

"Now that I'm here, I can't help wondering why I've never visited before. This city is beautiful, and so serene."

Nadine laughed again. "It *is* magnificent," she agreed, "but not always serene, Brad. The Sabbath begins at sundown. The city will stay virtually shut down until sundown tomorrow night. Then, it's as if someone flips a switch. Saturday night, the city comes alive again. The rest of the week can get pretty hectic, too. There *is* a spirituality here though that is ever-present and almost tangible. That's what it boils down to, I guess. The religious and political tensions over whose claims to this holy place are most sacred, who has the most right."

"Hmmm."

From the back seat, Zak piped up excitedly. "Brad, that's our school that we're passing. And down that big hill is the recreation center and the soccer field where we play. Did you know that my team is in the quarterfinals? If we beat the team from Haifa, we win and they're the best team in the league."

Brad turned and smiled at Zak, throwing Daniel a good-natured wink. "Do you ever stop to take a breath, young man?"

Zak was barely listening. He kept on talking, even after the jeep stopped at their doorstep and they climbed the two flights of stairs to their flat.

Their apartment was large and spacious. Its bright white walls and sand colored marble floor made the flat look even larger. Sofas and chairs were natural teak with pale woven cotton pillows that beckoned the weary to sink into their cushioned depths. The walls displayed an eclectic assortment of Middle Eastern tapestries and trinkets. The living room opened into a dining room whose furniture too, was teak. Its walls had a series of watercolors by one of Nadine's favorite artists. Beyond the dining room was a double-paned sliding glass door that led to a large balcony overlooking the Judean hills.

"C'mon," she said, "let's catch the sunset before dinner."

They stepped outside onto the spacious balcony and looked in the direction of the hills. Streaks of orange lit the horizon and the desert hilltops glowed as if in flames. Barely visible in the distance, the Dead Sea glistened in the fading light. They watched in silence as the burnt orange sky grew deeper and more intense. Moments later, they were plunged into darkness as though the flames had been extinguished at once.

"Whew!" Brad whistled. "That was almost eerie."

"Now you know the meaning of 'nightfall.' But it was beautiful, wasn't it? I'm starved. Let's eat."

In the small kitchen, Brad uncorked a bottle of wine and Nadine pulled steaming platters of food from the oven while Daniel and Zak set the table.

"Smells wonderful."

"I cooked for the occasion. Believe me, it isn't often." Musing, she said, "You know, sometimes I think I need a 'wife.' I'd love to have a hot meal waiting for me at the end of a hard day's work and God knows, the boys could use it."

"They look OK to me," Brad assured her, pouring the wine into two waiting goblets. He handed one to Nadine and raised his own in a silent toast. She returned the salute and they sipped their wine, enjoying the moment.

"Not bad," Brad commented approvingly, inspecting the label. "It's local," he said, mildly surprised. "I didn't know Israel produced such fine wine."

"Having just arrived from Italy, that's quite a compliment. But Israeli wines are walking away with all sorts of awards in the European competitions."

Brad raised an eyebrow. "I don't recall you being a connoisseur," he commented.

Nadine hesitated. Barak had introduced her to the finer points of Israel's wines but, not quite ready to share that with Brad, she said with a touch of cynicism, "Well, I've been trying to get interested in something other than studies on the economy and culture of this mad region."

"Mom, I'm starved," Zak complained from the family room.

"Let's eat!"

A few hours later, Nadine and Brad pulled up in front of the inn. Brad looked at her in the suffused light of the street lamp overhead. With conscious control he kept his hand from touching hers.

"I'll pick you up tomorrow morning at 10:00. Security at the Institute is very tight. It's rare for anyone to be there on a Saturday but I've checked the duty schedule. Tomorrow's watchman won't think twice about my showing up. You're a visiting family member just in for the weekend and I want to show you where I work so that you can go back and report to 'Mom' that I'm doing great. It's not an alibi that will give us much time but culturally, it works."

"Nadine, look at me. I look about as Jewish as the Pope."

"It doesn't matter Brad. We're both American, close enough for this guy. He's getting on in years. He just wants to retire and enjoy his grandchildren."

"Who am I?"

"My uncle."

"Do I look that old?"

Nadine smiled and shrugged. "Sorry. My mother's youngest brother."

"What's my name?"

"John Phillip Shaw." Brad understood immediately. Jack Shaw had been killed several years previously in active duty.

"OK, Nadine. You've always had good instincts." He leaned over, pressed his lips against her forehead then silently went into the inn without turning back.

When her husband hadn't appeared by eight o'clock on Friday night, Mrs. Mizrahi was frantic. He had never been late on the Sabbath before. Haim Mizrahi was a religious man and a man of habit. He had walked to and from his job as a security guard at the Israel Strategy Institute for close to twenty-five years, and had never once been late. As usual, their children and grandchildren were gathered at their home for the traditional Friday night meal. But tonight, instead of the general cacophony and laughter of the weekly family gathering, the house resounded with a strained silence. Mrs. Mizrahi had dispatched her eldest son,

Zohar, to the police station an hour earlier and anxiously awaited some word from him.

They would not wait much longer. Police were already investigating the murder of the uniformed man found in the bushes with a single stab wound to the lower left ventricle of his heart.

CHAPTER 14

▼

The three young men from Abu Jibril walked through the forest and exited at the far end of the track. As on every Saturday morning, the Jewish Sabbath, the area was deserted. The men were dressed in loose fitting slacks and dusty polo shirts, and their bare feet were loosely clad in leather sandals. Issam, the tallest and the leader of the three, wore a black and white checkered *kafiyah*. The other two were bareheaded.

They skirted the track to the far side of the hill leading up to Nadine's apartment building. Avoiding the main street, they scrambled up a snake path that would bring them to the rear of her building at the top of the hill without being seen. It was a longer, more difficult route, but much safer. As it was, they were taking a risk; most of the Jews in this neighborhood spent the Sabbath morning at home.

Issam knew the value of patience and observation. They would stay hidden in the brush and case the area. In a few days time, after planning the mission, he would return to execute the vow of revenge he had taken the night of his youngest brother's murder.

Issam crouched low in the brush and gazed about through cat-like eyes streaked in yellow, his muscles twitching in readiness. His loyalty to Al Rasuul had now been rewarded by a potent gesture.

"Be discreet. Do not endanger the mission. But never forget that Al Rasuul takes care of his own," he admonished Issam as he waved the small piece of paper with Nadine's address on it in front him. Al Rasuul's resourcefulness had made him an almost mythic figure.

With the scrap now safely stowed in his pocket, he peered through the brush at the geometric stone building and tried to discern which apartment belonged to Nadine. He pulled a photo from a news clipping out of his pocket and studied it once again.

"Sabri," he said in a low voice handing him the photo, "Look at this. I think she's the one."

Sabri was a thoughtful young man with wire-rimmed glasses who spoke little, but he often saw angles that others missed and was considered valuable to planning almost every mission. He looked from the photo to the dark-haired woman climbing into the American jeep. A young boy was climbing into the passenger seat. Another, taller boy waved to a youth carrying a soccer ball who headed down the hill towards the playing field, then he shoved off on a bicycle.

"It's hard to say, but it could be. This picture is so small and not all that clear." The crumpled print showed Nadine sandwiched between a smiling Shlomo Cohen and a very dignified Sami Nasser. The caption read, 'Peace in the making as American, Israeli and Arab representatives meet in Casablanca to do business.'

"But the jeep, it's American."

"And Al Rasuul said she has two sons," piped up Marwan, the third member of the group. Marwan was thick set and squat with a broad, flat face. He had always been uncomfortable with his ungainly build. Slow and uncoordinated, he had worked hard on building his physical strength.

"Allah has presented us with an opportunity. We are going to check out the apartment," Issam said.

Sabri blanched. "Slow down, Issam. We're all upset about your brother, Muhammad. But look around you. The sun couldn't be shining any more brightly. Most of the residents of the building are at home. If we're caught, we won't see anything but the dark walls of an Israeli prison. That will not help us avenge Muhammad's death or further our holy cause casting the Jews out of Israel."

Issam kept his eyes focused straight ahead and watched the jeep take off.

"I'm going in." He leapt out of the surrounding brush. His tall, lithe body raced with feline agility across the small strip of grass to the ground floor, open-air lobby.

Sabri cursed then turned to Marwan.

"Let's go," he ordered.

The apartments were separated by short sets of outdoor steps, each with its own private landing. They leapt up the stairs until they reached a door adorned with an artfully decorated plaque that read "Kanner Family."

Odd, thought Mrs. Wolf who was watering the geraniums on her rear balcony. What were they doing here on a Saturday? During the week, neighboring Arabs regularly came through this neighborhood, but they were rarely seen here on the Sabbath.

She followed them with her eyes until they disappeared from her line of vision, then she crossed her apartment to look out the opposite window, expecting them to exit the other side of the lobby, but she could not see them anywhere. She shook her head. They had clearly entered the ground floor landing of the building. How could they have crossed it and left so fast? Mrs. Wolf was heading for her front door to check the landing when the phone rang.

Oh, bother, she thought. She glanced at the wall clock. Nine-fifty. That would be her daughter. She would say hello to her grandchildren and snoop later. She was probably being overly anxious anyway.

Daniel was halfway to Michael's house when he realized he'd forgotten the *Titan III Space Explorer* diskettes. He slowed his bike and thought for a moment. He'd have to go back. They'd been planning this afternoon all week. He'd call Michael from the apartment to explain why he'd be late.

Daniel cycled back up the steep hill and nearly flew off the bike at the foot of the stairs while it was still moving. It skidded onto the grass next to the sidewalk and he left it lying there while he ran upstairs to grab the diskettes.

He put his hand on the knob and was about to insert his key when the door swung open.

That's weird. Mom forgot to lock the door. Just saves me time, he thought, with a mental shrug. He crossed the living room and ran down the hallway to his bedroom.

"There they are. Right where I left them," he said aloud to himself.

Daniel grabbed the diskettes and headed back down the hallway. He hesitated at the phone. Forget it. The whole thing had only taken five minutes. He trotted down the hallway to the front door decidedly ignoring the sensation that something wasn't right. He would think about it on the way to Michael's.

He was reaching for the knob when a bare hand smelling of sweat covered his mouth and yanked him away from the door. He lost his balance and fell but was quickly back on his feet. He leapt for the door again but this time the hand caught his jacket and a black and white checkered *kafiyah* was thrown over his face and tied around his head. He kicked in the direction of the hands that were holding him, but now another set of hands, large hands with thick fingers, grabbed his arms. His thrashing was useless and the odor of the *kafiyah* was making him gag. He sputtered and wheezed, then gradually managed to breathe again.

The wild beating of his heart reverberated in his ears, so loudly that he had trouble focusing on what was going on. He slowed his struggle to free himself from the hands that were pinning his arms, and the grip on him loosened slightly. Through the thin gauze cloth of the kafiyah, he could make out two figures besides the one holding him, though not clearly. He squeezed his eyes shut and tried to clear his mind of the fear and confusion that gripped him. Breathing through the cloth was making him feel sick. He desperately wanted to know what they were saying; maybe they were going to let him go.

The voices were low and urgent. Real fear spread through his chest as Daniel realized that they were speaking Arabic. He wished they would slow down and talk louder.

"Sit down, boy." The voice, that of Issam, was deep, but nonthreatening. Daniel didn't move.

"He doesn't understand," said another, more high pitched and clearly agitated. Marwan was sweating. He should have stayed outside as a sentry. He was petrified, but tried not to let his comrades see his fear.

"Never mind," said a third, calmer voice. "We only have a few minutes to decide. Do we take him or just tie him up and leave him?"

"We take him," said Issam. "But first you and Marwan go through the place. See what you can find."

Daniel's head jerked up. Issam looked at him for a moment, then said, "*Yeled*, do you understand me?" Daniel did not respond. He wasn't quite sure why, but for the moment, he felt safer not saying anything.

"Issam."

Without releasing his hold on Daniel, Issam turned to see Sabri coming towards him. In his right hand, he held a small scrap of paper. Issam took the note and paled. In confident Arabic scrawl was a name. Muhammad Ibn Assad. His brother.

Issam turned back to Daniel, tightening his hold around the boy's thin arm. The taste of hate was strong and sour in his mouth. "You," he said with contempt, "are my vengeance against your arrogant mother for my brother's murder."

Less than a minute later, they were ready to move.

"Sabri, you first. Give me the signal then I'll go next with the boy. Marwan, you're last."

Marwan thought he was going to lose his stomach. He wanted to protest that he should go first, but he knew that he would lose their respect forever. He would be shamed and there would be no place for him in the organization.

Each apartment opened out to its own outdoor landing. Stone stairways angled to other landings and down to the street. Sabri stepped out and headed down. Seconds later, he signaled from the bottom.

"Lazy Israelis. Instead of going to pray on their Sabbath, they hide in their houses." Issam spat as he spoke. He grabbed Daniel whose face was still covered by the *kafiyah,* and started out.

At that moment, Issam heard the loud click of a door bolt sliding back on the landing opposite and slightly above their own. A sixtyish gray-haired woman left her front door slightly ajar as she headed for the compost bin where she would drop the geranium clippings she held in one hand. The other hand held a fresh bouquet. Issam frowned. If she were going somewhere with that bouquet, she would have to pass right by here. He backed Daniel into the apartment, closed the door and peered through the peephole. He would let her pass by, then they would leave.

Issam nearly exploded when the old lady tapped on the door.

"Nadine?" Mrs. Wolf called. "Nadine, are you home? I've brought you some flowers, dear."

One arm across Daniel's chest, he could feel the boy's heart pounding rapidly. He had stuffed the end of the kafiyah in the boy's mouth as a gag and his thin chest heaved as he tried to breathe though the gauze that covered his nose. Issam unsheathed his knife, handed it to Marwan and mouthed, "Take care of her."

Marwan began to sweat profusely. To bolster his courage, he looked to Issam, whose wavy, copper brown hair was now exposed. He was the lion, their leader, Al Rasuul's second in command. His prowess had made him a hero among his people. Now Issam had chosen him, Marwan, to further the cause. He knew better than to disappoint.

Issam opened the door so that he and Daniel were hidden behind it. When it was fully ajar, Marwan's bulk filled the doorway. He clamped his huge hand down on Mrs. Wolf's gaping mouth before any sound could escape. Lifting her, he stepped out onto the landing and easily carried her up the short flight of stairs back to her apartment. He kicked the door shut behind him and half dropped her to the floor. Clutching the front of her garment, he grasped the knife and readied it at his waist. The warm smell of urine stung his nostrils. Her terror empowered him.

"*Allahu Akbar,*" he said almost inaudibly and with one powerful thrust, slid the sharp steel blade up under her left breast and into her heart, just as Al Rasuul had taught him.

Issam grabbed Daniel and started down. Daniel, still blindfolded, focused on moving his right leg behind Issam's left one, just inside his ankle. All I have to do, he thought, is hook it and sweep, and he's down the stairs like a sack of potatoes.

At that instant, Daniel felt an intense pain shoot down his left arm from underneath his collarbone where Issam had pressed his fingers against a nerve.

"Try it again, *yeled yehudi*, Jew boy, and you are dead."

The morning was brilliantly clear when Nadine arrived at the inn to pick up Brad. She laughed as he practically leapt into the jeep.

"Brad, what happened to you this morning?"

"I took an early morning hike through that valley," he said, indicating his route with his right arm "and came back up through the artist's colony on the side of that hill, after which I ate a stupendous buffet breakfast. Yogurt, tomatoes, olives, fresh bread, black coffee. I'm ready for a little espionage."

Nadine shook her head. "We've got to get you off that base a little more often, General."

The Sabbath morning traffic was light and ten minutes later they were walking up the flagstone path to the main entrance of the Israel Strategy Institute. Nadine took a double take when she saw a lean uniformed figure at the information desk. She put her hand on Brad's arm indicating that they should slow their pace while she assessed the change in security. It was too late to turn back. The guard had seen them on the monitor the moment they had turned onto the walkway to the building.

"You're going to have to sign in as yourself, Brad," she said quickly. "This guy is a stickler. He won't let you by without seeing your passport or some other identification."

The guard had not taken his eyes off of them since spotting the couple on the camera displays at the Institute's outer entrance.

When they reached the desk, Nadine smiled and said, "*Shabbat Shalom*, Ron."

Ron nodded curtly in response, then said in Hebrew, "*He* hasn't been cleared. Without authorization, he'll have to wait here." Though Brad could not understand the words, the guard's meaning was clear.

Nadine was irritated, but responded nonchalantly, "We'll only be a few minutes." Handing Brad a pen, she said, "Sign in and leave your ID with Ron. On the way down, I'll show you the courtyard. It's lovely."

As Brad scribbled his signature, Ron said, "I'm sorry, Dr. Kanner, it won't work. No clearance, no entry."

"We'll just be a few minutes." She took Brad's arm and led him to the stairway.

"SOB," she muttered, causing Brad to smile. "We're screwed. We've got ten minutes, max. And I haven't heard the end of this. Let's go."

They took the stairs two at a time. Less than a minute later, Nadine was loading the diskettes that Brad had handed her into the computer. She copied their contents onto her hard drive and returned the diskettes to Brad. Then she retrieved the document she had tried to decode manually and ran the decoding program.

"This should only take a few minutes. We'll just have to print it out and see what it says later."

They sat in silence as they watched an oblong bar indicating the percentage analyzed progress from 0-100%. Nadine hit the print command and her printer whirred into action. As she waited anxiously for the results, Brad asked, "Nadine, have you thought about what you're going to do with this information?"

She pressed her lips together. When she replied, her tone was determined. "There is someone out there orchestrating terror. I can't just pretend it's not happening or that it's someone else's problem."

Nadine jammed the printout into her bag but hesitated before shutting down the system. If she deleted the decoding program from her hard drive, she would have no further access to it. The diskettes were originals. Brad would have to take them back with him. If she didn't delete the program, it would certainly be detected soon. The system check the next day would reveal at exactly what time Nadine had accessed her computer. She decided to keep the program anyway. She had gone this far and she might need it again.

"Who's handling this at the Pentagon, Brad?"

Brad shook his head slowly. "I'm out of the loop, Nadine. Maybe they've even scrapped it."

"Once we've had a look at this we can notify them," adding, almost as an afterthought, "and maybe it wouldn't be a bad idea to get the Israelis involved."

They stepped into the courtyard in time to see Shlomo Cohen, dressed in jeans and a T-shirt, coming towards them, clearly put out by the morning's intrusion on his only day of leisure. Ron had called him moments after Nadine and Brad arrived. Shlomo had tried to avoid coming in, but he'd left strict instructions with Ron to notify him precisely of incidents such as this. The Institute handled a great deal of classified projects for the government and even the Secret Service. Nadine's blatant violation of the rules disturbed him. She hadn't risen to the highest ranks of the Department of Defense by being careless. He was certain that this was not an innocent tryst, but he also held her in very high regard.

Pre-empting him, Nadine waved and smiled. "Shlomo, what are you doing here on Shabbat morning?"

Ruffled, but calming, Shlomo answered, "That's what I'm here to ask you Nadine. I got a call about your visitor. Let's get to the point. Why didn't you get clearance for him?"

Brad, towering over Shlomo, extended his hand towards him, and said, "Nadine speaks very highly of you. I'm Brad McKenzie, a close friend and colleague of hers. It's my fault really. I didn't give her much notice of my visit."

Addressing Nadine, Shlomo said, "You have my home phone number."

"You're right, Shlomo. I just couldn't resist the opportunity to show off the Institute and I didn't want to disturb you. I apologize. It won't happen again."

Shlomo knew better than to be soft-talked, but he had other things on his mind, not the least of which was the murder of the Institute's long-time security guard, Haim Mizrahi. The police had already begun interviewing the Institute's employees.

To Nadine he said, "We'll deal with this later." Nodding to Brad, "Enjoy the rest of your visit."

He turned to leave, but something was bothering him. First, Mizrahi's violent death, now a serious breach of security by Nadine. He turned back.

"Nadine, Mizrahi likes you. Did he mention anything to you about not coming in this morning?"

"Why no, he didn't."

Shlomo shrugged. "I guess it was just a mix-up then." Almost as an afterthought, he asked Brad, "By the way, how long are you staying?"

"I leave early tomorrow."

The details can wait, thought Shlomo and he disappeared.

On the drive back to her apartment, Nadine said, "Shlomo is smart and well-connected. No doubt, he's already figured out where you came from, what you're doing here and for how long."

"Can you trust him?"

"Absolutely. The problem is that I've just given him reason not to trust me. I'm working at a disadvantage, even if I do level with him now."

"Pre-empt him. Call him before he calls you. It worked beautifully in the courtyard. And by the way, he wants to believe you. It was written all over his face."

"He seemed a little pre-occupied to me. I wonder what's going on with Mizrahi. Not like him not to show up."

"More curious than that is why he was asking you," Brad commented.

Nadine parked the jeep. She was about to run up the stairs when she spotted Daniel's bike.

"Daniel's home, Brad, but why did he leave his bike like this? I'm going to have to talk to him about that," she said, picking it up and leaning it against the nearby bike rack. They bounded up the stairs, both anxious to see what the program had turned up. Nadine opened the door, stepped inside and froze in her tracks. The sofa cushions were overturned. Drawers were open and their contents strewn about. Several items were broken and wall hangings were on the floor.

The knot in her throat tightened as she raced through the apartment to Daniel's room. Tacked to his door was an obituary ripped out of a local Arabic paper, accompanied by the photo of a redheaded man of about twenty. As she read the report, she began to tremble. Nausea rose from her gut and swept through her like a wave. Her temples began to pound and she broke out into a sweat.

> Muhammad Ibn Assad, 19, of Abu Jibril, was buried today as thousands of mourners thronged through the town's narrow streets in a martyr's funeral, shouting "Death to the Jews." The youth was fatally injured after being attacked in the Jerusalem forest. It is unclear how many were involved in the incident. Witnesses claim that he was beaten by at least two Israelis. The police refuse to comment on the incident, except to say that the matter is under investigation. The Liberation Brotherhood Army has promised to avenge the young man's death with personal attacks against Israelis.

Nadine wanted to scream. She ripped the newspaper off the door and shoved it open.

"Daniel?" she shouted.

Oddly, the room was untouched, but there was no sign of Daniel anywhere. She made a quick call to double check that Zak was still at the home of a friend where she had left him in the morning and immediately arranged to have him spend the night there. As the panic rose within her, she bolted for the door.

"Nadine!" Brad called after her. He caught up to her and grabbed her arm but she threw him off with a force that sent him flying. He had forgotten how strong she was. Stunned, he recovered quickly and leapt to his feet. Nadine was halfway down the stairs when he reached the top of the landing. He repeated her name, but this time it was a command.

"Nadine!"

She stopped dead in her tracks. Brad caught up to her in seconds. "You don't know where you are going."

"He's been kidnapped, Brad! Can't you see that?" Nadine eyes were glazed over and her pupils dilated with fright. Her voice was so shrill that it almost cracked.

"Of course I can! And by acting rashly you're endangering him further. Now tell me what is going on and we may be able to find him."

Nadine felt cold determination win over her urge to vent her rage. Brad was right. Panic would only decrease her chances of ever seeing Daniel alive again, if he were still alive. No, she vowed, she would not give his tormentors the pleasure of seeing her squirm. As her resolve grew, so did the thought that she would slowly and painfully squeeze the life out of Daniel's captors with her bare hands.

CHAPTER 15

▼

Brad took Nadine by the elbow and steered her towards the jeep. There was little likelihood of the kidnappers returning; he just wanted her away from the apartment. He had to get her to focus so that he could find out what the hell was going on. It wasn't going to be easy.

He started the jeep's ignition and sped down the hill to the intersection that headed back to the inn. There would be no distractions there. With a trace of cynicism and a touch of faith of the kind one could only experience in the land of miracles, he found himself hoping that its extraordinary view might offer up some inspiration.

He gave her a sidelong glance. She was biting her lower lip. How well he knew that habit. Her hands were clenching and unclenching. The important thing was to keep her from breaking down.

He had watched Nadine very closely after Jeremy died. She'd maintained a cool reserve that kept everyone else around her strong though he knew she was grieving deeply. They needed that cool reserve now. Only he saw her slipping. As great a loss as one's true love could be, it was not the loss of a life she brought into the world and nurtured from birth. As dedicated a professional as she was, Daniel and Zak were her soul's nourishment, the source of her strength. She anticipated their every need and would protect them to her last breath. She struggled with them through their difficult moments and rejoiced in their contentment.

The past year's troubled relationship between her and Daniel had him worried. He knew that she had been grappling with her failure to cut through the anger Daniel harbored against her since the night of his father's death. That measure of guilt combined with her intense anxiety for his well being, led him to wonder just how well she was going to hold up.

The inn came into view at the top of the hill. He knew that the police station was only a few kilometers further up the same road. It was hard to miss. They had driven right past the impressive municipal complex that morning on their way to the Institute.

He shook his head. Their visit to the Institute seemed like eons ago but barely an hour had passed. He pulled into the circular drive of the inn and stopped the jeep.

"Shall I continue on to the police?" he asked quietly.

The silent plea in her dark green eyes was so intense that he felt her desperation boring right through him.

"C'mon." Brad swung out of the jeep. He opened her door. She got out, still staring at him as if he had the answer. He was losing her.

Once in his room, he gently shoved her into it's only chair then sat opposite her on the edge of the bed.

"Nadine, what is going on?"

"I'm not sure."

"Start somewhere."

"I found a message."

"Why is it so important?"

She opened one of her fists and stared at the news clipping still in her palm, now moist and crumpled. Her eyes ran over the words, then she held it out to Brad and slumped deeper into the chair.

He stared for a moment at the unfamiliar script. "I don't understand this, Nadine," he said gently. "Please tell me what it says."

"Revenge. It says that they are going to get their revenge."

"For what?"

"His death."

"Whose death?"

"A young man. A young man named Muhammad Ibn Assad." Her voice was monotonic. She was beginning to tremble. Stay with me, Nadine, he urged her silently.

"What does this have to do with you?"

"I killed him." Brad was momentarily stunned. A thousand questions bombarded him.

She was shaking visibly now.

"Nadine, we'll go get Daniel. Just tell me where he is."

"They're going to kill him, Brad. I killed one of theirs and now they're going to cut out my heart."

She was trembling so hard he grabbed a blanket off the bed and wrapped it around her shoulders. She half sobbed, half coughed, like she was choking back the tears, trying to hang on to a shred of the steely endurance that had held her together for so long. He guessed that she was trying to understand where she had gone wrong, how she could go back and make it right, undo it all and make it not happen. Whatever it was, he was going to have to get her through it. Daniel didn't have a chance in hell if she didn't come around.

"Don't, Nadine. Stop torturing yourself," he whispered.

"Oh my God, Brad, I've got to find him. I've got to get him back." Her body was taut and her jaws clenched. "I couldn't protect him. I couldn't protect him when Jeremy died and I didn't protect him today. They're going to hurt him, Brad. I have to get him back."

Suddenly she jumped up and traversed the small room, back and forth, like a caged tiger, back and forth, restless and uneasy but waiting for just the right moment to spring.

"I'm going to kill them. I'm going to find them and kill them for doing this to him."

She paced the floor, her hands pressed against her temples. A grimace crossed her face as if she were in unbearable pain.

He dared not interfere. She was struggling to cut through layers of guilt and helplessness, to get to a place where the mind was not hampered by doubt and paralyzed by fear, where cold analysis took the place of sheer dread. He could not help glancing at the clock. Their chances of finding Daniel dwindled with every moment. Mentally, he willed her back so that they could get on with it. He watched her pace until she stopped as suddenly as she began, and looked at him. Her eyes were filled with pain.

Quietly but firmly he asked her again, "Where is Daniel, Nadine?"

When she answered, it was in a low voice, as if she feared that saying it aloud would make it true. "Abu Jibril."

"Where is that? Do you know how to get there?" Coaxing her, he said "Nadine, I need your help here. Daniel needs your help."

He waited for her response. She stood forlorn in the middle of the room, the blanket half-falling off of her shoulders. Slowly she shook her head from side to side as if understanding and disbelief emerged at the same time.

"I can't go to the police. I can't go to anyone." She paused, weighing her words. "He'll just be another victim, a pawn for each side to use to get out of the political quicksand they're all sinking in. I have to get Daniel back myself."

If they haven't already dumped him by the side of a road, Brad thought glumly.

He could see that she was regaining control, for now at least. He spread his hands. "It's your call, Nadine."

Her voice was steady but she spoke slowly. "If this is pure revenge, then I may have lost Daniel already. But if they plan to use him, then he may still be alive. I need someone who can get through to them, talk to them. Someone they'll listen to."

"What do you think they want?"

Nadine blinked again. "I don't care what they want," she said. "All I want is Daniel. That's why I need someone who can convince them that he's worthless to them, even a liability."

"What about Shlomo? He's well connected."

"Too establishment." She was biting her lip again. She wanted to call Barak. He was so in tune with the pulse of the region, he always seemed to know what to do. But he was out of the country. She might have wondered for a moment why, but she didn't have the time.

"What about some of your other colleagues?" He was trying to jog her mind, to keep her on track.

She began thinking aloud now. "I need a Palestinian."

"The Casablanca Summit. Every Palestinian who's anyone was there."

As he spoke, Nadine leapt for the phone. He heard her connect with directory assistance in Manhattan and request a listing for 'Dr. Sami Nasser.' She jotted down a number, disconnected and immediately began dialing New York.

Brad chose his words very carefully. "Nadine," he said softly, "he's hours away. Even if he can help, it will take time. There must be someone else, someone in the area."

Nadine shook her head. "He's something of a maverick. He's an insider but not associated with the Palestinian authorities. He has power without the taint of government. He's someone terrorists might listen to. He'll know what to do."

CHAPTER 16

▼

"My God," Nasser exclaimed, "Is it possible?"

He bolted upright in his bed, the sheet sliding off of his naked body. Next to him, Sheila turned and let out the light moan of sleep disturbed then returned to her dreams.

The room was dark except for the subtle glow of the full moon just outside his bedroom window. Nasser's elegant apartment on New York City's West Side was high enough above the street so that the city lights did not filter in, affording him the luxury of never having to draw the curtains.

Nadine tried to control her growing impatience. "Dr. Nasser, I would not be waking you at this hour if I had any doubt. Daniel has been kidnapped. I have to find him!" She almost added, "if he is still alive," but could not bring herself to voice it.

"Nadine, once more, more slowly this time please, tell me why you are not going to the authorities. The Israelis are experts at this sort of thing."

Nadine gritted her teeth, trying to keep the exasperation out of her voice and said evenly, "The moment I report this to the police, Dr. Nasser, the media gets hold of it and it becomes a political incident. They call in the army and Daniel becomes a sacrificial lamb. He will be paraded triumphantly across the television screen by his captors on a video trumpeting their cause, only to have his body discovered, too late, on the side of a road or killed in the crossfire with Israeli commandos." The tone of her voice lowered slightly, revealing her weariness. "We've both seen it before. The Israelis and the Palestinians each have their own agenda. I just want my son back, Dr. Nasser. That is my only agenda. The Israelis won't negotiate with terrorists nor will the terrorists negotiate with them. But you, Dr. Nasser, are a respected Palestinian, a well-known insider. You can talk to them. They trust you."

Nasser breathed a little easier now. At least they agreed on one thing, although for very different reasons.

"Nadine, how do you know...," he hesitated.

"He's alive, Dr. Nasser. I would know it if he were dead."

Nasser checked his watch. It was 4:00 AM in New York, 11:00 AM in Jerusalem.

"Nadine," he said, "there is a 10:00 AM flight out of JFK to Tel Aviv. I'll be on it. But just so time is not wasted, I'll try to make a few discreet inquiries before I leave. Perhaps I can stop the clock."

Nasser laid the telephone receiver back on its cradle and looked over at Sheila's sleeping form. How simple her world was. How little she knew.

He leaned back against the headboard, closed his eyes and breathed deeply. He was in many ways a fatalist and so he met fate head on, manipulating its twists and turns to his advantage. That, and never allowing his mind to become muddled with trivialities, always kept him one step ahead in the game.

He inhaled once more to completely clear his mind of any vestiges of sleep before slipping out from between the sheets and heading for the shower. He flipped on the bathroom switch and winced as the bright lights reflected off the black and white art deco tile. Squinting, he flicked off the master switch leaving only the soft amber glow of the heat lamp to light the room.

He pulled out his shaving kit and mentally checked off a list of things he should do. This was Saturday and he did not teach until Wednesday so there was no need to worry about canceling a class or finding a substitute. Nor did he need to pack. He lectured nationally and internationally so frequently that he kept a small travel case packed and ready for short trips. He would not even check it through. No family visits on this trip, either. Why complicate matters? He would keep a low profile, just deal with this glitch and get back.

He finished his shave, started a shower and carefully stepped into the steaming cubicle. Years of planning, a long slow evolution. Now events were taking on a momentum of their own.

A sudden blast of cold water brought him back to the moment. He cleared the steam from the glass shower door in time to see Sheila retreating back to the bedroom. She had flushed the toilet. Well, good. Time to get going.

With automatic movements, he toweled himself dry, dressed in a white shirt, subdued tie and lightweight suit. After slipping into a pair of soft leather shoes, he pulled his packed valise from the closet, walked quietly down the long hallway and placed it by the front door. He still had some time before he had to leave for the airport so he stepped into his study to take care of one more item.

This task would be easy. A recommendation letter to the United States Supreme Court for a brilliant law student he had mentored as an undergraduate. It was just a formality. The young man's application for one of the coveted clerkships had already been approved. That done, Nasser sat back in his large desk chair and swiveled toward the high study windows. A soft morning light was spilling across the New York City skyline slowly turning the treetops in Central Park from gray to green.

Detective Shimoni knelt over Mrs. Wolf's still warm body. The police photographer's camera flashed while another officer meticulously dusted for fingerprints and searched for evidence. The perpetrator had not entered by force and there were no signs of a struggle.

Shimoni glanced over at Mrs. Wolf's daughter who sat weeping quietly nearby. Years of police work had not hardened him to the personal misery he encountered. With a sigh, he walked over to her and gently touched her shoulder.

"The sooner you can tell me what happened, the sooner we will be able to find the beast who did this," he said quietly.

The young woman nodded. "My mother joins us every Shabbat for an early lunch. When she didn't show up…" Her voice caught in what sounded like a loud hiccup. She struggled to regain control. "Thank goodness I left the children at home. The door was open when I got here. I thought she must have had a heart attack but then I saw the blood…" She started to hiccup again.

Shimoni's left thumb tapped a small notepad he held in his right hand. He was troubled. This was not American TV, something his kids got in regular doses. Random murder simply didn't happen here. Homicide cases usually boiled down to a domestic squabble gone awry or the occasional petty criminal fight gone too far. Now he had two bodies on his hands, Mrs. Wolf and that old watchman from the Institute, Haim Mizrahi.

They would have to be quick about collecting as much evidence as they could before the Hevra Kadisha, the burial society, came swarming down on them. Under Jerusalem law, the body would have to be buried within twenty-four hours. Shimoni's left thumb tapped, then stopped. He turned back to Mrs. Wolf's daughter.

"I'd like you to come down to the station. Let me get your statement, then you can get back to your family."

Shimoni signaled to one of the officers to accompany her, then he took one last look around. Nothing more for him to do here. He would have to wait for the results from forensics.

CHAPTER 17

▼

Dr. Nasser scrutinized Nadine as they waited for their coffee. She looked tense and the strain was evident in her expression though her distress would not be obvious to a stranger.

"Nadine," he said, almost crooning, his voice suffused with the tone of one who knows better, "what really happened in the woods that day is immaterial. You must first accept the fact that reality is solely a matter of perception. The facts are irrelevant." He paused for emphasis.

"You killed Muhammad." He lifted his hand to momentarily silence her protest. "The family desires revenge. An eye for an eye. A son for a son."

"But he is only fifteen!" she hissed, not wanting to attract undue attention.

Dr. Nasser shrugged. "By their standards, a young man already. Even under Jewish law, a young boy becomes a man on his thirteenth birthday, obligated to undertake the responsibilities of adulthood."

Nadine thought of Daniel and was struck by her sudden recollection of the biblical Daniel. *They threw Daniel into the lion's den and in the den were seven hungry lions.*

"What about money?" Nadine asked

"They would spit on your money."

"You're one of them! Think of something!"

Nasser stiffened but let the rebuke pass.

"Dr. Nasser," Nadine began, her voice barely above a whisper. Though he was her colleague, she could not bring herself to call him by his first name. "How did they find me? I wasn't followed. The police found nothing."

"This is a small country Nadine. You know that. Everybody knows everybody else, or at least someone who knows him."

Her heart skipped a beat. Where had she heard that before? Ehud, her colleague at ISI, had said that too. Her head was bursting from too many unanswered questions. Who knew her? Who did she know? Were the police holding back on her? Too many questions. She turned away from Nasser and looked vacantly at the other guests in the café. Her eyes paused on a large, jovial looking Arab.

"Fouad," she whispered, unbelieving to herself.

"What did you say, Nadine?"

"Nothing. Just...nothing."

"Nadine, I cannot help you if you hold back."

Nadine hesitated.

She does not trust me, Nasser thought, but she has nowhere else to turn. Smart lady.

Nadine pulled out the newspaper article she had found tacked to Daniel's bedroom door and flattened it out on the table between them.

"The village of Abu Jibril. That is where this young man was from. That is where we have to start."

"I know people in Abu Jibril. I will go there and begin making inquiries."

Nasser reached across the table and held both of Nadine's hands in his. "Have faith, Nadine. Allah will look out for your Daniel."

Daniel in the lion's den. It took every ounce of Nadine's strength to believe him.

After making sure Nasser knew where to reach her, she exited the café and nearly collided with the Hasid who had brushed passed her in the shouk. Dressed in the same black suit and hat, his garb was severe but his round face, framed by a long gray beard and lit by clear blue eyes, appeared kind. Despite their near miss, he hadn't so much as glanced at her. Yet she could swear he was speaking directly to her. He continued on his way as if she wasn't there but his words remained behind, clear and unmistakable.

"Yagati velo matsati—al t'amen."

Nadine stood rooted to her spot and repeated the words to herself. "If a man should say, 'I toiled, but found nothing,' believe him not."

Al Rasuul eyed Daniel through a peephole in the door. He sat on the floor in the far corner, his back ramrod straight against the wall of a tiny, unfurnished room in a safe house for Brotherhood freedom fighters under heat from authorities, Israeli or Palestinian. Daniel's feet were shackled but his hands were free and the *kafiyah* had been removed from his face. He stared out into the Mediterranean twilight through a slightly parted curtain that covered the room's only window. A plate of food on the floor next to him remained untouched.

Dreaming of escape, Al Rasuul mused, or of Israeli commandos ready to burst through that window at any minute. We'll see.

Al Rasuul gave no sign of his irritation at this new wrinkle just days before the activation of Stage IV. Life had a way of doling out surprises. The difference between the winners and the losers was to know how to turn the unexpected to one's advantage. Discounting his initial impulse to kidnap Daniel, Issam had so far acted wisely. The boy had been brought directly here. For now, only Issam, Sabri and Marwan knew of the incident.

Had Issam succeeded where his brother Muhammad had failed in the wood, well, so be it. But kidnapping her son was another matter. It was precisely minor incidents such as this one that mushroomed into international crises. He was acutely aware of Dr. Kanner's popularity at the Casablanca Economic Summit. The U.S. President had acknowledged her and the Israeli Prime Minister had hugged her warmly. Even the King of Morocco had been impressed.

His ability to deliver her whereabouts had been another act of omniscience that renewed the awe and reverence in which his men held him. Each such act empowered him tenfold. But, as if the Israelis weren't difficult enough, now they would have the entire United States Armed Forces breathing down their necks on the eve of the most important coup in human history.

His calculations had proven to be precisely correct. The rise of Israel's right wing government to power brought its already tenuous relationship with the Palestinian Authority to the snapping point. The timing was perfect. Severing it completely was going to be a piece of cake. Al Rasuul nodded to himself. This time, history was on their side. But Kanner was very smart, too smart. He would deal with her himself.

Turning to Issam, he said, "So, Issam, you have your revenge. Now what are you planning to do with it?"

"I was unaware of the extent of the woman's influence, Al Rasuul."

"Of course," Al Rasuul responded, half to himself. Then, "Kill the boy. But not here. Take him to Jericho where the Israelis can't get to him."

He headed back towards his makeshift headquarters and considered the long road he and Issam had traveled together.

He stood alone at one end of the large courtyard near his Jerusalem home, still dressed in navy shorts and a white shirt, the uniform of the private school he attended. He was fourteen and small for his age but his position was solidly established. None of the boys would cross him. While others had won their places with their fists, he had never lifted a finger. His mind was so sharp and tongue so swift, his demeanor so assured and his glare so penetrating, that his allies were loyal without question and his opponents kept their distance.

So he was not particularly concerned by the group of boys led by a much taller teen with reddish brown hair and yellow eyes, approaching him now from the far side of the courtyard. This would be his first meeting with the tall boy, whose name was Issam.

Issam was an outsider, a scholarship student from a neighboring village who attended the school and lived in its dormitory, returning to visit his family only every other weekend. He was a natural leader, lithe and quick. His obvious intelligence drew a strong following about him.

The group stopped near enough for him feel the tall boy's warm breath on his cheek. His yellow eyes bore down into his face. He stood without moving a muscle. Despite his small size, he exuded an aura of uncompromising will. The other boys sensed his authority. And that was why they were here now.

They stared into each other's eyes for a full five minutes. Issam broke the silence.

"I have a proposal for you."

"What sort of proposal?"

"An alliance."

"Why would I be interested?"

"You are a leader. Yet you are a loner. Nobody crosses you yet you have no following. Your word is the last word, yet you have no constituency."

"What have you got to offer?"

"An army."

And so it remained to this very day. Only now Issam had made a serious error in judgment, one that could endanger their entire mission, eclipsing years of training and planning. Why hadn't he just killed the boy on the spot and ended it right there? He knew that Issam was agonizing over the same question himself, so it remained unasked.

CHAPTER 18

▼

Brad was edgy and relieved at the same time. Nadine was meeting with Nasser at that very moment. They had agreed it would be wiser for her to meet him alone. The wait had been a long one. He had to believe that Nadine was right. The police didn't negotiate with terrorists. Their intervention could only produce a gun battle or a military commando raid, violent solutions with questionable outcome.

But that hadn't made the wait any easier. He saw her energy ebb with each hour and the light in her eyes extinguish. She tried to be tough, analytical, to make the right decisions. Yet, a mere flicker of her old spirit remained. He could only watch as her agony sapped her of color and strength, while she tried to rise above it and reason to save her son.

Perhaps her hardest moment came when she telephoned Zak. Without offering any details, she let him know that an emergency had come up and he would stay with his friend for a couple of days. Through those few difficult minutes, the resonance returned to her voice and she sounded so calm that he accepted her words at face value, excited about the prospect of two days with his best buddy. This was the Nadine that the world knew. In control.

Then came the waiting. It was the waiting that could kill you.

While she paced his room, Brad picked up a bottle of scotch and poured the tawny liquid over ice, his own remedy for chasing away the demons that so oft hindered his rest. When he first offered her the drink, she had resisted, but he coaxed her into taking a few sips. It was enough. She slept for several hours and awoke in much better shape to face Nasser and what might come.

Now, perched on the edge of the bed in his room at the inn, Brad unfolded the printout Nadine thrust at him before running off to meet her colleague. Once they discovered that Daniel was missing both had forgotten about the sheet stuffed hastily into her purse that morning as they left the Institute. His eyes scanned the words but it took him a few minutes to fathom their meaning.

He read it over and over again, finally letting it go. The flimsy paper fluttered slowly, innocently to the floor. He pressed the palms of his hands against his eyes. Was it real? Or a hoax? If it was real, when was it going to happen? Could it be stopped? A multitude of questions ricocheted through his mind. All that was really clear to him was the horror, death and anarchy that would follow.

He was vaguely aware of a rap, rap sound at his door.

He rose slowly and looked about the tiny room. Nothing had changed. And yet he sensed that everything had changed. The stakes had just risen tenfold. What had, until now, been erudite speculation by Pentagon top brass was now a reality. Imminent? He didn't know. He just knew that the harm would be irreversible. Were they prepared? Not likely. Damage containment was the thought that sprang to mind. He recalled countless hours of testimony before Senate Intelligence Hearing Committees on the likelihood of anti-Western ideology being manifested by terrorism. They concluded the possibility was just that—a possibility. But in the absence of identifying a specific antagonist, no immediate actions were taken. Hearings closed.

The clear sky beyond the small balcony was a brilliant blue. He marveled at it like he was seeing it for the first time, and the last.

There was that rapping again.

"Brad, are you there?"

He opened the door. The look of surprise that registered on Nadine's face brought him back out of his reverie.

"Who first?" she asked.

He had the urge to hug her. For all the times that he had wanted to in the past but hadn't. For all the times that would not come again. And there was so little time left. He stepped aside and let her in. When she reached the center of the small room she turned to face him and wordlessly, he wrapped her in his large, strong arms. For a few moments neither moved each drawing strength and hope from the other, the will to go on in the face of unbeatable odds.

He wondered whether he should share her discovery with her at all. What possible meaning could it have when her child had been kidnapped by terrorists?

Brad released her, leaned over, picked the discarded paper up off the floor and silently offered it to her. She read it, her expression slowly turning to one of disbelief.

Ready the eight. Materials and supplies available for assembly at all destinations. Final targets: New York, Los Angeles, Washington, D.C., Paris, Rome, Tokyo, Jerusalem, Tel-Aviv. Simultaneous detonation. Exact times to follow. Photos, maps and sites attached. Maintain anonymity at all levels.

"When?" she whispered.

Brad didn't answer. Tomorrow? Next month? There was never enough time.

An attack in the forest. A kidnapped child. Suicide bombers.

Nadine moved quickly across the room and stepped out onto the narrow balcony. Nasser was heading for Daniel right now. He knew where to look, whom to contact. She felt confident that she had made the right choice. But what kind of world would be left for Daniel if the United States was reduced to anarchy? Or worse. They were not immune. This was just the kind of catalyst that could do it. It had happened in Germany. And the seeds of discontent were being sown all across the nation. Anti-government militias. Oklahoma. Ruby Ridge. San Jose.

The walls of Old Jerusalem surrounding the ancient City of David shimmered against the low sun, it's golden hues testifying to the presence of an other-worldliness. Beyond it rose the gilded dome of the Mosque of Omar, atop the Jewish Temple Mount.

Brad joined her on the balcony. The surrounding landscape was serene and inviting. Saturday evening breezes gently blew through the shrubs in the valley below where Israelis and Arabs strolled through the gardens with their families, unaware of the turmoil brewing. Nadine nodded in the direction of the mosque.

"The irony is palpable. Two holy places, one Muslim, one Jewish, permanently juxtaposed, eternally fused, melded into one solid entity."

Brad glumly agreed. "And now the conflict at its core is going global."

She could never have guessed that one day their war would be her own.

Her eyes searched the tiny crevices and recessed wells of the ancient rocks. It was here, where past and present were inextricably intertwined, where history, today and tomorrow merged, where events, ancient and recent were called upon by both sides to establish their claim to the one place each considered sacred and their own, that the answers would be found.

Stepping quickly back inside the room, Nadine grabbed a notepad and pen from the nightstand then scribbled Shlomo's address and phone number on it.

"You've got to tell him, Brad. We've got to get back to the Pentagon on this, get our program going again. We know that there is an offensive in progress. It's got to be stopped. Shlomo's well connected. He'll know what to do."

"What about Daniel?"

"Nasser is in Abu Jibril right now. Chances of Nasser finding him and getting him out alive are better than anything else I can think of but..." She averted her eyes and her voice cracked. "Hopefully, he's negotiating his release right now. I know Daniel's there Brad," she said with conviction. "And it's taking every ounce of strength I've got not to go there and get him myself."

Brad understood what she left unsaid. If she did, neither she nor Daniel would ever walk out of there alive but her voice revealed something else, too.

"Nadine, you're holding out on me."

Almost afraid to say it, she practically whispered. "Something is off. It's nothing I can put my finger on. Just gut. He seems removed, like he's playing a part. He seems to be following the dictates of another agenda."

Before Brad could delve any further, the phone rang. It was Nasser. Her heart leapt as she listened expectantly.

"Nadine," he said, "The people holding him will talk to me. But he is being moved. Sit tight, please, and I'll get back to you as soon as I can."

Nadine's head began to pound as the words of the *hasid* rang in her ears.

He was about to hang up when Nadine interjected, "Dr. Nasser, where are you going?"

The split second pause before he answered registered loudly in Nadine's trained ear.

"Jericho."

She gasped. Time had just run out.

Brad paid the cab driver and stepped out onto the wide sidewalk in front of Shlomo Cohen's private Jerusalem residence on the outskirts of the city. The home was elegant by any standards. He approached cautiously, then rang the doorbell. Shlomo's face registered only momentary surprise. He quickly recovered his professional demeanor and ushered Brad in.

As Brad followed him from the entrance down a short hallway into the library, he heard a woman's voice call out from the interior of the house.

"Mi ze, Shlomo?" Who is it Shlomo?

"Ze b'seder, Maya. Ze bish'vili." It's OK, Maya. It's for me.

Shlomo's wife returned to her newspaper and tea.

Shlomo closed the double doors of the library behind them and motioned Brad to an overstuffed leather chair. In this insulated haven it was hard to imagine the terror unfolding across the Western world. Before sitting down, Brad extracted an envelope from the inside pocket of his sport coat and handed it to Shlomo. Shlomo settled behind his desk and read silently. When he finished, he laid the printout on the desktop. For a moment, he did nothing, then, without a word, he picked up a secure line, dialed a phone number known only to a handful and spoke quietly in Hebrew. He had not acknowledged Brad's presence since seating him and Brad began to wonder if he had dismissed him or forgotten that he was there. When he finished speaking, he replaced the handset and turned back to Brad.

"Your Pentagon connection will ring through in a few moments." With that, Shlomo stood and left the room.

What was it with these people? Brad asked himself, confused by Shlomo's distance. Was it living on the edge that made them so difficult? There were some things they just would not share, a line that could not be crossed.

The phone rang.

"Brad, it's Phil Lathrop."

Brad was alarmed. Lathrop, the youngest Defense Department chief in its history, was always buoyant, even in the most tense situations, but tonight his voice was tired. In fact, Lathrop had barely slept in the seventy-two hours since being awakened by the Pentagon handler on duty.

"I want you and Nadine back here tomorrow. I'm arranging for one of your boys to pick you up and fly you back here to Washington. As soon as the Israelis clear it, Shlomo Cohen will get you to their air base."

Brad opened his mouth to say something then clamped it shut. He couldn't tell Phil where Nadine was. And he was not ready to call in help. He hoped he would not regret it but he had promised to give her until the morning before notifying the authorities. Checking his watch, he prayed that Daniel and Zak would be getting on that plane with him.

"What was that Brad?"

"Nothing Phil. I'll wait to hear from you."

As Brad replaced the receiver, Shlomo re-entered the room.

"I won't mince words here. It did not take me long to find out who you are. Why you are here has become abundantly clear. From this point on, until you're in the air, I'm running things." Shlomo paused. Brad knew he was wondering why he was there instead of Nadine.

"If you wanted me to know, you would have told me by now, but I'll ask you anyway. Where is Nadine? Why didn't she bring this to me herself?" Shlomo maintained an outward reserve, but Brad sensed that he felt betrayed.

He took a breath. He hoped that Shlomo would not dig deeper than necessary. They hadn't had time to cover all the bases.

"She wants to see this through," Brad replied. "It was Nadine who first discovered the coded messages when she was under my command at Aviano AFB. We developed the decoding software and tracked the messages as best we could for a while. At a certain point, we felt we had to refer the project back to the Pentagon. We thought they had canned it. Then Jeremy died, and I guess you know the rest."

"You haven't answered my question."

Looking Shlomo directly in the eyes, Brad said evenly, "She knows that she has to go back. As soon as possible. Nadine uncovered those codes because she sees things a certain way. And it's that way she has of seeing things—maybe it's a non-Western perspective, an understanding of where they're coming from—that makes her the one who has to do this. To help us get us one step ahead of them. But she and her family came here to heal. That healing isn't complete yet. She needs this evening with…," Brad choked on Daniel's name, "with her children," he concluded.

Shlomo simply nodded, acknowledging that was all the information he was going to get. He couldn't fathom her recent behavior, her betrayal of his trust. But that would wait for quieter times. Stopping this madness was the priority now. It would be like looking for eight needles in a haystack.

"The first teleconference for exchanging intelligence and coordinating action with the Americans is set for twenty four hours from now. Ages away and possibly too late. But we both need time to form our teams, analyze the data and coordinate strategy. I'll drop you at the inn. Stay there until I contact you."

Brad interjected. "Perhaps I could spend a few hours in Nadine's office. I know your security is tight, but I thought you might make an exception."

"What are you looking for?"

Brad shrugged. He stood up and now towered over Shlomo. "I know Nadine and how she works. Maybe I'll come across something."

Shlomo eyed him warily. "You make it sound like she's in trouble."

Brad didn't answer.

"I'll let you know."

It was the waiting that could kill you.

CHAPTER 19

▼

Detective Shimoni stared unseeing at the paperwork placed neatly in the center of his desk. Deep in thought, his thumb tapped the tabletop. An elderly woman had been brutally stabbed. In the light of day. In a quiet neighborhood. On a Sabbath morning. For no apparent reason. Tap. Tap. Tap.

"Cut it out, Shimoni. That racket's giving me a headache," a voice rang out from across the room.

Shimoni eyed the files neatly arranged in the metal rack on his desk. He was meticulous about his work. His cases were filed alphabetically in the large lower drawer of his desk. Active files that required immediate attention were on the desktop in a file holder arranged in order of urgency. No clutter.

His glance fell on the first file in the active rack. 'Mizrahi, Haim.' A flicker lit his eyes briefly as he reached for the folder. Mizrahi, too, was a seemingly altogether innocent elderly victim of a brutal stabbing with no apparent motive. Just last night. The night before Mrs. Wolf. He laid it on his desk and leafed through the next few folders. He paused at 'Kanner, Nadine,' then pulled that one too.

With the three files, *Kanner, Mizrahi* and *Wolf,* open in front of him, Shimoni began. Pencil to paper, he started with a triangle, Nadine at the apex, Mrs. Wolf and Haim Mizrahi at each corner of the base. Half an hour later, a web of lines and circles and scribbles laid out theories, questions and thoughts unfathomable for the moment to anyone but Shimoni. It was a practice that provided his fellow officers with a regular source of amusement and admiration. He quickly discovered that Mrs. Wolf was Nadine's neighbor and Mizrahi was employed by the Israel Strategy Institute. So was Nadine.

Shimoni leaped out of his seat, leaving the files still scattered across his desk. On his way out of the station, he sent out an all points bulletin for Nadine Kanner, with the license plates and a description of her American jeep. Spotting her should not be a problem. The vehicle was probably the only one like it in the country and certainly the only one around Jerusalem.

When Detective Shimoni pulled up in front of Nadine's apartment building for the second time that day, the crime lab was just cleaning up. It was dusk and a distinct chill penetrated the light cotton shirt he wore.

"What's the status?" Shimoni asked.

"We're O.K. here for now. The Burial Society was in to pick up the body. We're going to seal off the apartment. Mrs. Wolf's daughter agreed that going through her personal things could wait."

Shimoni nodded. "I'll need a report on my desk in an hour. I want everything you've got, even if it's preliminary."

He took the stairs two at a time to Nadine's apartment. He couldn't have known it then, but Nadine had been the only one missing that morning when the neighbors had streamed out en masse as the police arrived. He had no doubt that her absence, and the murders of Haim Mizrahi and Mrs. Wolf, were connected. Now, he was going to find out how. He knocked at her door and waited. Intuitively he knew there would be no answer. He made a quick note to speak with the officer who interviewed the building's residents.

Tap, tap. His thumb began to thump on the cover of his notebook. Where was she? Tap, tap, tap, tap. He could put out a warrant for her arrest and start a search beginning with the Institute president. What was his name? Cohen. But all of that would take time and he needed answers fast. He had a bad feeling about this case. One thing was for sure. It was going to get worse before it got better.

Shimoni pulled a light handkerchief from his pocket, gingerly reached for the knob and turned. To his surprise, the door flew open. He stepped in cautiously, and stopped dead in his tracks. A sinking feeling shot through him. Sometimes he hated being right.

He stepped back out to the landing, leaned over the railing and called out, "Hey, Jack, wait a minute. Don't pack up your stuff yet and get up here."

He pulled a cellular phone from his pocket and punched in his home telephone number. His wife answered.

"Dahlia, it's me."

"Shimoni, where are you? The babysitter will be here in half an hour."

His voice caught in his throat like a dry chicken bone.

"Shimoni?" Dahlia always called him by his last name.

"I'm sorry, *motek,* we have an emergency on our hands."

After a short pause, Dahlia responded reluctantly, "OK, I understand. Tova's husband is working the night shift tonight. I'll catch a movie with her."

"Dahlia?"

"Yes?"

"I love you."

"Hmmm-mmm," was all she said but he could hear the smile tugging at her lips and he knew it would be all right. One by one, he said goodnight to his four kids. When he hung up, he swore to himself he would make it up to them, maybe take them on a vacation to Eilat or Euro-Disney.

He hung up as Jack reached the landing.

"The lab crew will be up in a minute," he informed Shimoni. Each slipped on a pair of thin latex surgical gloves and stepped into Nadine's apartment.

CHAPTER 20

▼

As Nadine's jeep rounded the top of the hill she brought it to a sudden halt. Three police vehicles with flashing blue lights were parked right at the entrance to her building. On the landing to her apartment, she recognized Shimoni's tall, angular figure and the incline of his head as he listened intently to another officer. She threw the jeep into reverse and sped back down to the bottom of the hill where she made a U-turn in the wide intersection and headed back towards the center of Jerusalem.

She hadn't stopped long enough to identify the police vehicles. Maybe somebody had had a heart attack, but she doubted it. Thank goodness it was almost dark. The murky light of dusk made it difficult to see clearly and Nadine was fairly certain that she hadn't been spotted. But if they wanted her, they would find her.

"Time for Plan B," she said to herself. "Now, if I only knew what Plan B was."

Wry humor kept her mind clear and her nerves calm. Almost instinctively, she headed for Rona's apartment. She was sure that Rona would still be home this early in the evening. No self-respecting single Israeli went out before midnight. Many of the pubs didn't even open until eleven at night.

It took her a full fifteen minutes to reach Rona's place in the German Colony, an old section of Jerusalem originally settled by Germans, now popular among young intellectuals holding well-paying jobs. Nadine found Rona's address on a quiet side street. She climbed three flights of stairs to her flat and rang the doorbell. With luck, she would have what Nadine needed. She heard music playing from inside the apartment, so she rang again.

"Who is it?" she heard Rona call as she approached the door.

"It's me, Nadine."

The door flew open. It took her only a moment to grasp that this was no social call.

"Rona, I need a favor. I need to borrow some clothes." Nadine was still wearing the sleeveless mini-dress and sandals she had slipped on in the morning.

Obviously concerned, but without a word, Rona headed to her bedroom and Nadine followed.

"What did you have in mind?" she asked as they reached the closet.

"Something dark that I can run in and a pair of shoes. I need something with a rubber sole."

Rona dug into the bottom of her closet and pulled out a large shoe box.

"No problem, there. Last time I was at my mom's wolfing down her cookies and baklava, I made some sort of empty promise to finally start working out. She took me seriously and showed up with these," Rona said, handing the box to Nadine. "Never been worn," she added.

"So," Rona ventured as Nadine changed, "should I guess or just let you run off into the night like you're about to rob the Israel Museum?"

"The less you know, the safer you'll be; the safer we'll all be," Nadine said as she pulled on a pair of black leggings and sweatshirt.

"Safer? Who? Nadine, what are you talking about?"

"Rona, by this time tomorrow I hope to tell you the whole story over a Turkish coffee and some of your mother's baklava."

Ten minutes later, Nadine was back in her jeep. She had briefly considered asking Rona to give her a lift but decided against it. She could get back there without driving by her apartment. And hopefully, even if they did find the jeep, she'd be long gone by then.

Night had fallen and the Saturday night traffic was picking up. It took her half an hour to get back to the track. She parked the jeep in the lot behind the recreation center where it couldn't be seen.

Before trotting slowly towards the edge of the forest, she reached into a gym bag stashed under the back seat and pulled out a compass, a small flashlight and a sheathed knife. Training with the blade had made her cautious before an attack, agile in the face of one and always on guard for the unexpected.

The session concluded. Facing one another, each bowed from the waist. When she looked up, Tyler held out the knife. She gripped its worn leather handle and thanked him with her eyes. Then he hugged her, whispered "take care" and left her standing alone.

Nadine hesitated, resting the knife in the palm of her right hand. Feeling its weight, she felt her mentor's presence and decidedly slipped it into her waistband at the small of her back.

Abu Jibril only ten kilometers away, an easy distance for her, but the terrain was rough and uneven. Thick roots protruded from the dirt paths and the woods were pitch dark. That would slow her down considerably but it was the only way she could think of to get there without having to stop at the roadblocks recently set up between Jerusalem and the village. She knew that Abu Jibril was due east of the track. She also knew which trails turned back towards the recreation center, eliminating those. She would choose another and pray that it did not take her miles off course.

She took a few deep breaths and plunged in. Almost immediately she felt cramping in her shoulders and her legs. Her rhythm was off and her breathing irregular. Too tense, she told herself. Relax. Every step was slower and heavier than the one before it. Just *do* it.

Thoughts of Daniel cut through the uncertainty and pushed aside looming self-doubt, propelling her forward. She saw his face in her mind's eye; not the angry facade, but the real Daniel.

Right now, Fouad was her only hope. He would do this for her. He had risked his life once. He would do it again.

Every five minutes or so, she checked her compass. More than once, she found herself off course amongst the thick, green trees. Low-lying branches snagged her ankles and tore at the lycra leggings she wore. As she neared the hairpin curve that marked her last visit to this wood, she slowed slightly, but kept on running. Not quite sure how to get to the village, she let her senses guide her. She ran, one leg moving the other forward, each step carrying her closer to the other side.

CHAPTER 21

▼

Barak was fuming. His men had missed their rendezvous and his beeper was flashing an urgent message from Y telling him to report to his office within fifteen minutes. In half that time, he parked his BMW on a quiet Jerusalem street and walked with controlled nonchalance towards an unobtrusive stone house, indistinguishable from the other homes situated on the tree-lined street. A waist-high stone wall marked the perimeter of the yard thickly landscaped with trees and shrubs. He passed through its entrance under the careful observation of a network of hidden cameras and entered the domain of one of the most powerful intelligence agencies in the world. He flashed his pass at the security guard and headed directly to Y's office. His mind churning, he bypassed the elevator and took the stairs two at a time.

"Well, Barak, your target has turned out to be quite a score," Y said dryly as he entered the room.

Barak flinched at the characterization. He did not like thinking of Nadine in those terms. He noticed Y's ire was up so he took his seat without a word.

"Two years ago," Y began, "while reviewing academic publications on the economic developments of our friendly region, she happened across a series of coded messages being passed over the Internet. Once she had established that the messages were real and ongoing—that's how the missile shipment from Iran was intercepted in Amsterdam—the Pentagon took over. Only the Americans didn't bother to let us in on their little discovery."

Ahhh, thought Barak. The source of Y's irritation had revealed itself.

"Luckily, Dr. Kanner likes to read," he continued, his voice dripping with sarcasm. "She just happened to uncover their messages once again, this time, conveniently, at our very own Israel Strategy Institute. Lo and behold, eight suicide bombers, spread across the globe, are ready and waiting for the signal to blow." Y paused to close a manila folder he'd been consulting.

"The thing is," Y concluded as he slid the folder across the table to Barak, "your quarry has disappeared."

Barak, who had been reaching for the proffered file, froze midway. How stupid of him! He'd told her that he was going to be away for a few days so he could focus fully on supervising the infiltration mission. He cursed silently. He hated lying to her. More and more, he thought of her in personal terms, not as an assignment. He'd been happier in recent weeks than he had been in years. Now his lies had just cost him his contact with her.

He fucked up. He knew it. Y knew it. But something more significant was gnawing at his brain. His men didn't show for their meeting. Nadine had disappeared. Too coincidental. And Barak did not believe in coincidences.

"As of when?" Barak asked.

Y continued as if he hadn't noticed Barak's astonishment. "Everything we know is in the file. Shlomo Cohen is on his way over here now. I've got a team collecting and analyzing all of our intelligence on this. We'll be working with the Americans, but I want our own strategies on the table by tomorrow morning."

Y stood, signaling the conclusion of the meeting. "The U.S. Air Force is sending a taxi for her. We've cleared their landing for 14:00 tomorrow at Atarot AFB. Go find her."

Barak turned to leave. At the door, Y stopped him.

"One more thing."

"Yes, sir?" The look on Y's face told Barak he was clearly disturbed.

"Your American spy has uncovered operational plans all of us knew were waiting in the wings. What bothers me is that she found them here, in Israel, at our own ISI, but was not, by all accounts, planning to share them with us." Y gave Barak a look that bored right through him and in a tone that said he meant it, came to his point. "When you do find her, I want first crack at whatever is going through that famous brain of hers."

"What the hell…?"

Barak pulled over and watched the police van lock up and pull away from the curb in front of Nadine's building. One squad car remained. His eyes sought out Nadine's apartment. A lanky officer, apparently deep in thought, stood on the landing, tapping his thumb against a notebook.

Barak's throat constricted. No such thing as coincidences. He climbed out of his car and up the stairs. He coughed lightly as he approached Shimoni and extended his ID. Shimoni accepted it, then looked up at Barak with a raised eyebrow as if to say, "So what?" But understanding came almost as quickly. Nadine was a foreigner, and as he was quickly learning, no ordinary foreigner. An American working at ISI, an institute known to have intelligence ties, would naturally attract the attention of the security services. Nonetheless, he was reticent. This was still a police matter, not national security.

"Can I take a look?" Barak asked.

Shimoni stood aside. Barak walked through the apartment. With every step, his chest tightened. With every room, his jaw muscles tensed and twitched.

"It hurts, doesn't it?" Shimoni said to no one.

"You see this every day."

"If I got used to it, I'd cease to be human."

When he reached Daniel's room, Barak took a deep breath before gently pushing the door open. Surprised, what he saw was the haven of a fifteen-year old boy, disorderly but untouched by the violence that had torn through the rest of the apartment.

What happened here? he wondered.

Back out on the landing he addressed Shimoni. "Listen, we both need to find her."

Shimoni stiffened but didn't respond. The historical animosity between the two law enforcement agencies had only just begun to thaw. Recent political blunders necessitated information exchange and intelligence sharing between the security services and the police department, but through channels.

Barak was persistent. "I won't steal your thunder. This is your investigation. Police can have all the credit, if there'll be any left to dole out."

Shimoni seemed to be sizing up his visitor then he gestured toward the recreation center area at the bottom of the hill.

"I think better out in fresh air," he said.

They settled onto a wooden bench south of the track facing the woods where Nadine had been attacked. Barak's athletic physique remained upright, in a state of quiet tension, ready for action at any moment, while Shimoni's lanky frame slouched easily into the curves of the bench. Still, his inquisitive mind was as alert as his body was relaxed and his black eyes were probing and bright. There was nothing dull or slack about either man.

Shimoni began. "Whoever killed Mrs. Wolf trashed Kanner's apartment too. No results on prints yet, but the dog went nuts."

Barak swallowed hard. So Mrs. Wolf was dead. Did Nadine know? Was Nadine dead? Were they all dead? Where the hell were they? He shook his head as if to clear his mind of the questions and just focus on the facts.

Looking straight ahead he said, "The young man who attacked her in these woods was buried in a martyr's funeral in Abu Jibril. He was a member of Al Rasuul's Liberation Brotherhood Army. There were the usual promises of revenge."

Now it was Shimoni's turn to be surprised. He'd missed that, but of course, Mossad followed Arabic press. Its agents probably even attended the funeral. He'd stopped reading Arabic newspapers years ago. Their virulent positions were more than he could stomach and besides, the Israeli papers had enough bad news.

"Big funeral?" Shimoni asked.

"All the surrounding villages, and then some."

Shimoni nodded knowingly. Then he said, "Kanner was the target, Mrs. Wolf an unfortunate accident."

"How do you know?"

"Mrs. W. was killed at about 10:30 AM. Neighbors say they saw Nadine and the boys take off about twenty minutes earlier, one in the jeep, one on a bike."

"So maybe somebody was casing the place, saw them leave, popped the apartment and Mrs. Wolf interrupted a burglary in progress."

"Could be. But nothing was taken, at least not the usual items. So maybe this wasn't a random burglary. Maybe the intruder was looking for something else, something specific."

"Like what?"

Shimoni shrugged. "That's your arena. You're the spy. Dr. Kanner is not your average citizen. So you tell me."

Neither spoke for a few moments. Then Shimoni said, "We found Mrs. Wolf's body in the vestibule of her apartment."

"I don't understand. The intruder was searching Nadine's apartment."

"Freshly cut flowers were found scattered and trampled at the entrance to Kanner's apartment. Dropped."

"Meaning?"

"Meaning that someone else answered the door." Shimoni paused and looked at Barak to make sure he was following. Barak nodded and Shimoni continued. "So, if Mrs. Wolf knocked on Kanner's door and interrupted something unfriendly in progress, why wasn't she killed on the spot?"

"I don't know. Why?"

"Because someone else got there first."

"What are you saying?"

"One of the kids left with Kanner in the jeep, the other rode off on a bike. But both of the boys' bikes are in the bike rack. The neighbors ID'd those too. I picked up a call on Kanner's answering machine. It was from a kid named Michael looking for Daniel. Daniel was supposed to be there around ten this morning but he never showed. Yet another kid that lives in the building spoke to Daniel and saw him leave on his bike at the same time that Nadine and her other kid, Zak, drove off."

The realization of what Shimoni was saying left him with a pit in his stomach.

"Daniel came back and interrupted the intruder first."

Shimoni nodded. "Intruders."

Barak didn't say anything. He let Shimoni continue.

"Then Mrs. W. comes along. When she's greeted by obviously unwelcome guests, she drops the bouquet she's prepared for Nadine, but before she can alert anyone, the little old lady is whisked to her abode and done away with."

Kidnapping. Murder. His team members don't show. Nadine has vanished. He didn't like it.

"Anything on Nadine's whereabouts this morning?"

Shimoni flipped open his notebook. "She signed the register at ISI at ten thirty this morning with an American guest and left barely half an hour later. That's as far as we got."

Barak felt an unfamiliar pang. "Who was the guest?"

"We don't know," Shimoni said with undisguised disdain. "Shlomo Cohen got your guys to put a clamp on our investigation there." Turning to Barak he said, "So, Mr. Security Services, was our revered Dr. Kanner working on something top secret at the intelligence community's favorite spy center that we ought to know about?"

Was she? Barak didn't respond. Nadine was a pro. He realized now how much she had kept from him; that he'd never really know anything she didn't want him to know. Who was manipulating whom? he thought. But he quickly dismissed that line of thinking. He had no time to waste licking his own wounds.

Perhaps someone else, someone decidedly less friendly, knew she had uncovered a scheme to terrorize more than half a dozen cities. Maybe she had even discovered who was behind the plot. He was becoming considerably more anxious. He stared directly into the woods. Who were they? What were they after?

After a considerable pause he said, "Shimoni, what unit are you with in the IDF?"

"Sayeret Golani."

Barak nodded. A commando unit.

"Shimoni, if you came home to find your apartment ransacked and your son kidnapped by terrorists, what would you do?"

Shimoni adjusted his position on the bench. "Terrorists?" he repeated.

"Just answer the question."

After a thoughtful moment, he said firmly, "I have some connections in the villages. I'd call on them."

"You've got the entire police force behind you. You're a member of an elite commando unit in the Israeli army. The guys in your unit would go to hell and back for one another. Yet you would shun that aid to negotiate from inside."

Shimoni was adamant. "My children are my life. I would never sacrifice them to political will."

Understanding dawned on him as the words came out of his mouth. Barak continued.

"Precisely. Now, who do we have here? A highly trained, U.S. operative, who knows enough of authority to be suspicious of it. A mother, whose son, as she quickly realized, is in the hands of some very dangerous people. What do you think she was thinking? Does she go to the police? Or does she try to free her son, using her connections?"

Shimoni nodded in agreement. "Abu Jibril," he offered.

"Jericho."

"How do you know?"

Barak's hesitation was only momentary. Mossad, Police Department barriers had been put aside here.

"Two of our men infiltrated an LBA cell in Abu Jibril. They didn't show for a scheduled rendezvous, but they sent word that they were planning to move into Jericho."

"You think they're following Daniel."

Barak nodded, then added. "Protocol says, no show, I've got to send in back-up."

"Do that and you'll get Daniel and your guys killed."

Barak was torn. He knew the rules, but he didn't second-guess his men in the field. That was what set him apart from others. His men knew that they had leeway, and his trust. Interfering could get them killed. "But if I don't...."

Shimoni glared at him.

Barak half-smiled. "Got any plans for tonight?"

CHAPTER 22

▼

The young mountain lion had strayed from its usual territory in the hills of Jerusalem moving in closer to the outlying villages. It had not eaten for some days and the low growl of its stomach irritated the wild cat. Cool night breezes awakened its senses and the hunter focused its keen vision on the prey moving below. The wind had lifted the prey's warm scent sending a welcome signal to the cat of its approach. The feline crouched on a high branch. With night vision that could distinguish a rustling leaf from a field mouse over fifty feet away in the dark, the young lion brought the moving target into its site.

Its leap was perfectly timed to land on its prey as it passed just below. With a powerful lunge, the cat dropped silently through the air, its muscles completely relaxed, tensing only at the final moment that its claws sank into warm flesh.

Nadine screamed as the intense pain of an iron hot rake tore through her right shoulder and shot searing down her arm. She heard the cat snarl as it bared its teeth and she instinctively hunched her shoulders to protect her neck. The small cat glued itself to her back, its claws embedded in her burning skin. Rolling to the ground, Nadine's left hand flew up to her neck just as the cat's teeth closed down over it.

Nadine let go a roar of agony mixed with anger that she did not recognize as her own, shattering the still of the night, while her right hand drew her knife from its sheath in her waistband. Reaching across her chest, she stabbed at the cat's head.

Unable to slit the cat's throat with its teeth still embedded in her hand, she sunk her blade deep into its right eye. It screamed and threw its head back in pain, tearing the skin off the back of her left hand with it. She plunged the blade into the soft flesh underneath its chin. Its claws retracted, releasing their grip on her shoulders and back. For a few eternal moments the small lion jerked and gurgled, then lay still.

Dazed, muscles trembling, Nadine rose slowly and began to move. Her legs were unhurt, but the cat's sharp nails had driven deep into her hips. Her shoulders were on fire and her left hand throbbed and trembled as it stiffened and swelled from the bite. Her body was racked with pain. With every step her anguish intensified. Two minutes seemed like two hours. Almost immediately, she began to feel light-headed. How much farther was the village? How much longer could she go on?

Her head began to pound and her vision blurred. She was no longer sure in what direction she was moving, stumbling more than running. Daniel's image kept her on her feet. She would not let him down. She would run to the ends of the earth to save him, to wrap him in her arms one more time. She tried to block out thoughts of his fear but more, to stifle her own fear that she might not reach him. Instead, she filled her mind with the vision of Daniel to block out the pain and push on, step after agonizing step. Desperation propelled her forward.

A few scattered lights flickered dully in the distance and she forced herself towards them. She registered a controlled sense of relief as she reached the edge of the wood. One step closer to finding her son. Rolling hills of low grass and terraced fields with a few scattered houses came up to meet her. Spying a stone well, she stumbled in its direction, then fainted face down in the cool grass, her mangled hand stretched out towards the base of the well.

Al Rasuul reached his makeshift office in the safe house and lay down on the cot. He didn't bother to remove his combat jacket or even his heavy boots, only the kafiyah and dark sunglasses that he wore no matter the hour. It had been a day of surprises. He would be ready in case of another one.

He stretched his arms straight up over his head, spread his fingers and reached. Yes, that was good. The muscles down his sides and back felt immediately looser. He stretched his small, lean body a few minutes more, then exhaled, long and slow.

He folded his hands behind his head and stared up at the ceiling. As he lay in repose, he conceded that he was entitled to feel fatigued, although it was not a privilege he normally allowed himself. But then, life was strange. The peculiarities of his own life made that quite obvious. With his talents, he might have been the CEO of a global conglomerate, a millionaire many times over. A billionaire, perhaps. He'd proven that he had what it takes to make an organization tick. Genius. Charisma. Ambition. Instead, he ran a different sort of international organization. His powers of persuasion kept the coffers full. Money was never a problem. His financiers were more than eager to underwrite his plans to the tune of tens of millions of dollars, because everyone got what they wanted. Keeping all interests served was part of the game.

His quiet confidence combined with charm that was almost tangible made up for what he lacked in good looks. Indisputably, he possessed a gift not randomly bestowed upon just anyone; a gift that would continue to serve him well as ruler of Greater Palestine.

Yes, he most assuredly would have made it in the business world, but destiny had dictated otherwise. And Al Rasuul believed deep in his soul that one's destiny was as fixed as the position of the moon, the sun and the stars in the universe. He had been chosen to run a country that the world was not interested in seeing born. Which meant that instead of benign domination of the business world, he had created a frighteningly efficient terror organization the extent of which his adversaries hadn't yet begun to imagine. He smiled to himself. Indeed, they had yet to figure out who he was.

He shifted slightly on the cot. He needn't worry about those nasty Jews. There wasn't a nation on Earth that would cow tow to their whining and sniveling once they were down. No one was really sorry to see them go to the ovens half a century ago and no one would care now when he struck the ultimate blow. Except America perhaps. That's where the real problem lay to begin with. America had planted its spoiled stepchild in Palestine, slicing the already tiny land space in half. No one had wanted them. Not even the British. Of course, it was their own pomposity that brought *them* down in the end. But that's why they all agreed. And the UN never cared what the Arabs thought. Let the Jews have their little piece of desert and they won't bother the rest of us anymore.

Well, their presence did bother a few hundred million Arabs who didn't much care what the world thought either. And force spoke legions when you were the winner. Then everyone was on your side. No one liked an underdog. Soon those Jews would be back where they belong.

A smile played at the corner of his mouth then widened into a grin. He felt a swell of pleasure. No, he needn't worry about the Jews. By then the land of the free and the home of the brave would be writhing in agony from its gaping wounds. Saving the Jews would no longer be a priority item on its agenda. If anything, the gates would close.

He rested his hands across his chest. The brief detour into levity had passed. Who knew better than he the danger of delighting in victory not yet fully achieved? He turned his thoughts back to the present.

He had satellite offices worldwide. A steady flow of weapons. And a loyal infrastructure. Fringe defections, even larger scale desertion could not harm his core organization. Shrouded in secrecy, the LBA was virtually immune to the security raids and round-ups of the like that the Palestinian Authority targeted at Hamas.

He took no less pride in keeping a hand in every department, touring training camps when he could, supervising drills and regimens, and reviewing officers. He personally chose all special operatives. Needless to say, his visits were unannounced.

Of vital importance too, were his frequent calls on each grass roots cell. To see his people, the foot soldiers, the masses from which he drew the ones who showed talent, courage and foresight. They worshipped him. As well they should. He delivered. He gave them hope. Soon it would all be worthwhile.

Fatigued, Al Rasuul's heavy eyelids fluttered briefly in protest, then closed almost against his will. He hadn't felt this tired in a long time. Twenty minutes was all he would need.

The parlor was filled with little Leila's laughter as she danced around the piano. Jihan, calm and serene, didn't seem to mind that Leila danced and laughed as she played. He watched from the side, observing their fun but not participating in it. They were girls, albeit privileged, but it was he who accompanied their prominent father on matters of importance. His future was as clear as the map of Palestine that hung on the wall of his father's study. He would lead their country one day. He knew his destiny to be certain.

His father strode into the room. Tall and formidable, his arrival dominated the scene. Though he would never have his father's physical stature, he had his own commanding presence. Even at the age of twelve.

Al Rasuul groaned and tried to pull himself out of sleep but he could not resist his father's presence even now, any more than he ever could.

He watched his father carefully. A physician highly educated in matters of theology and politics as well, he was not one to wear his feelings on his sleeve. Beneath the outward veneer resided an unforgiving, rigid man.

Today, one day after the conclusion of the Six Day War, his anger was evident in the lines of his clenched jaw and his determination magnified. How many times had he heard his father's saga?

"*No family was more prosperous, more respected than ours. We can trace our lineage in Palestine at least seven generations back. We lived in mansions in Jaffa. We owned orchards and packing houses. We welcomed the Jews who settled here at the turn of the century. My great uncle Ahmed was a good friend of Haim Weizmann.*

But that did us no good in 1948. They threw us out like dogs. They said, 'it will just be for a few days.' 'For your own safety,' they said. We starved and froze in camps for nine months. My poor mother never saw her home again. Now it is occupied by nouveau riche Jews who have turned Jaffa into an artist's colony.

We remember that day as Al Nakba. The Catastrophe. But we are a resourceful family. We re-established ourselves on the West Bank and here in Jerusalem. And we will reclaim what is rightfully ours from these arrogant Jews."

He could see by the look on his father's face that they had now suffered the second, the ultimate, humiliation. Six stunningly short days earlier no one imagined that Jordanian East Jerusalem, the holiest of holy cities, and the entire West Bank of Jordan would fall into the hands of the Israelis. They were reeling from King Hussein's disgraceful defeat. Governed by Jews? Never!

His father beckoned to him. In a few minutes, they would be attending a meeting of community leaders that would establish a committee to deal with the new Israeli government.

He said, "Listen well. We will offer them cooperation. We will maintain an outward peace. But we will never give up the fight for a full and free Palestine. We will prey upon their weaknesses and jab at the soft spot in their hearts until they fall victim to their own shortsightedness."

Al Rasuul jerked into wakefulness. He felt certain that something had roused him. He raised himself up on one elbow and looked around. The room was dark and silent. Nothing seemed to have changed. How long had he slept? The fluorescent dial of his watch beamed back at him. Only a few minutes. He let out a long slow breath and eased himself back down on the cot, then crooked his right arm over his eyes.

The parlor was now filled with men, important leaders in the Palestinian community. Their position was unequivocal. The State of Israel had been a mistake. It was an abomination, a test to their faith in Allah. They would prove their worthiness. And Israel would be destroyed by its arrogance.

All eyes turned to him. They understood that it would take time. And planning. And resourcefulness. But the right leader could make it happen. One man. That was all it would take. That was all it ever took.

Under the profound gaze of this esteemed and trusted council, a sense of mission filled his soul and he felt destiny place a steadying hand on his shoulder.

Al Rasuul shifted on the little cot and finally rolled over onto his left side, falling deeper into sleep.

When they arrived at the scene of the demonstration, the area was already packed with thousands of students. The crowd alternately listened and cheered as the PLO leader addressed them. The reserved area was off to the left of the podium and he was seated next to a large man with a salt and pepper beard. Though the man's bulk easily cleared the small folding chair on which he was seated, his torso was solid. The man's expression was serious as he listened intently to his compatriot's oratory.

He looked around. Everywhere faces were lit by the flame of nationalism, their eyes bright and their bodies animated as they rose and shoved their fists into the air. With shouts of pride they called out in unison, bound by a common goal, driven by a common ambition.

Amidst the commotion, the large man turned to him and introduced himself.

"I am Youssef Abouad. I believe you might be interested in certain information that I am inclined to share with you. Will you join me today for tea?"

Taken aback, he appraised his neighbor. Despite his girth, a kindliness radiated from large light brown eyes set evenly above an aquiline nose. His skin tone was deep olive and his big head was adorned with thick graying hair and a neatly trimmed beard that gave him an air of royalty. Intrigued by the man's forthright manner and sincere demeanor, he heard himself agree.

In the neat sandstone house, away from the tumult of the demonstration, he silently admired the tightly woven tapestries hung evenly across the white washed walls. A young woman, covered from head to toe, poured their tea. There were no others in attendance, except for the bodyguards at the door. When the woman retreated in silence, Youssef Abouad began to speak.

"Last I saw you, you were a lad of twelve. A great mission was conferred upon you. You have grown to be a young man of great talent, intelligence and capability. Your accomplishments in the academic world are noteworthy and you have achieved great respect at a young age." Abouad paused to sip his tea, then continued.

"I represent a party who has an interest in executing the plan outlined in your father's parlor fourteen years ago. But a slightly modified version."

His chest tightened. The hand of destiny had him by the throat. "What about the PLO and Fatah? They are waging the war for a Palestinian state."

Abouad waved a hand. "They are small fish in a big pond. They operate as thorns in Israel's side but with no real effect on the country, which continues to develop economically and has built many modern cities. So what if a few shells fall on border towns? So what if a man here or a woman there is cut down in the street? True, the

Israelis take loss of life very badly, and every blow weakens them a bit. But they are resilient."

"It almost sounds as though you admire them."

Abouad shook his head. "It is not that. But to defeat your enemy, you must know him. We have something more global in mind."

He waited. With every passing moment, the man's words felt more right, more true, as if he had been hearing them all along.

"The real evil is America. Israel cannot be defeated as long as America is strong. The relationship between the two countries is powerful and deep, almost familial.

Glowering, Abouad declared, "Both are aggressive, arrogant powers. They do not know our people, they do not understand our ways, they do not know the extent of their wrong. To defeat one, we must defeat both."

"And my role?"

A broad grin creased his brown face. "It's really quite straightforward. You want Palestine. We want the West. Together, we can do this."

Al Rasuul opened his eyes. Yes, together they could do this. And they had. Almost. While the Palestinian Authority danced like a marionette every time America or Israel pulled its strings, he would strike at America's heart, and at the heart of democracy. They would understand their weakness and the error of their ways. The atmosphere was right. The timing was perfect. Americans were more distrustful of their government now than ever before in its history. Its own home grown militia was becoming more and more bold.

Israel's right wing government had left the peace process in shambles and completely alienated any Arab support it had garnered over the past few years. It was already teetering and about to fall. He would just give it a little push.

Abouad had been right. America was the true evil. Big Satan and Little Satan. But they understood what their predecessors had not. Both evils had to fall. Then change would come.

He was not an impatient man. Twenty years building and running the Liberation Brotherhood Army proved that. His own international organization was evidence of his success.

Meet fate head on. That had always been his credo, for there was no choice really, was there?

He swung his legs over the side and sat up on the edge of the cot. Meet fate head on. Now fate had handed him a fifteen-year-old boy. Was it just Issam's stupidity or was there something more to this?

There was only one way to find out.

CHAPTER 23

▼

From the window of his darkened bedroom, Naji watched his father walk slowly towards the well where he liked to sit and puff his pipe.

"Foolish old man," he muttered under his breath. "Completely out of touch with reality." He was convinced that his father had fallen for Zionist propaganda and was being used by the Israelis for their own purposes. "Probably dropped his pipe," he scoffed, seeing Fouad stoop down on the far side of the well. His loathing was palpable but catching his own reflection in the darkened window, he smiled. "Well, won't he be surprised when he learns that I am to be a *shaheed*, a martyr for the Brotherhood."

This was his last night at home and a wave of excitement surged through him. The smile that crossed his young face made him look even more boyish.

He was leaving the next day for a training camp in the Bekaa Valley and was still debating about whether to tell his father face to face or leave a note behind. He was inclined towards the latter. No sense in creating a scene on the greatest day of his life. Only thoughts of his mother's sadness dampened his joy slightly, but he reassured himself that her pride in him would outweigh any fear she might have for his safety.

Naji took a deep breath to quiet his pounding heart. His path was clear and open before him. He was heartened knowing that the West had no match for their weapons; theirs were the weapons of faith, far mightier than missiles. There was no defense against martyrdom and jihad. And there was no question of success. It was only a matter of time.

He reached out to the lamp on his desk and was about to flip its switch when he saw his father's large frame moving quickly though unsteadily back toward the house, his pipe clenched between his teeth. The moonlight faded in and out as clouds passed across its surface. Naji strained his eyes to peer through the dark but could see very little.

He slipped out of his bedroom into the dimly lit hallway and stopped a few feet short of the kitchen where he could see the back entrance without being seen. A small light burned over the sink. Keeping himself concealed, he watched as Fouad clumsily maneuvered his way through the back door then crossed the kitchen toward the spare back room. Naji pressed in a little closer, hugging the wall.

"Ya'Allah!" he uttered silently. A body!

Surprise and confusion were making him impatient, but he stayed low. The hair was short and dark, and the body well toned. For a moment he thought it might be one of his comrades and he almost leapt from his spot. But as Fouad passed directly by the hallway where he crouched, Naji got a clear look and quickly strangled a shout. Though bruised and streaked with dirt, there was no doubt about who it was. He had seen her several times at his father's kiosk—the American woman who had seduced him with her high Arabic and her white American smile.

She dangled lifelessly from his arms. Blood dripped from her mangled hand, leaving a neat trail of dark red drops on the floor. Though Fouad was clearly straining from the effort, Naji did not move a muscle. Distress and anger began to displace his surprise. Now he was certain. His father *was* a collaborator, a traitor poisoned by the Israelis, Europeans and Americans he served. He spoke their languages and catered to their wishes. He spent too much time in their company at his popular little eatery and too little among his own people. In the process, he had become one of them.

Naji trembled with rage. So what if the old man was his father? He had nothing but scorn for his ways. I would swat him dead like a fly if need be, he swore to himself and tore out of the house into the night.

CHAPTER 24

▼

He spent the hours repeating grammar drills, once memorized conjugations, vocabulary lists and mnemonics. He made up conversations in his head and softly sang the songs his mother had taught him. He closed his eyes and summoned the will to recall what he had tried to forget, its staccato rhythm matching the tempo of his own urgency before slowing finally to a steady cadence as the language returned and cautious hope replaced his fear.

He fought sleep and surrender, determined to survive, spurred by an inner strength he did not know he possessed, simply because he had to. He had to stay alive just long enough. Long enough perhaps for his captors to stop hating him. Long enough for his family to find him.

The plate of food he had initially shunned was now empty. He needed his strength and his wits for it was only by his wits that he would live to see his mother and brother again. He exercised his mind until he could think no more, then he closed his burning eyes and rested.

In 586 BC, Nebuchadnezzer, ruler of Babylon, conquered Jerusalem and commanded his chief of staff to bring back four of the brightest and finest of the Judeans. The chief of staff returned with four superior young men, among them, a young man named Daniel who far outshone the others in intellect and knowledge. Daniel was also gifted with the power of foresight and clarity of thought. His gift endeared him to Nebuchadnezzer, but caused others in the king's court to be deeply jealous. The king's men conspired and arranged a trap for Daniel. They had the king sign and seal an edict that no man shall worship any deity or human but the king himself.

That evening, as they knew he would, Daniel turned towards Jerusalem to bow before his God in prayer, for he was a man faithful to his God and to his King, whereupon he was arrested. The King had no choice but to carry out the prescribed punishment, for he had signed the edict with his personal seal. With a heavy heart, Nebuchadnezzer threw Daniel into a den of seven hungry lions and sealed the cave.

Nebuchadnezzer fasted and did not sleep. The following morning, he came to the cave and cried out, "Daniel, servant of the living God! Has He whom you serve so faithfully, saved you from the lions?"

And Daniel replied, "O King, live forever! My God sent his angels who protected me from the lions' jaws. They did me no harm, since in His sight I am blameless, nor have I wronged you either, O King."

The king was overjoyed and ordered Daniel released.

Daniel awoke with a start to the scraping of keys against the locked door of his cell.

CHAPTER 25

▼

Her thoughts were jumbled and confused. She heard voices, calling to her. They wanted something from her but she could not grasp their meaning. She heard Barak first, his voice low, insistent, warning. She strained to hear his words but it was useless. A bearded old man breezed by her, mumbling something in Hebrew. Daniel laughed, confident and wise. She tried to find him, but she couldn't move. Where was he? Always just out of reach. Women's voices whispered in Arabic. Her body felt chilled and she shivered, then she grew hot and sticky with sweat. She wanted desperately to call out, but was sure that no one would hear her.

The smell of pipe smoke tickled her nose and she opened her eyes. The room was dark but she could see Fouad's heavy form at the foot of the bed. She was aware of the pain but it seemed distant. Still, she could not move.

"Daniel," she said hoarsely.

"Allow me to speak, Nadine," Fouad said softly in Arabic. "Your thick sweatshirt prevented your wounds from being worse than they might have been. My wife has dressed them with medicinal poultices. Her knowledge of herbal remedies is quite sophisticated, but you need a doctor, antibiotics, and probably a surgeon," he said gesturing in the direction of her bandaged hand. "Fortunately, you have no sign of fever, yet."

Fouad paused. "I am not a wise or a learned man, Nadine, but I need not be such a man to understand that you meant for no one to know of your presence here."

Fouad's wife had slipped out of the room when she saw Nadine awaken and now returned with a steaming brew. She sat down next to the bed and Fouad helped her lift Nadine and prop her up with some pillows.

"It is not yet midnight," Fouad continued. "Drink this tea. It has a mild stimulant and will energize you. I will not be able to keep your presence here secret for long. Once you have drunk the tea, you will have your opportunity to speak."

She sipped the brew and felt its warmth disperse the chill that had spread through her aching limbs. Her pain reminded her of her predicament and for one panicky moment, doubt and fear threatened to defeat her, but as the hot drink took hold, her surroundings slowly came into focus and she felt herself calming and thinking more clearly.

Her eyes adjusted to the darkness. She looked around and saw that the room was small but neat and clean. Its walls were whitewashed and the floors were covered in tightly woven rugs of maroons and reds. A few small leather patchwork ottomans were scattered about and a neat wooden desk was tucked into the far corner, next to a window opposite the bed.

Fouad sat next to her, watching her as he patiently sucked on his pipe. She was grateful for his presence. When the cup was empty, she placed it in his wife's waiting hand.

Then she said, "Daniel's been kidnapped."

Shock and understanding registered in Fouad's oval face.

"Tell me what you know," he said softly.

"He was here, in Abu Jibril, but he's been moved to Jericho."

Fouad sucked intently on his pipe. "I can get you to Jericho," he said, "but how do we find Daniel? What do you know of his captors?"

"That he has been taken in revenge for what happened in the forest." She handed him the now crumpled newspaper clipping she had found tacked to Daniel's bedroom door. "I can only guess that they are family members. Perhaps terrorists, too. The LBA promised to retaliate. I didn't know they meant to take my son."

They were whispering. Perhaps because the situation was too awful to speak of in normal tones. Perhaps because of the need for secrecy, though they were alone. Perhaps both.

"I have a plan," Fouad said finally.

He motioned to his wife, who had been sitting quietly on a low ottoman off to the side. He gave her some instructions. She listened silently, nodded and glided out of the room. Nadine could not guess her age, but her movements flowed with the grace of a young dancer.

She mentioned this to Fouad and his eyes widened slightly as he responded, "Indeed, she is a dancer. But for an audience of one." After a thoughtful moment, he added, "She is a remarkable woman," and heaved himself to his feet.

"Rest. We leave shortly before dawn." Then he left her.

The moment he stepped out of the room, his mind began racing and he could feel his heart pounding rapidly in his large chest. His pacifist views were well known in the village and his warm relationship with the Israelis among whom he worked was apparent, but he'd never been accused of crossing the line. Tonight's actions, if discovered, would clearly mark him as a collaborator. He knew that he would not refuse to help Nadine save the life of her child, but some of his people would not interpret his actions in his favor. By this deed, his entire family, his wife, his children, his darling grandchild, could be swept up and executed in the dark of the night. There would be no outcry, no protest; only praise for eliminating the family of one who knew the enemy.

Amir and his wife were in their own quarters on the other side of the house. Naji's room was dark. He must be asleep, Fouad surmised, or surely, he would have come out to investigate. So, only he and his wife knew of Nadine's presence. That was good.

He lay down on his bed fully clothed, put his arms around his wife and placed his lips against her forehead.

"*Shukran*," he said softly. *Thank you.*

The truck bounced along in the darkness. Marwan knew the road well, so he paid little attention to his surroundings. His mind was on the boy in the back. Fifteen. Shackled. Soon to die.

He knew that Issam had plans for him. Al Rasuul had issued an order and walked away but Issam was not so easily deterred. Earlier, he had seen him in a huddle with Sabri, their heads bowed in towards one another, the taller Issam cajoling, while the smaller Sabri shook his head. Marwan dared not approach or listen in. He was not a leader and did not ponder issues that were beyond his limited sphere. He knew his position—a foot soldier in the holy war against the West and its abominations. But he always watched very carefully, even now.

He drove on in the darkness. None of that lessened the uneasiness he was now feeling about the boy's certain fate. He was stunned when the boy spoke to him in Arabic. His manners and speech reflected the upbringing of a young man in an upper-class Arab home. Perhaps, he thought, there had been a mistake. But no, he had been there himself. The boy lived among the Jews. His mother was an American. He was one of the enemy. Still, Marwan felt some regret. He seemed so much like one of their own.

He had decided to stay with Daniel while he ate. He imagined that the boy must be afraid; a little small talk in the hours before he was to die might hearten him. Peering through the dusty windshield, Marwan shook his head slowly from side to side. What a surprise to learn that Daniel too was a soccer enthusiast and admired so many of the legends of his youth, the Brazilian Pele, the English Charlton brothers and Beckenbauer of Germany. Daniel even knew Pele's real name, Edson Arantes do Nascimento. Eagerly, they compared the strengths and shortcomings of many of their favorite players and his earlier surprise slowly approached affection for his young hostage.

Like many boys, Marwan had dreamed of becoming a professional soccer player. A national hero. Only he never quite outgrew that dream. Marwan drove and heaved a sigh. He had apologized to Daniel for shackling him in the back of the truck. Were he a fifteen year old prisoner, he had explained, he too would try to escape.

Marwan reminded himself that the boy had been taken in revenge for the death of Muhammad, the youngest brother of Issam. An eye for an eye. Still, he did not have to feel good about it. Issam was surely committed to his revenge, but perhaps he could appeal to Sabri for mercy.

He had the entire night to work it out. His instructions were to get some rest once he had delivered Daniel to The Specialist. Issam and Sabri would arrive at daybreak. We'll need you in the morning, they had said. His heart swelled with pride. *They needed him.* Marwan smiled to himself. He would be a hero after all. And maybe Daniel would stay and become a Brotherhood freedom fighter. No doubt he would rather live and fight with them than die the next day. Now wouldn't that be the ultimate revenge!

Having resolved to approach Sabri in the morning, Marwan felt immediately better. He was one of them now. They had accepted him. Surely, they even respected him after this morning's daring raid. Once they got to know Daniel, they would see what he saw.

For the remainder of the ride down to Jericho, Marwan happily fantasized of fighting the holy war against the Israel and the West with Daniel at his side.

The truck braked noisily to a stop and jerked him back and forth. His arms ached from being tied in a single position for so long. The blood had rushed back into his burning shoulders and his fingers were numb and white.

He had been terrified at first when two men in black ski masks jumped onto the truck as it was leaving Abu Jibril. He had seen scores like them on the evening news. The reports of violence and street fighting in Jerusalem's surrounding Arab villages featured young men like these, burning Israeli flags and tires, throwing homemade bombs at patrols and journalists, and sometimes even tourists.

His first thought was that they were from a rival group, ready to do to him what his captors had not done yet. But something in their body language reassured him. Maybe it was the way they examined the chains that bound him to the frame of the truck's canvas cover or their posture as they sat on the bench opposite him, bodies loose, shoulders relaxed. Or maybe it was the way they watched him, steadily but without hostility. And though they whispered to one another in Arabic and gave him no reason to believe they were anything other than what they appeared to be, he sensed that there was more to them than met the eye.

Slowly, it dawned on him that maybe, just maybe, these guys were on his side. Maybe they knew he'd been kidnapped and were going to get him out. Buoyed, he tried to remain nonchalant, almost forgetting the discomfort along his arms, but he began feeling more apprehensive when he realized that they weren't paying attention to him any longer. His heart sank when, as the truck slowed, the two men poised to leap out. Hope turned to desperation. He couldn't have been wrong. He had to give them a sign. At this point, he had nothing to lose.

He spoke. One sentence in Hebrew. He saw their bodies stiffen slightly and pause before they disappeared into the night.

Alone again, he felt utterly deserted. A creeping dread replaced his earlier confidence. Marwan was sympathetic but still, he had made sure that he couldn't escape. The strangers had come and gone. Maybe they had decided not to help. Or maybe they weren't who he thought they were to begin with. He had no doubt that by now he had been reported missing but the farther away they took him, the more isolated he felt. He would not be easy to find and by then it might be too late. Worry and self-doubt jabbed at him relentlessly amplified by the fiery pain in his joints.

Come back, he prayed. Please.

The flap of the truck flew back and the trailer sank under Marwan's weight as he heaved his huge body into the back. He opened the padlock that linked Daniel's handcuffs to the metal frame and his arms dropped heavily into his lap the moment they were released. His fingers and hands tingled as the blood rushed back into them. He tried to move them to get the circulation going, chafing his wrists against the metal cuffs as he did.

Marwan helped him stand and he stalled, not wanting to leave the illusory safety of the back of the truck. A prickly feeling crawled along the back of his neck. A premonition or a warning?

Stay in the moment, Danny boy, he told himself. His father used to call him Danny boy and just the thought reassured him slightly.

Marwan patted him on the shoulder before lifting him out of the truck.

"*In'shallah*. It is God's will," Marwan said before guiding him towards a deserted house on a lot at the outskirts of what seemed to be a fairly large town. Daniel tried to take a moment to figure out where they were until he saw where they were going.

A tall, slim man in a starched shirt and neatly pressed pants waited patiently on the small porch at the entrance to the house. Though his features were handsome—square jaw, aquiline nose, smooth dark skin and clear brown eyes— the face was pure evil.

Daniel wanted to turn and run, to bury his face in Marwan's bulk, cry and plead, beg for his life, but he was too petrified to budge. His legs stopped moving and Marwan half-lifted, half-dragged him closer and closer to the inevitable.

The moment he was handed over, Daniel lost all hope. Fear saturated every fiber of his being. Panic gripped his chest and a tightening, burning sensation rose up into his head and to the tips of his ears and nose. His bowels loosened, threatening to give way. His breath became shallow, making it difficult for him to breathe. He felt the blood drain from his face and for all that he tried to block out the thought, at that very moment he knew how Mengele's children felt, as they were led into his evil laboratory; hopeless, terrified, regretful.

Mommy, mommy. His brain screamed out for her and then he fainted.

CHAPTER 26

▼

The ringing phone jerked him cursing into wakefulness. How could he have fallen asleep? His hand shot out for the phone.

"Hello?"

"This is Dr. Nasser. I must speak to Nadine."

"This is General Brad McKenzie, Dr. Nasser. Dr. Kanner asked me to wait for your call."

There was a long pause. When he finally spoke, Nasser's tone had changed. He sounded colder, more abrupt, perhaps even angry that Nadine was not waiting for him herself.

"I've arranged for Daniel's release. He will be delivered to me and only me. No one else is to be present."

"Where?"

Again, a pause. "It is safer not to say. If anyone else is seen in the vicinity, the boy will not be delivered, certainly not alive."

The finality of Nasser's tone sent shivers down Brad's spine. Still, he persisted.

"But what about Nadine? She'll want to know. I assure you, your instructions will be followed precisely. You've come a long way to help her. She won't do anything to betray that trust."

Brad suffered through another pause, though slightly shorter this time.

"He will be dropped off approximately one kilometer from the joint Israeli-Palestinian command near Jericho. He will walk alone towards the command. I will meet him along the way. Have Nadine meet me back at my hotel in East Jerusalem."

"What is the name of the hotel?"

"She knows. She met me there this afternoon."

Brad felt a stab of panic. What if she didn't show on time? He couldn't recall now if she had mentioned the name of the hotel. Something in Arabic he thought.

"Dr. Nasser, Nadine is very distraught as you can well imagine. I would not want to take the risk that she has lost or forgotten where she met you today." Fat chance, Brad thought to himself. Hopefully, Nasser didn't know her as well as he did.

"I will ring you when I have returned safely to my hotel with Daniel. Then we will arrange for him to return to his mother."

"Dr. Nasser," Brad called into the mouthpiece to catch him before he hung up. He was still there. "I assure you there are many people who appreciate what you are doing. People who would like to thank you, acknowledge your special efforts. You are no stranger to publicity. Securing Daniel's release makes you something of a hero."

This time there was no pause.

"Not to them it doesn't," came the short reply followed by a definite click.

Barak wasn't taking any chances. Alone in his darkened office, he went over his options. He knew whom he could count on. The critical issue was whether to mobilize them. He'd seen it backfire before. Too much action and Daniel dies fast. He pursed his lips and pressed his fingertips together. A missed rendezvous meant sending in a rescue team. Period. But knowing what he knew, or thought he knew, he had made a decision.

Pushing aside further contemplation, he packed a radio for himself and Shimoni and grabbed a couple of other items he thought might come in handy. He opened his desk drawer and picked up a lightweight semi-automatic. He had discovered it as an operative in Europe and had never used any other weapon since. Shimoni would pack his own piece and whatever else he felt comfortable with. They had no room for heavy ammunition. One more item—a vest for Daniel. He wished he could pack an entire suit of body armor for him. He did not want to free him only to see him shot on the way out. He heaved a sigh and stood. Only they had to find him first.

As he headed to his car and the rendezvous point with Shimoni, he silently admitted that as long as the enemy was as elusive as the achievement of an ideal, there would be no end. Fighting extremism in hand-to-hand combat was useless. It only fueled the fire. The *mujahadeen* proved that in Afghanistan. A rag tag army of Islamic teachers, shopkeepers and laborers triumphed over the Soviet war machine because they had faith and believed in the holiness of their cause. They waged a holy war against the infidel and died as martyrs in a guerrilla war against a superpower, but ultimately, by sheer will and indomitable faith, they were victorious.

Barak reached the car and slid into the driver's seat. Now the fringe was taking its holy war global. It was pay back time. Time to pay back the Western world for its condescension, for the insults, perceived or otherwise, to honor Allah.

Israel was no stranger to terror. Extremists had been treating them to a steady rain of kidnapping, murders and hijackings for more than fifty years. There was nothing inherently different about this threat. But the global attack would make the psychological toll very great. He knew that as long as there was an enemy, he would be there to fight it. He was one of the few that could and it needed to be done.

Barak pulled his car out into the street and joined the stream of Saturday night traffic. The streets of the city were alive with cars and pedestrians. He watched couples walk arm-in-arm, laughing with friends, delighting in the freedom of the weekend before returning to the constraints of daily living.

Maybe Zoe had been right to leave him. Maybe his career didn't leave room for a real relationship or pursuing personal desires. Maybe Nadine was just another mission, just a passing game, or whatever. He shook his head.

"Cut that shit," he said aloud to himself. Time was precious.

Midnight. Shimoni, who had already commandeered a vehicle with Arab license plates, was waiting at the Ma'ale Adumim intersection. Well traveled during the work week, the now deserted highway led out of the city in the direction of Southern Israel and Jericho.

Shimoni was dressed in dark plainclothes. Barak threw him a radio and a black ski mask, essential gear for the modern terrorist. If they wanted to get by them, they had to look like them.

He anxiously awaited the first message, a verse from the Old Testament. They had Y to thank for that. Raised in a religious home, Y could quote scripture in his sleep. Anyone casually listening might think that they had come across one of the many weekly radio programs broadcast in Israel on Bible study. Even on this open frequency, only a scholar would recognize the altered quotes but by the time anyone figured out their meaning, the operation would be long over.

Barak's radio crackled. "That's it!"

"And the prophet crossed the river Jordan, into the land of milk and honey," a voice intoned in Hebrew.

Barak felt his heart skip a beat. Al Rasuul was in Israel and had been sighted. If they could capture him, the relief would be audible from Jerusalem to Tel Aviv. He glanced over at Shimoni, who had a quizzical look on his face. The temptation to go after Al Rasuul was palpable. Though that kind of operation normally required careful planning, an opportunity may have presented itself that he could not afford to ignore.

Could he sacrifice Daniel to capture the terrorist whose organization threatened Israel's very existence? One life for the sake of the many? How many times had he heard that? The argument was wearing thin. But he might have no choice. His mind was racing ahead when the next message stopped him cold.

"*Kach na et bincha l'ir Yehoshua veha'alehu sham l'olah*" Genesis 22:3. God instructed Abraham '*take your son…and offer him up as a sacrifice*' but in this message, the location had changed. *To the city of Joshua.* Jericho. Confirmation. Daniel was in Jericho. And he was still alive. But probably not for long. Like Isaac, this son of Abraham was being prepared for sacrifice. He could only hope the comparison wouldn't end there. At the last moment, Isaac was spared. It was up to them to make sure that Daniel was spared too.

Barak signaled to Shimoni to drive while he listened for the next message. It was a moonless night and the mountain road was invisible beyond the glow of their headlights. Jericho lay twenty-six kilometers down the mountain on the flat, desert floor and slightly northeast of Jerusalem.

Shimoni pressed his foot to the floor. Curves rose up like a serpent flicking a fly off its tail and threatened to fling them off the mountain road, but Shimoni drove on and down as if he were the knight who had come to slay the serpent. The mountain didn't have a chance. Barak waited anxiously for the next message, hoping he would survive to hear it. *Dirballak*, he swore to himself, Shimoni has four kids. How could he drive like this?

"Hey, Shimoni."

"Yeh?"

"Watch out for sheep."

"Sure. No problem." Shimoni slowed their descent to eighty. Barak loosened his grip on the door panel, but remained mentally prepared for a last minute leap.

The familiar hiss followed by a short burst of static took Barak's mind off the road.

"*V'…shalach et hayona min hatevah.*" Genesis VIII: 11. *And…he sent forth the dove out of the ark.*

Al Rasuul would have to wait. They were going for Daniel. First. Barak's eyes glowed with determination, the hunter on the trail of the hunted.

At the foot of the mountain, Shimoni turned left from the main road onto the route leading into Jericho. The final message had instructed them to meet at the grove of date palms just south of the city. To their relief, they drove past the joint Israeli-Palestinian command post undisturbed.

The grove loomed into sight from the main highway. Bearing right, Shimoni turned off the pavement onto a desert road leading towards it. He killed the headlights when they were about fifty meters from the trees, their tall thick trunks crowned by wide, green fronds. They drove slowly, in near complete darkness until coming to a halt at the grove's edge. Barak stepped out and whistled softly. The answering call came moments later, then two masked figures exited the grove and approached from a short distance. They were dressed in jeans, sneakers and loose shirts.

Harel, tall and broad shouldered, was physically imposing. He had dark hair and piercing eyes but his quick smile and engaging nature touched everyone in his company. Avi was a full head shorter than his partner. He had strong, quick movements and a more intense, serious demeanor. He spoke little but he was sharp and his advice was best heeded.

They removed their ski masks and Barak introduced them to Shimoni who produced a thermos of steaming Turkish coffee and sandwiches. The two men were grateful.

Shimoni shrugged. "I told my wife I was going on a stake-out."

Barak turned to his men. "Report."

"We spent the afternoon at a Brotherhood indoctrination session. They're shipping a bunch of new recruits out to a training camp in the Bekaa Valley tomorrow. We'll give you a full report on that later," he said, nodding towards Harel, then he continued. "We got friendly with one of the recruits, a kid we'd seen around and talked to before. After the meeting, he was quietly bragging that he knew the location of a Brotherhood safe house. About an hour after everyone split, we checked it out. He was right." The man paused to take a bite of his sandwich and sipped some coffee.

"It's small. One story, stucco. We decided to case the place for a while. It was worth it." His eyes widened and he straightened up as he continued his account. "None other than Al Rasuul himself showed up. Even from where we were, we could tell that his lieutenant, Issam Ibn Assad, was caught off guard. But since Al Rasuul's visits are always unannounced, we knew that something else was wrong."

The Mossad had identified Issam Ibn Assad months earlier as being responsible for the Brotherhood's West Bank operations including a spate of suicide bombings in several Israeli cities. But they had decided to keep him under surveillance rather than target him, as their best chance of ever getting close to Al Rasuul and identifying the real force behind the Brotherhood. Barak hoped that reasoning was about to pay off.

"At nightfall, we moved in close. That's why we missed the rendezvous."

"Go on."

"The house is isolated, on the side of a hill covered with rocks and scrubby brush. They had no guards posted outside. Inside, there were only four men, Al Rasuul, his lieutenant Issam, a smaller, smart-looking guy with glasses and a big guy. After a brief exchange with Issam, Al Rasuul disappeared into a closed room. We couldn't see what, if anything, was going on in there. All of the others were accounted for. Issam and the guy with the glasses seemed to be having a disagreement, one Issam definitely did not want Al Rasuul to hear. They kept their voices low and their heads in real close. Issam seemed insistent, like he was trying to convince 'Glasses' of something. 'Glasses' kept shaking his head no."

"The big guy was staying out of the way, eyeing them but not interfering. We moved around to the back of the house where we wouldn't be seen if anyone stepped outside, to discuss our plan of action. From what we had seen so far, we determined that the house would be pretty easy to take. Not knowing how long Al Rasuul was planning to stay we were debating whether to do it ourselves or call in assistance."

"Then we saw what all the tension was about. A kid, maybe fourteen or fifteen years old. From our position we could see straight into the house through the back window. Looked like a hostage situation to us. Obviousiy, that changed things entirely."

Harel interjected. "The weird thing was that he didn't look scared. He was sitting straight, staring out the window. It was like he was thinking about something, not really looking at anything. He didn't appear to be agitated. He seemed…" Harel searched for the word.

"Determined," offered Avi.

Harel nodded in agreement and continued. "Sometimes he moved his lips. I thought maybe he was praying. I sure would be. But he looked more like he was trying to remember something."

Avi continued. "We decided to call in a backup team. We felt that that would increase our chances of getting the kid out safely and capturing Al Rasuul. We were about to move out and make contact when the big guy came into the back room. We watched to see what was happening. The kid started talking to him. The big guy was real happy."

"The kid is smart. He was being polite. Getting friendly with his guard, creating a connection," Harel commented.

Barak felt a swell of pride. Daniel had courage in his blood and his wits about him. That might keep him alive a little longer.

"Any idea what the other two were arguing about?"

"Just a guess, but we think they were disagreeing about what to do with the kid. I don't know whether they thought it through but whatever their plans were, Al Rasuul's arrival seemed to throw a wrench into things. Anyway, a while later, the big guy takes the kid out and loads him onto the back of a truck, like an army truck. The top and back were covered in canvas. As he climbed into the driver's seat and started the engine, we slipped on and hugged the back. The roads being unpaved, we had no trouble climbing inside without the driver knowing we were there once he started moving."

Barak protested. "The purpose of this mission was to identify Al Rasuul. You've put your life at risk to infiltrate a terrorist cell for that sole purpose. What was your reason for leaving him behind to follow the boy? If anything, the boy's removal made your chances of taking Al Rasuul successfully, even greater."

Avi's response came without hesitation. Without moving his eyes from Barak's face, he said, "We can bring Al Rasuul down and another maniac will take his place. But that innocent kid is somebody's son. No one is going to replace him. And I for one wasn't going to have the Brotherhood's next innocent victim on my conscience."

Barak nodded. Clearly, the sacrifice-a-life-for-the-greater-good argument was not working for them either. They were professionals, but he was relieved to know they were still human.

"Poor kid," Harel said, bringing them back to issue at hand. "He looked terrified at the sight of us."

"You are pretty ugly. You should have kept those masks on."

"We did. He thought we were his executioners."

"He was shackled hands and feet to the metal frame inside the truck. We didn't have the tools to free him. We kept an eye on where we were going through the canvas flap and stayed on until the truck slowed to stop. Then we jumped."

"As we were exiting though, he spoke to us. In Hebrew," Harel interjected.

Barak's face registered obvious surprise. "What did he say?"

"He said, 'My name is Daniel. Tell them you found me.'"

Barak stood. "Let's go."

They moved on foot into the southeast part of the town. Nothing stirred. Dusty streets lined with closely cramped, desert colored houses, were dark and still.

Avi and Harel led Barak and Shimoni to a free-standing building on the edge of town into which they had seen Marwan take Daniel earlier. The truck was still there.

"We'll have to see how well they're covered."

They split into two directions as they approached the house. It was an abandoned, unfurnished structure. There were no panes in the windows. Only one room had a light, produced by a small generator. Their first objective was to locate Daniel. They surmised that Marwan was not alone, but in the dark, it was going to be difficult to determine how many there were and what ammunition they carried. The four knew too well that the Brotherhood tended to be well armed.

Barak saw Shimoni move closer to the front of the house. One of the occupants had stepped out. The man was tall and slim, Shimoni's height, and nicely dressed in a starched shirt and slacks. He was about to light a cigarette. Shimoni removed his mask, stepped out of the shadows and called out to him. He approached, arms open, like he was greeting a cousin. Barak could not catch the words but the other man remained relaxed, his body language signaling that he did not feel threatened.

Barak held his breath as he watched. He saw Shimoni's arm encircle the other man's shoulder. They spoke a little more and a few seconds later, the man was down.

Barak joined him. Shimoni held up a syringe. "I pilfered it from my wife's medical bag. I thought we might need it for Daniel." They carried the man into the shadows. "He's only sleeping, but I gave him the whole dose. I don't think we'll be hearing from him for a while."

Shimoni pulled his mask back on.

"He didn't look like your typical LBA member."

"Must have a professional role, not a fighter. Maybe a banker delivering this month's bankroll."

"At this hour?"

"Maybe he's the owner and they're re-negotiating their lease."

Shimoni grunted.

"The answer is most likely inside. What's your guess?"

"No more than two others besides Daniel in the house, the driver and one more. From what we've seen and heard, this is an organization that works on the premise, 'the less anyone knows, the better'."

They crouched and moved in towards the steps leading up to the front door. Avi and Harel would keep watch on the sides and back until Barak signaled them. Barak led. They moved through the house slowly. The vestibule was empty. They moved into a small hallway. Off to the right, Marwan was snoring on a cot in the corner of a room. They crept by and headed towards the room at the end of the hallway. A horizontal beam of light near the floor marked its entrance. A third room off to the right was empty. Barak leaned into the closed door of the last room and pressed his ear against it.

Nothing.

Shimoni nodded and covered him as Barak slowly turned the handle, shoved it open, dropped to the floor and rolled into the room.

Nothing.

They could hear the quiet hum of the generator off to one side. Barak slowly raised himself, then stopped dead in his tracks. Instantly, he understood why no guards were necessary.

He had found Daniel, but he could not save him.

CHAPTER 27

▼

It was still dark as pitch when Fouad's wife gently shook Nadine awake and helped her into a heavy black gown and headdress that covered everything but her eyes. The two left hurriedly, not stopping to drink or eat, anxious to be on their way before any of the household awoke. Later, Fouad's wife would tell Amir that Fouad had taken the truck to pick up vegetables for the kiosk.

Fouad shifted the white pickup into neutral, released the brake and coasted to the bottom of the small hill on which his house stood. A yellow decorative fringe with dangling ornaments of plastic and tin swayed in the windshield as the truck rolled forward. Only when the house was out of view, did he start the ignition.

Fifteen minutes later they hooked up with the main road and made their way slowly down the mountain. Here, on the eastern descent out of Jerusalem leading into the desert, the hills were barren and rocky, looming like giant shadows in the night. They rode in darkness and in silence past Bedouin campsites perched precariously on bare slopes, the ragged black flaps of their huge family tents slapping in the wind. Idle camels, humps draped in tightly embroidered multicolored mats, sat motionless at the edge of the encampments.

Lone donkeys hugged the roadside in search of roots and scrub brush that sprouted here and there. They roamed like slowly moving phantoms, invisible in the dark that shrouded them. Fouad was careful to avoid them. They were stubborn animals. They often wandered aimlessly onto the highway, heads bowed, never raising their noses from the ground as they sniffed out anything remotely edible. A collision with one of those four-legged beasts would stop them for good.

Both had their thoughts on Jericho. It would come into sight as they came out of the hills. From above, it appeared flat and colorless, its tawny stone houses lined up in rows on the desert floor, barely distinguishable from its surroundings.

Jericho was the first West Bank city to be transferred from Israeli to Palestinian control, and it quickly became a haven for fugitives from the Israeli authorities. A crossroads between Jordan to the east, Jerusalem to the west, Gaza to the south, the Galilee and Syria to the north, the once sleepy oasis was home to a teeming underground where information was a commodity easily traded. Fouad was fairly certain that Daniel would not be difficult to find.

The sky was dark blue when they came out of the hills and turned left onto the road to Jericho. Over the desert, the sun rose almost as quickly as it set. In fifteen minutes, they would be driving in daylight. They passed a deserted refugee camp and five minutes later, drove undisturbed past the joint Israeli-Palestinian command post.

Barely a kilometer further down the road, Jericho was clearly in sight. Nadine did not like the uneasiness that now crept over her. The sky was getting lighter and the desert landscape left her feeling exposed. She glanced at Fouad. He seemed distracted. His eyes shifted nervously from the rearview to the side view mirror and then briefly back to the road ahead before returning apprehensively to the mirrors once again.

Alarmed, she looked into the large mirror to her right. It extended at an angle to provide a view of the road beyond the bed of the pickup. A light blue sedan with no markings trailed at a short distance behind them. At times, the sedan practically kissed the bumper of Fouad's truck. At others, it hung back, moving to and fro like a wave chasing a child's footprints.

Three young men, a driver and two passengers, sat ramrod straight, staring directly at the truck as if *it* were its destination and not the town that lay just a little further down the road. Nadine looked around. Nothing but scrubby desert. Up ahead, on her right was a small grove of date palms. The road itself was empty. The sedan could easily pass. If it wanted to.

Though the answer lay directly in front of her, she asked anyway. "Fouad, how far are we from the entrance to the city?"

"Only a few kilometers. We should be seeing the joint patrols by now," he added. She thought he sounded hopeful, as if by voicing it, they would appear.

She looked around again but this time noted detail, the gravel shoulder and a shallow ditch alongside.

Glancing back into the mirror, she saw the passenger in the front seat distinctly nod his head twice, up and down. The sedan accelerated up to the tail of the truck then swerved swiftly into the adjacent lane.

She turned and looked over her left shoulder, now watching them through the rear window. As they moved up alongside the bed of the truck she saw the two passengers raise submachine guns to their shoulders.

"Fouad, into the ditch!" she shouted, instinctively curling her upper body into a ball.

After a split second pause, Fouad turned abruptly to the right, trying to swing the truck into a U-turn, but its front wheels skidded in the gravel, sending it bouncing into the ditch at a forty-five degree angle.

The automatic weapons coughed rapidly at the bouncing pickup, spitting hundreds of rounds into its cabin, tires and bed. The truck swerved under their barrage. Bullets pounded its metal siding and smashed through the windows, shattering the panes into a thousand shimmering fragments.

Naji pressed the accelerator pedal to the floor and sped to the refuge of Jericho's shady palms. He hadn't turned his head, but through the corner of his eye, he caught Fouad's horror as recognition registered on his face. That split second hesitation had delivered the pair to God.

Naji smiled. Mission accomplished.

CHAPTER 28

▼

Barak stood stock still, staring at the specter before him. His mind screamed with rage as his eyes bored into the sight that his senses did not want to believe, that his heart could not accept. How could this have happened? How could he not have foreseen their insanity?

He squeezed his eyes shut and opened them again. The pounding of the blood in his head was so loud he could not hear himself think. He stumbled back out of the room, colliding with Shimoni.

Cautiously, Shimoni peeked around the door. In the middle of the room, pale and unmoving, he saw Daniel for the first time. Perched on a wooden chair, he was immobilized by the explosives, wired with painstaking cruelty from head to toe. Daniel was looking past him, insensible. Had he retreated into some other place or was he simply terrified into incognizance? He thought of his own son and felt sick. Without examining him too closely, Shimoni saw enough plastic explosives to blow the entire house and more. He waited for a brief moment to let the wave of disgust that engulfed him pass, then he rejoined Barak in the hallway.

Their eyes locked for a second, acknowledging the unspeakable horror they had just seen, then Barak spoke. "Stay here. I'm going to have Avi cover the big guy. Harel will keep watch outside."

When Barak returned he found Shimoni with his mask stuffed into his belt and a small tool kit open in his hands.

"This is your lucky night, Mr. Security Services. I'm a sapper for my reserve unit." He exhaled loudly. "Why don't you wait out here? This looks pretty complicated."

"Are you as good as the guy you put to sleep out there?"

"You had better pray that I am."

Shimoni stepped back into the room. Daniel's eyes were wide with fright and beads of sweat dotted his forehead. Shimoni held his breath as he watched one slowly glide down and drip onto Daniel's thick lashes. Daniel squeezed his eyes shut and gripped the arms of the chair with his fingers until his knuckles turned white.

Shimoni addressed him, speaking very slowly and very quietly from where he stood by the door, as much to soothe him as to make sure that he understood what he needed to say.

"I have a son your age. His name is Ayal. I love my son very much."

Shimoni took a step closer. "I am going to disarm you. But I am going to need your help. It's important that you stay very calm."

Shimoni took two more steps and kneeled so that he was eye level with Daniel.

"This may take a while," he said. "The man who did this was a professional. He may even have some of his own, personal ways of doing things, things that may take me a while to figure out. But with patience and team work, we'll be out of here soon."

Shimoni slipped his hand into his pocket and pulled out a handkerchief. "I'm going to dab your forehead. Please don't move." Shimoni kept talking as he pressed the cloth against Daniel's head and gently wiped his eyelids. "I may ask you a question from time to time. You may answer but for now do not nod or shake your head." He put the cloth down. "Try to keep breathing evenly. It will help you remain calm."

A flicker crossed Daniel's eyes. Shimoni would have liked to keep on talking. Alone in a minefield, when it was just he and the bomb, talking aloud always helped him analyze what he was seeing. But what he saw here was scaring him to death. He didn't want Daniel to know that he was shrouded in plastic explosives so powerful that an itch might flatten the house. Still, Shimoni thought, Daniel must have flinched when Barak shoved open the door.

He took a moment to glance around. His eyes fell on a heap of video equipment piled beneath the windowsill. A second wave of disgust pulsed through his gut and he swallowed hard to keep the bile down.

Had they already taken the video? Unlikely. At most, Daniel had been here a couple of hours. He was sure that it had taken most of that time to put together such an intricate wiring system. And he surmised that the key players were missing. If they had gone to this much trouble to rig the boy, they certainly did not want Daniel cooking himself before they squeezed him for all he was worth. Clue number two. He began looking for a timing device or a detonator. Or both.

Maybe it was all a facade, he thought to himself as he bent down and looked under the chair. Real enough for the camera, real enough to traumatize the hostage, real enough to fool the world, but not real at all, he prayed to himself, examining the apparatus.

No such luck. Everything was neatly intact. The plastic explosive, produced in sheets with an adhesive backing, could be applied easily to any surface. The largest piece was attached the bottom of the chair. From there, wiring ran to his feet, hands, chest and forehead.

Shimoni noted that Daniel's T-shirt had been removed. His arms were covered with thousands of tiny goose bumps. His upper body shivered, slightly at first, but with each passing moment, his breathing shallowed and a moment later, he began to shake uncontrollably.

Shimoni gently laid a hand on his cold shoulder. In a very soothing voice he said, "Relax. Breathe deeply. You'll shiver less. It's going to be all right." At least, he thought, the boy was responding to his presence.

A sick mind had molded a wad of explosive into the shape of a heart, then taped it to the center of his naked chest. The boy was thin and Shimoni watched his diaphragm slowly expand and contract with each breath. Faced with Daniel's defenselessness, he felt keenly vulnerable.

The tops of his sneakers had been loosened and a small wad of explosive was attached to the dorsum of each foot. The backs of his hands were similarly dressed. From there, two thin wires ran up past his neck. They met at the apex of his forehead, forming a loop that lay like a wreath on his head, connected by more of the deadly gum.

Shimoni circled the chair. This wasn't his usual gig. He knew just enough about this explosive to know that while the small amount used here was extremely powerful—the stuff attached to Daniel alone could easily take down a jumbo jet—it was stable until detonated. A small digital watch closed the circle. He sat cross-legged on the floor and stared at the watch. Almost 2:00 AM.

Something wasn't right. If the timer was set to detonate the explosives at a certain hour, then the guys running this show had to get in, make their video and get out before the fireworks went off. The building and most of the neighborhood would be leveled, killing the boy and an unknown number of residents along with him.

Shimoni thought about this for a moment. What did they have to gain? Daniel certainly was a prize. The Americans would be under pressure to force

Israel to negotiate. Demands would be made. Demands take time to be met. They probably wouldn't pan out, but would keep the kid alive for a while. In the meantime, Israeli commandos would come up with a plan. Daniel's captors would kill him the moment they smelled a trap. There would be a melee. And in the end, who knew how many mothers would be mourning? So maybe the timer wasn't set at all.

Shimoni closed his eyes, took a deep breath, sent mental messages of love to his wife, reached out and held the watch between the index finger and thumb of his left hand.

"Wait," Daniel whispered.

"What did you say?"

"The watch. Even if you disconnect it, there is another detonator."

"How do you know?"

"He told me. The Specialist. That's what he's called." Now Daniel was speaking quickly, as if his life depended on every moment. "He talked. He talked the entire time. He told me what he was doing and how the mechanism works. He said if someone found me and disconnected the timer, it wouldn't do any good. He thought it was funny."

Shimoni let go the breath he'd been holding. He'd almost blown them all to bits. "What else did he say?"

Daniel squeezed his eyes shut and tears came rolling down his cheeks. His voice was a mere whisper. "Bon Voyage."

Shimoni's anger propelled him into action. Fuck the bastard, he muttered silently through clenched teeth. He had to get Daniel out of there, out of this nightmare, fast. A chill desert breeze blew through the empty window spaces. Shimoni looked at Daniel to see if he was still shivering. He was probably too petrified.

Shimoni went over each point. He checked the wires from the backs of Daniel's hands, his feet, his chest and his forehead. Then he lay on his back and stared up at the bottom of the chair. That was it. All the wires led here, then from underneath the chair, two wires led to the watch. If he neutralized the timer, thinking he had neutralized the circuit, once he tried to remove the explosive, it would detonate on contact.

"All right," Shimoni said, "here's what I'm going to do. It's not going to be easy, because one tiny rub the wrong way and we all go to heaven. So pretend you're in the soccer game of your life. I need you to focus your will to win, to beat the other team and walk away with the ultimate prize."

The sound of gunfire interrupted his thoughts. Something told him he was out of time.

"Listen, Daniel. This is it. Nothing exists for the moment but getting you out of here alive. But I don't have the time to undo what was done so we're going to take a novel approach."

He examined his feet. Daniel's jeans were loose fitting and sagged over his high tops. He lifted the pad off of the top of his left foot without a hitch, but as he gently raised the right pad he felt a small tug on the wire. Shimoni gasped involuntarily, but the expected blast didn't come. Of course, he would never have known otherwise. He looked down and followed his long fingers as they nimbly made their way along the length of the fragile wire. It had snagged on the rough denim near the cuff of Daniel's jeans. He separated it from the fabric with great care and moved his fingers down to the pad on the top of Daniel's right foot. He eased it off and sat back, exhaling. Shimoni was sweating now, too. That was too close.

Next, he looked for a way to remove the explosive from Daniel's chest and lift it over his head, like a shirt, without tugging the wires that ran to the detonator underneath the chair. Those wires ran from the 'heart' in the center of his chest, under his arms and up his back. They were bundled together then separated at the back of his head where they wrapped around to the front, like a wreath.

Shimoni gently peeled the explosive back and away from Daniel's forehead, untied the bundle in the back and slid them forward over each of Daniel's shoulders. Now, only the heart taped to his chest was left to remove.

This was more problematic. If any of the tape actually touching the explosive, lifted off of it, that tiny bit of friction could be enough to ignite the pad, blowing them to smithereens. At least they would never know what hit them.

Gently, Shimoni lifted the ends of the tape like the ends of a band-aid and pulled them forward, one millimeter at a time. Luckily, Daniel's chest was smooth and damp. The tape nearly fell away. Still, the wad stuck. Shimoni was going to have to try to pry it. He prayed that there would be no interruptions, more gunfire or a sudden entry.

Using the small flat end of a tiny screwdriver, he gently prodded the edges of the adhesive explosive. Bit by bit, it let go of Daniel's skin. Several long minutes later, the malleable gum sat like a wad in his hand. Shimoni whispered a silent prayer of thanks, and lowered the suit of wires and explosive wads under the chair.

All the wires remained intact. The circuit was still closed. And Daniel was free. Shimoni realized that Daniel hadn't so much as flinched the entire time. He hoped the boy wasn't in some sort of trance. Before lifting him out of the seat, he looked him over one more time. Daniel blinked.

"Daniel, is there anything else I should know about before I ask you to stand up."

"I have to go to the bathroom." He smiled.

Shimoni smiled in return. "Let's go then." He held out a hand and raised him out of the seat.

"Tie your shoes."

Shimoni cautiously opened the door, his gun drawn. The hallway was empty but he was wary.

"Let's go the other way," he said, motioning towards the window space.

Shimoni killed the light from the generator. They would head back in the direction of the grove. As he helped Daniel lower himself out of the house through the paneless window, another pair of hands appeared suddenly. Harel lifted Daniel effortlessly through the opening. He slipped the bulletproof vest Barak had given him over Daniel's bare shoulders and back and zipped it up.

"You did real good," Harel said, one hand on his shoulder, admiration in his eyes. You've got it in you."

As they turned to leave, Shimoni asked, "Where's Barak? And Avi?"

"Unfinished business," Harel responded without slowing down. "*Y'allah*. Let's go."

At the grove, Shimoni retrieved some water and a sandwich from the car and gave them to Daniel. Dawn was painting the early morning sky with pale blue and yellow streaks. Shimoni was anxious to move. Harel was relaxing under a date palm, chatting with Daniel, who himself seemed calm, even patient. Was he the only one who wanted out of there? Shimoni wondered to himself.

Five minutes later, they heard a familiar whistle. Harel responded, then Barak and Avi joined them.

Barak went straight to Daniel and looked him over, once up, once down. Then, with a mixture of joy and relief, he grabbed him in a spirited bear hug and lifted him off his feet. He laughed aloud, as much from happiness as the look on Daniel's face at seeing him there. The uncertainty clouding him of late fell away and Barak knew that he wanted Nadine and her sons to be a real part of his life. All his misgivings had evaporated. His feelings for her were real, and ran deep.

The sound of automatic weapons laid them flat on the ground.

"Harel, cover Daniel!" Barak shouted and belly crawled over to the car. Harel's huge frame immediately covered Daniel, pressing him into the dry ground.

Looking in the direction of the rapid machine gun fire, they saw a white pickup truck careen into the ditch alongside the highway and bounce to a halt on the stony desert flats. A speeding sedan shot down the highway like a streak of blue paint, headed in the direction of Jericho.

"Shit," Shimoni muttered, "Never a dull moment."

"We need to check for survivors," said Avi

"There's going to be a patrol by in a few minutes. No way they didn't hear that gunfire, or see it from the watchtower," Shimoni added, nodding in the direction of the joint command.

"I want Daniel as far away from any more action as possible," Barak said. The open desert gave them long-range visibility but they were still some distance away from the crippled pickup.

"We'll contact the joint command by radio. They'll get there faster than we can anyway. Avi and Harel, you get out there and tell them what we saw. We'll pick you up further down the highway. Be there in twenty minutes."

CHAPTER 29

▼

When Nadine awoke the desert sun was beating down on the truck. She squinted and blinked a few times trying to clear the haze from her eyes. She raised her hand to her forehead to push her hair off of her face. Her fingers came away sticky and red. She was covered in thousands of glittering pieces of glass mixed with dust and gravel. Reflexively she brushed the glass away from across her chest and lap, and turned to Fouad. He was slumped over the steering wheel, still.

"My God, what have I done?" she whispered.

She slid across the seat and began searching for a pulse. Her heart leapt when she felt one but it was racing, telling her he'd lost a lot of blood.

She searched for the bottle of water he had slipped under the seat when they left that morning. Finding it miraculously intact she took a swig, and immediately spit it out. It was warm but would do the trick. Reaching over to Fouad, she pushed him back against the seat. Her action lifted a cloud of desert sand from her cloak that scratched her eyes and filled her nose and mouth with dust. She began to cough and tried to wipe her face clean with her sleeve but it only scratched her dry skin. Her eyes watered; salty tears streamed down cheeks, leaving streaks of dirt on her face. She gave in and waited for the tears to clear her vision before trying to return to the task at hand.

She tilted Fouad's head back. His mouth gaped and she dripped water from the palm of her hand onto his lips and tongue. Willing him to awaken, she patted his face with her wet hand. No response. She ran her eyes over his large form. The black jalabiyah and white headdress showed no signs of the violence of the previous minutes but the vinyl seat underneath him was soaked with blood.

The sun beat down on the metal and glass of the cabin, making the air inside it so stifling she could barely breathe. She tugged at the neck of the black robes she wore. Her head ached, her mouth was parched and her left knee hurt like hell. Fouad was still alive, but barely. She slid back across the seat and opened the passenger door. Swinging both legs outward, she hesitated for a few seconds before dropping down out of the truck.

Aiiee! She muffled her cry of pain.

Gathering it's gritty folds between her fingers, she raised the heavy robe above her knee to assess the damage. The fabric of her leggings was torn and her knee was bleeding.

How long had they been there? she wondered. It couldn't have been more than a few minutes or the place would have been crawling with soldiers from the joint command by now.

She lifted the robe and pulled it over her head, then bent over to examine her knee more closely. She hoped that the bullet hadn't shattered her kneecap. With no small effort, she ripped off a piece of the robe's thick material and tied it around her thigh to stem the bleeding.

How was she going to get into Jericho now? Fouad needed to get to a hospital. Without him, her chances of success were nil. Maybe she should have trusted Nasser. Where was he now?

She was so absorbed in her thoughts that she almost didn't hear the bleating. A herd of sheep and some tiny goats had surrounded the truck and a young boy in loose clothes gaped at her. A man in his twenties, herding the animals from the rear, joined the boy a few seconds later. His eyes ran over her from head to toe as if examining an article he might want to acquire.

Nadine spoke first. "We had an accident." The boy's wide-eyed gaze reflected unabashed incredulity. She took a deep breath and tried again. Pointing towards Jericho she asked, "Can you take me there?"

The boy shook his head, pointing up the hill they had just descended.

"Jerusalem?" she asked in surprise. He nodded vigorously.

She heard the crackling of their radios before she actually saw the army jeeps pulling up on the road behind her. She didn't have much time. It was now or never.

She shut her eyes. Her head swam and her mouth was parched and dry. She had tried to keep this a private affair, not turn it into a political one. She thought it would be less risky for Daniel. But, in truth, wasn't it all about politics?

"No," she said to the boy. "I will wait for them." She pointed to the three jeeps pulling up alongside the road. One had a large red Star of David, the Israeli equivalent of the Red Cross. The other two were Palestinian police and regular Israeli army.

The young shepherd simply shrugged and continued on with his flock. The sound of boots crunching on the sand mixed with the rattling of weapons and equipment grew louder as half a dozen pair of feet trotted towards them. Before she knew it, two uniformed men were lifting Fouad out of the truck and onto a stretcher. She heard them call for an airlift to a hospital. Relief washed over her like a cool breeze in the hot desert sun. She rifled through the glove compartment, found a scrap of paper and a pencil. She scribbled a quick note and gently laid it on Fouad's chest. "We will meet again, my friend, in peace."

As soon as he was gone, she felt sapped of her last ounce of energy. The scene around her appeared surreal. She was outside looking in, unmoving, disconnected.

One of the soldiers handed her a canteen of water and called over a medic. He dressed her wound and replaced the dirty strip she had tied around her leg with a clean bandage, then ordered one of the soldiers to drive her to an emergency medical clinic at the top of the mountain, near the entrance to Jerusalem.

No one had spoken to her directly, until they lifted her into the jeep. Then the commanding officer said, "We'll have you treated first. Someone will meet you up there to get a report from the doctor on your condition and when you are up to it, a description from you of what happened here."

Her heart sank as the jeep climbed back into the mountains, back up to Jerusalem. Jericho faded away into the desert, further from Daniel, further from hope. She was torn by misgivings and the totality of her failure. Her time was running out. Would Daniel still be alive? She tried to shut out that possibility but her body betrayed her. Her heart began palpitating, a lump stuck in her throat and tears of frustration, anger and grief welled up in her eyes.

They pulled up in front of a small medical clinic on the outskirts of Jerusalem. The two soldiers lifted her out of the jeep and helped her to the reception desk. The man on her left spoke rapidly and she was handed over to two orderlies. They were gone before she could say a word. Proper thanks would wait for another time. They had not expected it nor could she have given it. It seemed strange to her that as her care was passed from hand to hand, no one actually spoke to her, not even here. She went from scene to scene and the characters simply floated by, moving around her as she progressed from place to place. Soon, she was alone in a spotlessly clean examining room, lying prone on the examining table.

A white-coated man strode into the room. Immediately a charge shot through her.

"You're a doctor!"

His azure eyes shone above his full, gray beard. His sidelocks were neatly tucked behind his ears. The white coat made him appear slightly taller, less rotund. Instead of a hat, he wore a large, black yarmulke that covered most of his thinning gray hair. He studied her face and she felt that her soul was bared in his presence. Though fully clothed, she looked around instinctively for something to cover her. She saw that he had left the door open and a nurse hovered at the entrance.

He examined her wounds, ordered intravenous antibiotics and began tending to her injuries. Moments later the nurse returned, inserted an IV into her left arm and started the antibiotics flowing. When he was finally satisfied that he had done all that he could, he addressed her.

"The injury to your leg is superficial. The bullet grazed your thigh and I expect it to heal fairly quickly. Your hand, though, is another matter. We have some excellent hand surgeons in this country, necessitated, unfortunately, by the high rate of casualties that we see every day in this pretend peace that that bit by bit, is eating both sides alive." He sighed deeply. "However, you will be leaving shortly so you may prefer to have your American experts tend to it."

Her mind swirled, full of questions, searching for explanations. She opened her mouth to speak, then shut it, finding herself at a rare loss for words.

"The IV is a mixture of antibiotics. This injection is a painkiller. Before you leave, I will give you prescription antibiotics to start right away. You'll be on 2000 mg/day. Take them. They will suffice for at least the next forty eight hours, when you'll be examined by a specialist."

Nadine stared at him. Finally she said, "You warned me."

"And you heeded my warning, but you have not pursued the light."

"Why didn't you do something?"

"I did. It is up to you."

"I can't stop them."

The intensity of his clear blue eyes seemed to brighten as he counseled her, "*V'abit v'ein ozer, v'eshtomem v'ein somech, v'toshea li z'roi.*

She repeated his words. "I searched but found no help. I was afraid but there was no one to trust, so my own hand brought me victory." She leaned back, exhausted, as much by what she had been through as what she still had to face.

Her jaw tightened. "Daniel. He comes first."

"He is on his way back to you."

Tears welled up in her eyes. In a barely audible voice, all she could ask was "How?"

"How, indeed? You are not alone in this, good lady. You never were. In fact, this was never just about you, at all. This conflict goes back thousands of years before either of us was born, and will likely continue."

Alone, she leaned back against the pillows and closed her eyes. She knew by now that the meaning of his words would become apparent when she was ready to understand them. The mixture of fluids rushed silently into her bloodstream. Could he have been right?

She felt disoriented and wanted to call Brad but she did not see a phone in the room. Confused about Nasser and whether she had misjudged him, she was getting anxious when she heard the back door of the clinic open and familiar voices speaking quickly in Hebrew. She pushed herself up and strained to look out the door of her room, but by the time she caught a glimpse of the hallway all she saw was the doctor's back as he followed the voices into an examining room and closed the door behind him.

She leaned back against the pillows and looked around. In the corner was a sink with a small mirror above it. Dust and gravel still powdered her hair and clothing. Although the nurse had given her a wet cloth to wipe her hands and face, she still looked dirty and disheveled. She eased herself off the table, and gingerly hobbled over to the sink, carefully rolling the IV stand alongside her. She pumped soap out of the dispenser and scrubbed her skin thoroughly, wincing as she cleaned the fresh scratches that covered her face. Then she dampened a towel and used it to clean some of the sand out of her hair and clothes. She combed her fingers through her hair and nodded at her reflection, now decidedly less alarming.

Just as she finished washing-up, the doctor appeared in the doorway. In an unusual gesture, he picked up her free hand in both of his and said gently, "I will take you in to see Daniel now."

She stepped through the door and he was in her arms. Overwhelmed by feelings that went beyond relief and humbled joy, she simply held him. She buried her face in his hair and inhaled the scent of jojoba that lingered from the day before, the brown strands still wet when he silently rode off on his bike and into terror. Silently, she thanked every deity that came to mind.

"I'm sorry," she heard him whisper.

She wanted to reassure him, to tell him there was nothing to be sorry for, but she knew what he meant and she accepted his expression of intent to leave the bitterness he had cultivated, behind them. It was she who was sorry. Sorry for the blows he had suffered in his short life before he had the armor to defend himself, sorry for the heavy dose of unfairness life had meted out to him, sorry that she hadn't been able to protect him.

She'd been unaware of the presence of the others until Daniel gently pulled away. Drawing her good hand across her face, she smiled through a veil of tears. Someone handed her a tissue. She stayed close to Daniel, aware and mildly surprised that he seemed relaxed. She was grateful at that moment for the quiet strength he'd inherited from Jeremy. They were so much alike.

"Mom," Daniel said turning to Shimoni, "he saved my life."

His half-smile acknowledged her surprise. She didn't know yet how all the pieces fit together but she was sure that his being there from the beginning, since the time of the attack on her, had led him to Daniel.

He extended his hand. She took it and drew him into a grateful hug. Speechless, it was all the thanks she could muster.

Accepting her gesture, he thought they still had a lot to talk about. The murders of Mizrahi and Wolf were still unresolved. Loose ends fluttered aimlessly, leading nowhere. Under the circumstances, arresting the perpetrators was going to be next to impossible. But all of that would have to wait. He was anxious to get home to his own boys.

"These guys, Avi and Harel, were there too." She looked at the young men and recognized who they were at once. The elite. Their eyes reflected just the right mix of heroism and caution. They knew how to take intelligent risks and were never afraid to exercise them, yet they valued life above all.

She shook their hands and thanked them. Avi remained serious but Harel grinned from ear to ear.

"He's a hero," Harel pronounced. "Eh, Dani?" he said, turning to Daniel for confirmation. "You'd think he'd been through commando training." Harel put his arm over Daniel's shoulder and gave him a brotherly hug. *"Ata gever, Dani. Al tishkach et ze."* You're a hero, Daniel. Never forget it.

The smile on Nadine's face froze as she turned toward a sound at the door. Barak's form filled the doorway. He moved towards her, his arms open to embrace her, but the anger that flashed through her eyes, transforming them from deep green to thunderous gray, stopped him short. Tension thick with hostility and confusion filled the space between them. The silence was quickly broken by the doctor and Y, who followed directly behind Barak.

The doctor spoke first. "Detective Shimoni, one of my orderlies is waiting for you outside. I've instructed him to give you a lift home." After a brief round of warm farewells, Shimoni disappeared.

Y's presence dominated the room. He exchanged greetings with his men, gave them quick instructions and they were on their way. Extending a hand to Nadine, he appraised her fully, while maintaining a respectful distance. "Shlomo Cohen speaks highly of you," he said. Finally, he turned his complete attention to Daniel. Grasping his hand in a firm grip, Y said solemnly, "Few twice your age could have endured as you did. You're a fine example to my men. We're all proud of you."

Barak led them to a car waiting at the back of the clinic. Daniel ducked into the back seat. As Nadine was about to follow, Barak stopped her.

"Nadine, please, I can explain."

She gazed at him calmly. The mocking look on her face was more than he could stand.

"Is that what you think? I can understand who you are, Barak. I can even accept what you did. But your lie of convenience led me to believe that you were out of reach when you were just around the corner, and left Daniel in the hands of terrorists until it was almost too late."

She turned abruptly to get into the car, but Barak grabbed her arm just above the elbow and swung her around towards him.

"I love you, Nadine."

Without a word, she climbed into the car and shut the door.

Naji was fuming. He watched with mounting frustration from his vantage point as Fouad was evacuated. He had wanted to go back and finish off Nadine, but his cohorts had stopped him. They were his superiors. If he disobeyed, the training camp in the Beka'a Valley would remain nothing more than a dream. Resigned, he vowed that she and her children would never be safe. His hate now had another objective.

CHAPTER 30

▼

"Nadine, I should be telling you this in person…"

"Never mind, Dr. Nasser, Daniel has been re…" she choked back the word rescued. "Released."

"So I understand. I am grateful for that."

"And I am grateful to you, Dr. Nasser. You are a remarkable advocate. Your efforts on Daniel's behalf surely helped save his life."

"Perhaps you will fill me in on the details later. I must get back to New York and you must get back to Daniel."

"Dr. Nasser, I will never forget…

"Extraordinary circumstances demand extraordinary action. Peace to your family."

"Thank you. Good bye."

Nadine's brow wrinkled as she replaced the phone. She was still confused about whether the terrorists had really intended to release Daniel to him or were just stringing him along.

She looked across the room at him with relief. He was wolfing down the breakfast Brad had ordered from room service and pestering Zak at the same time. She delighted in the sight of them as if she were seeing them for the first time.

She sat on Brad's bed with her bandaged leg stretched out in front of her and allowed herself to smile. Shlomo would be picking her up at noon. Until then, she could pretend the world was rosy. Somehow this trauma had helped Daniel rediscover himself. She remembered precisely the last time she had seen him this animated. She would have wished for it to happen almost any other way but watching him now, she could only hope he had been set free of his torment for good.

Shlomo was speechless when he learned of the events of the previous twenty-four hours. He had given her a hug and went straight into closed-door consultations with Y. Y remained unruffled. Nadine thought he was practically gloating, as if he had planned the entire operation himself. Fortunately, he also made sure that none of this became news. Israel was a democracy but he wasn't going to help the media do its job. Today, she was thankful. Her personal opinions on censorship for the sake of security could wait for another time.

Brad cried when he saw Daniel. Now he sat down next to her and held her bandaged hand. She returned his gaze, sensing his relief. Still, she could not ignore the dull ache that settled in her chest, dampening her spirits. The lives of three people who had been kind to her had been ruthlessly snuffed out and that knowledge hardened her resolve for pay back.

She was reeling from the news of her dear neighbor's murder and that of the kindly watchman, Haim Mizrahi. The image of Fouad laying in a coma never left her for a moment. He remained under twenty-four-hour guard at the hospital on the summit of Mt. Scopus. His room was graced with a view of the mosque where he often prayed and his village nestled in the valley just beyond the next hill. She could only hope those icons of his goodness might offer him some strength to recover. Like so many others before him, he was punished for his willingness to help her and because he was a man who loved peace.

She had squeezed his hand as he lay inert in his hospital bed and promised to return, equally sure that her words to his wife sounded empty and meaningless as she sat vigilantly beside her husband's still form.

In a couple of hours, after a briefing with the Israelis, they would be on an Air Force jet to Washington D.C. In the meantime, her apartment was still a crime scene. The police hadn't finished collecting evidence so she wasn't allowed back there, even to pack. The police took down a list of items, passports, some clothing and limited requests from the boys that would be brought to them before take-off.

She was left with an uneasiness to which she was unaccustomed. Everything about the future was uncertain. She did not know just when—or if—she might return. The next few months were going to be very tough. She realized now that she needed Daniel and Zak as much as they needed her.

She shot another glance in their direction. She hadn't told them yet. Maybe on the flight back. She wondered if Daniel realized just how cruel his kidnappers were. Then she remembered how he'd been found and she shuddered.

CHAPTER 31

▼

As the Air Force jet lifted off, Nadine felt a mixture of purpose and misgiving. Daniel slept, his head in her lap. She stroked his hair gently as she looked out the window at the terrain below. Familiar stone buildings shrunk to miniature models and Jerusalem became a toy city nestled in tiny green hills. Minutes later, they left the mountains behind and the royal blue Mediterranean burst into view beneath them. Miles of white sandy beach dotted with sunbathers and surfers snaked up and down the coast as far as the eye could see. Soon it too vanished in the distance. An unfamiliar pang momentarily distracted her, but she pushed it aside and focused on the mission ahead. Her drive had returned but this time it had an added dimension—personal revenge.

Her head ached and her eyes burned, but she wasn't ready to rest just yet. She simply couldn't get enough of Daniel, the sweetness of his face as he slept, the warmth of his breath on her fingers, the tranquility that sleep imposed. She had come so close to losing him that she was afraid to close her eyes, only to awaken and find him gone. She looked at him now, grateful that he was alive, keenly aware that it might have turned out differently. Her jaw tightened. Thoughts that she wanted to drive away, persisted. Even as her heart swelled with joy, she was in turmoil. Her soul insisted on revenge, a channel for her rage; there was no escape from her internal chaos, yet. She squeezed her eyes shut, breathed deeply and exhaled. No. She shook her head to physically cast off the demons. Her priority was to keep her sons safe and to keep herself safe for them.

Brad caught her gesture as he approached from the galley. He settled into the seat opposite hers, contemplating her for a moment. "What was that about?"

When she responded, her voice was brittle. "I keep asking myself how I get on with a normal life as a decent parent raising my sons, knowing that the men who tortured Daniel still sleep in warm beds every night? I thought that all I wanted was to have my son back."

"Nadine, you need rest."

"No Brad," she said adamantly. "I can understand political militancy, revolution for a cause, social unrest, even violence. I cannot reconcile the torture of my son with any of those things." She looked down at Daniel and relaxed slightly. "I don't want to hate, Brad. I don't want to be so consumed by vengeance that I abandon the joy of being given a second chance."

They sat in silence for a few minutes, watching Daniel.

"Things are going to be pretty crazy when we get back to Washington."

Nadine nodded slowly. "I've thought about that. I've already asked my mother to stay with me for a while. For about ten seconds, I considered sending the boys to my parents, but I don't want to be separated from them."

"Hopefully, we'll be wiser tomorrow, after the briefing."

"I want this to end, Brad."

"Me, too."

"I want us to be able to get on with our lives, but I'm not sure what that is." She paused. "We were very happy. Where do we go from here? Which pieces do we pick up, which do we leave behind?"

Brad didn't respond.

"We wouldn't have left if it weren't for this mission. Despite what happened. Daniel wouldn't have wanted to leave either."

They were interrupted by a young soldier who handed her a fax. She read the words of the multi-page document, but they weren't penetrating her consciousness. She needed sleep. She leaned back into the leather headrest, and let her hand rest on Daniel's shoulder.

"There's something else, Nadine."

She nodded.

"Barak."

Nadine shrugged, but her eyes looked pained.

"He loves you," he said, stiffening slightly even as he spoke.

Some of her earlier fury had been replaced with bewilderment. Did the ends really justify the means? Fatigue muddled any option of clear thinking now.

"It didn't really matter that I was a mark." Through her sadness, a small smile played at the sides of her full lips. "The thought had crossed my mind more than once, you know. It might have hurt my feelings had the Israeli Security Services concluded that I wasn't important enough to attract their attention." Her expression resumed its seriousness and her eyes wandered over to Zak, then back to Daniel. "Despite the circumstances of our meeting, he's been a good friend. He made a difference." As professionals both had lied. But alone together, as man and woman, they had been honest. They trusted. They loved.

She slid out of the seat and gently placed a pillow under Daniel's head. Zak slept soundly nearby. Brad stood, squeezed her shoulder and placed a light kiss on her forehead before heading off to his own corner for some rest. She looked around for a blanket. As she leaned across the small table and reached for the recently sanitized, army issue woolen wrap on the opposite seat, something on one of the sheets she had just reshuffled registered in her mind's eye.

She'd look at it later. Sleep was getting harder to fight.

She settled into the leather bucket seat and waited for Brad to finish speaking with his second-in-command at Aviano AFB. She was feeling much better now. Her earlier melancholy had lifted. She was alert and in the moment. The present was all that mattered. She looked over at Daniel and Zak who were engaged in a battle of wits, laughing and shoving. Nadine's relief was immense. She knew that their emotional roller coaster ride hadn't ended, but she was glad for the temporary suspension.

Watching Brad, she was glad he'd been included in the team. Though steely at times, she'd never seen him ruffled. She thought about the mission. It could be a week or months. There was no way of knowing. The message had said, "*Ready the eight.*" What did that mean? Ready to go? Start preparations? She was anxious to learn what else they knew.

Brad eased into the seat next to hers.

"Everything OK?" she asked.

"Quiet as a herd of rampaging elephants. But Holman is competent. And this is just the opportunity he's been waiting for. He'll do fine. What did you think of the Israeli team?"

The makeup of their team had been on her mind too. The Israelis were experienced in dealing with terrorists. That didn't make it easy but most likely, they were prepared for any number of scenarios.

"Shlomo was an obvious and excellent choice. He's been specializing in terrorism for a quarter of a century. I would bet on his predictions as to how these scenarios could play out. He'll be a big help to all of us. Barak's intelligence network will be helpful too, in identifying the perpetrators or at least the group orchestrating it.

"What about the general? Lev Barzel. Do you know much about him?"

"Hmm, now he's an interesting pick. Controversial, but a good choice for this team. I guess even the Israelis know when to put politics aside. It took me a while to figure out, but I think I understand now why he was included."

"What's his background?"

"He's been on the extreme political right all his life, a staunch hard-liner, taking tough stands. He's stubborn and an independent thinker, an idealistic pragmatist. He was born and raised in a farming community in central Israel. Every fiber of his being is devoted to building a strong Israel with defensible borders but he holds no religious beliefs about the land. The notion of occupation is foreign to him and he has made it plain that Israel should not dominate another people."

"So what makes him a logical choice?"

"He's both brazen and an insider. More importantly, he understands the Arabs. Even some of his fiercest opponents, who've spoken of him scathingly, believe he might be the only one who can bring real peace between the Israelis and the Palestinians, branded as the only true 'Middle Eastern' leader."

Brad nodded.

"One more thing to bear in mind, though. He's not terribly enamored with the U.S. He has infuriated the Secretary of State on countless occasions and disdains what he considers American meddling in Israel's internal affairs."

"Maybe we should introduce him to baseball."

Nadine smiled. "We're going to have to work together on this one, Brad. Phil's been in touch with Gerard Hire in Paris and Alessandro Valena in Italy. We'll have to use any means possible to stop them."

"What are you driving at Nadine?"

"There's more going on here than eight bombs. Martyrdom is scary. It is so very effective because even when the casualties are low, the psychological impact is devastating. The entire country of Israel was paralyzed a few years ago by a series of four suicide bombs. They didn't kill many, but it so traumatized the nation, it brought down the government."

As she spoke, her own words took on new meaning. "That's it, Brad. This could bring down the government. Imagine Oklahoma City repeating itself in Los Angeles, New York City and Washington, D.C. and across Europe as well. This isn't just about our government. They're aiming to cripple as many Western governments at one time as they can. The ripple effect in the aftermath would immobilize a significant part of the Western world leaving it economically wrecked and vulnerable for years."

Brad reacted visibly. "I don't think anyone is taking this lightly, Nadine."

Nadine's thoughts flashed to Daniel's captors, whoever they were. "These militants are difficult to identify. They work in secrecy. After an event like this, there's no one to challenge, nowhere to channel the rage. Its victims, correction, everyone, is left feeling helpless and afraid, anxious about when and where it's going to happen again. The free world becomes susceptible to the illusory salvation offered by the voices of totalitarianism, especially if they are of a religious nature. Should these eight cataclysms succeed, we can expect chaos of the magnitude only imagined in apocalyptic novels."

"So how do we stop it now?"

"As long as we're perceived as vulnerable, our adversary will use that to its advantage. The best use of that would be to focus on sites that won't necessarily be devastating in terms of numbers, but would be demoralizing."

"Any ideas?"

"Yeah, hundreds," she said gloomily.

There was no stopping a suicide bomber. If he were about to get caught or couldn't reach his destination, he would just blow.

Brad excused himself and Nadine began to examine the fax she'd received earlier, more closely now. Usually, she hated long flights. They seemed to drag on interminably, leaving her restless and feeling muddled at the end. But this flight, empty, quiet, but for the muted drone of the engines, was like a pause in time.

She leaned her head back against the cushioned leather and for a moment, allowed herself to believe she was safe. Seated opposite her, lounging easily in the seat, Jeremy gave her that half-cocked smile, the one that said, you can do it, you'll whip their fannies. She closed her eyes and willed him away. She wished him near, but not like this. It was time to let go.

She lifted up the paper and realized with a jolt what she had seen. Among the eight names listed as the members of her team, one stood out.

Dr. Sami Nasser.

Nadine summoned the young soldier who had delivered the fax. "I need to get in touch with Phil Lathrop right away." As she waited for the call, Nadine began to ask herself what exactly she was going to say. What evidence did she have that he was a security risk? None. She had called him herself to find and free Daniel for the very reasons he was crucial to the team.

A few minutes later, Lathrop was on the line.

"Phil, we may have a security problem. Have the team members been briefed on this crisis yet?"

"Yes, except for one. Dr. Nasser is out of the country. He'll be arriving at JFK on a commercial flight this evening."

Of course. His flight had left only a few hours before hers. Nadine was relieved.

"Do you think that you could hold off on speaking to him until we've had a chance to review the intelligence?"

"I suppose. The rest of the team is intact and preparing for our first teleconference with the Israelis. What's up?"

"I have some hunches, but nothing concrete. I don't want to make any quick judgments yet though. Can it wait until I land?"

"It will have to. And be sure to get some rest. I'm afraid you'll be going to work right away, and from what I know, you've had the weekend from hell."

CHAPTER 32

▼

He gazed dispassionately at the footprints in the cement. Icons of a celluloid city. Around him, tourists laughed aloud as they tried to match their own soles to the fossilized imprints of stars and starlets whose well-bred feet were now preserved in mortar. A steady stream of pedestrian and vehicular traffic jammed Hollywood Blvd. He eyed a teen-aged couple in dressed in studded leather pass by indifferently. Safety pins adorned flat nipples peeking from his tattooed chest. Rainbow tresses fell across vacant eyes and a miniature screw protruded from her lower lip. Across the street, in the entrance to a souvenir shop, speakers blared.

So this is what it was like to live in a democracy. He'd seen enough. Turning from the vulgar display of Western decadence on the boulevard, he focused his attention on the building behind him. The imposing façade of the Chinese Theatre overshadowed the famous patio. Striking masks and golden wind chimes hung from the eves of its light green, pagoda-style roof. He turned and looked with greater interest at the small ticket booth. Checking the marquis, found what he was looking for.

Closed Monday, October 5. Special Engagement.

It was unusually quiet as the members of the team sat in strained silence around the oval, teakwood table waiting for the conference to begin. Phil Lathrop appeared to be deep in thought while the others scanned the few sheets of sketchy intelligence collected thus far. In a few minutes, the large screen at the far end of the room would bring Israel's intelligence team into the meeting.

Phil looked up, made eye contact with each person at the table and began to speak.

"Ladies and gentlemen, let's begin. In several minutes we will be joined by a team of experts in Israel that will be working with us on this operation. Our priorities are to identify the perpetrators, the exact time and location of each event, and given that, if we're lucky, formulate intact plans for interception and prevention. Should we fail in all I have said so far, teams will be in place in each of the cities cited to minimize damage, evacuate the wounded and control panic. Now, to date we have First Alert teams active in a few U.S. cities. They are already working with selected teams in our target cities to train them ASAP." Phil paused. When he continued, his was tone contrite. "We've been caught with our pants down. We've been slow in implementing the kind of response systems that we should have had in place two years ago. Now we're scrambling."

A hand went up. It was Roya Lazaro, Chief of Operations at INTERLET, the International Anti-terrorism Law Enforcement Team based in Amsterdam. "Mr. Lathrop, what about Europe and Japan?"

"The European and Japanese intelligence communities have all of the intelligence we've collected so far and will be briefed immediately after our consultation with the Israelis. What little we know seems to indicate that these assaults have generated from the Middle East and are motivated by anti-American and anti-Israeli extremism. We want to get their input first."

Another voice from the opposite end of the conference table. This time it was Jeff Reese, National Security Advisor. "Phil, I can't go back and tell the President, well, if we can't stop them now then we'll do our best to sweep up afterwards. We've got an entire network of intelligence agencies. I want to be sure that all the information even remotely related to this catastrophe in the making is being centrally reviewed and analyzed."

"CIA, DIA, FBI and NSA anti-terrorism sections are giving this top priority, Jeff, and forwarding all information into our unit here." Phil motioned in the direction of a young man seated opposite the National Security Advisor who looked like he was barely out of high school. "Claude Hennicker is in charge of that."

Reese's eyes widened slightly, but he made no further comment. He had been briefed on Hennicker. Touted as the Defense Intelligence Agency's intelligence wizard, the fair-haired, athletic looking boy-man sitting opposite him was an alert analyst with an unparalleled memory. He mentally registered every bit of information he had seen or heard and could recall it with computer-like speed. He had worked with Dr. Kanner for several years before she took off for that stint in Italy with her husband. He'd just finished reading the file on her too, and everyone else at the table for that matter. Nasser had given him pause, but Phil had been adamant. Reese was certain of one thing: DIA sure knew how to recruit 'em.

"What about local law enforcement?" Roya asked.

"We'll bring them in, but at a later stage. We don't want to take any chances that this will leak, so the less people involved for now the better."

"But will they be adequately prepared?"

A trace of impatience crossed Phil's face. He pressed his lips together to quell it. "It is my hope and belief that our police officers are in a constant state of preparedness. When we know precisely what it is that will be required of them, we'll let them know."

Adam Westlake, the computer codes expert on loan from the NSA/CSS, spoke up. "We're ready to begin."

In contrast to the sealed underground chamber deep in the bowels of the Pentagon in which they sat, the Israelis were gathered in a sunlit room around a long rectangular table. Pitchers of orange juice, fresh rolls and cheeses were spread across the white tablecloth.

Nadine suppressed a smile. You can't stop a terrorist on an empty stomach. Her eyes met Barak's. He nodded in reply.

Y spoke first. "Nice of you to join us for breakfast. I trust you received the materials we passed along with Dr. Kanner to give you all an opportunity to familiarize yourselves with our team. I will just point out each member to you so that you can attach a face to every name. On my right, General Lev Barzel and Barak Oren. On my left, Dr. Shlomo Cohen, Dr. Ehud Ben-Meir and Dr. Rona Sharabi, all of whom Dr. Kanner knows quite well from our own Israel Strategy Institute." Addressing her directly, Y said, "Dr. Kanner, we hope your exodus from our tempestuous little oasis is only temporary."

Phil scanned the list. "What happened to General Gideon Perry?"

An almost imperceptible change in body language shot through the Israeli team. "General Perry is out of the country. We should have him back here shortly."

Phil nodded knowingly and one side of his mouth curved up in a half smile. "He's on vacation and tuning you out. OK. We can proceed. Dr. Kanner will start. We also have an intelligence report from Hennicker. Nadine?"

Nadine bypassed the formalities. "Terrorism is a phenomenon that has the potential to strike any time, any place. In recent years, it has been characterized by more violent and catastrophic events, aided in no small measure by our advancements in technology and weaponry. Its singular objective is to harm the enemy, real or perceived."

Nadine paused for a moment and looked around the room. "Our worst nightmare is about to come true. But, Lady Luck is on our side and has given us advance warning. We have more information than meets the eye."

"Can you be more specific?" This from Y.

"A single event—the bombing of the Oklahoma federal building, the sarin nerve gas released into a Tokyo subway train—makes a statement. Granted, a horrific one, but just a statement nonetheless. Eight events, precisely timed, precisely placed, change the world."

Nadine let the meaning of her words take hold as the group contemplated the possibilities.

"Nadine's point is well taken," Shlomo agreed. "By extrapolating the global changes, we identify our perpetrator."

"Or perpetrators." Dr. Nasser straightened as he spoke.

"So what you are saying is that if we know 'why', it will tell us 'who,'" Lazaro remarked.

"Yes," Shlomo agreed.

"If you'll allow me," Nasser interjected, "given what we know, we can narrow the field considerably. This could be one rogue terrorist organization, a hostile government or a collaboration. Who are the likely players? Who trains suicide bombers? Terrorist organizations. And there are plenty of them. But this kind of operation takes more than money. It takes passports. Travel and lodging. Sophisticated networking. Materials of the kind that raise eyebrows unless purchased by a legitimate source, like a government or a contractor. So if suicide bombers are going beyond their own borders, I would say look for a sponsor. In my mind, there's a collaboration at work here." He sat back to indicate he had finished speaking.

"Now, now, don't you think you all are getting one step ahead of yo'selves?" interjected a voice with a thick Southern drawl. "Sounds to me like Dr. Nassuh here is makin' a heck of lot of assumptions. I can see where you Jews and A-rabs have a problem worth discussin'. But we're talkin' about the United States of America. I, for one, think you all are makin' a mountain out of an itty bitty molehill."

Nadine and Phil exchanged a quick look. Senator Frank Ashford, senior Louisiana statesman, was not supposed to have attended the teleconference. But as chair of the House Senate Intelligence Committee, he had raised Cain when word of the threat reached him. Phil knew that their operation would be front-page news before the weekend was out had the famous Senator been excluded. Notorious for his blustery style and romance with the press, he claimed it was all in the name of the people's right to know, but it was common knowledge that his bluster was more to keep himself first in the minds of the American people.

"Claude, I think this would be a good time to bring us all up to date on the intelligence we've collected," Nadine said.

"Yes, ma'am. The first part of last year saw a steady stream of deposits, traced back to straw corporations with fictitious shareholders, an increased flow of arms shipments into the West Bank and heightened activity in training camps both in the Bekaa Valley and around Teheran. Our message intercepts also led us to a tanker with Liberian flags loaded with missiles and other materiel from Iran in July of this year. The cargo was headed for areas under Palestinian control. After that intercept, the messages either stopped or we lost track until this last communiqué."

Brad spoke up but as if thinking aloud, said, "Makes you wonder whether we aren't being given a warning."

"Now there you go again, makin' those assumptions. How do you know this ain't all a big hoax?"

"Nothing would make us happier, but with all due respect Senator, it's our job to take these communications seriously."

"And with all due respect, I am here at the taxpayer's behest."

Phil wanted to remind him that the press was not present but instead said, "OK, Claude, what's the potential fallout?"

"Opportunistic chaos, undermined confidence in government. Sounds like a recipe for anarchy. We've got terrorists of presumed Middle East origin planning to strike at eight Western targets. When that occurs, we'll not only have chaos, but every secular government from Paris to Tokyo will get a clear message: "Death to the West."

"Being an ally of Israel makes us a logical target, vulnerable to attack. If the operation goes according to plan, the U.S. will be in turmoil. Helping Israel out of a jam will be the last thing on this nation's mind. Not to mention that the atmosphere would be ripe for a wave of anti-Semitic sentiment. With Big Satan out of the way, Little Satan is a sitting duck."

Bristling, General Barzel interrupted. "Terrorism is not new to Israel. Every government since the founding of our state has had to deal with it."

"True. But things have changed. *Before* peace talks began between your country and your Arab neighbors, you were in a state of war, so your people came together in response to terrorist attacks. Since the peace talks began, the level of internal frustration has risen with every act of terrorism. As long as your government is negotiating for peace and terrorism continues, it is perceived as weak. And each terrorist act has a more intense reverberating effect on the government. Another successful hit will push the pro-peace and anti-peace camps even further apart."

Claude shook his head then realization lit up his face. "My God, it's brilliant. If I were one of them, I'd think Allah had just handed me an Palestinian state on a silver platter. It could actually work."

"What are you getting at?" Phil asked.

"The Arab-Israeli peace process is in a shambles. Unrest on the West Bank is the order of the day. Israel is fractured socially, politically and religiously. The weakened internal infrastructure could not withstand a heavy blow."

Bristling, General Barzel interjected. "You can throw around your theories all you like. Israel still has a strong military."

"There's no question of that. But imagine this. This next series of suicide bombers deals the final blow to the present government. Israel's Arab parties form a coalition with the left. Despite the enormous power of the Israeli religious right, they just won't have the numbers. It almost happened in '96."

"It's not that simple," Ehud interjected. "The Israeli public would not stand for it. That government would fall."

"Precisely. And the civil war that's been brewing since the assassination of your Prime Minister Rabin will erupt."

Everyone stopped speaking. The thought of a Bosnia-like war in the Middle East, only worse, was enough to subdue further discussion. With the kinds of weapons available to both sides, the results were unthinkable. And no one in the room had any doubt that the chaos would spread far beyond the region.

Stop the eight or change the world.

Two hours later, Nadine picked up the phone in her office. Phil, seated opposite her, listened as Y and Shlomo came on the line.

"I think Dr. Nasser was right," Shlomo said. "All the evidence points to a collaboration. Two parties, whose goals are different, but related. Two parties who alone can achieve nothing, but together can fulfill both aims."

"You say it like you have some thoughts on who they might be," Phil queried.

Shlomo paused before he responded. "The only terrorist group realistically positioned to carry out this sort of operation, the Liberation Brotherhood Army, backed by the religious establishment in Iran, is the combination the intelligence points to."

"Why is that?"

"Because the LBA has nothing to lose politically. Indeed, they stand to gain everything. As far as Iran is concerned, the only solution to the Middle East problem is annihilation of Israel. But they know that to destroy Israel, they must hurt America—badly."

Again, Shlomo carefully arranged his thoughts for a moment before continuing. His face reflected a deep sadness, as if what he was about to say was more than well thought-out speculation, but rather prophecy on the verge of fulfillment.

"The singular aim of the LBA is to replace the existing establishment in Israel. That is why, unlike Hamas and Fatah, it has not established a mainstream political wing. For the most part, the organizational end has functioned in secret, while amassing huge grass roots support among the people. Its leader, Al Rasuul, is an almost mythic figure and is widely believed to be the redeemer of Greater Palestine. Hence the name, Al Rasuul, One who has been sent by God. They see him as The Deliverer, the one who will deliver Greater Palestine to the Palestinian people. Working together with anti-Western extremist governments, both achieve their greater goals: the radical movement effectuates a significant weakening of the Western infrastructure, providing an opening for the dictates of a new doctrine, already spreading rapidly across the globe. These same events provide the catalyst for Al Rasuul to carry out the scenario so aptly described earlier by Claude, replacing Israel's weakened government in a coup of sorts and installing himself as ruler of Greater Palestine. The State of Israel, as we know it…" his voice trailed off.

"Where does Iran fit in?" Phil asked.

"When the Iranian President took steps to renew ties with the United States, the Supreme Ayatollah rejected the possibility outright. The Islamic Revolution freed Iran from "Western evils" when it overthrew the Shah in 1979. His move was a clear warning to the President that any overtures to "Great Satan" were a threat to the revolution. He called for a full-scale assault on Western arrogance, going so far as to suggest that the United States would be helpless against a united front of the Islamic countries. His latest oratory had supporters burning U.S. flags and openly calling for "Death to America." The Supreme Ayatollah's message is clear and certainly could be interpreted as sanctioning a plan such as this. It would be wise to remember that while the President runs the country, the Supreme Ayatollah is just that—supreme."

"So we've got two conflicting Islamic philosophies at work here. One that favors openness to the West versus the autocratic legacy of the Ayatollah Khomeini."

"Yes. The Ayatollah Khomeini's death only strengthened the Islamic Revolution that he led. Vehemently anti-Western elements are entrenched."

"A hit like this would prove that what they see as Western arrogance—the attempt to impose our egalitarian systems on the world—has not defeated those that reject Western thought as harmful to Islam."

"It is not an untenable plan," Nadine said. "Destabilizing the existing structure leaves room for another doctrine to creep in, to ultimately reach the goal of *umma*, one united Islamic community. It is already the faith of more than one billion people globally. More than eighty countries have established Islamic governments that command more than one-fifth of the world's wealth."

There was momentary silence on the line as a young woman entered the Y's office and handed him an envelope. He opened it and removed several photographs. One by one, he examined them, then handed them over to Shlomo.

"Nadine, Phil, what we have here are recent photos of the man we believe to be Al Rasuul along with his first lieutenant, Issam Ibn Assad, and another key figure in the organization. They were taken by two of our men who infiltrated the Abu Jibril cell; the same men who were instrumental in rescuing Daniel. We'll send these electronically now. Remember," Y said before disconnecting, "they're aiming for the heart."

Nadine's hand trembled as she disconnected the speaker. In a few minutes, she would come face to face with the man she hated most in the world. A man she did not know, but because of whom she would not rest until he was dead, by her own hand or another's.

Watching her, Phil said, "We may know *who* is behind this, but we are still left with *where* and *when*."

"Huh? Oh." Nadine returned his gaze. "Well, this group is telling us we don't like you and we don't like what you stand for. What does that leave us? Shopping malls? Theme parks? McDonald's?"

"I think fast food chains have been reserved for gun-toting lunatics who take out a dozen or so diners then guns himself down before the local police arrive."

Nadine ignored the sarcasm. "Each team is focusing on its targeted cities and starting with its most obvious landmarks. Security will be tripled at each site. We're checking border entries for the past six months. Surveillance and disaster preparedness protocols are commencing immediately."

"That still leaves us with *when*."

"We're working on it."

"I also want to know whether they're waiting for a final order or if the clock is ticking as we speak. Those are the answers I want, stat."

CHAPTER 33

▼

He slept through most of Sunday, awakening in the late afternoon to the sound of his children's laughter as it trickled in from outside his bedroom window. His oldest boy was teasing the three younger ones, playfully taunting them in a game of his own creation. Shimoni smiled, then his thoughts switched over to Daniel and he felt a slight catch in his throat. The boy was on a flight home, away from this insanity. He said a silent prayer for him and let go the breath he had unconsciously been holding. Tension flowed from his chest and shoulders and he relaxed back into the pillow. The nightmare was over, but his work was far from done.

Now fully awake, a web began forming in his mind. Daniel's captors were more than likely Mrs. Wolf's murderers. But who were they and where did that leave Mizrahi? He could start with the big fellow who had transported Daniel to Jericho *if* he was still alive. He never did get around to asking what happened back there. And no one offered to tell him. Besides, Jericho was out of his jurisdiction. He would need the cooperation of the Palestinian police; a slow process that in this case might yield questionable results. If his perpetrators were still in Abu Jibril, he could make the arrests. Mentally pausing, he wondered how much he could get out of Barak. They were probably through with him, but he figured Mossad owed him one.

Rising, he went straight to the kitchen to pour himself a cup of strong black coffee, grabbing a pad and pencil along the way. At the small breakfast table, he charted his thoughts, scribbling names, drawing lines and arrows based on what he now knew. He wrote with his left hand, the right wrapped firmly around the warm body of his coffee mug.

Mizrahi was killed late Friday. Mrs. Wolf met her demise the following morning. That same Saturday morning, Daniel was kidnapped. Similarities: both were killed in the same manner, fatally stabbed in the heart. Both knew Nadine. Both, he was sure, were ancillary victims, tossed aside in pursuit of Dr. Kanner herself, first at her office and then at her home. Why? He tapped the eraser end of his pencil against the pad. Who wanted Kanner? What did she know? Or what did she have? Was all of this really LBA revenge for what happened in the woods or was he missing something? He made a note: talk to forensics. Check the apartment again.

He heard a shriek and then a cry. The game had gone too far. With a sigh, he put down his pencil and headed out to comfort the wounded feelings of his youngest child.

Shimoni hesitated momentarily before slowly pushing open the door to Fouad's hospital room. Barely twenty-four hours had passed but it seemed like eons. Seated by his bedside, a woman robed in a black floor length dress and white head covering held Fouad's hand. He lay in repose, his large barrel chest moving in slow rhythm, up and down. Standing opposite the woman, on the other side of the bed, was a man in his thirties. He looked up when Shimoni entered the room, but did not greet him. A younger woman with suspicious eyes, dressed identically to Fouad's wife, stood next to him.

Shimoni felt the man's gaze scrutinizing him, measuring the color of his skin, the length of his nose, the height of his body, the wave in his hair. They were the same. They could have been brothers. Thousands of years ago they were. But even then, they had clashed.

He greeted the older woman first, speaking softly in Arabic, expressing his regret. She nodded in response and squeezed her husband's hand. Shimoni straightened, held his hand out to Fouad's eldest son, Amir, and introduced himself. He was about to ask Amir to step outside with him into the hallway when he felt a tug on his left sleeve. Extracting a picture from her pocket, she looked up and locked onto his eyes. Shimoni was surprised at the smooth texture of her skin and the youthfulness in her face, though her pallor was sallow, her eyes full of sadness.

"This is my son, my youngest. He is seventeen and his name is Naji. He was home in his room, the night my husband found the American lady beside our well. He is gone. He has disappeared. I have not seen him since that night."

Shimoni's face did not register the jolt he felt. Another fucking coincidence of the kind he didn't believe in. "Do you have any idea when he left?"

She shook her head but said, "I believe it was before sunrise. I went to his room shortly after my husband and the American left. He was not there."

"Is there anything else you would like to tell me?"

She took a sharp breath, as if she was about to speak, but thought better of it. She simply shook her head and returned her attention to her husband. How disappointed Fouad would have been had he seen the note that Naji had left her expressing his intention to join Al Rasuul in his fight to liberate Palestine. Naji had misjudged her. She was not like the other mothers. She would not rejoice in her youngest son sacrificing himself to Allah.

Shimoni turned to Amir. His response was a stone cold stare.

Back outside on the sunlit streets of Jerusalem, Shimoni's mind was churning. He recalled the shooting that they had seen from the palm grove after releasing Daniel. The blue sedan had streaked into Jericho. Were Fouad's attackers connected with Daniel's captors? Or were they after Nadine? Were they connected to Mizrahi and Wolf's killers? Shimoni shook his head. The Palestinian police should have come up with something by now, but even the vehicle seemed to have disappeared into thin air. His stomach turned. If he wanted answers, he was going to need cash.

Once at the station, he sent out a description and Naji's photo to every border crossing in Israel. It was as good a place to start as any. Then he was going to have a chat with Barak, if he could find him.

Sgt. Ron Keital was grateful for every day that border patrol ended quietly. He liked going home to his girlfriend, happy that he hadn't seen any action and especially happy that no one had gotten hurt. He'd seen it happen too many times. The wounds of the skirmishes healed, but they always left scars. Every quiet day along the border meant one more day of peace. Perhaps if they could act like there was peace, maybe someday there would be. Then *his* children wouldn't have to grow up to patrol with rifles or be suspicious of the kids across the river. They would go to Amman for dinner and to Tel Aviv to dance.

He had just learned that morning that his girlfriend was pregnant and these were the thoughts that occupied Ron's mind as he waited for the bus to grind to a halt at the Allenby Bridge border crossing into Jordan. He boarded the bus, greeted the driver and routinely inspected the documents of the passengers. A group of young Swedes was headed for Petra, the ancient red city. Several Israelis were on their way to Amman and the remaining passengers were Jordanians returning home.

He had reached the back of the bus and was about to turn around when he noticed a young boy crouched in the corner of the very last seat. He held out his hand for the boy's travel documents. He was a skinny kid.

Can't be more than fifteen, Ron thought. As he waited for the boy to pull his papers from his pocket, Ron surmised that he might be a runaway.

The documents were in order. A little surprised, the he looked from the papers to the boy and back again. He was an Israeli citizen and nineteen years old. He looked awfully young for his age, but that was no crime. There was something about his demeanor though.

"Stand, please," he ordered. Naji stood, shoulders slightly stooped, arms at his side. The border guard looked him over, searching him with his eyes only.

"Where are you going?"

"To visit relatives."

He thought the boy looked a little angry, but there was nothing threatening in his behavior. He returned the documents, walked to the front of the bus, waved to the driver and stepped off. He then signaled the soldier at the bridge to lift the gate. The driver shifted into first gear, released the clutch and lurched onto the bridge, when a second guard, Sam, whistled through his fingers loud enough to alert the soldier at the gate. He waved at him to lower it and the bus jerked to a halt, sending the passengers into the seat backs in front of them. He held two sheets of paper in his hand. The first had the description of a wanted man, the second was a printout of his photo.

"What's going on?" Ron called.

"This just came in," the younger man responded. "It's an alert. I wanted to bring it to your attention before the bus went through."

"Everyone looks clean, but let's have a look. I don't want to keep them waiting too long."

"Your little contribution towards peace, eh, sir?" the soldier jived him, although Ron was his superior.

Ron returned the jibe. "Nothing like showing a little courtesy to your neighbors, Sam. Not a bad thought to keep in mind."

He took the papers and shook his head as he reviewed the description of the wanted man. The name and description did not match anyone on the bus. They flipped to the second sheet. Naji's face peered back at him.

Ron hit the sheet so that it made a snapping sound. He *knew* there was something odd about that kid. As Ron re-boarded, Naji shoved the window open and jumped out on the far side of the bus. He headed for the river bank as the guards scrambled after him.

"Don't shoot him," Ron yelled. "He's not armed!" He leapt off the bus. To the soldier at the gate, "Call over to the other side. If he gets across, I want him back."

Naji plunged into the cool dark water. The Jordan River was narrow. A child could swim across it. Jordanian soldiers watched from the opposite bank. Sam scrambled down the bank and dove into the water after Naji. All eyes were on the pair until Ron heard a shot fired. He looked up to see where it had come from. He saw a Jordanian soldier, rifle on his shoulder, aiming to take another shot at Sam.

Mother-fucking son of a bitch! Was he some sort of a nut? What the hell was going on? The guy was starting a war! "Don't do this! Don't do this!" he yelled, waving his hands. "Stop!"

No chance. He was going for another shot. Why wasn't anyone trying to stop him? Was he an officer? Ron tried to make out his rank. He could easily blow the soldier away with his Uzi but he didn't want to give anyone an excuse to start a gun battle. And that, Ron knew, was what this guy was counting on.

He heard another shot fire off as he ran for the crossing booth picked up a rifle with a telescopic sight. Sam went under. Ron had no idea whether he'd been hit or was dodging the bullets, but hoped that he would head for the bridge. Where was the kid? He couldn't see him.

He ordered the soldier at the gate to call for backup and medics. No one was going to believe this. They were in deep shit.

"Hang in there, Sam," he said silently. He dropped to one knee and steadied the rifle on his shoulder. He would allow *no* excuses for escalating this incident. He had the soldier in his sight. Ron was a good shot but he was no sniper. His goal was just to stop him. He aimed for his shoulder, wrapped his finger around the trigger and squeezed. The sniper looked up in surprise at the sound of the bullet that whizzed by him. Then he smiled and turned his sights towards Ron. Raising his weapon, he aimed directly for Ron's head. Ron hit the ground and rolled for the bridge. A bullet shot up the dirt where he'd been kneeling just a moment earlier.

Sam crawled back onto the bank as three jeeps and an ambulance came screeching over to the bridge. Two medics and half a dozen soldiers leaped out and ran towards Ron and Sam.

"What's going on?" the commanding officer demanded to know.

"A passenger jumped from the bus and headed for the water. When Sam went in after him one of the soldiers from the other side began sniping at him."

"Where's the passenger?"

Ron shook his head. They turned to Sam who was being treated by a medic for a wound to the shoulder.

"I pulled him under with me when the guy started shooting, but I couldn't hold him."

"Do you know if he was hit?"

Sam just shook his head.

Ron pulled out the two sheets he had stuffed into his pocket. "These are the stats on him."

The CO nodded and turned to his men. "OK, take a quick look and get out there. Spread out along the banks and find him. I'll make the appropriate contacts to the other side in case they find him first."

The Jordanian border guards had returned to their posts but the lone officer still stood rooted to his spot, weapon at his side. The CO stopped one of the soldiers. "Get the camera equipment. See if you can get a photo of this lunatic. But do yourself a favor and don't let him spot you first."

Naji pulled himself into some scrub along the bank and tried to hide. Luckily, he was thin enough to conceal himself. The sun was setting. Another factor in his favor. He didn't have the energy to wonder how they were on to him. He would just wait for dark and swim over. He was sure the Jordanians would sympathize with his position. The earlier adrenaline rush had worn off and he was feeling faint. He hadn't eaten much since the previous morning when he, Sabri and Issam had gone after Fouad and Nadine. Thinking back to what had transpired, he swelled with pride. He reported what transpired at his father's house to his cell leader, who brought the incident to Issam and Sabri's attention. Their reaction had been swift. Naji was astonished that the two had insisted on carrying out the retaliatory operation themselves. How right he had been. Even as a new member, he had already proven his value.

He leaned further into the bushes. Unfortunately, his father had picked the wrong side. That was war. He prayed that Allah would forgive Fouad his sins and reward him for working hard all his life.

Naji began to shiver. He'd been in the river for quite a while now and in the desert, the air lost heat quickly. Still he could not understand why he felt so tired. He moved in closer to the bank and tried to position himself so that he could rest. Maybe he could close his eyes just until the sun set.

He was aware of the voices disturbing his jumbled dreams, but he could not move. There were shouts, instructions, then several pairs of arms lifting him out of the water. He heard one of them swear and say something about his leg. Now that they mentioned it, he did feel some pain in his leg. But his head hurt more than his leg. No matter. The leg would heal. And he would be back again.

Shimoni wasn't allowed in to see Naji for a full two days after he'd been fished out of the river. The doctors told him that he'd lost so much blood, he was nearly dead when they brought him in. When he awakened Wednesday evening, Shimoni was allowed into the room for a few minutes. The interrogation would have to wait, but Shimoni wanted Naji to get used to seeing him around. Soften his antagonism a bit. He dressed in plainclothes and did not say anything about who he was or why he was there.

He learned from Barak that Marwan was dead. Daniel had described his kidnappers in great detail before leaving and Barak's men confirmed their identities, but they had disappeared. Barak gave Shimoni copies of their recently obtained photos and wished him luck.

There was a lot he wanted to know from Naji. But for now, that would have to wait.

CHAPTER 34

▼

Nadine hung her suit on the small hook protruding from the back door of the car and set her brown pumps on the floor. Dawn was breaking over Washington, D.C. as she slid into the front seat and headed for the city center.

She was looking forward to the next hour. She had barely seen the inside of her rented Georgetown apartment since dropping her gear there one week ago. For the past seven days, from the basement of the Pentagon, she and other members of their top-secret team had been analyzing every scrap of information that might bring them closer to pinpointing the events in the message. The computers were running twenty-four hours a day. And they were running with them.

She needed a breather. Something to kick her brain into a higher gear. She pulled into a space along the banks of the Potomac. Stepping out of the car, she dropped her keys into a small pouch and stretched a bit before easing into a slow jog to warm up. Her running shoes hugged her feet like old friends. The air was crisp and cool. Clouds of warm breath vaporized instantaneously each time she exhaled. She almost laughed as the memory of trying to blow 'smoke rings' as a child came to mind.

The stairs to the Lincoln Memorial rose before her. She ran in their direction and counted each step as she skipped up from one to the next. A slight throbbing in her left thigh reminded her that the past was not yet resolved. At the top, hopping in place, she saluted the likeness of the sixteenth president, the man whose homely visage and strong character led a divided Union through its darkest moments. Those were times that changed the course of the nation, yet preserved the ideals upon which it had been founded. She sensed that today's times were equally profound, but complex in a way that they were as yet unprepared for. Time as a dimension had lost its relevancy. Today, tomorrow and yesterday had no meaning in a world where instantaneous communication across multiple time zones erased those kinds of distinctions. Cyberspace, meant to help the world function faster, better, more informed, making us closer, friendlier, eliminating borders and prejudice, became the perfect tool to sow evil, spread hate and commit crime that could change the course of history.

Freedom was the life spring of the American people. Freedom to speak, to object, to love, to protest, to arm, to disarm, to believe, to deny. Americans were vociferous about protecting their freedom. It all boiled down to that, didn't it? Nadine thought.

Now they were faced with a new sort of threat. The most insidious to their freedom yet, because it was invisible. One that was ever more dangerous because the enemy could not be faced head on. Americans remained ready to fight, but where indeed was the enemy?

Nadine turned around. The glass face of the reflecting pool was dark against the overcast sky but no less serene, and the Washington Monument stood tall just beyond it. She could see the Capitol Building in the distance. She decided to loop it, run past the United States Supreme Court Building and the Library of Congress, then back again. Finally, crossing the bridge at the north end of the Tidal Basin, she would swing down to her car and head for the Pentagon. It would take her less than an hour, leaving her just enough time to shower and dress before most of the staff was in. She sprinted back down the steps and along Henry Bacon Drive past the Vietnam Veterans Memorial. Memories flooded her every step of the way. Turning right on Constitution Avenue, it was a straight path from here to the Capitol.

She tried to empty her mind completely. These past few days, her thinking had been muddled. Jet lag always hit her hardest two or three days after a long flight, but something else was bothering her too. She couldn't put her finger on precisely what it was. She hoped that some fresh air and a quiet run would clear the cobwebs so that she could get back to work

The sidewalk glistened from an earlier rain, but the clouds were moving on and patches of blue were now visible. The Sunday morning streets were empty and she could admire the majesty of the buildings that housed the greatest democracy in the world. No government was without its flaws, but she could not help feeling a swell of pride that she served a country that stood for liberty and the protection of basic human rights. She silently cheered her good fortune.

She picked up her pace now and synchronized her breathing with the sound of her footsteps on the wet pavement. She felt a slight tightening in her chest that she tried at first to ignore, then, when it persisted, to will it away, but it stayed, its heavy presence bearing down harder with every breath.

"OK," she told herself out loud, "face it." An image blazed in her mind's eye. The image of Daniel, of her hugging him and finding it so hard to let go until she heard him say, "Mom, please."

She couldn't recall whether she had been aware of it then, but now the event was as real as if it were being played out before her. She was making an oath, promising Daniel that she would revenge the violence visited upon him; that she would find the men who had kidnapped him and she would kill them. That it might take some time, but she knew how to track them down and to make sure they suffered before paying ultimate price. And she would do it herself. She had promised him that.

She exhaled loudly and the image was gone. So was the weight on her chest. She remembered her oath, looked at her bandaged hand and reaffirmed it. They would pay. She had the patience of a saint. Her burden lifted, she ran faster now.

On 1st St., she turned right and paused before the United States Supreme Court Building. She had always loved that building and was awed by the knowledge that here sat the highest arbiters of justice in the country. Some said that the justices lived in an ivory tower, removed from the realities of the common man, but Nadine believed that these nine men and women were the pursuers of truth and protectors of the Constitution that they were beholden to be.

Despite the weight of their mission hanging over her, Nadine felt jubilant at this moment. Tomorrow, on the first Monday in October, a new justice was to be sworn in. That new justice was her mentor and her friend, Melinda Samson-Knight. She was ten years Nadine's senior, but that had never hindered their relationship. In fact, they'd enjoyed many runs like these together, the older Samson-Knight often outdistancing her, her mental stamina fueling her physical endurance. Just thinking of her propelled Nadine forward with renewed vigor.

Senator Ashford had vigorously opposed her nomination. He thought her too liberal, too young, too outspoken and too candid. Never mind that Samson-Knight had twenty-four years on the bench and an illustrious legal career before that. Senior Senator or not, he wasn't going to attend the swearing-in ceremony and that was that.

Nadine could hardly believe he was going to miss all that press. The President, Vice President, Speaker of the House and many others would be in attendance.

Maybe he just didn't like the competition. She chuckled to herself and started to move on but unwillingly, she found herself turning back to look at the courthouse, the Capitol Building across the street, the bare trees all around her.

What was wrong with this picture? Beneath her dark bangs, a small frown creased her forehead. She squinted slightly as she scanned the sky. Low on the horizon, just above and to the left of the apex of the courthouse facade hung a just-waning full moon. She swung her gaze to the marble steps that led up to the grand entrance of the Supreme Court. A young man dressed in a suit and tie tripped lightly up the stairs and entered the building through a door at the far end of the bank. He had a briefcase in one hand, a lunch pail in the other.

Nadine shrugged. At least she wasn't the only one working this Sunday. She had wasted too much time. She checked her watch and continued to run.

CHAPTER 35

▼

Tokyo, Monday October 5, 1998

He snapped the briefcase shut with satisfaction. Constructing the bomb had gone without a hitch. It was a classic mercury-based incendiary device placed in an attaché case attached to a digital watch. Set the timer, walk away and boom. And that is exactly what he was planning to do.

At the start of trading, he would deposit the briefcase by a central computer, walk out of the building and straight into the Japanese countryside, back to his home, to the tranquillity he didn't appreciate as a restless, adventure seeking youth. Twenty-seven years in Lebanon had been more than enough for him. Better than prison perhaps, but nonetheless, all too long.

He had made it through customs without a hitch, thanks to a new identity and slightly modified looks. Besides having aged very little in the last two and a half decades, he was now eighty pounds lighter. That, and plastic surgery to gently round out his eyes, gave him an entirely new look. He doubted that his own mother would recognize him.

Carefully, he set the suitcase upright by the double doors to his suite. Ascribing to the theory that conspicuousness was often the best way to hide, he had checked into a very posh hotel. This particular establishment was sure to guard his privacy closely should anyone exhibit excessive interest in his business, however unlikely. Plus, the sizable tip he had left was a worthwhile premium for that extra bit of insurance.

He would leave with sunrise. He checked his watch and took his position by the window. Assuming the preparation pose, he emptied his mind, vaguely acknowledging as he always did at this juncture, that it was immersion into *qigong* that set him on his new path to health, vitality and strength. The ancient

Chinese breathing exercises renewed and directed the flow of his *qi*, the body's energy, and brought his mind and body into complete balance.

Forty-five minutes later, the sun reddened the sky. He lifted the briefcase with due caution. As he did, he caught his reflection in the mirror and almost laughed out loud, greatly amused by his elegant appearance. He was dressed in an expensive suit, crisp white shirt and dark tie, adorned with gold cufflinks and a tiepin. His feet relaxed into the soft leather of his shoes. He stepped out the door and left his fugitive life behind him, forever. At the lobby entrance, the chief porter offered to hail him a cab but he declined, indicating that he preferred to enjoy the early morning air.

He turned the corner, walked a couple of blocks and waved down a taxi. He gave the driver an address in the business district, not far from the Nikkei Stock Exchange, then leaned back in the seat and relaxed. He secured the briefcase under his left arm, safely wedged by his side. The cab wound its way through the slick streets, gleaming from a light rain that had fallen earlier in the morning.

He hadn't been to Tokyo in twenty-seven years since joining Kozo Okamoto and dozens of others to form the Japanese Red Army. Anti-establishment zeal had infected his young mind like a virulent disease for which there was no cure. Aligned with extremist pro-Palestinian factions, they spread their bloody terror across Europe and Israel, leaving a hideous trail of dead and wounded behind them. Only he and Kozo had survived the attack on Israel's international airport near Tel Aviv. The bloody massacre played through his head like a tape in slow motion. May 1972. They simply sprayed the crowded baggage claim area with machine gun fire. People all around them screamed and dropped like flies. He snorted a laugh. It wasn't long before he and Kozo were released in a prisoner exchange. They and dozens of other murderers chomping at the bit to strike again, freed in exchange for the bodies of a few dead Israeli soldiers.

He paid the driver and stepped out of the cab. He chose to walk along the water's edge before turning toward his destination. Yes, he'd been away a long time. Ostensibly, he was a free man in Lebanon. Leaving meant certain punishment, so in Lebanon he'd stayed. Now he was going home. Fate was returning him to the countryside; to the quiet life in a place where people still traded produce for goods. How fortunate. In a few hours, the economy would crash, and he would live out his days as his forebears had for thousands of years.

Absorbed in his thoughts, it took him a moment to understand that the vibrations under his feet were not those of a subway train passing below. Realization brought terror. He looked at the case he carried in his right hand, stricken. Around him, buildings swayed, sidewalks buckled and at any moment, the volatile mercury, now prematurely flowing through its tube, would come into contact with the wire connected to the watch, closing the circuit. Waves lifted and crashed over the barrier along the walkway, soaking him. The trembling earth quaked faster under his feet.

"I will not die for anyone!" he roared.

Without another thought, he raised his right arm and heaved the case like a javelin into the enraged surf. The rumble of the earthquake muffled the sound of the explosion. He hit the throbbing cement and blacked out, but not before he saw its wake surge in his direction.

CHAPTER 36

▼

Paris, Monday October 5, 1998

He rose, washed and knelt to say his morning prayers. When he finished, he wrapped the deadly belt around his waist and latched it into place. He slipped into his jacket, took one last sweep around the room and closed the door behind him.

He moved unhurriedly, as if to remember his last hours on earth not in a nostalgic sort of way, but with the cool of one belonging to those who could choose to stay or leave. He made his way towards Champs-de-Mars, the park that was home to the world's most famous monument, the Eiffel Tower. He squinted up at the wrought iron latticework, its arrogant spire straining towards the sky like a modern Tower of Babel. There was no escaping its oppressive silhouette. Its empty form dominated the scene. He wondered at the veneration of so many for such an obviously grotesque form and scoffed at their fondness for this empty fabrication. Yes, this was the appropriate target, its inert, vacant façade so symbolic of the emptiness of the Western world. He would take down the hideous monstrosity and free the populace below from its infatuation with the cold, vacuousness of their mistaken belief system.

The air was chill, the sky gray, but his mood was lofty. Angels would greet him at heaven's gate. His family, the relatives of a *shaheed*, would know honor all their lives and ascend directly to heaven upon their deaths, as well.

He joined the line at the base of the tower and waited for his turn to ride the glass elevators to the second level. From there, he would take another elevator to a third platform near the top. An American couple with two small children stood behind him. Behind them, a pair of giggling girls threw glances at him, then coyly turned away when he met their gaze. He stepped back to allow the Americans to move ahead of him.

"*Belles filles*, what is so amusing?" he asked, his dazzling smile captivating them completely. He offered each an arm. "What do you say we travel to the heavens together, eh?"

In a fit of giggles, they hooked their arms into his and chattered happily. They were almost at the elevator entrance when the little American boy in front of them began to cry.

"Scary, scary," he managed to say in between sobs. Unable to console him, his mother lifted him and stepped out of line. They waved to his father and sister who skipped delightedly through the glass doors. The trio followed, passed over by the two gendarmes scanning the visitors as they filed into the elevator.

Gerard Hire was worried. He was due to retire as head of the Service de Documentation Exterieure et de Contre Espionnage (Department for Foreign Information and Counter Espionage) and now an affair certain to mar his long, unblemished career had been dropped into his lap. Until now, he was probably the only SDECE chief to last so long without some sort of a scandal under his belt. Well, providence might yet intervene. As of this moment, that looked like his only hope.

The smoke rising from his cigarette stung his eyes. He stubbed it out in an ashtray brimming with a dozen or so similarly crushed filters. He had almost quit smoking entirely when Washington alerted him of the threat. A terrorist bomb. Somewhere in Paris. When? Where? How?

"*Merde*," he said again for the hundredth time.

What could he do without imposing widespread panic? He shook his head. The French were so finicky. He practically had to strangle some of the obstinate city officials personally before they had allowed him to institute even the most minimal of safeguards at their beloved monuments and museums. What would people think? they always wanted to know. There would be panic, they protested. Perhaps *monsieur* was overreacting just a bit, they wondered.

Indeed, the information was sketchy. It did not help that France was teeming with Arabs, mostly from neighboring Morocco. If it were he, he would go straight for the Eiffel Tower, but who knew? The Chief smirked. It would do wonders for the Paris skyline. Privately he thought it looked more like a birthmark on Paris's otherwise flawless beauty regardless of its sheer architectural and engineering genius.

The buzz of the intercom sliced through his thoughts. His secretary announced that Robert Devereaux, in charge of the French team, was on his way in. Almost simultaneously, the door opened. Without any introduction, he said, "This is it, sir. In just now from Washington."

Hire scanned the order.

"Call my car," Hire instructed his secretary. "Let's go."

"Where to, sir?" Robert inquired, following Hire out the door.

"The Eiffel Tower."

Hire swore to himself. What was he going to do? Hang around the Tower all day? But he had a hunch. And his hunches had never let him down before. His driver negotiated the Parisian traffic with expert ease and dropped the Chief and Robert next to the Tower. Hire strode ahead, his trench coat flapping out behind him, Robert in tow. At the head of the line, they flashed their identification and squeezed into the already crowded elevator. Hire faced a handsome young man with a girl on each arm. Suspicious of everyone, Hire noted that the man was Mediterranean looking, but this one apparently had other things on his mind.

The glass elevator ascended on a curve up the legs of the tower to the second platform. The doors opened and Hire was relieved to see that the metal detector he had insisted upon was set in place. Anyone wishing to ascend to the third platform had to pass through it. The trio headed straight for the elevators that would take them to the top of the Tower. The cars going up to the top of the tower were newer and smaller than the glass elevators. Hire looked around while Robert wondered what exactly the Chief had in mind. Behind them, the metal detector let out a familiar alarm. The Mediterranean man flashed a dazzling smile and jangled a large set of keys.

"*Seulement mon clefs*!" he said with good-naturedly. To Hire's horror, the gendarme waved him through.

"*Arrete*!" Hire roared. "Stop him!"

With his two companions still faithfully clinging to him, the younger man dove into the elevator just as the doors closed behind him.

"You see," the young man grinned broadly to his new friends, "nothing to worry about." He spread his hands wide open, revealing the belt around his waist.

"What is that?" asked one of the girls.

"This, *ma cherie*, is your destiny."

Hire did not waste time getting pissed off. He hoped to have plenty of time for that later.

"Disable that car," he commanded. "Immediately!" One of the gendarmes ran for an emergency exit that led to the control room. "You," Hire shouted at two others, "Evacuate the area!"

Hire did not know for sure if the man had a bomb, but knew that if he did, he could detonate at any moment. At least at a lower level damage to the tower would be more contained. He was fairly certain that the tower itself was as much a target as the passengers in the elevator car. After what seemed like an interminable time, the elevator car jolted to a stop, then began to descend slowly. Hire was sweating. He was waiting for the blast.

"Draw your guns but do not fire. I do not want a slaughter of innocents here."

Time practically slowed to a standstill as the elevator settled down and the doors eased open. Inside, a dozen visitors stood frozen to their spots, unable to move as they stared at the group of gendarmes and security agents, their guns drawn and directed at them.

"*Merde!*" Hire murmured to himself again. Where was the bastard? He looked up. Several stories above, three figures clung to the wrought iron ladder, slowly, tentatively, climbing upward.

"Get these people out of here. And get me the elevator engineer."

A frightened, bleary-eyed civil servant approached them.

"Listen," Hire barked, "here is a walkie-talkie. We're going to head for the top platform. I may need you to move us as I instruct you. I don't want to have to wait for the elevator to respond."

"I will do my best, *Monsieur*," the engineer replied unconvincingly.

Someone was tapping on Hire's shoulder. He turned to see a tall, fair man holding a small child. Hire recognized him as one of the elevator passengers.

"*Oui?*"

"That guy," he said pointing upward, "he's wearing explosives. They're in some sort of belt." The little girl he held buried her head in her father's neck. A pained look spread across his face. "Sorry, my French isn't that good. He tried to detonate it, but it failed. Luckily for us, I guess, the elevator started down before he could fix it. That's when he flipped. He started yelling, jabbering something about our destiny and forced the two young women he was with, out of the hatch. One of the girls was hysterical but the other is in control. I think he has a weapon, too."

Hire could see that the American was trying hard to stay calm, but as realization sunk in deeper, he began to tremble.

"One small question, *monsieur*. Do you happen to know what the difficulty was?" The American managed a weak smile. "He wasn't using a Duracell."

"Eh?"

"He couldn't complete the circuit. I think the battery was dead." Hire thanked him and passed him off to the gendarmes to get him out of the tower.

Allors. Perhaps Providence had intervened after all. But the American said something about his trying to fix it and he still had two hostages. He signaled to Robert and the other agent and the three climbed into the elevator. It rose slowly.

They had just passed the trio when Hire ordered the car stopped. One of the young women, unfortunately dressed in a miniskirt and high-heeled shoes, was sobbing into the ladder. The wind whipped her long blond hair about her face. Paralyzed with fear, she gripped the rungs for dear life. She began to scream as the elevator passed. Her friend was scampering up the ladder, putting distance between herself and the would-be suicide bomber. Just below her on the ladder, the bomber pressed against the sobbing girl. Her hands were clenched so tightly he could not peel her fingers away from the metal. Impatient now, he climbed right over her. They watched from the elevator car in horror as the man, pushing against an upper rung with both arms, brought the full weight of his body down on her shoulders. Her fingers began to give. Her right foot flailed as if trying to find the step below. The muscles of her shoulders and upper arms stiffened and trembled from the intensity with which she clutched the metal bars. Now his weight on her upper torso weakened her grip further. The flush of youth drained from her milky complexion. Fear erased every joy she had ever known and gripped her in its intractable vise. Her lips as pale as her transparent skin gave her the look of one already dead.

"My God! He's trying to throw her off!" Robert exclaimed as he worked on opening the elevator hatch. Hire was galled. He barked into his walkie-talkie. "Are any of our snipers down there yet?"

A maddening shriek sent their hearts racing. Too late. Stunned, they could only stare as the girl fell back, body arched, arms out at her sides, head first. Still alive, her body turned as if by righting itself it could be saved. Seconds later, she hit the expanding base of the tower and lay tangled in its steel filigree, as cold and lifeless as her metal bed.

The terrorist cursed as the elevator rumbled towards the upper platform. He could feel its vibrations in the rungs under his hands and feet. The rubber soled shoes of his other young escort never stopped moving. Her pretty blue eyes never looked down. She climbed, up, up, never breaking her rhythm, never interrupting her pace. Her entire being focused on reaching the upper platform.

Perhaps, he mused, this one was worthy of her fate. Her soul would fly with his to the heavens, unlike that of her friend, whose spirit would linger.

He leaned into the ladder and went over the wiring that extended from each explosives-laden canister held snugly in place by loops in his belt. He found the culprit. A thin wire had slipped from its insertion point, interrupting the circuit. He slid it into place and climbed. Now he would catch up to the girl and accomplish his mission. Inside the elevator, the blast of the bomb would have magnified the power of its impact many times over, blowing out the surrounding beams of the tower. But even in the open air, the damage would be devastating.

He was gaining on her now. The climb was strenuous and the wind was a force to be reckoned with. He paid little attention to the elevator car, though it did seem to be moving rather erratically, sometimes slowing to a stop, lowering then rising again. It dawned on him then that it seemed to be keeping tabs on the girl. Now he understood that someone must be inside, controlling it. He quickened his ascent. She would not get away from him like the other one. Even better. If the people in the elevator tried to pick her up, he could climb back inside too. And *boom.*

The elevator was just above him now. The ceiling hatch lifted open and a man climbed out. Robert reached for the girl but as he did, the bomber firmly gripped her ankle with his right hand. The car swayed and Robert struggled to keep his balance. He had not yet fully stabilized himself when the terrorist grabbed her. He tried to steady himself and still hold on to her, but was not sure that he could. The velocity of the October winds was swift at this height, moving quickly through the spaces in the Tower's latticework. The gusts could easily send them plunging to the ground below. He willed the terrorist to let her go. How important could she be to him? They would all die in the blast anyway. As if reading Robert's mind, the terrorist suddenly released his grip on the girl. With a leap, she fell onto the roof of the car and collapsed into the open hatch.

Robert steadied himself against the cable and drew his gun. The bomber's smiling face was now level with his own. His hand on his belt, he deftly guided the wire to the battery's negative pole. His grin remained, but the look in his eyes turned to one of surprise as the bullets from Robert's gun ripped through his chest. He fell back off the ladder, his fingers still gripping the decisive filament.

The blast sent Robert hard into the cables. The elevator car swung wildly. He grabbed the hatch and held on for dear life as his body, splattered with the bomber's skin and blood, was hurled against the beams. He used the momentum of the swinging car to slide himself toward the opening but for every inch of progress he made, he lost more each time it rocked. He heard Hire calling his name, but didn't respond. He needed all his strength just to hold on.

With a lurch, the car began to descend. Robert was desperate now. He took a huge breath and with a roar, propelled himself toward the opening. Head first, he dove into the car, Hire's body breaking his fall.

CHAPTER 37

▼

Rome, Monday October 5, 1998

George Michel Elias prepared his vestments, the purple biretta and cape of a Roman Catholic bishop. He had only recently been elevated to the position and was still awed by the rich hues. A priest of true humility and love for his fellow man, he had never aspired to such splendor. His diocese was mostly working class. He always had a smile on his lips and a good word for most the destitute, among whom he found contentment when he could lessen their distress. But his colleagues had implored him not to refuse. So few, even among the clergy, were not motivated by power or personal gain. It would be sinful if one so deserving declined the rank. He crossed himself and asked God's forgiveness for presuming himself worthy. As he prepared for the procession, his heart soared at the opportunity to accompany His Holiness in this morning's ceremony.

He adjusted his robes before the mirror and winked in fun. Perhaps purple wasn't a bad color for him after all. It suited his dark, Semitic features that had always made him a standout. His parents had fled Jaffa in 1948 for Detroit, where he was born ten years later. The rest of their family remained in the city just south of Tel-Aviv. When he was a boy, he visited them often, spending summers with his cousins on the beach. His knowledge of Hebrew facilitated his study of the Old Testament and other writings, but when he entered the seminary, many of his cousins, with whom he'd played and grown, became increasingly distant. It saddened him greatly. He still contacted them when he made pilgrimages to the Holy Land, but personal visits were increasingly rare. He heaved a sigh and replaced the thoughts of his lost boyhood days with those of the procession about to commence.

Despite the chill in the air, the skies over Vatican City were a deep blue and worshippers filled the square. He took his place in line, only a few paces behind

His Holiness. The altar boys preceded them and made their way slowly out of the church and onto the long platform. The Pope followed, his spry body upright, his face welcoming, silently greeting the crowd.

George spotted a young man in the front row and smiled with his eyes. He had a striking similarity to his cousin Sayeed, as he had looked twenty years earlier when they were teenagers.

"Sayeed, Sayeed," he called out, his voice drowned out by the caws of the seagulls above. A warm afternoon breeze swept across the sandy beach and blew his hair back from his forehead, as he tried to catch up. They were fifteen and this would probably be his last summer visiting Jaffa. Next year, he would get a summer job and start to save for the seminary.

Sayeed turned, grinning mischievously. "Come on, slow-poke. All the girls will be gone by the time you get your ass in gear."

The sun was setting. Sayeed whooped and ran further up the beach. George ran after him, his feet slipping in the sand.

The memory of blue skies and their laughter faded.

The worshipper did not return George's warm look. His eyes never left the Holy See. Now his warm gaze turned to concern. George knew the souls of people. He could read them in their eyes. This worshipper did not have the glow of those that stood around him. There was no joy in his face. No love in his eyes. Indeed, he did not appear at all involved in the auspicious event that was about to take place. He was intent only on the figure of the Pope on the platform directly above him. And as he saw the lips of the Sayeed look-alike part and his right arm rise to his chest, George felt his body move, not slowly like the day he tried to follow his cousin in the sand, but swiftly, like the breeze that flew across the ocean. His arms flung open, wide like Christ on the cross. He prayed for forgiveness as he shoved the Pope from his feet and begged for God's mercy for the soul of the young man who was about to commit suicide.

He sailed from the platform. Together they uttered *Allahu Akbar,* for indeed, God is Great, and their bodies, now joined, disintegrated in a flash of heat.

CHAPTER 38

▼

New York City, Monday October 5, 1998

She walked the six blocks along the broken sidewalk to her subway stop at 149th Street and the Grand Concourse for the last time. Catcalls and stares followed her into the station but no one stopped her. By now, she was used to the smell of urine that permeated the air at the bottom of the cement stairs. She hugged her large jacket around her. The canisters, filled with gunpowder and shrapnel that she had so painstakingly prepared, pressed into her ribs. The sides of her lips tuned up slightly. She dug her hand into her pocket and pulled out a single worn token. Without thinking, she dropped it into the slot and passed through to the platform where she waited with the few other seemingly indifferent passengers. No one cared who you were. They didn't want to know. They had plenty of their own problems.

The Number 5 train pulled noisily into the station. She and the other passengers stepped robotically through its open doors. Yellow plastic benches lined the sides of the metal car. Despite the rush hour, it was practically empty. Not too many people in this part of the Bronx had jobs to go to in the city. She took a seat near the door and stared unseeing at an ad above the window opposite her. "Learn skills for the next millenium. BTC offers daytime and nighttime courses."

A little over an hour later, she exited the train at South Ferry in Lower Manhattan and crossed the street into Battery Park. She paid no attention to the mix of historic brick buildings interspersed among metal and glass skyscrapers behind her. A chill wind whipped through the park's large trees, bare under overcast skies. She walked purposefully, though careful not to overexert herself, past the war memorial to the ticket booth in Castle Clinton. The next ferry left in 45 minutes.

She joined the long line of passengers, mostly tourists and several elementary school classes. Vendors parked their carts alongside them on the pier in hopes of eking out a day's wages. A trio of young men amused the crowd with jokes, music and antics while they waited. A babble of languages mixed with laughter filled the air. She was patient. Her calm composure and buoyant spirits gave her a radiant aura. A pair of police officers on the beat strolled by. The younger of the two smiled at her as they passed. She smiled back.

The ferry approached. It was a handsome boat, large and white with a bright yellow stripe and 'The Statue of Liberty' scripted across it in green. Yasmine boarded and took a seat on the upper deck. It was warmer inside but she wanted to experience every moment. Leaning into the wind, she was captivated by the cold beauty of the statue, her strong, feminine curves adding movement to the stone, determination visible in her uplifted arm and her large hollow eyes. She saw no conflict in that. Her joy rose from her mission, not the vision of the form before her. Americans took their icons seriously but Islam rejected all forms of idolatry. It made her mission that much easier.

The wind freed strands of her long wavy hair from the band that held it in place at the nape of her neck. They whipped haphazardly around her face. Today, the day of her death, she felt no hate, only peace in her soul. She looked beautiful and serene, her shiny dark tresses framing her oval face and dark eyes. Only her naturally olive skin was sallow and her lips slightly blue, prompting the woman next to her, a teacher chaperoning her third grade class, to suggest that she sit indoors. Yasmine pulled her jacket around her more tightly and simply smiled in return. The pockets so dutifully sewn by her mother's callused but nimble hands, pressed into her. There was no cause for anxiety. The blast would occur only when she closed the circuit. Gently, she touched the detonator switch, confirming its position. So simple. So deadly. A flush rose in her face, the glow of anticipation masking her illness.

The ferry docked at Liberty Island. She disembarked and followed the large groups of schoolchildren to the base of the statue where they waited in line to ride the elevator up into the pedestal. She turned about several times, keeping her eyes on the huge shoulders of the Lady of Liberty. Soon, she would be looking down from the heavens.

> *Give me your tired, your poor*
> *Your huddled masses yearning to be free*
> *The wretched refuse of your teeming shore*

Send these, the tempest tossed to me:
I left my lamp beside the golden door.

She might have been moved by the words, but Emma Lazarus was a Jew so she knew them to be a lie. All of America was a lie. Duped into submission by politicians touting democracy as freedom, devoid of spirituality, driven by the pursuit of material goods that they had learned to exalt above all. She would save as many souls as possible; the rest would follow when the revolution prevailed. As she knew it would. The truth was plain to see. Strange, that it was not plain to them.

She planned to trigger the bombs from the top level of the pedestal. With the amount of explosives she carried, the blast would radiate 100 feet around her. She moved as if in a trance. Stepping out of the elevator into the monument, the New York Harbor came into full view. She was shocked by the size of the room. Now she was not sure that damaging the pedestal would bring the statue down. Again, she touched the switch but did not press it just yet.

When she spotted the winding staircase that led inside the Lady's crown, she knew what she must do. It was a long climb, twenty-two stories, but Allah had given her the strength to carry out her mission from the highest height. Her body was tingling with excitement and she felt stronger, healthier than she could ever remember. She approached in a dream, and climbed step by step.

As she stepped onto the very top step, and entered the crown, she saw that it was filled with school children, chaperones and tourists. The stares mildly surprised her, but she couldn't know that her lips were blue and her smooth skin, transparent. Yet again, her hand found the switch and her smooth fingers grasped it. All twenty cylinders were set to explode. As blackness surrounded her, she marveled at how very quiet it was.

A persistent beep penetrated her consciousness and her eyelids fluttered rapidly. Bright light washed over her. She anxiously anticipated her first view of Paradise.

Beep, beep, beep, beep. The warm sun bathed her face. She was having difficulty opening her eyes. She so desperately wanted to see the heavens, the higher domain of *Allah* to whom she had dedicated her life and martyred her soul.

Something disturbing penetrated her consciousness. For a moment she was unsure. She recognized that sound. Countless childhood hospitalizations, many in the United States, had burned the beep-beep of the heart monitor into her brain. Tetrology of Fallot. Congenital heart disease. As a child, she was cyanotic and suffered from fainting spells. But as she grew, her stamina increased and she fainted rarely. She had been a superlative soldier, a devoted freedom fighter.

Her eyelids flew open and her eyes darted wildly about their sockets, taking in every millimeter of the room. Realization flooded her. Failure! Her body felt leaden with anguish and disappointment. Her head arced back, pressing into the large, soft pillow and her mouth opened wide, emitting a loud, mournful wail that grew in intensity as her lips parted and the sound from deep within her soul filled the room, a lamentation of utter despair. The baleful, undulating moan rose in pitch and vigor reaching a crescendo that shook the walls of the sterile white room and penetrated its large door so that the two guards posted outside leapt to their feet in fear, their own hearts pounding, adrenaline pumping. The moment they burst into the hospital room, her death shriek arrested abruptly. The only sound now was the flat, incessant whine of a heart monitor in search of a beating heart.

STATUE OF LIBERTY BLAST AVERTED
By Sidney Barr, Associated Press

New York, October 5—Police released the identity this morning of a young woman suspected of attempting to blow up the Statue of Liberty. She was 22-year-old Yasmine Khalil. Police found a Jordanian passport and other papers in a Bronx tenement they believe Khalil used to assemble 12 bombs, sewn into the lining of the jacket she was wearing. They were led to the apartment by the landlord who contacted police after hearing a radio news report. It appeared that Ms. Khalil was about to detonate the bombs in a suicide mission when she collapsed after climbing twenty-two stories into the Statue's crown. She was rushed to New York Hospital where doctors discovered that she suffered from a congenital heart condition known as tetralogy of Fallot.

"This disease causes severe pulmonic stenosis of the main artery to the lungs, resulting in fainting and cyanotic spells upon exertion," said Dr. Andrew Watkins. "It's surprising that she made it as far as she did without collapsing."

Based on an analysis performed, the explosion could have been killed or injured everyone within a 100-foot radius. Experts also state that damage to the Statue would have been "irreparable." The FBI said a "massive investigation" was under way to find out whether Khalil was acting alone as an individual or as a member of a group. Possible motives are also being investigated. FBI Assistant Director Drew Morgan said the probe was global and progressing at a rapid pace. The Mayor released a statement confirming reports issued by the police and the FBI, but at the same time urged the public and the media not to jump to conclusions about the deceased.

CHAPTER 39

▼

Los Angeles, Monday October 5, 1998

Gideon sucked on a cigarette and regretted every drag. God knows he'd tried to quit, especially when Sharon first got pregnant with the twins. He glanced over at her from the sidewalk and saw her laughing with the boys as they tried to match their feet to the imprints in the cement. Their twin sons were nine and Maya, the greatest surprise of his life, was three.

God, she was gorgeous, he thought, admiring Sharon from the distance. A real California girl. Long legs. Great body, even after three kids. Recently, she'd traded her long locks for a really short cut and he thought she looked even more beautiful.

He certainly wasn't what her parents had expected or hoped for. He was ten years older, an Israeli with heavily accented English and they lived halfway around the globe. Not the sort of guy movie mogul Ted Rimer and his celebrity wife had in mind for their only daughter. But three grandchildren later they were resigned to the reality of it. They knew that he adored Sharon and made sure that she and their children had all the comforts she had grown up with in Beverly Hills. Not easy on a military officer's salary.

He took another drag. God, he loved American cigarettes. He'd looked forward to this vacation more than his kids had. He needed to get out, away, feel like a kid again himself. No cell phone, no pager. Gideon was convinced that mobile phones were the eleventh plague, raining down on Israel's streets, restaurants and theaters. The tiny country was jammed with people jabbering into their phones. There was no privacy anymore and certainly no down time.

He blinked a few times. He was still tired. The older he got the harder the jet lag hit. Still, the last few nights he'd slept better than he had in months. Hell, at home he was practically an insomniac. It was no wonder. There was no room for a mistake, or a guess. Miscalculations meant lives. The last few months they'd had a few disasters. Two elite units wiped out due to faulty intelligence. Just thinking about it gave him a headache. He sucked on his cigarette. He was getting too old for this. Fifteen years in military intelligence was enough for anybody.

He had once considered politics. He was highly decorated, well respected, and the Israeli public had a penchant for war heroes. But Sharon was probably right. No, she was always right. Israeli politics would put him six feet under. He'd retire soon and head for academia.

He finished his cigarette and tried to relax, something that didn't come naturally to him. He looked at his watch and wondered when the doors were going to open. His father-in-law was due to arrive with his co-producers in a studio limo for the screening of his latest release.

He wasn't used to this sort of thing. Half of Hollywood would be there. Invitation only. The baby stayed home with Grandma, but Grandpa gave the thumbs-up for the twins to see the film despite its R-rating. The boys couldn't wait to sit in the balcony. He thought they were more excited about that than the action thriller they were about to see.

Photographers and TV crews set up their equipment and fans were beginning to line up behind barricades along the sidewalk. Looks like we're gonna make the evening news, he thought. The October sun was beginning to dip and a light breeze swept through the air. A young man in a red jacket began directing invitation holders towards two brass stands separated by a red chord. Sharon was waving to him to join them.

He crushed out his cigarette and headed from the sidewalk into the Chinese Theater courtyard. He had taken several steps in her direction when a man hurriedly crossed his path, forcing him to stop dead in his tracks. The man was dressed in an oversized Hawaiian shirt, black jeans and tennis shoes. But it wasn't the man's clothing that caught his attention. It was his face. Christ, he knew that man.

Sharon was calling his name. Never mind, he thought. Gideon continued towards her and his boys. They were near the front of the line of invitation holders. They'd be going into the theater at any moment. The man in the Hawaiian shirt stood several feet behind them. Sunglasses hung from a beaded chain around his neck. Gideon was tweaked. He didn't like it not being able to place the stranger and liked it less that he didn't appear to belong. He shook his head as if to shake the thought from his mind. This was America. It was no crime to lounge around a movie theater in a loud shirt. He had to be wrong. Anyone up to something funny wouldn't be wearing an outfit like that.

He joined his family. Maybe he should introduce himself. Get reacquainted. That way, he could keep an eye on him. Gideon avoided turning around and staring in his direction. But the hairs on the back of his neck bristled and he knew he couldn't let it go.

He tapped another cigarette out of the box.

"C'mon, Gideon," Sharon said lightly, "put it away. We're going inside in a minute." She scrutinized the man she had spent the last fifteen years with. "Are you O.K? What's goin' on?"

"Uh, nothing." He looked around. The man in the shirt was looking straight ahead, but not at him, not at anything at all. A small smile played at his lips like he was remembering a private joke. Gideon stepped out of line and walked back in the man's direction. Now he knew. Gideon had interrogated him himself. The man had spent two years in jail for murder, but was released later in a swap; 135 Palestinians for two Israelis.

Gideon looked around for a cop. With all the celebrities about to arrive, he was sure there'd be a few black and whites. He was about to turn and look for them, but stopped himself. Was he nuts? What was he going to say to them? Maybe the guy was just visiting, like he was.

Instead, he approached him directly and said, "*Ahi*, my brother, got a light?"

The man's smile widened into a grin. Almost imperceptibly, his hand glided under his shirt. Gideon needed no more. With his left arm, he pushed the man's hand down and twisted it behind his back, grabbing for the other arm as well, but he slipped. The man spun around, ran for the entrance of the theater and disappeared through the large, open doors. Gideon chased him to the doors, but was stopped by the young man in the red jacket.

"Sorry sir, you can't go in there."

"Listen," Gideon hissed, "call the police. Clear these people out." He purposely avoided looking back at Sharon.

"Sorry sir, you'll have to wait while I call management."

"I'm plainclothes. Tell them it's a Section 3 emergency." Gideon didn't know what the hell that meant, but he prayed the kid would buy it. He did. Gideon dashed into the entryway. He felt a heaviness in his chest as he ran. Too many cigarettes. It took a moment for his eyes to adjust to the dim light of the cavernous lobby. He looked up and down the large art deco halls. A teenage girl waited expectantly behind the refreshment counter.

"Did you see a guy in a Hawaiian shirt run through here?"

She shook her head indifferently.

Gideon headed left when he heard the jangle of keys and heavy footsteps behind him. He turned to face two large uniformed officers. He was about to inform them of what he knew when the two grabbed his arms, pinned them behind him and shoved his face into the wall.

As one officer began frisking him, the other said, "You're under arrest for disturbing the peace and impersonating a police officer. You have the right to remain silent. Anything you say may be held against you in a court of law. If you don't have the means for an attorney, one will be appointed for you." The officer continued to recite a litany of rights as he snapped handcuffs over Gideon's wrists. With all the celebs on their way, they weren't taking any chances having a kook running around. All they needed was a deranged fan on the premises.

The officer looked up from rifling through Gideon's wallet and said, "You gotta passport on you?"

"No, I don't carry it with me. Listen, I'm...ooof!

The officer who had cuffed him slammed him into the wall. "We ain't interested. You tell it downtown. There's a party here tonight and you're not crashin' it.

"Bomb. A guy with a bomb..." Pain shot through his head as the officer brought something down on him, hard. Don't lose consciousness, he willed himself. He was having trouble standing and leaned into the wall. The officer was squeezing his left arm, keeping him upright.

"Hold on a minute, Franky." Still examining his ID, Sanchez asked him, "What's your name?"

"Perry, General Gideon Perry, Israel Defense Forces, ID No. 2570073," Gideon answered, emphasizing the *General.* Franky still had Gideon's face pressed up against the wall. Sanchez signaled him to lighten up.

"OK, General Perry, let's hear about the bomb."

Franky made a face at Sanchez, but Sanchez held up his hand.

Gideon's head was exploding with pain. He closed his eyes and opened them, hoping he could speak, answer the officer coherently.

"Somewhere in this building is a man I interrogated a few years ago. He's on our terrorist list. I believe he's dangerous. He is wearing a loud yellow Hawaiian shirt. He may be wired with a bomb."

Gideon was overcome with nausea and doubled over, gagging and coughing. Sanchez signaled the girl behind the counter for some water and said to Franky, "Move him over to that chair and call for back-up."

Franky didn't like it, but he complied. Let Sanchez take the rap if this guy turned out to be a nut. He didn't much like kikes or chicanos. He was just paid to keep the peace.

Sanchez inspected Gideon's international driver's license, his military ID card. "O.K., for the moment, I am giving you the benefit of the doubt. What you are telling me is very serious. If you are lying, I have friends in the DA's office and I will personally make sure that you are hit with everything in the book. But this is Hollywood where stars rule and entertainment icons call the shots. You may be a nut, but if this theater comes down, Hollywood goes down with it."

Gideon nodded and held one arm across his stomach. His speech was staccato-like, but clear. "He's thin. Hawkish features, taller than me, broad shouldered, rough dark skin, wavy black hair. Hawaiian shirt."

"What makes you think he's got a bomb."

Gideon was reeling. What indeed? Minutes were flying by. Nothing he could put his finger on except that the guy just didn't belong in Southern California. Maybe he was wrong. Maybe he had a rich uncle who had talked him out of liberating his country and into joining him in business in Anaheim.

"Gut," was all he managed to say

The manager hurried over. "We're ready to let the guests in. We want them all seated before the VIP's start arriving."

Sanchez looked at Gideon. "What do you say, General?"

The water had helped. His mind was clearing, by necessity. Gideon looked up at the high ceilings, then all around him. Addressing the manager, he asked, "Do you have plans for this building?"

The manager shrugged. "Maybe. I don't know." Then he brightened. "Yeah, the theater was renovated not too long ago. I may have something in the office."

They followed the manager to the back. "Usually, the architects keep these things, he said over his shoulder, "but they left one roll behind. It's been lyin' around for a while."

Gideon turned to Sanchez. "Do you think someone could let my wife know I'm all right? She's out there in the line. She saw me chase this guy into the lobby."

Sanchez nodded. "She already made a commotion at the door. So you're Ted Rimer's son-in-law, to boot. That name carries a lot of weight around here."

Gideon smiled. Fifteen years living with him in Israel had injected some *chutzpah* into his laid-back California girl.

The Hollywood precinct captain arrived in dress blues and caught up with them at the manager's office door. He was on his way to the theater for the opening when the call came through to his car. "I want to know what is going on here."

Sanchez introduced Gideon to the Captain. "This is General Gideon Perry, Captain. Israel Defense Forces, Military Intelligence. He's here on vacation, sir. He says he spotted a man on their terrorist list and when he approached him, the guy bolted into the building."

"Nothing more concrete than that to tell me?"

Gideon just shook his head. The captain pursed his lips. Some of Hollywood's biggest stars would be here tonight, dozens of entertainment industry big wigs and a number of the city's politicians. If there was a nut in the building, he wanted him out. If there was a nut with a bomb…He studied Gideon, who stared back at him.

"Get our SWAT team and the bomb squad out here, but tell them to keep it quiet. Rendezvous around the back. Have them stay put. Send in only the team leader and one other for deployment instructions." Then to Gideon, he said, "You'd better be for real. Sanchez, run his ID. Verify with whoever it is you need to…"

"I'll make it easy for you, Captain." Retrieving his wallet, Gideon pulled out the card of the Israeli Ambassador in Washington. On the back, he penned the ambassador's private home number.

Another officer came running toward them. He pulled the Captain aside. As he spoke, they saw the Captain go pale. Turning to Gideon, he said, "Speak."

Gideon looked at the plans that the manager had laid out on his desk. They included the ceiling above the theater in which the screening would soon begin.

"A lot depends upon what kind of explosives he has and how he is planning to use them. If he is setting plastics, he doesn't need much. I'd put it here," Gideon said, pointing to a center supporting beam, "and bring the theater down. If he's on a suicide mission, he'll want to be closer to the crowd, to the screen area, where the VIP's will be."

"I think you should know, General, a suicide bomber just blew out the Eiffel Tower in Paris. Another went off at a papal ceremony at the Vatican. No final word on the number of casualties yet." He clenched his teeth and his jaw muscles began to twitch. "Something is going on here, but whatever it is, Los Angeles is not going to be added to that list."

Gideon stood stock still. He gathered now that Y's message to cancel his vacation was somehow connected to this event. He momentarily considered contacting Jerusalem for more information, then rejected the idea out of hand. At this point, he knew more than they did. And he knew something about the man who thought he was taking a one-way trip to Allah.

Gideon was clenching his jaw so tightly, a sharp pain shot up the left side of his face. Suicide bombs struck without warning, in the most innocent of places, against the most innocent of victims. Its purpose unfathomable, the bomber was gone, his own blood spattered and mixed with the blood of his victims, leaving only grief and devastation behind.

A young woman in a red jacket shoved her head through the office door. "The theater is full, Mr. Oatman. Ticket staff says they never received instructions to hold."

Gideon headed straight for the door.

"Where are you going?"

"My wife and boys are inside," he said without slowing down. "I'm getting them out."

The Captain signaled Sanchez to follow him. "Help him out and get him back here. Where the hell's the bomb squad? And the SWAT team?" he barked.

Gideon headed straight for the balcony. His family was seated in the front row, overlooking the mezzanine. As he took the stairs two at a time he tried to recall as much as he could about the man in the Hawaiian shirt. Ahmed Kabir was one of nine brothers. Born in 1968, he was raised in the village of Rafat, a bastion of the militant Liberation Brotherhood Army. One brother was a high-ranking Islamic militant. Another headed an Arab-Israeli peace coalition. A third was an agronomist. He worked closely with the Israelis who supplied hi-tech irrigation systems to his farm in Gaza. Crazy world. Ahmed, he remembered, liked to talk. Gideon could hardly shut him up the last time he was in their hands. He didn't care about their questions. He said whatever he had on his mind. Mostly, he yammered on about freedom fighters, Palestine and whatever had made headlines that week. Gideon would never have tagged him as suicide mission material. He was unstable. Too flighty. His cheeks burned as he raced to the top of the stairs. When would the madness stop? It was one thing to wage war on land you claimed for your own, but did they really think they could take on the entire world? Maybe not, but they sure knew how to make it hurt.

From the balcony landing, he could see that most of the guests below were seated, but many were still milling about, congratulating the film's stars and making sure the producers noticed them. He spotted his father-in-law below, his tall, slim, still athletic frame easy to identify near the front of the theatre. His head was inclined as he listened to a much shorter man, the director, talking to him. Gideon knew that each intended to say a few words about the film before it opened. He figured that left about ten minutes before the theatre darkened. Would Kabir wait? He had no idea. Where was the bastard anyway? Gideon's eyes scanned the theatre, as he tried to analyze the best spot for a hit like this.

Shit. His father-in-law nodded as the director patted him on the shoulder. They had wound up their conversation and looked expectantly at the crowd, ready to begin the program. Gideon scanned the theatre stage directly behind them. At stage right, he caught a ripple in the curtain's edge and glimpsed a spot of bright yellow.

He turned and grabbed Sanchez, running back down the stairs. "Stage right," he said.

"What about your family?" he asked, racing down the stairs with him.

"No time, and too much commotion if I try to take them out now. Let's get this over with before it's too late." They were safer in the balcony anyway, Gideon acknowledged to himself, almost guiltily.

Before they reached the bottom of the stairs, his father-in-law was on stage, recounting an anecdote about the film. It would only be another minute before he introduced the director. A few words from the director would take no more than a couple of minutes before the lights went down.

Sanchez headed back to the office to update the Captain while Gideon came to a halt at the double doors leading into the main floor theatre. How was he going to get backstage without going down the main theatre aisle? He doubled back to the manager's office. The manager quickly led him through a small door and into a darkened area to the side of the stage. Almost directly in front of him, back turned, he saw a bright yellow Hawaiian shirt. He tiptoed slowly in Kabir's direction. By now, the police should be deploying its SWAT team. His father-in-law was smiling and shaking the hand of the film director who had just joined him on stage. He was barely two feet behind him now. Almost there.

Gideon heard the door behind him bang open as it slammed into the adjacent wall, and watched with horror as Kabir swung around. Morons! Gideon wanted to scream. Two police officers burst through the door and into the darkened wing. They slowed momentarily to adjust their eyes to the limited lighting. Distracted by the noise, the two men onstage paused to look in their direction, just in time to see an intruder sprint out from the wings in their direction. In seconds, he was behind them. He shoved the director into the crowd and grabbed Sharon's father behind the collar.

One of the officers spoke into his radio. "He's onstage. He shoved d'Angelo into the crowd. He's got Ted Rimer by the neck."

Gideon understood immediately why. Sharon's father was slightly taller than Kabir. He made an adequate body shield. But why use a shield if you're going to blow yourself up? Why not just get it over with? Gideon knew he was missing something.

"I have a bomb," Kabir screamed into the microphone that Ted was still holding. The agitated crowd froze. Gideon used that moment to step onto the stage, but kept his distance. He hoped the crowd would remain stage struck long enough for them to get the upper hand.

"Ahmed, my brother," Gideon called to him, using his first name.

"You are not my brother," Ahmed spat.

"Forgive me," Gideon said, shrugging and lifting his hands, palms up in apology. The crowd was mesmerized by the drama unfolding before them, unwilling or unable to absorb its gravity, no one moved. "My Arabic has gotten a little rusty since we last met."

Gideon moved a few steps closer. "Why don't you complete your mission? You are in the perfect position. And that man you are holding is a very important gentlemen."

Kabir's mouth split into a grin. "You will help me. I wish to make a statement. Tell them to bring in the reporters and photographers that wait outside. They will be released to memorialize my actions and the message of the Supreme Ayatollah."

Gideon was stunned. It was just as they had predicted. Competing Islamic philosophies. The Supreme Ayatollah was in direct disagreement with the moderate Islamic leaders and their open dialogue with the West. So the Ayatollah had taken matters into his own hands and forged an alliance with Al Rasuul's LBA. He had filed a report just before he left that included Kanner's paper from the ISI warning of the potential for precisely this kind of allegiance. Gideon swore to himself. Why the hell did they collect all of this intelligence if nobody was going to pay any attention to it?

Gideon kept his voice calm and even. "This is your lucky night, Ahmed. The Captain of the Hollywood Police Precinct is here. I'll tell him what it is you are interested in. The reporters will need his permission to enter."

"They need only *my* permission," Kabir roared. "Just get them in here."

Gideon looked over his shoulder. The Captain was a few feet away, in the wings. Gideon stepped back, whispered something into the Captain's ear and came back out onto the stage. He dared not look in the direction of the balcony, or imagine what Sharon and the twins were going through. She and her dad were very close. He had even been a little jealous of their relationship until he came to understand it better. No point in thinking about that now. Or about the twins. He wanted to bring this guy down fast.

"I saw your brother, Ishmael," Gideon said, "just before I set out on this vacation. That's a nice family he's got." He spoke quietly, so that Kabir had to strain to hear him. "And he's making good money, working with that Israeli contractor. He takes good care of your mother and father. They are still heartbroken, of course, about Faisal," he said, referring to Kabir's older brother, a physics and chemistry teacher who accidentally blew himself up while constructing a bomb in his lab. "But surely, you will succeed where Faisal did not."

"I will join Faisal in heaven and take this audience with me as souvenirs. Satan has tainted you. You have cursed the people of Allah and now you shall pay."

Swathed in black from head to toe, the sniper knelt in the aisle next to Sharon and steadied his rifle on a small lightweight tripod. He adjusted the aluminum stand to just above the height of the balcony rail. Kneeling on one bent knee, he adjusted the sight so that the tall gentleman on the stage was in the center of its cross-hairs. Others dressed just like him silently fanned out across the parapet. The twins' eyes widened. The older twin opened his mouth to speak.

"He's going to shoot Grandpa!" he cried out. The last three words were muffled as Sharon abruptly clasped her hand over his mouth and pulled him down to the floor in front of the seats. Simultaneously, the lights in the theatre went out, except for those focused on center stage.

"What's going on?" Kabir demanded.

"They're bringing in the reporters and cameras. The filming works better when the lighting is focused on the subject."

Kabir was becoming agitated. "I can't see them! I want to see them! I have a message! I want to speak!"

In response to Gideon's signal, the lights came up just slightly so that the hall took on the glow of a distant shadowy moon.

"Ahmed," Gideon said quietly, "You'll need a mike."

Without turning or looking at him, Kabir nodded his approval. He moved forward with Sharon's father towards the front of the stage, then stopped. In thickly accented English, Kabir said to Ted, "I have two wires. I have only to join them, and we fly to heaven. Perhaps you and I, we shall close the circuit together. Or perhaps you are too big a coward."

Without warning, Kabir pushed Ted off the stage into the seats below. Several pinging noises whizzed through the air as he reached under his large, yellow print shirt. His body undulated in a slow motion death dance. He opened his mouth to speak but managed only a cough before crumpling quietly to the floor.

CHAPTER 40

▼

Washington, D.C., Monday October 5, 1998

Jamie Harris, law clerk to Justice Joseph Barrows, strode nonchalantly down the wide corridor of the United States Supreme Court. As usual, he strode with a confident upbeat stride. He loved the feel of the Court's understated elegance. Even more than that, he loved the atmosphere of challenge. Every day, the justices and their clerks struggled with the formidable task of interpreting the law and the Constitution. The intricacies of conflict, where the answers were anything but clear, took nine of the nation's most brilliant minds in vigorous debate to resolve complicated issues, often by the narrowest of margins.

And here he was. He relished every moment. Yet he was even more elated by where he was going next. A smile creased his handsome face. Two names would mark the victory of the Palestinian nation over the State of Israel. Nasser and Hassan—he would, of course, revert back to his family's original name before emigrating from Palestine—would be those most revered.

Two brilliant minds. Like King David and King Solomon of yore. Hey, the Jews had their day, he thought with a mental shrug. In fact, they'd had a few pretty good millennia. But that was going to change now. Half a century after the U.N. approved the state, they were fighting amongst themselves like shrews. Internally weakened, the time was ripe. So Allah had decreed. He had turned the tides against them. Oh well.

Jamie strode through the double doors into the chambers where less than one hour from now, Judge Melinda Samson-Knight would become Justice Samson-Knight. Briefly.

With great care, he set the small glass water bottles in their appropriate places and loosened the caps. He then walked around behind justice's bench, opened the thermal lunch box he'd left there the day before and loosened that bottle cap.

He checked his watch, removed a small incendiary device with a timer attached to it and laid it in the lunch box next to the water bottle. Timer set. With that, he strode out the back of the courtroom, stripping off his gloves as he did.

The morning sky was brilliant blue and clear. The perfect day for a ceremony. The previous day had been an exhausting one, coordinating emergency procedures for the targeted cities, analyzing possible sites and anticipating damage potential. They went through procedures for over a dozen conceivable bombs and scenarios—car bombs, like those used in Ireland and Turkey, attaché cases, gun powder based explosives, TNT-based explosives, plastic explosives, fertilizer bombs like those used in Oklahoma City and the World Trade Center. But their worst fear revolved around the one that was impossible to stop—the suicide bomb.

Unless they could pinpoint the locations *and* the bomber…Nadine left the thought unfinished. She reminded herself to check with Claude to discuss the SWAT teams although she knew they had already been placed on alert.

Despite her fatigue, Nadine had not slept well the night before. Since her run, she had not been able to rid herself of the feeling that she was missing something that was right before her eyes. She reviewed the scene over and over, but it's secret eluded her. She decided not to dwell on it and settled into the large courtroom with the hundred or so other guests. The nine justices of the Supreme Court, the President and Vice President would enter last.

The ceremony would last one hour, followed by a reception, but she couldn't stay away from the Pentagon that long. She was feeling apprehensive as it was. No need to add to her anxiety.

Claude Hennicker drove furiously into the government center and left his car in a no parking zone in front of the Supreme Court building. He flew up the stairs and prayed that the ceremony had not yet begun. He had never moved so fast in his life. He dashed through the security sensors, flashing his Pentagon identity card to the guard, and ran up to the courtroom. The doors were shut. His heart sank. As he approached, a uniformed secret service agent blocked his path.

Claude pulled out his ID. "Claude Hennicker, U.S. Department of Defense, Intelligence, Top Secret Security Clearance. This is an emergency. I need Dr. Nadine Kanner right away."

The secret service agent narrowed his eyes as he inspected Claude. At the same time, he raised his cuff to his mouth and spoke into it softly.

"I have an urgent situation out here." Within a hair's breath, another secret service agent, this one in plainclothes, exited the courtroom. Claude repeated his message, only now beads of sweat had begun to form on his brow.

"And while you're at it, get Jeff Reese, National Security Advisor out here too!" Claude was trying to keep his voice under control. The sound of applause echoed from the chamber as the nine justices, the President and his VP entered the room. The agent disappeared back into the courtroom. Moments later, Nadine appeared at the door, her eyes wide in anticipation.

Claude didn't say anything. He just shoved a manila folder stamped 'TOP SECRET' in large red letters, into her hand. She opened the folder and scanned the printout. It opened with a date.

"24 Jamad II"

"Tell me," she said.

"October 5."

Heart racing, she scanned the rest of the message.

Shaheed, Allah calls to you. Enter heaven and collect the rewards that await you in paradise.

Nadine felt weak in the knees, then she looked at Claude.

"This is it," Claude said.

"Yes." Damn it, damn it, damn it. She knew and yet she didn't know. She thought about what was going on the room behind her. Her good friend about to take a position on the highest court of justice in the land. The President, the Vice President, the eight other justices, the leaders of this country, assembled in one room, to celebrate democracy. Gathered to continue the tradition of freedom, the pursuit of justice, to protect the inalienable rights guaranteed to each and every citizen of the United States. Now the foes of everything the people in that room stood for, were poised to strike at America's heart.

She turned and stared at the closed door. And then she knew.

"Clear out this room. You have got to clear out this room right now!" she barked at the secret service agent.

He stared back at her, unbelieving. "Sorry ma'am. You are going to have to explain yourself."

"The President, the justices, everybody in that room is in immediate peril."

While the agent whispered into his wrist, Nadine shot off half a dozen instructions. "Who has the guest list? I need it immediately. Seal off all the exits and lead the guests out one by one."

Claude pulled her over. "Are you sure?"

"Yes, yes, positive." Her senses were reeling. Why hadn't she seen it before? She cursed, then decided to stop wasting time.

"Get Phil Lathrop over here," she said to Claude. Turning to one of the agents, "I need to get behind the courtroom."

They ran, the agent in the lead, through a side doorway and down a long hallway leading to the chambers behind the courtroom. Nadine racked her brains. Where would they strike? How? With what?

"Has everyone in the room been scanned and cleared for entry?"

"Yes, ma'am."

So it wasn't going to come from within the room. She knew that the building was secure, but on occasions like this one, it was "swept" electronically before the President arrived, every hallway and room he would pass through, checked. Where was it going to come from?

"What's directly below us?" Nadine asked.

Claude and Jeff Reese, NSA chief, joined them. "Phil is on his way," Claude said. Reese skimmed the printout and looked at Nadine. "Is this all you've got? This building has been secured from top to bottom. Do you really think that it's going to happen now, here?"

Nadine understood his dilemma. She couldn't cancel the ceremony on a hunch. But it was more than a hunch. The signal had been given. And what better place? Anarchy and chaos would be the order of the day. The door to revolution would open wide. Extremist militias. Islamic fundamentalists. An opportunity in the land of opportunity.

Governments fell in other countries, not in the United States of America. There was always someone next in line. That was the precise calculation. The President, the Vice President, the Speaker of the House were all inside. Who was next in line?

"Ashford!" she gasped aloud. "That's why Senator Ashford isn't here! Don't you see? He's next in line for the Presidency." Nadine was flabbergasted by her own revelation. How could he? No time for that now. "Claude, what have we missed?"

His answer was immediate, but he kept his voice very low. "There is one possibility that's been nagging me but that we haven't discussed because the message says, *simultaneous detonation*. But given an opportunity like this," he cocked his head in the direction of the courtroom, "I'd go for sarin gas myself."

Jeff Reese blanched. "But wouldn't we know? How could they get it in here?"

"Sarin is colorless, odorless and an extremely efficient killer. It's one of the most toxic chemical agents known to man." Claude said. "It won't set off metal detectors or electronic sweeping devices. Technically, it's not a gas at all. It's stored as a liquid and actually disperses more like an aerosol, tiny droplets in the air, as opposed to a real gas. Heck, you could store it in a water bottle. It's extremely volatile though. I wouldn't recommend detonating it."

Reese practically jumped all over the agent. "Have your men been down in the basement, checked the ventilation systems, everything?

The agent looked confused. "Sir, you know the procedures. We've checked the entire building. Everyone and everything *inside* the building has been cleared," he concluded.

"It's someone on the inside," Nadine said. "Someone who's got clearance. Get me a list of everyone present in the building and everyone who has access. Start checking the entire place again. And for God's sake, clear out that room!"

The President was grateful for the bottle of water. His recent diagnosis as a diabetic explained why he felt constantly thirsty. Naturally, now was not the time to pour a glass. But at least it was available for the appropriate moment. Just then, a secret service agent leaned over his shoulder and whispered in his ear.

"I'm sorry Mr. President. You're going to have to leave. It's a matter of national security."

The President knew better than to argue. He rose discreetly, nodded to the Chief Justice and allowed himself to be led out of the courtroom. The country was used to this sort of thing. He was hurried down a back flight of stairs into the garage and out of the building in his waiting limousine.

Gratefully, he accepted the bottle of water the driver handed to him as he slipped into the back seat. From a corner of the garage, Jamie smiled. He had left nothing to chance.

No one in the courtroom had batted an eyelash when the President left, but the murmuring began when the scenario was repeated for the Vice President and the Speaker of the House. Finally, an announcement was made.

"Ladies and gentlemen. Although it is strictly precautionary, we are going to have to evacuate the room. Please file out as quickly as possible, row by row, through the doors at the back of the courtroom."

For a moment, nobody moved. Senators, Congressman, guests, all just looked at one another until the agents began herding them out, quietly at first, but more urgently with each row. As the Chief Justice swept by the table beside which he was about to inaugurate Judge Samson-Knight, his robe knocked over a bottle that had been set there. The cap had been loosened and its clear contents quickly spread across the table.

"Odd," he thought to himself. He didn't recall ever seeing water bottles at official ceremonies. The justice's sleeve soaked up a small amount of the liquid.

Quickly, he pulled it away. Once in chambers, he slipped out of the robe and hung it in the closet. The other justices, along with Judge Samson-Knight joined him.

"I'm sorry Melinda," he said, taking both of her hands in his. A frown creased his face. "Let's find out what this is all about." They did not have to wait. Several secret service agents burst into the chambers. "We're evacuating the building. Please follow us. Quickly!"

The agents split the justices into groups of three. The Chief, Justice Barrows and Samson-Knight, followed the lead agent. As they descended the staircase, the Chief began sweating. His face blanched and the muscles around his eyes began to twitch. The agent grabbed him and hurried him along, but the Chief doubled over in pain.

"Get me a medic and a stretcher," he commanded into his wrist. "The Chief Justice has collapsed."

Nadine breathed a momentary sigh of relief. The room had been safely evacuated with no casualties so far. But they weren't out of danger yet. Most people were still milling about the building. Special agents in yellow hooded chem suits and boots were already testing the room. She tapped her foot impatiently, waiting both for the lists and the report form inside.

"Confirmation, Dr. Kanner. Sarin. But it's odd. It's much more effective when dispersed as an aerosol. Whoever set this up…"

The explosion behind them sent them diving for the floor. It was small, more like a loud popping sound, but it was enough to unnerve them.

A suited agent radioed from within the room. "That's it! Get out, everyone out. The sarin vapor is dispersing."

Nadine ran down the hall and headed for the exit. People were pouring out into the street. She caught up to Phil and Jeff Reese conferring with the secret service agent in charge. "It's sarin. Contact each car, President, VP and the House Speaker. They mustn't touch or drink anything."

The driver glanced in his rear-view mirror. He thought the President looked rather pale, but when he bent over and didn't straighten up, he knew something was wrong. What was with the two goons that were in the back seat with him? He was tempted the open the glass partition, but used the speaker instead.

"Excuse me, Mr. President, is everything all right back there?"

He locked eyes with the agent seated next to him. "Tell the hospital to be ready in three minutes." The driver hit the accelerator. "Make that two."

CHAPTER 41

▼

Nadine sat unmoving in the dark, her knees pulled up to her chest.

The country was in a state of shock. After lying in state for three days, the President had been buried on a rainy Thursday afternoon. Congress was debating a declaration of war, but on whom? The perception of uncertainty emanating from the Hill was fueling adversity. Hysteria continued to dominate the airwaves as people called for closed borders, massive deportations and heightened isolationism. Extremist groups spewed more hate and bigotry. "I told you so," became their new mantra as their ranks swelled at an alarming rate.

Still visibly traumatized, the Vice President was sworn in. The Chief Justice was in ICU, but expected to survive. Senator Ashford was under indictment. Just about everyone who had ever set foot in the U.S. Supreme Court Building was under investigation. And a brilliant Supreme Court law clerk had been found dead of a knife wound to the heart.

New York and Los Angeles had averted the worst by chance. The Pope had survived but the young priest from Jaffa and several others had lost their lives. Israel had averted the worst. How, Nadine did not know. Damage to the Eiffel Tower was reparable. In Tokyo, the earthquake had inflicted so much damage, whatever happened there remained a mystery.

Indeed, democracy had taken a hit. The free world was shaken, if not quite brought to its knees. Fear and paranoia, precursors to totalitarianism, were on the rise. Home grown hate groups from Tampa to Seattle were vying for the front.

Privately, Nadine was being hailed as a hero. So why did she feel like shit? Because deep down inside, she knew that nothing had been resolved. This was just a setback, perhaps even a victory for *them*, whoever *they* were. But that wasn't it, either. It was something far more deeply personal. Her world had been turned upside down. Her son had been violated. And no one had paid.

Ashen shadows wrapped her in their sinewy arms. More and more, she felt like the black that enveloped her. Only a single silvery moonbeam kept her from giving herself over entirely to the gloom. It was the same moon, she knew, that hovered over the village the night her assailant died and revenge was born. The same moon that illuminated the room where she made love to Barak, bathing their bodies in its ardent glow. The same moon that lit her way through the forest to Fouad's house. The same moon that lit Daniel's way back to safety.

Here in the dark, alone with her pain, from an empty space in her soul—that void created when Jeremy was taken from her—something began to churn. The sour taste of hate slowly filled the chasm, and she knew what she had to do. Everything she had done until now, her training, her special knowledge, her whole life, led her to this moment. All along, she had called it patriotism. Nothing had changed. Only its name. Now it was called vengeance.

She laid the photos three across on the table. Two stared straight back out at her. Young faces. Faces she did not know. The third was less conspicuous. The shot was blurred, its subject in profile. But the man was unmistakable.

"Truth is light to the eyes," the doctor had said knowing that her personal mission was not yet over.

She dialed Ann Arbor and spoke to her mother. One more, short trip to the Middle East, she explained, and she'd be back. Her voice was cold and flat. No, there was no need to worry. She was just tired. She sent her love to her sleeping boys and laid the handset in its cradle.

She booked a reservation on a flight leaving the following morning then left word for Brad that she was taking a few days to rest and not to worry about her. She packed only as much as could fit into a carry-on bag; anything unforeseen she could pick up there, and went to bed.

She awoke early the next morning, rested after a dreamless sleep. There was one last-minute item left to pack. Deftly, she wrapped her knife in a fibrous cloth woven from leaden thread and calmly slipped it into the false bottom of her flight bag. The x-ray beams of the airport security system could not penetrate the flexile material. Next, she unlocked a small portable safe that held several items she'd been trained to use in the event of certain emergencies and extracted an alternate passport. No need to alert the Mossad of her visit; she planned to stay only a few days. Before stepping into the shower, she poked around the cupboard under the bathroom sink and found what she was looking for. A box of Clairol Nice n'

Easy. Just how much fun did blondes *really* have, she wondered as she straightened up. Funny, even in home territory, her apartment had been prepared as if she were in the midst of the enemy. Perhaps she was.

The results were stark. Platinum blonde and some hard gel transitioned her into another generation. Black liquid liner accentuated her deep green eyes and red lipstick exaggerated her already full mouth. She slipped into a pair of tight fitting jeans, boots and a short leather jacket. Except for small gold earrings, she kept jewelry to a minimum. She was ready to go. She gave herself one last look in the mirror before hefting her carry-on bag onto her shoulder. Running and a smooth complexion, had shaved a decade off her real age.

"Not bad," she said aloud, accepting her own compliment.

She walked a mile before flagging down a cab to the airport and purchased her ticket at the counter in cash. Settling into her coach seat, she felt calm, more buoyed than she actually had in days. She was looking forward to the next several hours to formulate the final details of her plan.

Israel's international airport was jammed. Five flights had landed at the same time and customs officials looked more harried than usual. Nadine hoped that meant less likelihood of being among those travelers randomly stopped and questioned. Normally, leaving the area with just a shoulder bag would draw the attention of the watchful agents at the exit. She sidled up alongside a woman with several large suitcases, precariously piled onto a luggage cart. The top suitcase teetered as the woman tried to steady it and keep tabs on three small children at the same time. Exuberant over having escaped the confines of air travel, they ran about in circles, discharging hours of pent-up energy in the large baggage claim area.

"Here, let me help you with that," Nadine said, catching the suitcase just as it started sliding off the top of the heap. The suitcase would help her blend in with the hundreds of other passengers lumbering through the exit.

The young mother lunged for her smallest boy who was about to ride off on someone else's luggage cart. When she returned, she smiled gratefully at Nadine. Nadine smiled back and towed the suitcase behind her carefully avoiding eye contact with the officers who alternately waved people through and stopped others. It rolled unsteadily on plastic wheels as she guided it towards the customs gate.

Engaging the young mother in conversation, she even took the hand of her little girl as the two strolled by the inspection area. She hoped the ruse would work and not draw undue attention to their little troupe. They had almost passed the inspectors when the woman's young son turned around and made a beeline for the baggage area they'd just left. Before he could get far, a customs officer scooped him up and directed him back to his mother. She thanked him profusely, but the officer barely nodded having already turned his attention toward a gentleman behind them carrying only a canvas duffel bag. Nadine let go her breath, long and slow. One minute later, they were outside.

Normally, her heart soared whenever she touched down in the warm Mediterranean sunshine, but today she was indifferent. She shared a shuttle to Jerusalem with five ultra-Orthodox men obviously unhappy with her presence in their midst. But they relaxed when they realized that the young woman was content to stare out the window in silence.

She checked into a small hotel in East Jerusalem's Arab sector. The building was ancient with high ceilings and stone walls, but the room was clean and tidy. She took a quick shower, closed the metal shutters over the windows to darken the room completely and lay down for a nap. It was going to be a busy night.

It was evening when she awoke and the streets were alive with activity. She dressed quickly and headed into the city center. At the new municipal complex, she bought a sandwich and sat down on a bench in the courtyard, eating slowly and observing her surroundings. A group of boys nearby argued about who was better in soccer and whether to go to the movies.

"Hey there," Nadine said. "Movie tickets are on me in exchange for a small favor." She held up a folded sheet of note paper and nodded in the direction of the police station. "Deliver this, *in person,* to Detective Shimoni. When you come out with an answer," she held up a bill in her other hand, "this is yours."

The tallest boy snatched the note. "Be right back," he said, and the three trotted into the building.

It took them a few minutes to talk their way past the front desk, but the sergeant quickly tired of the argument. He had more important things on his mind, like getting laid that night. If they wanted Shimoni, what did he care? He didn't like Shimoni much anyway. Too serious. He opened a door that said, "No Admittance" and pointed to a tall, thin man intent on the sheaf of papers in front of him.

The boys wasted no time. They crowded around Shimoni, eager to get a peek at what was in the note. He looked at it and then at them.

"Who gave this to you?" he asked before unfolding the paper.

They answered at once, speaking rapidly.

"Some lady." "Kinda pretty." "Come on, open it up." "She looks American, even though her Hebrew's real good." "We get one hundred shekel when we come out with your answer."

Shimoni shot up an eyebrow. He already knew who had authored the note. He unfolded it and scanned the clean scrawl. Even her handwriting was intelligent. "Café Casablanca, East Jerusalem, 5:30?"

Shimoni stepped over to the window.

"Is that her?" he asked the boys, pointing at a blond woman in jeans seated on a bench below.

She sat with her arms open across the back of the bench, one ankle resting one the opposite knee. She looked completely relaxed, as if she were early for a date and was enjoying a few moments alone.

"Yes, yes. What's your answer? Come on, the movie starts in fifteen minutes."

"Tell her half an hour."

He watched from the window as the boys excitedly delivered the message and collected their prize. She stayed a few minutes longer, then without so much as a glance in the building's direction, she rose and strolled back in the direction of the Old City.

Shimoni eased into the chair opposite Nadine.

"How's Fouad?" was her first question.

"Don't you know?"

She shook her head. "I just arrived."

And not making any announcements, he thought to himself. He wondered what name she was using. No, actually, he didn't really want to know.

"Should I be flattered?"

She shrugged. "I owe you. You saved Daniel's life. That means everything to me."

Shimoni nodded. No need to kid himself. Her every move was self-serving. But he had nothing to lose. "So you're here to finish the job."

"With your help."

With yours, Shimoni thought to himself. Catching them was all he'd thought about since she'd left. Some, like Barak, could shrug their shoulders and walk away. They had bigger issues on their minds. But two innocent, elderly people had been brutally murdered, and he couldn't sleep at night knowing that their murderers were a few kilometers away. Untouchable. His frustration mounted with each passing day. The intelligence black hole he was encountering in the autonomous zone left him with very few options.

"I'm listening."

"First tell me about Fouad."

Shimoni gave her a lopsided smile. "He'll live. He came out of the coma, but he's not entirely back yet, if you know what I mean. The doctors aren't saying what damage there is; it's a game of wait and see."

Nadine was silent.

"I'm not sure how much he understood, but I told him about Daniel."

Her response was a flicker of her eyelids. She's changed, Shimoni thought to himself. She's gone cold. He studied her for a moment. No, that wasn't it. He'd seen it before. He just wasn't used to seeing it in a woman. It was the look of a professional. Devoid of emotion. Her eyes, unreadable, would betray nothing. She was a woman on a mission; a woman who had come to kill.

She opened a manila envelope that lay on the table in front of her and extracted a stack of eight-by-ten photos. Shimoni recognized the first three. They were the same photos Barak had handed over to him, with a shrug and skeptical remark. Full face photos of Al Rasuul's first lieutenant, Issam Ibn Assad and the graduate student, Sabri, whose role was unclear, but they suspected was technical, mocked him. The third photo showed a slight, dark man in profile. The quality of the photo was less than perfect.

Shimoni glanced apprehensively in the direction of the waiter. Nadine caught his gaze.

"Don't worry. I've already tipped him three times his normal night's tips to leave us alone. I told him you were a private investigator I'm hiring to follow my husband. Naturally, he graciously offered to do it himself, but as you can see, I declined."

Still, Shimoni didn't like it.

"Let's go for a walk. Where are you staying?"

"At a small hotel not far from here."

"Let's go."

When they reached the entrance to the hotel, Shimoni leaned over as if to kiss Nadine on the cheek but instead, whispered in her ear.

"Walk straight through and out the back. If I'm not there in three minutes, leave."

He turned and left. Without looking back, Nadine walked through to the back alley. Three long minutes later Shimoni showed.

"Well, your waiter was no waiter. He's on somebody's payroll. Get your things. I have somewhere you can stay."

"Where's our tail?"

"He's sleeping it off next alley over." Shimoni's eyes narrowed slightly as he probed her face. "Who knows you're here?"

Nadine shrugged with a measure of indifference. "How did you know he'd follow you?"

"I didn't. That's why I had you go straight out to the back. If he followed you into the hotel, I'd know where to intercept you. Besides, I was fairly confident you could handle him yourself."

They wound their way through a myriad of narrow alleyways, passing from the Old City's Arab quarter into the Jewish quarter. Though the transition was subtle, the stone passages widened and took on a lighter hue. Night had fallen and street lamps now lit their way. They turned into another series of narrow lanes until Shimoni stopped and knocked on a large wooden door. A woman of indeterminate age opened it and greeted him warmly.

Her plain beauty struck Nadine. A magenta shawl laced with gold thread was wrapped tightly around her head concealing every strand of her hair. Her modest garb completely hid any hint of the woman's true form. She wore no makeup at all and her skin glowed clean with a dewy radiance. She listened as Shimoni spoke and then opened the door widely to let them in. She led them to a small room behind the kitchen with a single bed, a small table and chairs. She left them alone, but did not close the door behind her.

Nadine set her bag down at the foot of the bed, then spread the photos out on the table.

"Are these what I think they are?"

Nadine nodded. "Satellite photos. We only have a window of fifteen minutes each day when the satellite passes over Jericho."

"How did you get these?"

"I've earned the loyalty of some very valuable people over the years," she said matter-of-factly, without a trace of pretension. "Normally, these shots would not have been taken. In fact, officially, they don't exist."

There were several shots of Issam and Sabri inside a house and two more of the exterior, clearly identifying the address. He knew that house. He'd been there before.

"How did you find the house?"

This time it was Nadine's turn to smile. "Let's just say, trade secrets. But I will say this, it didn't happen overnight."

"You spied on every household in Jericho until you found them!"

Now Nadine laughed. "Cut the judgmental crap, Shimoni, or you and your wife won't have another private moment for as long as I have anything to say about it."

He studied the pictures more closely. "The detail is amazing."

"We could read the fine print on your morning newspaper if we were interested. Sabri made a few phone calls from that cell phone. We picked those up, too."

"Anything interesting?"

"Yeh," she said gathering up the photos. "It's not over yet and we have to move fast. The problem is, these photos are already twenty-four hours old. They could be worthless by now."

Shimoni was thoughtful. Then he nodded to himself.

"Are you going to give me a hint or just sit there agreeing with yourself for the rest of the evening."

"Fouad's son, Naji, disappeared the night Fouad found you. We think he was involved in the drive-by shooting against you that morning. We caught him trying to cross into Jordan on forged identity papers later that day. He was shot in the leg and hospitalized. I haven't yet linked him to the incident directly, but I've been biding my time, hoping he would lead us to some bigger fish. This may be our chance."

"What's his condition?"

"Quite good. He's been eating his mother's cooking—no Zionist hospital chow was going to pass his freedom fighting lips. He should be home free any day now."

"What about his family? They might keep pretty tight reigns on him."

Shimoni shook his head. "He's officially in custody. I can see to it that he has an opportunity for an outing. I'll stop by the hospital in the morning and see how quickly he can be released." Shimoni rose. "Aliza will give you some clothes; you'll blend in a little better should you decide to go out. I'll call you by nine."

Nadine nodded. He was right where she wanted him.

She rose early, but the members of the household were already up and out. Aliza had left her an outfit by the door and a note telling her where she could find something to eat. She dressed in the modest clothes—a loose fitting, long sleeved, button down shirt and ankle length skirt—but decided to go out for breakfast, making sure to be back by nine when Shimoni would ring. Before leaving the house, she wrapped her head in a scarf careful to cover even her bangs; the sign of a married woman. A woman of her age with a bare head would attract undue attention.

She stepped out into the sunshine and made her way along the flagstone pedestrian street toward a city square with shops and restaurants. Stopping at the first café, she drank black coffee and ate toasted sesame bread stuffed with cheese. Sated, she stood to leave, then stopped. A jolt ran through her. She backed up a little into a position from which she could see but not be seen, then, when he was well ahead of her, she left the café and followed.

Now, she had a dilemma. Shimoni would be calling soon. But Nasser was barely fifteen feet in front of her and moving fast toward the area of the Western Wall. She glanced at her watch. She had a few more minutes. Maybe she could get a sense of where he was going before she turned around. He was here and she would find him again, before the Mossad did. If they knew who they were looking for.

Rather than follow him down the stairs into the open expanse facing the Wall, she stepped out onto a wide ancient veranda directly opposite. From her vantage point, she could see the entire area: the Wall, the mosques above it and the surrounding vicinity. To its right, a stairway rose to the Temple Mount on which the Mosque of Omar was perched. To the left of the Wall, she had full view of the entranceway to the tunnels that ran under the Temple Mount. Sure that Nasser was headed toward the stairs to the mosque above the Wall, Nadine half-turned to leave but halted mid-turn, puzzled and surprised when she saw him disappear through a small door with a sign overhead: "Yeshiva Gedolah."

Shimoni had no trouble having Naji released into his custody for the next twenty-four hours. Naji's wound, though still tender and painful, had healed quickly. He wore the slight limp that remained like a medal. Feisty and anxious to get out of the hospital, Shimoni knew he'd have to keep a close eye on him. He cuffed Naji's hands behind his back and led him to his car.

"Where are we going?" Naji demanded to know.

Shimoni assessed the teen, his skinny frame, his young face, the inexperience that manifested his entire being, but there was something wild in his eyes, so all he said was, "You'll know soon enough."

He'd already gotten approval for his plan from his superior. Now all he had to do was make it work. And hope that Nadine was feeling cooperative. His thumb tapped the steering wheel. She was a tightened coil just waiting to spring.

When she saw Naji, she saw Fouad as a young man. Only the eyes were different. Fouad's eyes were kind, filled with laughter and love for everyone. Naji's eyes were frenzied, suspicious, filled with anger and hate. His look only deepened her resolve.

The receiver attached to the tiny explosive device fit nicely into the bottom of the hollow cane. That had been her only problem, but the solution presented itself when Shimoni mentioned that Naji had been shot in the leg. She had no problem replacing his cane with the one she had purchased that morning.

Within the hour they were at the Joint Command near Jericho. Once they saw the photos, the Palestinian police decided to cooperate to show that they were serious about cracking down on terrorists. They loaded into two unmarked cars. Naji and Shimoni in the first, Nadine and two other officers, all plainclothes, in the second. Though they departed from the same point, the Palestinians headed in another direction. She did her best to let Shimoni believe that she had provided the intelligence and was leaving the rest up to him. But she knew he was wary, convinced that she would leave nothing to chance. Never mind. To her, the end result was all that mattered.

The neighborhood they entered was nondescript, the houses separated by desert scrub. Palestinian sources confirmed that Issam and Sabri were still there.

They took up their positions and Naji began the short journey from the intersection to the safe house. As he stepped away, Nadine slipped the transmitter out of the small pack she carried and into her pocket. Shimoni caught the movement. He moved alongside her.

"Show me," he demanded.

Nadine responded with raised eyebrows, then slowly withdrew her hand. He looked from Naji to her palm and back and his anger grew. It was too late to stop him. Shimoni's normally dark skin took on a reddish hue as his rage threatened to erupt.

"Are you crazy?" he hissed through his teeth.

"If I was, I would go in there and do it myself."

"You don't know who you will hit. You could maim or kill innocent people."

Nadine stiffened and her eyes flashed but her voice was cold. "How can you talk to me about innocence? What crime did Daniel commit the day he rode off on his bicycle to visit a friend? What crime made him deserving of the torture they put him through? And what if you hadn't saved him? Are there innocent people in there?" she asked, pointing at the safe house where Daniel had been kept. "Is Naji innocent? We both know he tried to kill his own father. Are the men inside that house, innocent? You saw what they did first hand. Is what *we* do the work of innocents? You, me, the officers here, we all know the risks."

"But not murder, Nadine. You don't want to commit murder. It's not our way. It's not your way. That's why I'm a police officer, and that's why you serve a democracy. Bring them to justice."

She turned away and looked through a small pair of binoculars. Naji was limping slowly down the dusty street. She scanned the windows of the house. Most were open. The plan relied on that. Naji's presence would draw their attention away from the back of the house. The police, who had already surrounded the house, would smoke them out and take them, hopefully, with a minimum of gunfire. In the moments before the police fell on their quarry, if things went her way, Naji's cane would save them the trouble.

Well, she thought, we'll see. It was dangerous, she knew, to change her mind at this point. If she lost her chance, there would not be another. But if they brought her son's torturers down, so be it.

She jolted at the sound of the automatic machine gun fire. Naji was lifted into the air and suspended there momentarily as a hail of bullets spewing from the safe house riddled his thin body. But no one was prepared, in the seconds that followed, for the explosion that rocked the house and sent her and Shimoni face down into the dry ground. Several blasts followed the first. Even from their distance she could feel the heat. She heard Shimoni radio the others to move away from their positions and regroup at the intersection. Soon, the wail of sirens could be heard approaching.

Nadine raised her head and stared at the burning house. Were they in there? Was this over? She had wanted to see them with her own eyes. Maybe that would have been enough.

She heard Shimoni barking orders into his walkie-talkie, worried about the injured officers. He already had other things on his mind. He'd told her about the equipment and explosives that he'd seen in the house when he rescued Daniel. She dropped her head down onto her folded arms and cried with relief.

CHAPTER 42

▼

Barak nursed his scotch. It was rare for him to drink, but he'd been keyed up since spotting Nadine at the airport. All he'd wanted to do was wrap her in his arms, profess his love and desire to live with her happily ever after. But that was a pipe dream. He didn't have a chance.

He took another sip. The scotch seared through his system. Getting there wasn't as pleasant as he'd hoped, but the alcohol was beginning to take effect.

He was impressed with her makeover. Few would recognize her, even up close. He was almost surprised that he had.

He played the scene over and over in his mind. He'd gotten off the flight from Paris but bypassed customs by going straight through security on his secret service credentials. He was about to leave the area when he was distracted by a commotion behind him. A little boy had broken away from his mother. She was rather frumpy and harried looking but her companion was exceptional. It was her profile, and the way she held herself. He had memorized everything about her.

Yep, Nadine was a professional. He had to give her that. The tail he'd set up was useless. And after hearing about Jericho, he knew she'd accomplished what he had given up trying to do. Of course, her stakes were higher. Personal stakes always were.

He was fairly buzzed by now, but suddenly he wanted to be alert. Maybe there was a way.

Nadine did not have time to mull over previous day's episode. It would take days, if not a week, to identify what was left of the bodies that were in that building. She knew that the real threat had not yet been averted.

She climbed the three flights of stairs and wondered how the professor still managed to maneuver them every day. Professor Amitai Lebovitz was well into his eighties and greeted her warmly at the door.

"Nadine, my dear, come in, come in. Ah, I can see by your eyes that this is no social call. Give me a smile and tell me how my old friend is, then we'll get right to what it is that you want."

For a moment, in the scholarly home of her father's dear friend and colleague, Nadine felt she could put the world aside. She gave him a hug and delivered her father's regards, then got down to business.

"Dr. Lebovitz, I need to know about a Yeshiva in the Old City, the one next to the Wall."

Without hesitation, Lebovitz went to his desk and scribbled a name and address on a piece of paper. "This is the man you want to talk to. He was born in the Old City and knows every stone and alleyway, in every quarter. His knowledge of history, right up through what happened yesterday, far surpasses that of mine and your father's combined. I've tried to talk him into joining the university faculty. We even offered him an honorary Ph.D., but he refuses. He gives my class one guest lecture every year, on a topic of his choice. That is as much as I can get out of him. Go to him."

"Just call me Joe," he said when they met, laughing heartily as if at some sort of inside joke. When she made her request, he grabbed a safari hat, propped it on his head and with some enthusiasm, said, "Let's go!"

They sat atop a rampart on the Old City wall overlooking the rooftops of the Armenian Quarter. Their perch also afforded them a view of the area about which the professor's friend was now elucidating.

"The Western Wall, also known as the Wailing Wall, or in Hebrew, the *Kotel*, is the only remaining excavated wall of the Second Temple," her wiry guide explained. "The First Jerusalem Temple, built by King Solomon, was destroyed almost 400 years later by the Babylonians in 586 B.C.E. They marched the Jews off to slavery, including the famous Daniel of the lion's den. Fifty years later, a new king ruled Babylon, one who believed in religious and cultural freedom. He issued an edict to the Jews to rebuild their temple, which they did. The Second Temple was built in Jerusalem on the same site, only to be destroyed by the Romans some 400 years later, in 70 C.E. Once again, the Jews were marched off into slavery, this time to Rome, as depicted in the Arch of Titus. Several hundreds of years after that, the Muslims adopted Jerusalem as a holy site when it was told that Muhammad was instantaneously transported here and stopped to rest at the Church of the Holy Sepulchre. The Muslims built two mosques, the Dome of the Rock and the Al Aksa Mosque directly on top of the site of the Jewish Temple, known as the Temple Mount."

"Since the establishment of the State of Israel in 1948, there has been a great deal of excavating going on here. After almost 3000 years of foreign rule by various empires, six hundred under the Ottomans and most recently, in the last century, the British, we Jews were left with a burning desire to uncover everything we could of ancient Jerusalem. This was not without protest from some Orthodox groups, who feared the archeologists would desecrate our holy sites. So an Antiquities Authority was formed and now the excavations are handled in cooperation with the Rabbis. Among the most interesting discoveries were the tunnels that run beneath the Temple Mount."

Nadine listened without comment. It was clear that Joe was not one to be hurried.

"In 1967, it was agreed that the Muslims would be in charge of the Mosques on top of the Temple Mount, and the Jews would be responsible for what goes on below. But a few years ago, when the second tunnel was opened, Palestinians protested, claiming it desecrated their holy sites. The protests turned violent and scores of people, Palestinians and Israelis, were killed."

Until now, her guide had been reporting to her, like a history professor at the lectern. Now, he dropped his voice and brought his head in close to hers. "That is why the authorities have kept the existence of a third tunnel, secret."

Nadine was about to speak, but he held up a hand. "Yes, yes. You want to know about the Yeshiva, the one that is practically a part of the Western Wall, the one that sits in near total obscurity in one of the most well-traveled squares in the world. I'll get to that."

"There," he said, pointing to a small door in a stone wall, adjacent to the *Kotel,* is the entrance to the tunnel." Above the door a simple white sign with blue letters read, "Yeshiva Gedolah."

"Where does it go?"

"Ah-ha. Good question. You see, the larger tunnels basically control traffic. The one opened most recently, leads directly out to the Via Delarosa. You know the road. It is the route along which Jesus was carried to his crucifixion. This one leads directly to the center."

Nadine frowned. "What do you mean by 'to the center'? What's there?"

"At the center of the Mount, is a small room, a chamber. A piece of the original Temple. Perhaps even the Holy of Holies. The tunnel ends there."

Nadine was skeptical. "Have you seen it?"

"With my own eyes."

"What does it look like?"

"It's fortified. Walls of hewn stone."

"Can I go there?"

Now the guide laughed. "Unfortunately for you, you are a woman. They would never let you pass its threshold. That Yeshiva is not like many of the others here in Jerusalem with educational grants and beautiful campuses. That Yeshiva accepts no money from the State of Israel, or indeed from any source other than its own sect. They do not recognize the government or the State. They study and pray, waiting for the Messiah to come to herald the building of a Third Temple."

"Who can go there?"

Now the guide eyed her more carefully. "You're not the typical American tourist."

"Perhaps not."

"They're a scary lot. They believe, of course, that Armageddon, the war between good and evil is a precondition to the coming of the Messiah. Nor are they passive in their beliefs. With the millenium upon us, and the possibility of the advent of Armageddon, they are bent on removing whatever obstacles to the Messiah's coming they see to be within their power."

"That would put the State of Israel directly in their way."

He nodded. "Yes, they've been known to support terrorism."

"Then why are they allowed to study here?"

Now the guide smiled. "We are a democracy. Like you, we have our hate groups, our anti-government factions. But they are also Jews, albeit religious zealots. And this is their homeland. Perhaps a little tolerance makes it easier to keep an eye on them."

"You haven't answered my question. Why did you tell me about the third tunnel? Maybe it doesn't really exist." Nadine stood and looked out over the wall. This chatter was getting her nowhere. To herself, she muttered, "Useless, like the words of a sealed book."

The guide didn't say anything for a while. Then, he jumped up and started walking quickly along the top of the wall. "Follow me," he said without looking back. He hurried down off the top of the wall, through a small courtyard and into the Arab shouk. He was quick and nimble, dodging the people shopping at the market's stalls. It took all the energy she had to concentrate entirely on following him for he never once looked back. When they had traversed the market, he did not continue down the main thoroughfare but dove into a small passageway. Stone walls rose on either side of them. Very little light filtered down into the alley and it took a few moments for Nadine's sight to adjust. Several minutes later he stopped at a door. When he turned back to her, she saw real fear in his eyes.

"This is what you are looking for."

"What do you mean? Where are you going?" Nadine demanded to know, for he had already started walking away from her.

He hesitated, then turned but did not approach her. "Many years ago, when I was a very young man, a seer told me that a woman would say these words to me, *'k'divrei hasepher hachatum—useless, like the words in a book that is sealed.'* They are the words of the Prophet Isaiah, Chapter 29, verse 11. Without question or hesitation, I was told, I was to show that woman the way. I'm sure I would have forgotten about it. Jerusalem is full of seers and it was so long ago. The whole thing sounded absurd. So when you uttered them, I did not recognize them right away. But it was what he said after that, that left the incident buried in the corner of my mind, not entirely forgotten."

He screwed up his face just a little, as if trying to remember the seer's exact words. "Should you fail, the forces of evil shall have their way. Our land will be soaked with the blood of Muslim, Jew and Christian and the holocaust shall spread well beyond the borders of our region. The fires shall burn for decades and when they die out, your children's children will emerge scarred and damaged. Her success is their salvation."

Now he shook his head. "Even that didn't convince me. Gibberish to a twenty year old whose best friend bought him half an hour with a seer as a birthday gag. But I've been shot in the chest in war, trampled by a horse within these walls, survived the crash of a small airplane piloted by my friend, that same friend. I should have died half a dozen times over, but I am here and so are you."

"Is that what's frightening you now?"

He nodded.

"What's in there?" she asked quietly.

"Through that door, is *your* entrance to the tunnel."

"What do you mean, *my* entrance?"

"From here, you are behind the Yeshiva. This part of the building was sealed off from the rest," he waved his hand, "a long time ago, never mind why. Go down to the cellar. There is an old wine closet. Pass through it. At the far end, is your entrance to the tunnel."

She opened her mouth to speak, but he put up a hand. "No more. *B'hatzlacha.*" He bid her success and was gone.

Nadine shivered involuntarily and pulled on the jacket she had wrapped around her waist. She wasn't sure if it was the lack of sunlight or the guide's distressing forecast that chilled her. Probably both.

She wrapped her hand around the door handle and turned. Nothing. Damn it, she swore. Was this some sort of bad joke? She looked up and down the darkened lane. No one. After one more futile turn of the handle, she put her shoulder into it and nearly fell through the opening. A push of her hand would have done it.

Not a very auspicious beginning, she mumbled to herself. The stairwell was dim and chill. She took a moment to remove her knife and a small flashlight from her pack. She slipped the knife into her waistband at the small of her back and flipped on the light. She stood at the top of a stone staircase, leading downward into nowhere.

Her uncertainty about what she might find below was surmounted only by her certainty that the answer lay ahead. Without another moment's hesitation, she descended into the dark.

Noam peered over the top of his rimless glasses, his head bent, his shoulders still hunched over the open tractates of the Talmud. It's large Hebrew letters remained unread on the page, their teachings not of interest to him at the moment. What *was* of interest to him was the meeting between another Yeshiva student, Manny, and the well-groomed man with the thick eyebrows and polyester yarmulke perched precariously on his head. He'd seen his photo in the files, though not very clearly. Still, he was sure of who he was.

A tiny frown wrinkled his brow. He wouldn't have played it that way in Abu Jibril. He'd have gone for the big fish and worried about the kid later, if at all, but he wasn't there and the rules in the field were open to interpretation.

He watched the two men walk down the corridor, then slipped off the study bench and out the front door of the Yeshiva into the sunshine. Most of the Yeshiva students were heavy smokers and often took a break in the open air to light up. His short recess would not look unusual to anyone watching him leave. He walked around to the far side of a large group of tourists visiting the area and shoved his hand deep into the pocket of his baggy black pants. He punched Barak's pager number into the tiny cellular phone and coded him to meet him at the Yeshiva. Before emerging from the crowd, he lit a cigarette.

Barak felt the hum of his pager vibrating against his hip. He slipped it off the belt of his jeans and checked the number. Pulling on a shirt, he felt better than he had in months. He'd slept like a baby and his head was clear. This was going to be his last assignment. No more fuck-ups, professional or personal. Maybe he would go into the satellite technology business for real. He had the connections. And he would do whatever it was he had to do, to regain Nadine's trust.

He met Noam at the entrance to the Yeshiva.

"Manny's been taking deliveries of large sacks through the kitchen entrance for the last three days. I don't know where they've been storing it, but I lucked out. One of the sacks broke on the stairs down to the cellar. Fertilizer."

"Anyone else involved?"

Noam shook his head. "These guys have no natural curiosity, man. They've got their noses in their books and they don't stop turning the pages without the Rebbe's permission. But Manny's something of an outsider. He runs the place, and studies only part time. The rest of these guys are full timers, so they kind of look down on him. I've had to be careful. Couldn't get too friendly with him without ostracizing myself. These guys are serious. No mercy around this place."

"Heard anything about the deliveries?"

"Nah. They don't care what Manny does as long as they've got what they need."

"What about our mark?"

"I'd bet my behind it's Al Rasuul.

"And he's here now?"

Noam nodded. "Affirmative."

Barak withdrew his gun from under his jacket and checked the chamber. "O.K. cowboy, you lead the way."

The air got distinctly colder as Nadine neared the cellar. She was surprised to feel a draft. She found the wine closet, long deserted, with little trouble. Strewn with crates, she had to get her bearings about where the doorway might be before she began moving things around.

"At the far end was what he said," she reminded herself. The crates were piled practically to the ceiling and it took her almost half an hour to clear a part of the back wall. She was immediately dismayed. Nothing. Just huge square stones. Maybe it was further to the right, or to the left. She didn't know and it could take hours. She ran the beam of her flashlight up and down the wall, checking it for seams. Every few feet, she pressed the tips of her fingers into the stone. Futile, unless the stones were rigged to open. They weighed at least a ton each.

Moving methodically across the wall, she failed to notice a small metal object protruding from the floor until she tripped over it. Even with her heavy boot, pain shot up through her toe.

"Ouch, ouch, ouch," she said in a loud whisper. Though no one was listening, she just didn't feel right about talking out loud.

Directing her beam to the place where her foot had been, she saw a metal stake with a handle extending about six inches above the floor. She bent down and shed light on the stones adjacent to the lever, using her fingers to search for any seams her eyes might miss. She fiddled with the metal handle a bit to get a feel for its direction. She had no idea when it was last moved and she didn't want to jam it by forcing it the wrong way. Gently, she pushed, pulled, tugged and pressed. Nothing. What was the mechanism? She thought for a moment then slipped her hand beneath the lever, palm up, fingers wrapped around it, and lifted. She heard a scraping noise from underneath the wall where the stone was being released from its position. Still holding on to the handle, she pushed the stone out with her left foot. An opening about three feet high and several feet wide yawned before her. As she slowly released her hold on the lever, a metal pole came up through the floor into the center of the space, where the stone had been.

Nadine took a breath and slipped through on her belly to the other side of the wall. She was immediately struck by the difference in temperature. It was slightly warmer and less drafty in the tunnel yet it wasn't the natural warmth that came from a source of heat. It was the warmth of movement, of human bodies.

She pressed back up against the wall, assailed by a dozen new signals, feeling exposed. The tunnel was lit by electric lamps strung at intervals along the wall where it met the ceiling. She flipped off her flashlight but kept it in her hand. The distinct smell of musk filled her nostrils. She recognized that scent. It was in Casablanca and at the café. It was strong and recent. It was Nasser. Another odor was present, odd because it should have been outdoors. It was fertilizer.

Which way should she go? The tunnel was not straight and she could only see a few feet in either direction. She noticed boards on the floor and scaffolding on the walls in areas that needed support or repair.

She followed the scent to her left. She stepped carefully, feeling her way around the sides of the tunnel, stepping over the boards so as not to make a sound. She had no plan. Time had lost all meaning. It seemed to her that she'd been groping along for close to fifteen minutes. She tried to estimate how far she had gone and concluded that there could not be much further to go.

The malodorous scent of fertilizer grew stronger. She paused at a point that the tunnel turned sharply to the right. She peeked around the corner and saw another turn farther up, this time to the left, from which a bright light emanated.

She surmised that it was coming from the chamber and took a deep breath before proceeding. As she stepped closer, she could see that the passage continued straight ahead, beyond the turn, but that corridor was dark, unlit by the lamps strung up to this point.

She thought that the guide had said that the tunnel ended in the chamber. Maybe he was wrong. Or maybe there was more than one chamber. She decided to pass the entrance into the lit chamber, to observe what she could from the cover of the darkened passage.

When she reached the intersection, she took one large leap from the turn, into the darkened passageway. She landed almost silently except for the toe of her boot rubbing on the stone floor underfoot. A bearded man, slightly overweight in a baggy white shirt and black pants, looked up. Nasser stood next to him, unmoved, focused on the task before him.

"Mice," he said without interrupting his work.

Peering around the corner, Nadine's mouth dropped open. The small room was stacked with sacks of treated fertilizer, slit open to reveal their contents. Nasser was setting a timer. She recalled the words of the seer and her blood turned cold. *Our land will be soaked with the blood of Muslim, Jew and Christian and the holocaust shall spread well beyond the borders of our region.*

Yes, she thought to herself. This would do it. This would not be the first time a single madman had changed the course of history. They were standing at the center of the world. Holy site to three faiths and a source of recurring strife and conflict, but nonetheless a symbol of what all could aspire towards—harmonious coexistence, just as the Mosque had fused itself to the Temple walls shared by the Church beside them.

She narrowed her eyes and measured the distance between herself and Nasser. Her aim would have to be precise. Then she assessed his accomplice. She would have to take him down by hand. Hopefully, there would be enough time for her to call someone to defuse that monstrosity. Slow down, she warned herself. One thing at a time. She slid her knife from its sheath and watched. And waited.

Nasser set the timer down and signaled to Manny to approach. In a move that was sharp and swift, he shoved the blade up through his soft flesh and into his heart. Manny's eyes widened in disbelief and stayed that way as Nasser lowered him deliberately to the floor.

Nadine silently exhaled the breath she had been holding and readied her dagger. Its handle felt secure in her steady grip and she mentally counted out several beats, picking up Nasser's rhythm, the timing of his movements. Her arm raised, her elbow close, her timing in perfect synchrony with the rhythm of his breath, she positioned herself for the shot. A movement to her left interrupted her.

Barak! And who was that other guy? He was making so much noise. Was he born yesterday? She looked at Nasser. His Baretta drawn, he moved to his left, out of her line, but at the perfect angle to shoot anyone who stepped into the intersection. She would have to step around the corner to get her shot and it would be too slow. By the time she aimed, he would take her down. And they were about to step into his line of fire.

She crouched as Nasser fired off his first shot. It hit the back wall and ricocheted off. Noam leaped into the space beside her but she saw Barak go down. She flew across the open space and Nasser fired off another shot. Noam peered around the corner and took a shot at Nasser, but missed.

Nadine lifted Barak's head and placed it in her lap. His eyes were already glazed over and his pulse was dropping.

He looked at her gratefully. "No more fuck-ups," he whispered. "Back-up on its way." She nodded and put a finger to his lips, signaling to him not to speak.

"I love you," he mouthed.

"I know," she answered.

Thirty seconds later, the firing stopped. Noam was down and Nasser stood over her.

"I've always respected, even admired you, Nadine. But for you to have found me here, well, you're even better than I thought."

Gently, she lay Barak's head on the stone floor and rose slowly, arms at her sides. The Baretta followed her and stayed level with her chest, but they were eye to eye as he spoke.

"I knew that day I spied you in the woods it meant I had to be careful. When I saw how easily you brought down my recruit, I understood that to be a personal omen. I admit, you are my match in every way. But, you see, I have won." He studied her for a moment. She remained impassive. Only her eyes were watchful.

"Never mind, Nadine. We can't all change the world. Your boys won't have it too bad in America. They might even like…"

At the mention of her boys, she hesitated no longer. In a fraction of a second, she crouched, turned, and with her back flat in one line with her head, she thrust out her left leg behind her, flinging the gun from his hand. Even if he had gotten a shot off, it would have cleared right over her. Now grabbing his outstretched right arm with her left to increase her momentum, she straightened and moved in close, into his face, too close for him act, while her right hand thrust the dagger straight up into his heart.

His mouth opened, but no sound emerged. She jumped back and he dropped to his knees, then flat on his face, lifeless.

Nadine didn't waste a moment. She knelt beside Noam. He was still alive, even conscious. Nasser's bullet had only grazed his shoulder.

"OK, hero, let's see you make yourself useful. Do you know how to disarm that thing?" she asked, cocking her head in the direction of the still ticking timer.

Nodding, he pulled himself to his feet. She knelt beside Barak and searched for a pulse, though she knew she would find none. She touched her lips to his cold ones and said goodbye.

Halfway back through the tunnel, she met the reinforcements and breathed her first real sigh of relief in weeks. Two ran ahead to defuse the bomb. She promised a third she would wait for them outside and let the medic know he had only one live one. They rushed forward to save the day while Nadine walked more briskly now, wanting nothing more than to feel the fresh air and sunshine on her face.

A few minutes later, she reached the spot where she had entered the tunnel. She stopped. If Y wanted her, well, he'd have to find her first. She dropped to her belly, slid through the opening and flipped on her flashlight. She pulled up the lever, shoved the stone back and latched it into place.

Her hands were sticky with Nasser's blood. Looking around the cellar, she found an old tap and turned it on hopefully. It took a few seconds for the gurgling fluid to reach the end of the pipe. It gushed out brown at first, then finally ran clear. She washed her hands, and splashed the cool water on her face, but it was useless. Salty tears cascaded over her cheeks. Her anguish was huge and heavy. They had shared a passion rare and pure. He had touched her in a place no one had ventured before, that she herself had not known existed until he settled there. But when last she kissed his lips, they were cold and blue. She knew the man, but she would know him no more.

Wracked by silent convulsive sobs, she crumpled to the floor like a damp rag in the dark, stone cellar. The vault-like room was her doorway into oblivion. She remembered and cried. When tears no longer sufficed to alleviate her pain, she unfolded her coiled limbs, smoothed back her hair and walked head high, out into the day.

Epilogue

▼

December 1998

Nadine awoke from her airborne nap and lifted her laptop onto the tray table in front of her. The boys had been skiing with Brad in northern Italy for a week now. She was looking forward to finally joining them.

A smile tugged at the corner of her lips. Brad had been waiting for her when she returned from Israel, physically exhausted and emotionally weak. His devotion was her succor. He tended to her broken heart and ministered to her wounds, slowly healing her with his love and encouragement. In time, she understood the complicated place Barak had captured in her heart, and she was able to accept and let go.

She turned her attention back to the monitor and scanned the screen. Their e-mail said they'd be waiting for her on the tarmac at Aviano. With less than an hour to go, she decided to look at the file that Brad had attached to his e-mail letter asking her to review it before she arrived.

She heaved a sigh. She wasn't really in the mood, but being occupied would move the remaining time along more quickly.

The document was another like hundreds she'd seen before. She started to scan it, then read more carefully as she began to see a pattern emerge. She closed her eyes to abate the pounding in her head. Why her? Maybe she should ignore it, or just forward it to the Pentagon with a note: *More secret messages. Have a great day.*

She wanted to stop but knew that she couldn't, so slowly, reluctantly she picked up a pencil and notepad, and began to transcribe the letters.

Forty minutes later, she sat back and smiled. It read, "The loving are the daring. Will you marry me? Brad. P.S. Permission granted. Daniel & Zak."

A voice overhead said, "Dr. Kanner, please fasten your seat belt. We'll be touching down now."

She looked out the window. The mountains to her right loomed large and snowy. Below her, the runway moved up to meet the wheels of the Air Force jet. And just ahead, her family waited.

0-595-28808-1